A MIDNIGHT ENCOUNTER

"Eden, for Chrissake—"

"No, I mean it . . . there's something in my bed."

"Why do I feel like one of the three bears?" Steve muttered. "All right, Goldilocks. I'll get up and see what it is." She didn't move, so he slid his hands up her arms to grasp her elbows. Her grip tightened. "I can't get up until you let go," he said in what he hoped was a reasonable tone that did not betray his growing arousal pressed so close to her soft body.

Bending her head so that her hair brushed against his jaw, she shuddered. He could feel her warmth, and it was all he could do not to put his arms around her shaking body and draw her even closer. He clenched his teeth.

"Get *off* me," he said, and she tilted back her head to look up at him with wide, frightened eyes. A shiver trembled through her quaking limbs.

He couldn't help it. He didn't care what was in her bed, or what had scared her, or why she had ended up in his lap. She was here, all warm and soft and needy, and it ignited every male instinct he had been doing his best to smother.

Tangling one hand in the hair at the back of her neck, he held her still and kissed her. His mouth closed hard on hers, harshly tender and demanding. Then her lips parted, and he was lost . . .

JADE MOON
VIRGINIA BROWN

ZEBRA BOOKS
KENSINGTON PUBLISHING CORP.

ZEBRA BOOKS are published by

Kensington Publishing Corp.
850 Third Avenue
New York, NY 10022

Copyright © 1995 by Virginia Brown

Zebra and the Z logo Reg. U.S. Pat. & TM Off.

First Printing: December, 1995

Printed in the United States of America

To Rob Sangster, who graciously let me pore over his photographs and "pick his brain" about the Yucatán—and to Lisa Turner, who so graciously loaned me Rob for a few hours. . . .

One

The scream had an electrifying effect. High-pitched, it began piercingly, then dropped to a moaning wail. It sliced through fringed coconut palms, tall mahogany branches, sword-shaped henequen leaves, and drifts of Spanish moss, then through thick, looping vines and fragrant orchids to reach Steven Ryan as he dozed by his fire.

Jerking upright, he tensed. The usual cacophony of night noises in the jungle subsided into heavy silence. The hair on the back of his neck prickled a warning. After a long moment, he slowly relaxed again. A prowling jaguar, maybe. Or a howler monkey, although they didn't usually range this far north.

When no other scream sounded, he shrugged and reached for a glass of sour mash bourbon imported from the United States. A satisfied smile curved his mouth. This was the life. Serenity. Silence. Solitude.

Stretching one arm above his head, his fingers brushed against vines as thick as his forearm. Woven densely, the living walls and roof of his hut cascaded with exotic blossoms on the three sides, leaving the front open. Yeah, he liked it this way. Though there were moments when the solitude made him feel more lonely than peaceful, this was what he needed. He'd gotten his fill of crowds. Of noise. Of chaos and cannons . . .

Best not to think of those things anymore. All that was behind him; war and its aftermath was the main reason he had first left the States. He was happy enough here. He had all the basic necessities, and food grew wild—literally. Oranges, limes, coconuts, avocados, papayas—if he was hungry all he had to do was reach out and pluck a ripe fruit.

If he wanted water, it could be found in deep, shaded pools pure enough for drinking, cool enough for bathing. In the rainy season—usually June to October—gigantic, palm-shaped leaves formed natural umbrellas. Wild game was abundant, and deer ran rampant. For entertainment, he had the singing of exotic birds for private symphonies, and the playful antics of familiar raccoons for laughter. And when he needed man-made goods, he made the trek to an Indian market to trade for more.

Yes, Steve Ryan had it all.

So why did he feel this damned restless yearning? When he already lived in paradise, why did he feel as if something—or was that some *woman*—was missing from his life?

Scowling, Steve jabbed his bare foot at a smoldering log. A stab of pain brought him upright. He squinted at the splinter now in his toe. Stupid of him, really. He knew better. But splinters were nothing compared to the trouble women could cause. Poor Adam had discovered that truth in the Garden of Eden, the most famous of all paradises. See how much trouble *Eve* had caused? Yeah, he'd better leave well enough alone and forget all about women.

Steve scooted closer to the fire and carefully removed the splinter. He tossed it into the flames. In the velvety blackness of towering trees beyond the leaping glow of the fire, a macaw shrilled loudly. The fire's glow permeated only a small distance into the shadows, barely lighting the steep hill that formed one side of the homestead he'd painstakingly carved into the dense rain forest. Tree roots shaped a snaking tangle that tumbled over the hill's edge and intertwined with morning glory vines.

Not a bad sight first thing in the morning, a fall of flowers as pretty as a bridal veil. No, not bad at all. They presented a refreshing view during the long hot days. Time was relative here. It had a way of meandering slowly by. Yeah, solitude was great—even though there *were* those brief, annoying moments when he thought wistfully of sharing this tropical paradise with someone. Female, of course. And definitely temporary. No long-term arrangement . . . ah, hell. Neither was likely.

Holding up his glass of bourbon, he murmured mockingly, "Oh powerful Itzamná, Lord of Life, deliver me a woman of light and beauty and independence . . ."

Another loud scream sliced the night, sounding much closer than before. And dangerous. Steve put down the bourbon and quickly reached for his rifle. Jaguar, maybe. But jaguars normally didn't come too close to fires. He'd never been bothered by a marauder in his camp, though he did see them from a distance at certain watering holes. *El tigre* was wary of man, and for good reason.

A noisy crash in the brush atop the hill brought Steve to his feet. Another scream rent the night, followed by the sharp snapping of branches and a familiar coughing sound. *Jaguar.* Most wild cats could be very unfriendly, he'd found. And the snarling coughs they made almost always preceded an unpleasant encounter. Like now.

Before he took more than two steps back to get a better view, a flurry of motion tumbled over the brushy crest of the hill with another broken scream.

It all happened so fast, he barely had time to react. Instinct took over. Sweeping his rifle to his shoulder in a practiced motion, Steve curled his finger around the trigger and narrowed one eye to sight down the long barrel.

Fortunately, disbelief kept Steve from pulling the trigger. As the terrified, panting creature plummeted down the root-tangled hill and rolled to a stop against his feet, firelight illuminated blue eyes staring up at him.

He stared back, shocked into silence.

"Help me," came the rather breathless plea, "you've . . . g-g-got to help me."

Recalling the prayer he had uttered to an ancient Mayan god just before this long-legged female with honey-colored hair and huge blue eyes had landed at his feet, Steve couldn't help saying, "That's the quickest answer to a prayer I've ever gotten . . ."

Eden Miller staggered to her feet and stammered out, "R-r-run. L-l-leopard."

"You mean jaguar. Or maybe a margay or jaguarundi. All of 'em are fairly big cats—where are you going now?"

Still poised for flight on trembling, fear-weakened legs, Eden paused. She spared a glance at the tall silhouette against the leaping flames of a fire. She vaguely understood that the man was calm and not at all perturbed by the possibility of being mauled by a wild animal; a sense of relief at seeing not only a friendly face, but one that spoke her language began to penetrate her haze of fear.

"A l-l-leopard was chasing me . . ."

Shaking his dark head, the man put down his rifle and said, "You mean jaguar. It's probably gone. Jaguars don't like camp fires. Leopards either, for that matter. Are you all right?"

Relief flooded through her with a rush. Eden's legs refused to cooperate with her mental orders to remain upright, and she collapsed into a quaking heap at his feet again. A wave of nausea washed over her. Putting her face in her cupped palms, she mumbled, "I'm f-f-fine. What d-d-difference does it make what k-k-kind of animal it is?"

"To us, not much. To them, a great deal I should think."

When she lifted her head to frown at her rescuer, she

was caught by the intensity of his stare. As fear receded, other things came more sharply into focus—dark hair, gold eyes, sun-brown skin, and the amused tilt of his mouth. Did he think this was funny? If he only knew what she had been through . . .

"Here," he was saying in a matter-of-fact tone, "put this blanket around you. There's not much left of your clothes, and I have a vivid imagination."

Eden flushed. She was well aware of how scanty her attire was, but in light of everything, it had not seemed important.

"Thank you," she said tartly as she took the blanket he held out to her. "I would hate to offend your sensibilities."

"I'll bet you would."

Oddly, his cool reception was calming, if his attitude was not. Apparently oblivious to the fact that *he* was wearing only a pair of cut-off pants that had seen better days, he crouched down in front of the fire and began to jab at the logs with a long pointed stick. She could see the shortened pants he wore had once been brown, but now were a muddy gray cotton that barely covered him. He wore no belt, and the waistband of his brief trousers hung low on his lean hips. She felt a spurt of annoyance that in light of his lack of proper dress he should criticize hers. At least she had an excuse for being barely clad.

"Have a seat," he said without looking at her, and flung an arm out to indicate a camp stool. She hesitated. Firelight flickered over him in distorted patterns, red and orange and gold shadows playing over his bare chest and the wide curve of his shoulders.

Eden looked away. Wrapping the blanket around herself, she plopped down on the camp stool. Really. She was beginning to wonder if she had fallen out of the frying pan and into the fire. This man looked like Satan himself, with his unholy face and hard-muscled body. Still, he was better than meeting a jaguar face to face.

With an effort, she struggled to regain her composure as well as her breath. The last few days had been trying enough.

Resorting to the commonplace, Eden took a deep breath and asked, "What did you say your name was, sir?"

He shot her a quick, frowning glance from beneath his devilish brows, then went back to poking at the fire. "I didn't."

That took her back a bit. He certainly wasn't being overly friendly. Or curious, it seemed. Nor did he seem surprised by her sudden appearance in his camp. Could he be—she swallowed hard—in league with the villainous men who were the reason she had fled into the night?

She cleared her throat and decided to brave the unknown. "My name is Eden Miller. As you've—"

"Eden?" He turned to stare at her in obvious disbelief. "How appropriate. The only better name would be Eve. So what are you doing here in my private paradise?"

"As you have probably surmised, I'm lost and . . . and alone." The last word was said in a dismal croak. She hadn't meant to allow emotion to intrude. Any display of fear or grief would only send her spiraling into the abyss that had yawned before her for the past week. Or two. She'd lost track of time since—

Shifting position so that his body was silhouetted against the bright flare of the fire, the man said abruptly, "You shouldn't even be in this damn area, much less wandering around alone."

"It wasn't my idea," she flared, then caught herself. This was certainly no way to begin. She took a deep breath and felt the sharp rake of smoke from the fire burn her throat. "We were on an archaeological expedition when—"

"You? An—archaeologist?" His gazed scoured over her.

Clamping down hard on her rising emotion, she said, "No, not me. My husband and I were associated with those sent here by the Metropolitan Archaeological Association expedition."

"Husband."

His face was shadowed, with the leaping flames and sparks at his back making him appear even more saturnine. Eden suppressed the urge to flee as he stared at her. There was a disquieting intensity to that gaze. Why did he look at her like that?

"So where is your husband now, *Mrs.* Miller?" he demanded, tapping the end of a long stick on the open palm of one hand. He studied her as if suspecting her of desertion. Or worse. Her mouth tightened.

"Dead."

That answer didn't seem to surprise him very much. He merely nodded. "And you two were dumb enough to come out here alone?"

Outrage won the battle over tact. Eden rose to her feet. "No, we were not alone. Colin and I were part of an expedition numbering twenty people. P-p-people who are all dead now, for your callous information. I am the only one who managed to survive the attack except . . . except for Paco."

For a moment he didn't speak, then said mildly, "Paco?"

She drew in a deep breath. "Yes. An Indian boy who was one of our guides. He was with me for a time, then . . . then he disappeared. I think—I think a crocodile got him."

Studying her for a long moment, he finally gave a slow shake of his dark head. "That's possible. It happens out here. Most likely it was a human predator, though. More numerous, and infinitely more dangerous."

Shuddering at the visual images those comments provoked, Eden looked away from his dispassionate expression and thrust the images away. "Yes," she said softly, "so I've learned."

For another long moment, her rescuer said nothing. Then he shrugged and pivoted on the balls of his bare feet to gaze into the fire again. Smoke coiled around him, reinforcing the impression of a denizen of the underworld. "Are you hungry or thirsty?"

She shook her head, then realized that he wasn't looking at her. "No. I managed to find edible fruit and fresh water."

"More resourceful than you look, then. Didn't anyone warn you about Quintana Roo?" He slashed her another glance. "It's a no man's land out here. The natives hate all whites, and kill them at the first opportunity. Why the hell come here for your expedition?"

Eden struggled with a mixture of anger and grief. It hadn't been *her* idea. In fact, she'd warned Colin and the others. But they hadn't listened. Ambition had inured them to the dangers.

"We were," she said through stiff lips, "on an exploration to retrieve as many Mayan artifacts as possible. Our expedition was funded by a well-known and respected association, and every possible precaution was taken." She paused, aware of how silly that statement must sound in light of all that had happened.

The man gave a grunt of disbelief and slapped idly at an insect on his arm. "Except the sensible precaution of staying home, I see. Are you certain that all the others—?"

"Dead." She slowly sank back down on the camp stool. Her fingers dug into the folds of the rough wool blanket. "All dead. It was . . . horrible. They fell on us at night when we were asleep and set our tents on fire. There was screaming and shouting and hacking with swords and guns firing . . . I saw . . . I saw Colin fall."

"Your husband." Silence fell between them. After a moment he looked away from her and said into the flames, "You were lucky to escape. The Cruzobs like to take white women as—as prisoners. Your husband was a fool to bring you here."

Eden shuddered again. His inference was not lost on her. And she recalled the warning of a frowning official in Merída who had tried to prevent their expedition, but was overruled by her husband. Colin had sneered at the possibility of crude natives overpowering intelligent white men who were proficient with firearms and modern weapons. Yet he had died horribly from a crude sword wielded by one of the very natives he'd scorned.

She looked up with sudden tears blurring her vision. "Colin may not have been the most foresighted man, but he didn't deserve to die like that. None of them did."

"Maybe not. But they should have stayed home. It was stupid to come out here."

Frowning, Eden said slowly, "There is a great deal of competition between certain institutions for exciting new discoveries. We were trying to find the temple of the jaguar. Richard—he was the head of our expedition—barely won permission over another group for us to make the trip. It can get quite political at times, and incurs fierce rivalry, which is why they decided to come ahead without making proper inquiries first, I suppose. Even so, none of them deserved to die as they did . . ."

His shoulders lifted in a careless shrug. "At least they aren't prisoners of the Cruzob and being forced to work their fields as slaves. Believe me, that's a living death, and much more cruel."

"So how is it that you're not dead?" she blurted out, and saw his gaze swing toward her in narrowed surprise. "If you say it's so dangerous out here, how is it you're alive and not a prisoner?"

A faint, sardonic smile curled his mouth, and he rose to walk close to her. With casual grace, he hunkered down on his heels in front of her. His face was level with hers, and she stared at him. Firelight flickered over his features, revealing gold eyes beneath dark-winged brows, a straight nose, well-cut mouth, and slash of cheekbones that ended in a strong sweep of beard-stubbled jaw.

She noted with a little sense of shock that he had a wild, dangerous beauty. However, that brief thought was immediately dispelled by his words.

"I am alive and free," he said softly, "because the Cruzob

consider me a crazy man who communes with ancient gods."

Eden felt the hair on the back of her neck prickle. Dear God, she'd thought herself safe when she'd realized he was an American—now it seemed as if she was in even worse trouble than before . . .

Steve correctly ad her expression. It didn't help his already raw tempe o know that he was frightening her. The abrupt arrival o nis attractive—and even covered with insect bites and cratches, and with dirt streaking her face, he could see at she was *very* attractive—woman, shook him more t n he wanted to admit. The Yucatán was no place for 1 . Hell, it had been no place for him until he somehow ianaged to establish himself as a holy man, a lone lur c who was fairly harmless to the hostile natives.

Shif g to stare into the dark trees beyond the fire, Steve said a ad, "White men are not allowed in the Yucatán any mor Not since some idiotic officials bungled the handling of Mayan about ten years ago."

Not allowed? We were told only that it would be danous to travel into the interior."

"Yeah, it's sure that. Guess whoever told you that failed to mention the blood baths that wiped out entire towns on both sides. It was all-out war when the Mayans aligned themselves to two leaders with a 'talking cross,' and then formed the Cruzob cult. Some still call them the Chan Santa Cruz Indians."

"A talking cross? That sounds more like fantasy than fact."

Steve slung her a quick glance and shrugged. "Unbelievable as it may sound, it's true enough. Of course, the cross can't actually talk. A Mayan ventriloquist only made his followers think it could. Now the Cruzob—taken from *cruz,* Spanish for cross, and *ob,* the Maya plural suffix—rule the

Caribbean coast as the Empire of the Cross. They get notably cranky about unapproved visitors."

"So I discovered."

Steve studied Eden for a moment. Her face was pale, eyes a wide, scared blue. He could see she was trying hard to retain her composure. Unexpectedly, he felt a spurt of pity.

"You can call me Steve. You're welcome to stay here for the night."

Her eyes widened even more. "For a night? But what will I do after that?"

Already regretting the impulse that had given her his name, Steve abruptly stood and looked down at her. "That's your problem."

He was being an ass. He recognized that fact, but could no more stop himself than he could stop the summer rains. Hell, he wasn't used to being around people anymore. He could relate to animals easier than he could to people, especially women. Females had always had the ability to turn him inside out with an ease that amazed him. This particular female would be devastating even if he'd met her under different circumstances, but being out here alone with her— oh no. Not him. He got panicky at the mere thought. Damn. Maybe the Cruzob were right about him after all. Look at what happened when he prayed to one of their ancient gods . . . who'd have thought Itzamná would even listen to a white man? Especially after the last time during the drought, when he'd found himself in an exceedingly awkward position and prayed to the God of Rain, Chac . . .

Eden stood up, and her voice shook slightly as she repeated, "But what will I do after tonight? Will you escort me back to Mérida?"

"Mérida is too far. I'll give you provisions and directions to Uxmal. It's the closest town." He didn't look at her. It would be fatal. If he could, he would banish from his memory the image of long, bare legs and an ample glimpse of womanly curves that had first startled him. Yeah, it had been much too long.

"You're too kind," Eden said in a tone that conveyed the exact opposite. Steve didn't blame her. He took two steps back and indicated his hut with a jerk of his head.

"You can stay in the hut tonight."

"Your chivalry is overwhelming."

"Chivalry is out of fashion, in case you didn't know." Steve fought the urge to shake the condemning look out of her eyes. Even stronger was the urge to kiss her. And more. Damn. It was worse than he thought. Why had he tempted the god of mischief by wishing for a woman?

Two

Eden stared around the small hut, vaguely surprised by the cozy furnishings. An oil lamp lit the interior in wavering patterns of rose-gold and gray. Woven baskets were stacked neatly around the walls, holding blankets, clothes, and various utensils. A long string of garlic and peppers dangled from one of the cross-poles of the roof. Brass pots hung from hooks in one corner, and there were stacks of books all round the room. Tightly woven hemp mats dyed in colorful patterns covered the packed-dirt floor, and the sleeping area was defined by a plump mattress festooned with a mosquito net and several pillows. It looked exotic. Innocent. Dangerous.

"Where do *you* intend to sleep?" she asked, feeling the strangeness close in around her. She turned to look at Steve, and recognized irony in the amused tilt of his mouth.

"Don't mind biting the hand that feeds you, I see. Never mind. Don't say it. It may have been a long time since I've been with a woman, but I won't lose control. Tonight, anyway. Here." He tossed a rolled up blanket to her. "Use this one. It's softer than the one you're wearing. I'll use another blanket."

Strolling toward the sleeping area, he bent to scoop up a blanket. Eden watched him with mixed feelings. On one hand, she had a certain appreciation of his masculine beauty. His lean body was well-muscled and proportioned. Broad brown shoulders, sinewy arms, and long legs—hard, lean bands of muscle on his chest and roping his flat stomach. Yes, he was certainly suited for this primitive lifestyle, she supposed. But it did nothing to dilute her nagging impression of him as dangerous—balanced as he was on the knife-edge between civilization and barbarism. It would take, she thought, only a slight nudge to push him off that ledge into uncivilized territory.

"I'm not at all sure I'd like to know what you're thinking," came the slow, amused drawl, and Eden flushed as she realized that she was staring at him.

"Just thinking how tired I am," she lied, and knew from his quick, sideways smile that he was aware of her lie.

"Don't forget the netting," he said. "It keeps away bats."

"Bats."

"Don't tell me you haven't seen any bats since you've been here."

"But I haven't seen any bats since I've been here—"

"Well, they're out there. Vampire bats. Nasty little beasts that feed on fresh blood. Just like mosquitos. Make sure the netting is tucked in all around you. The worst kind of mosquito is an early riser. It can get damned uncomfortable without netting."

She looked down and rubbed an idle hand over her arm. Dozens of tiny bumps attesting to numerous insect bites already pocked her skin. "I'm convinced of that fact. I've endured the past nights without any kind of protection." Unable to help the sudden shudder that racked her, she looked up to catch his narrowed gaze resting on her. Then he shrugged.

"There's some ointment in a blue jar in that square basket. It heals insect bites. Help yourself. And I've got an extra shirt and pair of pants you can have. I'll share everything but my bourbon."

She gave a weary smile. "Your generosity is greatly appreciated. As well as your hospitality."

"Yeah. Right." He raked a hand through his hair, suddenly looking uncomfortable. "Look, it takes a lot to survive out here. I'm surprised you had it in you to do it alone."

"Because I'm a woman, you mean?" Her brow arched. "How archaic. Believe me, sir, I am quite capable of doing what I must to survive, even if it means hiding in tree stumps from wild animals and natives. Or doing without mosquito netting."

"Pardon me, Mrs. . . . Miller, is it? I seem to have trod upon your finer sensibilities. And I'm overjoyed to hear that you have what it takes to survive. Perhaps you also have what it takes to get back to Merída by yourself. Good night."

Turning on his heel, Steve strode from the hut toward the campfire. Eden wished she'd resisted the urge to defend her gender. At this point, it hardly mattered how brave she'd been in the past few weeks. At this point, what she needed to do was impress him with how much she needed his assistance. He couldn't really expect her to travel on to Merída by herself, could he? *Could he?* Dear Lord, she hoped not. When she was more rested, she would have to convince him to guide her to safety. And that promised to be difficult. He'd made it apparent that he preferred solitude to unexpected company.

She glanced at the comfortable bed tucked beneath the gauzy folds of mosquito netting. Later. She'd ponder her circumstances when she'd had some rest. The past two weeks had been spent hiding in tree stumps and under rocks to snatch scant moments of sleep. It would be heaven to sleep without worrying that she would wake up as some marauding animal's dinner. In the morning she would deal with her problems. Now, she would sleep.

It was still warm beneath the blankets. For the first time in much too long, Eden felt safe. Secure. Even in the half-awake world between slumber and awareness, there was a feeling of security just knowing someone else was nearby. Morning had come with the usual burst of light and noise. Toucans screeched a rasping greeting, and macaws chittered noisily. Raucous birds. Beautiful, but loud.

Snuggling deeper into the mattress of moss-filled cotton ticking, she tugged at the folds of blanket over her shoulder. It was caught on something, and she gave it a sharper tug. This time, the blanket was freed. But it was then that she realized she wasn't alone. A massive presence stretched beside her, big and warm. She could hear the rasp of heavy breathing.

Her eyes opened with a furious snap as she rolled over and prepared to send Steve packing with a scathing denouncement. But the words died a quick death, clogging her throat. Fear returned in a sweeping rush, and she filled her lungs with air before letting it out in a scream of terror.

The scream seemed to intrigue the hut's intruder. Cocking its huge black head to one side, it reached out a massive paw and batted playfully at the mosquito netting. Eden sucked in another breath to scream again, too paralyzed with fright to move.

This scream was more like a whimper. Before it faded, the animal responded with a rumbling reply that made Eden's heart stop. Snuffling curiously, the enormous black cat gazed at her with interested gold eyes. Eden could hear cursing outside the hut. Her panic-driven thoughts told her Steve was the only person who could rescue her.

Suddenly galvanized into action, she twisted from the mattress to the floor in a quick motion, tangling her legs in the blanket folds and mosquito draping. The big cat obviously considered this an enticement to follow, and it sprang up from its supine position with almost lazy grace. Eden scrambled blindly toward the open entrance of the hut. The netting came cascading down over her head, further impeding her progress. Batting frantically at the mosquito netting, she wallowed in a desperate attempt at flight. The

material clung with an inanimate determination to her arms
and legs.

"G-g-gun," she shouted through the netting. "Get a
gun!"

"Dammit, you're noisy as hell in the mornings. Quiet
down. Some of us are trying to sleep."

Eden clawed the net from her eyes and tried to find Steve.
He was sitting up in his blankets, looking very annoyed.
Unable to speak more coherently, and expecting at any mo-
ment to feel the big cat tear her apart with fangs and claws,
Eden pointed behind her.

"Panther. Gun. Shoot."

Steve looked at her sourly. "Friend. No. Won't."

Eden paused. She glanced behind her and saw that the
huge animal was sitting in the entrance and yawning. As
she stared, it lifted a paw and began to thoroughly clean it
much as a parlor tabby cat would do. Eden promptly lost
the use of her legs and collapsed in a quivering heap. The
netting settled around her like a huge, gossamer spiderweb.

"My God."

"Do you do that a lot?" Steve asked, and she looked at
him.

"Do what?"

"Fall down."

"Only since coming to the Yucatán."

"Charming." He rose in a lithe motion that reminded her
of the gigantic cat, lazy and graceful and subtly dangerous.
Scratching his bare chest, he eyed her. "Now that you've
awakened even the nocturnal animals, I suppose you expect
breakfast."

Eden strove to be just as casual. "Yes. That would be
quite nice."

"Then take off that netting, get up off the ground and
make yourself useful. If you expect eggs and bacon, you
better be ready to cook."

"What about—that?" She pointed to the cat still lounging

in the hut's opening. As if sensing it was the center of conversation, the animal paused in its washing and regarded Eden with a direct, unblinking gaze.

"*That* is Balam, and he doesn't like being referred to as an it. He considers himself quite the ladies' man, and cuts a wide swathe through the female jaguar population."

"Jaguar? But he's solid black. I thought jaguars were spotted like leopards."

"Some are. He isn't." Steve snapped his fingers and Balam responded with the feline equivalent of delight, bounding forward with a rumbling sound.

The jaguar caught Steve around the middle with his powerful front legs, tumbling him to the ground where they rolled around for a few minutes. Eden watched with a mixture of horror and interest. The massive black jaguar could easily have killed Steve, but it was obvious they were only playing.

As it was, when they were through and Steve stood up, she could see red weals and scratches on his chest, legs, and back. "You're bleeding," she commented.

Puffing slightly with exertion, he nodded. "Yeah. Skin grows back with the help of a little ointment. Clothes are too hard to mend."

"An interesting philosophy." She stood and shrugged away the netting with some difficulty, then moved as gracefully as possible toward the hut, keeping a wary eye on the jaguar. She paused at the entrance and turned to Steve. "When I have performed my daily ablutions, I will help with the morning meal. Unless you prefer otherwise?"

He stared at her. His eyes were a deep, almost translucent gold in the light of day, pale and shimmering and light-tricked beneath a heavy brush of black lashes. Narrowing them slightly, he said, "I was just kidding about cooking breakfast. There's fruit if you're hungry, and maybe some leftover beans or tortillas. If I cook, it's usually later in the

day. Maybe even night. Other than that, you're out of luck.
Unless you plan to cook."

Eden nourished a spurt of hope that he would allow her
to stay longer than one night. In her experience, forcing a
man to do something he didn't want to do usually ended
in disaster. If, however, he could be persuaded that it was
his idea. . . . She smiled.

"Very well. I have learned a bit about camp cooking. If
you like, I will be happy to try my hand at it."

Shrugging, he said, "Do as you like. Just don't burn
down my camp."

It wasn't an invitation to stay, but it was better than being
ordered to leave. Eden was determined to delay her eviction
as long as possible. The thought of being alone in the jungle
again was terrifying. And if she had to dissemble a bit, then
she would do her best.

She smiled. "I wouldn't dream of burning down your
camp."

Steve stroked Balam's sleek hide idly, watching as Eden
knelt in front of the hut with an array of cutlery and fruit.
Apparently, she had abandoned the notion of cooking. Instead, she'd arranged wooden bowls and a pile of fresh fruit
on the chopping block, and was busying herself with cutting
things up.

Somehow, the infernal woman looked as if she belonged
there. Ridiculous. She was as out of place in his world as
a quetzal in New York City. In fact, the elegantly plumaged
quetzal bird would probably be more comfortable roosting
among the stone and brick buildings of New York than this
woman was in the Yucatán. She looked too—refined. That
was it. Graceful, fragile . . . all those words that defined
unsuitable in the Yucatán.

He unwisely allowed his gaze to drift over her in a lazy
glide that did nothing to help him relax. She was wearing

one of his shirts, made of thin cotton. The top two buttons were missing, leaving the shirt open to the shadowy cleft between her breasts. He drew in a ragged breath. It covered her, but only served to accent the slight motion of her breasts beneath the loose-woven material. Each movement she made gave him an enticing glimpse of forbidden territory. He closed his eyes, but that only made him feel foolish and did nothing to dampen his admittedly fertile imagination. So he determinedly shifted his attention elsewhere, focusing on the jaguar lying beside him.

Balam yawned hugely and rolled onto his back, forelegs bent and draped over his massive ribcage in a position of utter abandonment. At the big cat's movement, Steve noticed Eden's sudden tension. He smiled.

"Balam has been with me since he was only a month old. He was an orphan. As long as you're nice, he won't hurt you."

"Right. I'm not worried." Eden went back to dicing up a succulent avocado. "Not that I enjoyed waking up to find him in bed with me. You could have warned me."

Steve shrugged. "He doesn't always show up. He's a friend, not a pet. He comes and goes as he pleases."

She looked up. "Like you."

"Yeah. Like me."

"Your friend, however, seems tame."

"You're inferring that I am not?" Steve rather liked that, and grinned.

"Uncivilized was more the word I had in mind." She wielded the knife in a decisive slash that split the avocado in two, pit and all. As he watched her position the fruit, he noticed that her hands were small-boned but capable, with slender, blunt-tipped fingers.

"Ah, now you're just trying to flatter me." He sat up and placed his elbows on his bent knees. "So tell me—how did you manage to survive for two weeks? No machete. No knowledge of the jungle—did the missing Paco teach you?"

"At first." She kept her head down, intent upon dicing the fruit on the small wooden board. Pale hair tumbled over her forehead, loosened from the tight braid she'd woven. As well as his shirt, she was wearing a pair of loose *calzones* that she'd had to tie around her slender waist with a length of twine. Though he'd rather liked the enticing picture she had made in her ankle boots, tattered pantalets, chemise, shredded skirt and blouse, this wasn't bad. Somehow, instead of detracting from her femininity, the loose clothes only emphasized it. She glanced up at him. "It was only a few days after the massacre that Paco disappeared. But he'd shown me a few things, and I tried to adapt."

"Where was your camp?"

The knife paused over a liberal hunk of glistening greenish-yellow avocado. "I'm not certain. It was near an immense mound of what looked like dirt, but when Richard—he was one of the archaeologists—scraped away some of the thick growth, he found carved stone steps and figures. Richard was quite excited. We thought it might be the temple of the jaguar." She looked down at the fruit for a moment, then said softly, "Paco seemed to think we would earn vengeance for disturbing the dead."

"The native boy? Must have been a tomb of some kind, then. I've seen quite a few scattered around, but mostly ceremonial places and temples."

Eden looked up, her blue eyes so wide that they made him think of Wedgwood saucers. "You have? Have you explored them?"

"Not since I learned better."

She leaned forward slightly, and her lips parted. "The temple of the jaguar—there are rumors that it has a throne made of jade and gold, fashioned in the shape of a jaguar. Have you heard of it? Or seen it, perhaps?"

"No. And don't go getting any ideas. One of the reasons I'm still alive and living here in peace is that I don't go poking my nose where it doesn't belong. The Cruzob get miffed when white men prod around sacred places." He paused, then said in a spurt of candor, "Not that they mind looting a few tombs themselves when they feel the need. Gold and jade bring handsome profits in foreign markets."

Carefully setting the knife on the wooden chopping board, Eden folded her hands and asked, "Aren't you ever tempted to find a few artifacts yourself? They could be invaluable to historians. And very profitable for you."

"Why should I? What food I can't find already growing, I can buy from some of the Indians. Or send an Indian to another market for me. Gold only brings trouble. And greedy men."

Eden looked down. She toyed with a broad banana leaf; then she ruthlessly stripped it from the main stem in quick, jerky movements. "I agree with that last part. Sometimes I think that Colin—well, he was definitely interested in the artifacts we found, but I'm not certain what his motives were."

Steve eyed her for a moment, while he ruffled Balam's furry belly with one hand in an idle motion. "Why did you come down here with him if you didn't approve?"

"Who said I didn't approve?" She looked up with a trace of defiance in her tone. "We were searching for knowledge, not fortune."

"Doesn't sound like it." When she made an inarticulate noise, he added, "Not Colin, anyway. Look—don't get mad at me. I only say what's obvious. And it's obvious you had your doubts, or you wouldn't have said what you did. Why were you here with him? For company? Or did you intend to profit from looting the tombs?"

Never, he reminded himself when Eden lurched to her feet, knife clutched in one hand, annoy a woman with immediate access to a sharp object. It could be very unsettling.

Brandishing the knife, she snapped, "Listen to me. We were not—I repeat *not*—looting. We were recording our finds and carefully packing them to return to the institute so they could be examined in order that as much as possible might be learned about the Mayans. Their culture could tell us much if we only knew how to interpret what we find. And don't you *dare* insinuate that we had ulterior motives . . ."

Still eying the knife with wary attention, Steve said, "All right, all right. Don't get all riled up about it. I was just trying to find out why you were brought down here. No man in his right mind would include a woman on an expedition like that one unless she had a specific purpose."

After a moment of taut silence, Eden abruptly sat down and began to chop fruit again. "You're right," she said as she halved an orange. "I'm an artist. It was my responsibility to make accurate drawings of all that we saw."

"An artist." Steve relaxed only slightly as she plied the knife with an unnerving dexterity. "You don't say. Can you draw accurately?"

"Within reason." Scooping up a handful of neatly diced fruit, Eden placed it in one of the wooden bowls lined with a strip of broad green banana leaf. "In archaeological work, it is imperative to record the tiniest detail. Photographic equipment is rather bulky and impossible to use in some locations. Caves, for instance. Bright light is required for the equipment to work properly. That's where I was useful. And since my husband didn't feel it necessary to pay me, I was cheap labor. Here. Breakfast is served."

As she shoved the bowl across the chopping board, she looked up, and Steve could have sworn he glimpsed a mirror image of himself in her eyes. It was not very flattering.

"Thanks." He uncurled his body and leaned over to pick up the bowl. "It's been a long time since I've had room service."

"I'm not surprised. Do you have any eating utensils? I couldn't find forks or spoons among your baskets."

"Probably because I don't have any. Fingers are nature's best utensils."

"Ugh."

Amused, Steve picked up a particularly juicy bit of orange and said, "Too genteel to eat with your fingers, yet you don't think it a trifle immodest to arrive at my hut wearing no more than your undergarments. How contradictory."

A flush rode the high curve of her cheekbones and made her eyes look very, very blue. "I had little choice about my garments, as the jungle was rather wearing on flimsy material and seams. I do, however, have a choice about my eating habits."

"Not really. If you're hungry, you'll eat with your fingers. Or that knife."

"Yes, I've considered that possibility." She frowned, a dainty little gesture that he found highly intriguing. "I don't mean to sound ungrateful or arrogant, but do you really feel that you should abandon all manners simply because you're in a remote, uncivilized area?"

"Eating like a barbarian, you mean? Maybe I am one."

"I meant nothing of the kind." Eden met his gaze with unnerving directness. "I think you are an educated man, despite your preference for these crude living arrangements."

"Do you. And why would you think that?"

"Because you have a great many books. My guess is you attended an excellent school."

"Ah, you are fairly perceptive after all. When the war started, I was a cadet at West Point. Fifth in my sophomore class, as a matter of fact." He saw her eyebrows lift and couldn't resist adding, "Everyone said I'd go far, so I did. From home, anyway."

"Now you live here." She waved a hand to encompass the wild tangle of tropical growth that continuously threatened to overrun his patch of cleared ground. "May I ask why?"

"I have a feeling I couldn't stop you," he said dryly, and popped a banana slice into his mouth. It was sweet and luscious on his tongue. He met her gaze and shrugged. "Let's just say I left because I found I couldn't live in a country that was no longer mine. If I was to be forced to dwell in a strange land, it could at least be a land of my own choosing."

Eden swallowed a slice of orange and wiped the sticky juice from her chin with a fingertip before saying thoughtfully, "An exiled Southerner. May I hazard a guess you hail from Texas?

"An excellent guess. What gave me away?"

"Besides your accent, you mean? Well, to be perfectly honest, I noticed some of the titles of your books. *A Biography of Sam Houston. A Detailed Sketch of Stephen Austin. The Struggle for Texas Independence.* Not titles that would interest just anyone, except, perhaps, a man from Texas."

"How astute of you. I shudder to think what else you may have noticed about me." Irritated without quite knowing why, Steve shoved his unfinished bowl of fruit away. That act piqued the jaguar's interest, and Balam rolled over to sniff at the bowl before deciding he wasn't a vegetarian. Rising to his feet in a lithe motion, the jaguar padded softly into the jungle. Steve watched the big cat disappear beneath a spreading ceiba tree's buttressed roots. He was acutely aware that Eden was observing him very carefully. Damn. This could turn out to be a more uncomfortable situation than he'd first considered.

Hell, who was he kidding? It already was. And he didn't have the foggiest notion of how it had happened. When he glanced up, she was watching him with a faint frown that pulled her brows together in a dainty pucker. He scowled and looked away again, and heard her cough slightly as if embarrassed to have been caught staring. *Damn* he repeated silently as he felt the first fingers of guilt tap lightly on a conscience he had thought long-buried. Why the devil did this woman have to appear in his world? An instant reminder of things he should do? Should feel. It wasn't fair. He was happy here alone, where the only choices presented to him were ones of survival or idleness.

She wanted him to take her to safety. She expected him

to be civilized and a gentleman. But she didn't know him. And if she did know the real Steve Ryan, she would run as far and as fast as she could in the opposite direction . . .

"Suddenly lost your appetite?" Eden inquired, and it didn't help his temper any to realize she sounded awkward and uncertain.

"For the moment."

"Too bad. This fruit salad is quite tasty."

She lifted a generous slice of papaya and took a bite. Steve's gaze riveted on her mouth. *Small white teeth . . . moist pink lips . . .* When her tongue flicked out to wipe away the juices, he closed his eyes. Oh yes, it had been much too long since he'd enjoyed feminine company. His mind leaped from one fantasy to another, just like an adolescent boy's.

To make matters worse, he'd spent a restless night on the ground, with her just a few feet away in his bed. Not even the discomfort of a fallen limb pressing into his back had eased the direction of his thoughts, and when he'd finally fallen asleep, damn if he hadn't dreamed about *her*. Pale angel hair, blue eyes, long slender legs, and an enticing view of high firm breasts had flashed through his dreams with heated repetition and embarrassing embellishment. Even thinking about it now made his body taut and feverish. Made him think about things he should ignore.

Abruptly rising to his feet, Steve reached for his rifle. "I'm going to fetch water. And go for a swim. I'll be back later."

Eden immediately launched herself to her feet, panic evident on her expressive features. "Oh. I'll go with you . . . to help carry water back, I mean. I don't want to stay behind. Alone. With no one nearby in case . . . in case of trouble."

"What trouble? It's doubtful the Cruzob know you're here. They rarely come close anyway. I'm something of a . . . a local legend, I guess you could say."

Her brow arched. "You mean because they think you're crazy?"

"Kind of you to mention it. Having Balam for a friend has added a bit of mystique to my reputation. Not that I mind. It helps when it comes to dealing with some of the natives."

"Because he's a wild animal? I would think even primitive peoples would understand about taming wild animals."

"Sort of." Steve raked a hand through his hair, impatient to get away by himself. "Look, Balam means jaguar in the Mayan language. And the jaguar has always been considered a god. Sacred. Anyway, since the Cruzob view me as inviolate, it stands to reason anyone in my camp would be viewed as untouchable. It's perfectly safe for you to stay here alone. I'll even leave the Winchester for you."

Her eyes widened to huge blue pools that made him think of a sacred well, deep and bottomless. "Please—take me with you. I won't get in your way. I won't talk or bother you, or make any noise. I just . . . just don't want to stay here alone."

"Christ." How could he admit that *she* was what he needed to get away from? He couldn't. Then she'd know she had some kind of power over him, or at the least, realize what a degenerate he was. Steve shrugged, his words a reluctant growl. "Grab two towels out of the basket in the hut. If you can swim."

"I can't swim. Do you have any soap? I really need a bath and I'd like to wash out some of my things."

Steve bit back the impulsive words that sprang to mind and said impatiently, "Yeah, yeah. It's in the hut. Hurry. And you better keep up or I'll leave you behind a palm tree."

Eden gave him a blinding smile that made his stomach knot. No, this wasn't going to be easy at all.

Three

Thick foliage hung from trees and jutted up from the forest floor to present a seemingly impenetrable wall, but Steve didn't appear to have any trouble finding the path. He was carrying his rifle slung over one shoulder, and using a machete mostly to push aside dangling vines and huge leaves. Eden could barely discern the small track beneath her feet, and wondered how he knew it was there.

Only tiny streaks of sunlight penetrated the sweltering shade beneath the dense canopy overhead. It was hot and humid, with no breeze to stir the leaves. Rivulets of perspiration ran from her head to her heels in thin trickles, and her clothes clung to her in clammy shrouds of material. Permeating everything was the damp smell of decay from fallen limbs, dead trees, and rotting leaves underfoot. She ducked a hanging branch just in time, shuddering at the sight of stinging ants swarming over the leaves and bark. Steve didn't even seem to notice. After a few more minutes of silent walking, she began to see the rain forest with a more appreciative eye.

Spanish moss draped in delicate lace streamers, and all around them the murmurs and calls of birds could be heard. Eden had quickly learned over the past few days that the rain forest was not the desolate area she'd once thought it. It teemed with life. Now and then she glimpsed a bright flash of feathers. Scarlet macaws, splendid with their crimson, blue, and gold feathers, fluttered from branch to branch, shrilling at the interlopers below. Toucanets, toucans, tanagers, and parrots grated harsh greetings mixed with melodic songs. A bright chattering high above signalled the presence of monkey troupes, though Eden caught only brief glimpses of them.

What had seemed terrifying when alone seemed exotic now, and she could recall how fascinated and thrilled she'd been when their expedition had first arrived in Quintana Roo. Colin had been faintly amused at her obvious delight, though he'd chided her for wasting paper by drawing birds and animals instead of what she'd come to the Yucatán to do. But to Eden, it had not been a waste. Depicting the beautiful and exotic creatures on paper had been as enjoyable as carefully recreating the magnificent stone carvings they'd found. Colin had never understood her enjoyment of nature. It had once amazed her that he was so dedicated to finding and preserving antiquities, when he made it so obvious that he cared little about preserving most living things. As a young girl, she had thought Colin absolutely wonderful. His passion for beautiful artifacts had intrigued her until she'd begun to suspect he cared more about them for their monetary value than for their beauty. But by then they were married, and it was too late to have reservations about her husband. In the eight years of their marriage, she had learned to close her eyes to many facets of Colin's character that were disturbing.

There were times she'd begun to feel as if her own character was eroding by her refusal to confront him. Or the truth.

Not that it mattered now. Colin was dead, and she was alone. Dear God, alone and in the jungle with a stranger she was forced to rely upon for help. And this enigmatic man with the gold eyes of a jungle cat was not very reassuring. She had the inescapable impression that he would gladly be rid of her at the first opportunity.

Cautiously, she lifted her eyes to watch him. He was

slightly ahead of her, easily wielding the machete in a back
and forth motion as he hacked a path through a tangle of
vines. Green, shiny leaves shimmered beneath the blade in
a shivering cascade as they fell to the side. The cotton fabric
of Steve's shirt stretched taut across his shoulder blades as
he swung the machete again. At least he was wearing a
shirt and pants now. She found it much less disturbing than
his former scant attire. His casual over-the-shoulder comment, however, was quite disturbing.

"Be careful. Most snakes would rather run, but a fer-de-
lance is more aggressive."

Eden's attention instantly riveted on the ground again.
"Snake?"

"Yeah, but a small one. Can't ever tell about the fer-de-
lance. Tricky rascals. Just as soon leap into the air at you
as not."

Her voice was a squeak when she asked faintly, "Do you
see one?"

Steve stopped and looked over his shoulder. A dark brow
rose inquiringly. "No. Why?"

"You said—"

"Oh, that. I saw a snake, but it wasn't a fer-de-lance.
You sure are jumpy. How'd you survive two weeks alone
out here?"

"Quaking in my boots," she snapped. "How do you
think? I was scared out of my mind, but I couldn't stay
where I was and hope someone would find me."

"No," he said in a thoughtful tone, "guess you couldn't.
It was sheer luck you stumbled into my camp. A few more
feet one way or the other, and you'd have missed me entirely."

"I know." She swallowed the caustic observation that it
was plain he wished she had, and said instead, "I didn't
even see your fire until I tripped over a tree root and fell
down the hill."

"Yeah, there's lots of tree roots. Soil's too shallow for

them to go deep, so they just kinda run along the top of the ground for quite a ways. You're more likely to be stuck with plant spines and thorns than you are to be snake-bit. That's why I'm wearing long pants in this heat." Turning back around, he began to walk again, swinging his machete at looping vines. "I have to clear my area every few days. Heat and humidity make plant life grow quickly down here."

Eden didn't reply. She thought of what Richard had said when they were attempting to clear the stone ruins of thick tropical foliage.

"It's as if it grows back overnight," he'd complained, but behind his spectacles, his eyes had been alight with enthusiasm. "All these layers of dead plant life may mean that we are the first living souls to see these temples since their original owners abandoned them aeons ago."

Poor Richard. He'd never lived to see the entire temple, only a small portion of it. One of the native guides had brought up a crusted remnant of a statue, and once cleaned, it had proven to be fashioned of gold and jade. Excitement had mounted, and she recalled Colin's jubilation at the discovery, as well as his belief that they would all be wealthy beyond their wildest dreams. And it was that last sentiment that had most disturbed Eden. True archaeologists were rarely wealthy. Funding always came from private investors or museums, and there was never enough money. To the true archaeologist, however, the real riches were the exciting discoveries of ancient history brought to life by painstaking research.

"Watch it here," Steve said, motioning at the path with the gleaming blade of the machete.

Eden sidestepped a tree root, as thick as a man's leg, jutting across the path. On a moonless night, these roots could be dangerous to the unwary. She glanced up at Steve's back.

"Thanks. I never seem to see these roots until it's too late."

"Yeah, so I noticed. Ever thought about watching where you're walking?"

"Is that a hint that I'm not paying attention to where I'm going?"

"I do seem to remember you falling at my feet last night."

"If you are referring to my solitary sojourn before I found you, let me assure you that it was most difficult to watch my feet when I was in danger of losing my head," she snapped, and heard him laugh.

"You sure are easy to rile. Bet you're fun at a party."

Eden drew in a deep breath and glared at the back of his head. "Are you always such a boor?"

"Always. It's my true vocation."

"You show an amazing aptitude for it."

"Thank you. Watch out."

Eden barely missed treading upon a snake that was slithering its way across the path. She sucked in a sharp breath as it slipped safely beneath a tree root and disappeared.

"Non-poisonous," Steve offered casually, not even turning around to see if she had managed to avoid it. "The cenote is just ahead."

Slapping at a tree branch that he released too early, Eden muttered past the leaves dangling in front of her nose, "What the devil is a say note?"

"Cenote—say-no-tay. For a budding archaeologist," he said, "you sure don't know much about this area. What publication did your team of experts plan to publish their momentous finds in? I can hazard a guess that it was more of a sales catalog."

"You are insinuating that the Metropolitan Society is not professional? On the contrary, they are responsible for bringing to the United States many valuable finds. Many of which are now being categorized and studied at great length."

"Uh huh. I'll bet. Most of those finds are probably cozily

nestled in some wealthy shipping tycoon's mausoleum of a house, or being auctioned off to the highest bidder. I'm familiar with the way some of those operations do business, and I can tell you, if you're dumb enough to believe that drivel you've been spouting this morning, you probably deserve all that's happened."

Steve released another hanging branch and it swung toward her face with dizzying speed. Eden barely managed to duck in time. It whizzed over her head with a vigorous rustle of leaves, depositing a family of beetles down her collar. She dropped her bundle of laundry and screamed.

Even knowing how ridiculous she must look, Eden could not keep from clawing at her shirt in a frantic effort to dislodge the tiny creatures that clung with dismaying persistence to the cotton material.

"Oh for the love of—" Steve broke off his disgusted comment to step back and grasp her by the collar. He gave her shirt a few brisk shakes—ignoring her feeble protests— then pulled it over her head. Not even glancing at her, he shook it again, then peered at the garment before handing it back.

"Clean," he said, "as an Irishman's pantry. Now put it back on and keep up. You're a lot of trouble."

Mortified, Eden snatched the shirt and choked out an opinion of his ancestry that only caused him to lift an eyebrow. She turned away from him to struggle back into the shirt. With a great deal of effort, she clamped her lips together. To alienate him completely might soon find her alone in this inhospitable land.

"I'm ready," was all she said when the shirt was buttoned snugly around her again. She picked up the laundry bundle and took a deep breath. "Lead on."

Steve grinned, a measured show of teeth as predatory as a wolf's. Turning around, he said over his shoulder, "I'm beginning to think you have a strange affinity for going about partially unclothed, Mrs. Miller. And may I say that I approve most heartily."

Not even genuine outrage could stifle Eden's sudden awareness that behind the devil's grin and heavy-lashed gold eyes, Steve was hiding an increasing attraction to her. She felt it, saw it in his surreptitious glances, and heard it in his barbed comments. And it presented intriguing possibilities.

"This is a sacred cenote." Steve stopped at the crumbling edge of a huge pit that yawned at his feet. The stone sides went straight down for fifty feet, cradling murky water in the bottom. He held out his arm to bar her way when Eden came too close to the edge. "Careful. Sometimes this ground gives way."

As if to prove his statement, a shower of grass and rocks broke loose and plummeted to the water some distance below. He stepped back from the edge.

"You intend to jump into that?" Eden demanded in an incredulous tone. She clutched at his arm, peering over the sheer drop, and he turned to look at her.

Humidity had already moistened her hair; it dangled in limp golden tendrils that clung to her cheeks. Perspiration beaded her face and upper lip in tiny drops that glittered like diamond dew, and the cotton shirt clung damply to her breasts. The enticing picture was much too—enticing. He looked away from her and shrugged.

"Don't be silly. It'd be too hard to climb back up. Those rocks lining it are limestone and break easy. Look." He pointed, and she turned to follow his gaze.

Two motmots, gorgeous birds with blue-green plumage, battled for the same limestone ledge jutting from the side. Pieces of ledge crumbled to drop into the cenote with hollow plops. In the jade-green water below, an egret perched atop a clump of floating twigs, preening itself in the sun.

Delicate butterflies with brilliant blue wings as large as dinner plates fluttered above the opaque surface of the water. He heard Eden's murmur of appreciation and turned back to look at her again. A faint smile curved her mouth, and her eyes briefly met his.

"Come on," he said. "We can't stand here all day."

He took a path to the right, leading back into the forest. They followed the thin trail for a few minutes, then he led her down a winding track and under a huge rock ledge to a cave. He stepped inside and motioned her to follow. It was much cooler here, with a mystical quiet that always affected him. It was as if the spirits of countless beings still existed here in the rock walls and shadows. Stalactites punctured the cave's roof, and strange rock formations dripped down the cave walls. A hazy ribbon of sunlight pierced through a rough circular opening in the top of the cave and gleamed mistily on the surface of a vast pool.

"Down there." Steve pointed, and heard Eden's gasp as she came up behind him.

"It's beautiful. So clear and shallow, I can see all the way to the bottom."

"That's deceptive." Steve handed her the calabash gourds. A thin rope pierced the narrow tops of the yellow gourds. They also had a hole in which to pour water, which was plugged by a small piece of cork. The empty gourds made a soft clacking sound as he held them out and said, "You can fill these. The water here is deep, and probably the purest you'll find in Quintana Roo. An underground spring feeds it. Ancient Mayans considered these cenotes sacred. They believed these were the gateway to the underworld, where Mayans enjoyed an afterlife. Of course, they also sacrificed an occasional virgin to keep them flowing."

"Fascinating," Eden murmured with a faint smile. "Don't get any ideas. I've been married."

Steve heaved an exaggerated sigh. "Too bad. Guess a used virgin wouldn't work. You're safe."

Eden turned slightly, tilting her head to one side. A shimmering reflection of sunlight on water played over her face in shifting, erratic patterns. "Am I safe?" she asked in an odd tone. "I wonder."

He didn't like the turn of this conversation. "Yeah, you're safe. Used virgins are a dime a dozen. Here's the soap. I'm going this way. You take that trail. Third stalactite to the left."

Eden looked up at the mineral deposit dangling like a dragon's tooth from the roof of the cave. Directly below it, a narrow trail led downward to the pool. "What if I get lost?"

"Yell."

"I may just do that," she said.

A slow smile curved her lips, and he noticed for the first time how incredibly lush her eyelashes were. They made long, fringed shadows on her cheeks, like butterfly wings on pearl luster. Damn.

Steve felt the absence of solid ground beneath him, as if he'd stepped into empty air. Oh, he was in trouble. It had been a long time since he'd felt this particular churning in his stomach, but he could still recognize it for what it was.

His voice sounded hollow to him when he said, "I won't be that far away. Try not to use all the water."

Feeling more foolish than anything else," he backed away as if she might follow him. She didn't move, but stood with the soap, towel and yellow gourds in one hand and her soiled clothes in the other, watching him. Steve finally turned and walked around a rock wall that would give each of them privacy. Something had changed. Something very important had somehow intruded into the distance he was trying so hard to keep between them. And he knew what it was. It was that damned female awareness that could always cut a man's feet out from under him. Well, he'd be damned if he'd let another woman do it to him. Not this time. This time, he was smarter.

It wasn't until he'd stripped and eased into the clear, cool waters that he began to feel any better. From above, the water had a definite blue tinge. Once immersed, it was as clear as rain. He rolled onto his back and floated. This had always been one of his favorite pastimes. It was serene and peaceful, and he could easily believe that this spot was the gateway to the Mayan underworld. There was a suspension of disbelief as well as gravity when he came here.

Time seemed suspended as well, and he drifted aimlessly in the cool waters while shadows flirted with sunlight against the vaulted rock walls. Steve narrowed his eyes against the glare of light filtering down from above. He heard muted splashing not far away, and couldn't help visualizing Eden at her bath. He'd directed her to a spot in the pool that had a small shallow area lapping at the edge of the rocks, perfect for bathing. And damn him, he couldn't stop imagining her perched atop one of the rocks like a mermaid, washing bare arms and more . . .

Steve abruptly turned over and began to swim. He was vaguely surprised that the water around him hadn't begun to boil, he felt so flushed. Why hadn't the wretched woman stayed in camp? Did she *have* to come with him when he needed this time alone to collect his thoughts and rearrange his priorities?

He remembered his father using that phrase. Such a long time ago, almost like another lifetime. "Rearrange your priorities, son," Samuel Houston Ryan had boomed frequently. "Think about something besides women, whisky, and war."

Too bad he hadn't taken his father's advice. It would have saved him a lot of trouble.

But then, everything happened for a purpose. Or so he'd once believed. There were times lately that he'd begun to think most of what happened was just a celestial jest meant to torment humans. Godly beings toying with the lives of mortals made just as much sense as anything else did, lately.

Which brought him back to the abrupt arrival of the girl in his camp. That she had rolled to his feet at almost the exact moment as he'd mockingly uttered a prayer to an ancient Mayan god could be taken as evidence of divine interference, he supposed. On the other hand, it was more likely due to his rotten luck.

Steve ducked beneath the water, then surfaced several yards away, spouting water like an orca and shaking wet hair from his eyes. Treading water in leisurely strokes, he raked both hands through his hair and blinked to clear his vision.

Then he wished he hadn't.

Lord, these temptations . . .

Eden Miller, oblivious to anything but the pleasure of the cool water and the serenity of the cenote, perched in ivory and rose splendor atop a bare rock. *The Birth of Venus.* There had been a painting like that done by—hell, the name escaped him now. Everything that made any sense escaped him, save for the beauty of the woman adorning the ancient rocks in the same attire as she had come into the world in. But sweet heavens, what a difference twenty-odd years must have made since her first arrival on this earth.

Fair hair, pale and shining like muted gold in the gentle light from above, swung in soft, damp curls over her shoulders. She sat with her arms behind her, palms flat against the stone, and one long leg drawn up, her face tilted toward the light. In silhouette, her bare breasts were high, firm, perfect, with rose-tipped peaks that drew his instant attention.

Steve realized he'd forgotten to tread water when he began to sink, and quickly moved his legs and hands in the familiar pattern that would keep him afloat. He wished he hadn't swam so far. He wished he hadn't seen this. He wished—he wished he hadn't made the first wish that had summoned this goddess to his camp. For an instant, he wondered how to give her back. Then he wondered why he would want to.

Then she looked up, and their gazes locked.

It seemed like an eternity before she reacted, reaching

for the drying shirt spread over a rock to hold in front of her. Steve tried to think of a casual remark, but found it impossible. Any sound he made would more likely resemble a frog's croak than human words anyway, so he didn't bother trying.

In doubt, retreat seemed the most prudent course. He retreated, if not with dignity, at least with all due haste. Damn. His lungs were out of air, and sounded like a faulty bellows as he tried to drag in enough air to fill them. He should have stayed in his camp. At the least, he should have stayed around the rock wall that had given her privacy.

It was as if he'd been drawn to her by unseen currents, and now there would be hell to pay. He knew, with sickening certainty, that he would never be able to pry that vision from his mind . . .

Four

For several stunned moments, Eden sat staring at the spot where Steve had just been. Only gradually widening ripples on the water's surface gave any evidence that he had been there. That, and the oddly breathless constriction in her chest.

It shouldn't have been unexpected. After all, it wasn't as if she hadn't known he was only a few yards away on the other side of the rock wall. Yet his sudden appearance was not what had left this funny feeling in the pit of her stomach. That had occurred when she looked up and realized that the clear water hid nothing of him from her. Beneath the flickering surface of light and shadow, it had been obvious that he was naked. And there had been no mistaking the evidence of his desire. The strong, hard lines of his body were clearly visible.

She hadn't meant to stare. He'd caught her by surprise, that was all. Frozen with shock, and a strange, consuming heat, she had finally fumbled for something to cover herself. Her arms had felt oddly weighted, her motions slow and clumsy, as he'd stayed there in the water, silently watching until she looked up into his eyes.

Even with water dripping from his heavy lashes and his gaze narrowed, she had recognized the hot molten light in his eyes. But it was the unexpected surge of her response that left her reeling. She'd known he found her attractive. She wasn't a naive young girl, and could recognize when a man wanted her. Steve wasn't the first man to look at her that way. He was just the first man who had sparked a similar feeling in her.

Eden looked down at her hands which still held the shirt in front of her. Her fingers were trembling, curled into the thin material, and shaking like wind-blown leaves.

She should not have yielded to the desire to perch atop the rock even for a moment, of course. But her clothes were drying, and the cool water and soft air had felt so good, she had not thought of anything but her own enjoyment.

At least, that's what she told herself.

Maybe, somewhere inside, she had hoped that Steve would swim out too far. That he would be there, and see her. Brutal honesty compelled her to examine her motives, but there was no simple answer.

Not even Colin had ever had this affect on her. At first she'd been so young and innocent, so absolutely unaware of what exactly it was that a man wanted from her, she had not had the experience to recognize the difference between love and desire. Though theirs had been an arranged marriage, she had loved Colin at first. The reality of a physical relationship had never been explained to her, and their wedding night had been a disaster that she had never forgotten. She had never desired him, and perhaps that was part of the reason why their marriage failed.

Eden slipped into her clean, damp undergarments. Steve's loose shirt and trousers clung to her moist skin in places, but at least she was covered. It took several tries before she managed to lace up her heavy ankle boots, but she was grateful they were so sturdy. Hardy footwear was a must in this climate and terrain. Certainly, mere cloth could not survive the rigors of the rain forest.

She'd gathered up her few other garments and climbed to the top of the rocky trail before she heard Steve approaching. He was whistling, as if to warn her. Deciding that to say anything would be to make the incident seem more important than it was, she put a casual smile on her face and waited.

"Finished?" he asked shortly when he joined her, and she noticed that he didn't look directly at her. She nodded.

"Yes. Thank you. My clothes needed a thorough washing."

"What your clothes need," he muttered, "is more material. I hope you don't intend to wear what's left of your skirt again."

"I'm afraid that's a lost cause. Perhaps I can find another use for it."

"Yeah. Good idea. Give me the water gourds. I'll carry them." He walked past, still without looking at her. His eyes were averted, his face stiff and unsmiling. "Well come on. I don't have all day."

She bit her tongue to hold back a sharp comment. It was obvious that he was edgy, and she spared only a brief moment's impatience for the reason. He'd known she was there. It was as much his fault as it was hers. Why should she feel guilty? Or awkward?

A cursory glance at him told her that he was still aroused. It was evident in the taut set of his shoulders and his refusal to meet her eyes. She'd noticed the rapid beat of his pulse in the hollow of his throat, and the grim set of his mouth. Yes, he most definitely was as guilty as she, though neither of them would admit it. For it was not so much what had happened, as what had not.

It occurred to her more than once as she followed his swift progress back into the rain forest, that he was making no attempt to slow his pace for her. It seemed that he wanted—was almost determined—to leave her behind.

Eden was not about to be left behind, or let him know that he was making things hard for her. She kept up with dogged determination, several times almost running when he seemed in danger of disappearing behind a screen of broad leaves and thick, hanging vines. The dirt path was treacherous, and at times all but invisible. Her chest hurt from the effort of keeping up in the wilting heat and humidity, and it was as if she'd never taken a bath. She was drenched with perspiration again, and dirt smeared one palm where she had stumbled and put out a hand to catch herself against a rough-barked mahogany tree. A splinter jabbed the middle finger of her right hand, and she pulled it free.

It had grown cooler in the densest part of the forest. Huge palm leaves towered overhead like serrated green umbrellas. Birds screeched incessantly, and when she glanced up toward the spikes of sunlight threading through dense foliage, she could barely see the fragile blossoms of orchids clinging among the topmost leaves. A paradise, she had once thought. That was before danger and death had visited in the velvety blackness of night. Now she knew what could lurk behind the lush tropical vegetation, and it made her uneasy.

When she glanced up the path again, all she saw was dropping vines and gently waving leaves. She paused and took a deep breath. Surely, he had not left her to find her own way. He must know she was unfamiliar with this path. But there was no sign of him. No indication of which way he had gone, save for the sway of slender tree limbs in a soft breeze.

Shouldering her still-damp laundry and towels, she marched forward. There would be a mark. A slash of his machete would leave traces of his passage. Cut limbs, trampled grasses—there would be something to indicate which way he'd gone. Damn him. He was only doing this to punish her for what had happened in the cave. And it had been as much his fault as hers.

Angry—and beginning to feel scared—Eden pressed her lips together to keep from calling out for him. Wouldn't he love that. It would make him feel superior, probably, to think she was lost. She kept her eyes on the ground at her feet, following the faintest sign of a trail. Weren't those crushed grasses left by footsteps? That broken limb—had it been snapped by a boot?

A loud cry sounded, high and lilting, and it made the hair stand up on the back of her neck. Eden swallowed heavily. A monkey. They could be loud at times, as they screamed and chattered in the treetops. So could toucans, she'd discovered. And parrots were expert at mimicry, sounding like a human or even a jaguar. So clever. So—unsettling.

Her hands tightened on the knot of the towel bundling her damp garments. She bent to pick up a thick, sturdy-looking tree limb. Just in case. One never knew when it might be needed . . .

The tree limb was longer than she'd thought, running back up and under a squatty bush, and she gave it a sharp tug to free it. It came loose quickly, taking her by surprise.

Losing her balance, Eden felt herself tumbling backward, and to her shock, realized that the dense leaves covering the ground were nothing but a flimsy framework concealing a steep ditch. She clutched wildly at them, but they refused to support her. Head over heels, she rolled down the sheer embankment. Dirt flew up around her and branches slapped painfully against her bare skin. She heard something rip, and hoped it was just material.

When she came to a stop, dazed and aching, she sat up slowly and looked around. Her hair hung in her eyes, a pale tangle thick with leaves and debris. She pulled it back with a shaking hand and took a deep breath to keep from crying. Hot tears blurred her vision for a moment, and she wiped them away with the back of her hand. She would not cry. She would not.

Deep scratches striped her knees, and she saw that one leg of the loose trousers was ripped almost to the waist. Gingerly testing her arms and legs, she decided nothing was broken, only bruised. As well as her pride.

She stood up slowly and looked around. It was as if the lush jungle growth had closed in around her. She didn't even see her laundry anywhere. After a moment of indecision, Eden began to climb back up the hill the way she'd come. It had to be this way. There were broken limbs and crushed vines . . .

But when she reached the top of the hill, she saw nothing familiar. No laundry bundle lay discarded within sight. Had she made a mistake? She turned slowly, peering upward to try and ascertain her position by the sun.

Two steps took her onto a patch of cleared ground that looked as if it might be a path. Pride no longer seemed important, and she took a deep breath and called for Steve.

The only reply was the screech of birds in the treetops. A series of hiccoughing cries that made her think of a loon vibrated in the thick, humid air. Then there was silence except for the rhythmic murmur of birds.

She took another deep breath and called again. "Steve. Over here . . ."

No answer. Panic welled up, but she pushed it determinedly back down. He might resent her, but he wouldn't abandon her. When he realized she wasn't behind him, he would turn around and look for her. And then she would tell him what she thought of him . . . once she was safely back in his camp.

Taking another deep breath for courage, she walked several steps along the level pathway. Grass covered it, but it was surprisingly free of rocks. Perhaps this was the way back after all. It had all the earmarks of a defined pathway.

She walked for several minutes, limping at times from her fall, but growing increasingly confident that she was headed in the right direction. She just didn't remember everything, that was all. Nothing looked familiar because everything here was strange to her.

Several times she cupped her hands over her mouth and called for Steve, more to guide him to her than because she was frightened. It was still daylight, with the sun directly overhead and filtering through tree limbs and heavy leaves to spatter over the forest floor. Birds flitted above in a flash of brilliant color and excited screeches. Rustling in the branches resulted in a shower of falling leaves or an occasional branch, and she could hear the curious chattering of monkeys. Paco had told her that as long as small creatures did not suddenly flee, there would be no large predator lurking nearby. It was vaguely comforting to hold that thought to her. Though most predators were nocturnal, there were enough abroad in daylight to make her wary.

When the path abruptly ended in a high tangle of thick, wild vines and brush, Eden hesitated. This wasn't the way after all. Steep banks dropped from each side of the wide path, studded with large stones and choked with vines. She slanted a glance upward, and was dismayed to see that the sun had dipped deeply below the treetops. It would be dark within an hour or two. She must have been walking far longer than she'd thought.

Her leg throbbed, and her clothes were damp with perspiration. She stood indecisively, listening to the sounds of chirping insects and the whir of birds. A slight breeze lifted the hair from where it clung in damp strands to her neck, and she gave a distracted shove at a stray tendril dangling in her eyes.

What was it Colin had told her? Something about staying in one spot when lost so that searchers could find her. Well, she'd gone far beyond that now. She was tired. And hungry and thirsty. And—lost.

The old fear began to creep over her. She'd thought herself safe for a brief time; now she was alone again. Even Steve would look good to her, though he certainly should shoulder the blame for this. If he hadn't been irritated at something that was entirely his own fault, he wouldn't have walked away so quickly. Of course, there was the possibility that he had meant to lose her. He'd made it clear enough that she wasn't wanted there.

But, whether he meant to or not, he'd also made it very clear that she was wanted in a different way. Damn him.

Eden's legs felt weak and wobbly, and she looked down for a safe spot to rest. Preferably on something besides rotting leaves that might hide snakes or other undesirables. Though vine-choked, there seemed to be a flat stone beneath a particularly large chunk of leaves. She bent to pull away the vines, and found it easy enough. Though she scraped her hand, she soon had a spot cleared. She would sit and wait, and every so often, call out for Steve. With any luck, he would hear and get to her before dark.

As she removed the last clinging vine, her fingers brushed against an odd curve in the stone. Frowning, Eden bent to investigate the strange protrusion. Then her throat tightened, and her heart gave a sudden lurch.

There, staring back at her from under the leaf-framed shroud, was the fierce image of a stone jaguar. Fangs bared and eyes glaring, the glyph still held traces of ancient paint along carved lines that must have been hewn a thousand years before.

With trembling hands, Eden reached out to touch the lichened stone just behind it. She could barely discern the outline of another carving, hidden behind the ravages of time . . .

Swearing, Steve doubled back again. Damn her. He'd known she would be trouble. Any woman who was the lone survivor of a massacre and who had then managed to make her way through nearly impenetrable forest to his camp, could be nothing but trouble. He should have sent her right back up that hill with a map and his best wishes. Or just a map. But no. He'd let her stay, against his better judgment.

Now look. Night would soon fall, and he was tramping around in the brush searching for a woman who didn't have sense enough to keep up with him. He tried to ignore the quick sting of guilt. It wasn't his fault if she was slow. She could have kept up if she'd really tried.

A vision of her flashed through his mind as he'd seen her atop the rock, and he scowled at the memory. His lust for her wasn't exactly unexpected, considering how long he'd been alone out here, but it was damned inconvenient. Maybe because it was different, somehow, than the normal, everyday lust he felt for other women. With Eden—it was odd, but he felt as if she could be more to him than a momentary pleasure; an easing of the mind rather than the body. And that was dangerous.

Frowning, Steve shifted her abandoned bundle of laundry to his other hand. He'd found it a while back, lying at the spot where she'd obviously fallen off the trail. Clumsy female. Didn't she know enough to recognize what was solid ground and what wasn't? Even the rankest amateur should be able to see that a patch of vines would hardly bear any weight. And if she'd wanted to stop and relieve herself, why hadn't she called out to him? He would have waited. Probably.

Another curse formed in his mind, but remained unspoken. It was nearing dusk. Mosquitos had begun to swarm with an irritating ferocity that made him wish he'd brought the jar of repellent with him. He'd better find Eden soon or they'd both be dinner for the voracious little pests. Damn her. If he didn't find the wretched woman before dark, he would be tempted to smear her with something enticing and stake her out for the blasted swarms of mosquitos to devour.

That particular thought provoked an image that was vivid and mind-numbing. Flashes of the way she'd looked perched atop that rock returned to haunt him, and he cursed again, this time loud and fervently.

Above, a green and gold parrot picked up the phrase and repeated it in a screeching lilt that made him glance up. It stared back at him with bright, beady eyes, squawking again, *"Damn it all to hell . . ."*

"Yes," he said to the colorful bird, "my sentiments exactly."

With a noisy flutter of wings, the bird vaulted from the limb and streaked skyward; echoes of Steve's curse drifted back to him as he bent to examine a broken branch. She'd come this way. Good thing he meant her no harm. A blind man could follow this trail.

Even as he was slightly amending the "meant her no harm" part, he heard something just ahead and rose slowly to his feet. It sounded like a soft cry. And female.

Grimly, Steve swung his rifle down from his shoulder and clenched the hilt of his machete as he moved stealthily forward. He'd gone no more than a few yards when he saw a flash of movement, a blur of white, then another cry. His grip on the rifle tightened, and his muscles tensed with expectation.

Then he saw his white shirt and *calzones* seemingly suspended in mid-air. Before he completely recovered from this surprise, he saw that Eden was still in them. Her hair was bound atop her head with a strip of white, and dirt liberally streaked the loose garments she wore. She was climbing up a slanted wall of vines, pausing to exclaim now and then before continuing upward.

"Another one," she cried excitedly, and snatched with furious energy at the vines.

Steve's eyes narrowed. He swung the rifle back over his shoulder and stalked forward until he stood directly below her. Now he could see that she was climbing up some kind of structure all but obscured by tropical vegetation, but the knowledge didn't lessen his irritation.

"What the hell do you think you're doing?" he demanded harshly, and was startled by her sudden scream. He should have seen it coming, but it was still a shock when she toppled backwards. He barely caught her before she hit the ground, a solid weight in his arms that took them both down in a bruising crash.

With the wind half-knocked from him, it took a moment to recover. Eden, however, had the benefit of landing atop him instead of the hard ground, and took full advantage of his silence.

Scrambling to her feet, she glared down at him. "How dare you scare me like that? And why did you run off and leave me? But never mind that. Look at what I've found."

He didn't care what she'd found. Just as she got off him, her foot struck him in the groin and he was having a great deal of trouble catching his breath. When he did manage to draw in a ragged gulp of air, it brought with it a stabbing pain. He had the vague hope it had nothing to do with the machete, which he thought he'd had the presence of mind to toss out of the way when he saw her falling toward him.

"Glyphs," she was saying blissfully, waving a hand toward the stone and vine tower. "On steps, I think. They're so narrow it's hard to tell . . . well, not actual glyphs, perhaps, but some kind of carvings. Glyphs are usually found on stelae set in solitary sort of statues . . . are you all right? You don't look well. Your face is all red—haven't caught your breath yet? Sorry. It's your own fault though, for scaring me."

Hearing all this through a haze of pain, he managed to roll to his belly and get to his knees. He felt like hurting her. If he could only summon the strength, he just might. Finally, he was able to draw in a breath that didn't feel riddled with needles, and he glared up at Eden.

She wasn't looking at him, but at the damned structure she had found. There was a pleased smile on her face, and she sort of—glowed. As if she'd swallowed a lit candle. Thoughts of murder altered slightly. He recalled feeling that kind of fervor, though it had been a long time ago. Before he'd made the grim discovery that there wasn't much room for genuine enthusiasm in this world. People and events always seemed to find it necessary to eradicate that sort of thing.

"What," he forced out when he saw her turn around and bend down to retrieve his machete, "are you doing now?"

"Oh. Just thought I'd hack away some of these vines. This is rather heavier than it looks, isn't it? But it seems sharp enough. I'm certain if we can just clear enough away, we'll find—oh!"

Lurching to his feet, Steve was able to snatch away his machete before she smashed it against the stones. "Give me that. I have no intention of allowing you to dull my blade on that damned stone. Nor do I want to tear up what's left of my clothes applying a tourniquet to whatever part of yourself you don't slice off."

"Well." She drew herself up stiffly. "Really. Don't you feel the least bit of excitement or interest about this discovery?"

"The only thing," Steve muttered as he carefully wiped clean the blade of his machete, "that would excite me right now is sitting in front of my own fire before my own hut. Alone." He thought a moment before adding, "With a glass of bourbon."

"I hardly think—"

"That's just it," he cut in, looking up at her. "You hardly think before you do anything. Did it occur to you that you might get lost out here? Or do you have some sort of gift for stumbling across unwary inhabitants who you expect to deliver you to safety?"

She stared at him. Before she lowered her lashes, he saw a sheen moisten her eyes. Then her mouth quivered slightly before her lips pressed into a tight line.

Narrowing his eyes, he snarled, "Don't you dare cry. If anyone deserves to cry, it's me. I wanted a swim—alone, I might add. That was all I asked. You insisted upon coming along, and I seem to recall a promise not to be any trouble. An obvious lie. It's almost dark now. We won't be able to make it back to my camp where there is food and comfort. And mosquito netting. Instead, it seems that we will be spending the night here. I hope you're satisfied."

For a moment, he thought she might cry anyway. But she didn't. Beyond a muffled sound, she kept any tears to herself.

"I beg your pardon," she said softly. "You're right, of course. About my promise not to be any trouble." She lifted her head then, and he instantly realized his mistake. In the drenched blue of her eyes was a blaze of anger, not tears. "However, I did not expect that you would do your best to lose me. My mistake. I should not have expected you to behave as a gentleman. It's obvious you are not."

"No," he said shortly. "I am not. I never said that I was." He took a step closer to her, and saw the anger in her eyes alter to uncertainty. "In fact, Mrs. Miller, I am known throughout a large portion of the United States as a very *un*gentlemanly sort of fellow. You would be very wise to remember that in the future. It could save you a great deal of inconvenience."

There was a heavy silence. He was close enough to her to count each individual eyelash that curved over wide blue eyes which were filling with fear. He'd seen eyes like that too many times before, the quick dilation of pupils, then the opaque glaze of terror.

It was not one of his most comfortable memories.

Her lashes lowered to shield her eyes. "Thank you," she finally said in a barely audible voice, "for the warning."

He stepped back and continued cleaning his machete with his shirt tail. "You're welcome. Now, if you'll please be kind enough to gather a few sturdy sticks each about a foot long, I'll do my best to find us something to eat. And drink, since I left the water behind when I began to search for you."

Not glancing up when she finally moved, he had the thought that he'd done a fine job of scaring the hell out of her. He just hoped he hadn't done too good a job, or he might find himself dismembered in his sleep. Fear did strange things to people. And he, of all men, should know that well enough.

Five

Firelight cast high, glowing shadows in the trees and over the ground. Eden focused on the wavering shapes of flames dancing over stilted tree roots and wide-leafed palms, and occasionally dared a glance toward Steve.

Since their confrontation, he'd not said much to her. She was grateful for that. If for no other reasons than because she found it hard to meet his hostile stare with the necessary show of backbone. It wasn't that she didn't have any backbone. She did. But she found it much too disconcerting to face an irate male when she had no idea what exactly it was she was supposed to be afraid of. His allusions to being villainous were, she knew, intended to frighten her. But the reason for this was mystifying. Was it to keep a certain distance between them? If that was his motive, she would be more than happy to cooperate. Such theatrical maneuvers were hardly necessary.

Smoke rose from the fire; flames made a hissing sound as the fowl Steve was turning on a makeshift spit dripped grease. He did not look up, his face a collage of hellish light and shadows.

"I like mine well-cooked," Eden ventured to say when Steve tore off a strip of meat that looked much too pink. The upward glance he flung her from beneath the black bristle of his lashes was brief and dismissing. He stuffed the meat into his mouth and continued to turn the green stick holding the roasting bird. It smelled delicious. Her stomach growled in anticipation, and she refused to think about the beautiful creature she'd seen dangling from his hand only a short time ago.

The foot-long sticks she'd provided had been used to form a snare, along with narrow strips of cloth torn from the clean skirt still in her laundry bundle. Steve had made quick work of the feathered prey, wringing its neck with a deft twist that had been slightly unnerving to Eden.

"Not used to killing your own dinner, I see," he'd muttered at her faint squeak. "Guess you think it comes already plucked and gutted."

She had made no reply to that. In his absence, she'd gathered what looked like edible fruit from nearby trees while there was still enough light to see. Most of it he'd thrown away upon his return, but there were a few nuts that he'd kept. These were roasting in damp leaves nestled among some embers at one side of the fire.

"What kind of bird is that?" she asked as Steve turned it with another deft motion. "It seems rather large."

"Turkey."

"A turkey?"

He slashed her another glance from beneath his lashes. "Yes, a turkey. I don't know what part of the States you're from, but I'm certain you must have heard of turkeys before."

"Of course I have," she snapped. "I just didn't know they ranged in the Yucatán. And this bird didn't look like any turkey I've ever seen."

"I imagine not." Giving the spit a last turn, Steve stood up to remove the cooked bird. "Turkeys here have prettier feathers. They taste a little gamier, though."

Eden glanced toward the neat pile of plucked feathers. She had to admit he was right. Domestic turkeys were usually shades of brown or gray. This bird had more closely resembled a peacock with brilliant greens, blues, and coppers marking its plumage. The head had been a soft, pale blue, and the comb atop had been blue as well, though dotted with small gold knobs that had also crusted the eyelids.

"Well," she said while he deftly sliced the bird with a few quick strokes of his machete, "if it tastes half as good as it smells, I won't be disappointed."

"Beggars can't be choosers."

"How clever. I wish I'd said that."

Glancing up, a half-smile touched the hard corners of his mouth. "I know others—Waste not, want not. A stitch in time saves nine."

"A penny saved is a penny earned . . . Marry in haste, repent in leisure—I suppose you have a *Farmer's Almanac* tucked among your books."

"Probably. Full of good advice as well as bad clichés." He lay several slices of turkey atop the clean patch of skirt that was serving as a tablecloth over their stone-top table.

Steam rose in thin wisps that curled toward Eden, and she breathed deeply. Her mouth watered and her stomach rumbled with a noise loud enough to draw Steve's amused glance. She wiped her mouth with her fingertips. "Shall I pull the nuts from the fire?"

"Only if you want a burnt hand. Here. I'll do it." He leaned forward and used the tip of his machete to scoop the smoldering leaf from the embers. He had them unwrapped with only a few soft curses and minimally burned fingers, dumping them next to the pile of turkey meat. "Dinner is served. Oh wait—you must be thirsty. Native wine." He rolled two green coconuts to one side. "I do hope it's properly chilled—shall I?"

With an adroit move, he brought his machete down, splitting the top off one of the coconuts. He caught up the larger portion and held it out. "As tasty as the finest wine, madam."

Bemused by his transformation from villain to valiant, Eden accepted the coconut. She needed both hands to hold it, and the sparse hairs of the outer covering tickled her palms. She shifted the heavy coconut to a better position.

"Is this coconut ripe?" she asked doubtfully. "It's still green on the outside."

"If it was ripe there wouldn't be any milk." Steve brought his machete down on the other coconut. "As it ripens, the milk is absorbed by the meaty part. Go ahead—drink. It's a bit sweet, but tasty and good for you. And safer than water from the lake."

"What lake?"

"We're right next to one, didn't you know that?" He waved an arm in a vague half-circle. "That's why the mosquitos are so bad right here. The ancient Mayans occasionally built next to one. There are several lakes in this area. Try the coconut milk. It's good."

To her surprise, he was right. Eden took another sip, then carefully placed the round shell in a dip on the ground. Satisfied it would not tip over and spill out the milk, she looked up to find Steve watching her. Her stomach did a funny kind of flip. She looked away, then back, feeling awkward.

"You have a milk mustache," he said solemnly, and she laughed as she wiped her mouth with the edge of her shirt.

"Thank you. That was good, but I want to try the turkey now."

He motioned toward the still steaming turkey piled on the stone between them. "Help yourself. Ladies first."

"Why do I suddenly feel apprehensive?" she asked as she leaned forward and picked up a generous slice of meat. It was delicious. She sighed with pleasure, even licking her fingers when she'd finished. To her surprise, Steve shelled one of the roasted nuts and handed it to her.

"Try it. It might taste bitter at first, but it's really quite good. It's a breadnut. Kind of like a chestnut."

It was bitter, but piquant enough to enjoy. She took the next one he offered her as well, then some more meat. By the time she'd finished, she was quite full. Feeling lazy, she stretched out on the ground close to the fire and sipped from the coconut shell. She looked up, gazing at the canopy of leaves overhead. The moon was a faint arc in the sky, glistening with a greenish light through the web of leaves, looking for all the world like a huge slice of jade. Beautiful, exotic, a priceless treasure in a land of mystery and marvel. She'd never looked at the moon in quite that way. But then, there was a lot she'd never viewed with the perspective she'd acquired since coming to this fascinating land of contrasts. Unable to resist, she turned to look at her rescuer again.

Steve still sat cross-legged in front of the flat stone they were using as a table. He was stripping the turkey carcass of the meat and placing it in a neat pile. She watched his hands move efficiently, and wondered as to the real reason he had chosen to live in this remote wilderness. It couldn't be simply the war. Disillusion might cause a man to leave his country, but wouldn't he want eventually to return?

A log in the fire popped, startling her, and she turned to gaze into the leaping flames Tiny sparks rose, burning quickly into ash. In the distance, a faint, plaintive call rose in a shivering wail, then faded away.

"Tapacamino," Steve said without looking up.

"What?"

"The bird you just heard. A tapacamino. It always sounds so sad." He popped a chunk of glistening turkey meat into his mouth and looked up at her. There was a dark intensity to his gold cat-eyes as he regarded her for a moment. "Everything here has a name and purpose, you know. Wind, rain—even animals have souls or masquerade as gods."

She ran her fingers over the rough round shape of the coconut. "And do you?"

"Have a purpose? Or a soul?" He rose to his feet, wiping his hands on his pants. "Neither, I think."

It wasn't exactly reassuring, and she tilted her head back to look up at him. Smoke from the fire curled around him in gauzy drifts. Shadowed, his face was a dark blur of devil's brows, white teeth, and the gleaming eyes of a jaguar. He moved slightly, and beneath his open shirt, his muscles flexed as gracefully dangerous as those of a predator. She looked away again, then flushed at his soft laughter.

"Do I scare you, little girl?"

"Are you trying to?"

"Maybe."

Defiantly, she sat up and met his steady gaze. "Why? What have I done to you, except ask for your help in getting out of here? You've been rude and mean since I first chanced upon your camp, when I think you would be eager enough to get me away from here . . ."

"Oh, I am," he replied coolly. "But that doesn't mean I'm enthused at the prospect of escorting you through a hundred and fifty miles of jungle and desert to get rid of you."

She took a deep breath. "I understand that. It's a long trek to Merída. I am not unaware of the rigors of such a journey, but I am certain that the officials of the Metropolitan Society would be quite willing to repay you a generous amount for your trouble."

"How nicely put." He came to her and knelt down so that their faces were on the same level. She drew in a sharp breath at the fierce glitter in his eyes. "Let me put it to you in a way that you will understand. If I escort you to Merída, I would be a fool to let anyone know my name. Or that I helped you. Or that I am still alive."

Puzzled, she shook her head. "I don't understand what you mean . . ."

"Allow me to be blunt—if I show my face anywhere that I might be recognized by government officials, I will more than likely be shot on sight. Does that help?"

A chill raked down her spine with sharp teeth, and she shivered. "Yes. That puts matters in a very different light."

"Excellent. Now that we understand one another, we can

come to an agreement as to the best means for your departure."

Eden stared at him. It was obvious he had no intention of explaining himself further. Questions crowded her lips, but she wasn't at all certain she wanted to know just why he would be shot on sight. The answer might be more terrifying than the mystery.

Maybe he shouldn't have done that. Actually, Steve wasn't quite sure why he had, except that things were getting too comfortable between them. Too—easy. Yeah, that was it. He found it easy to talk to her, easy to laugh, easy to look at her and wonder . . .

Eden Miller was intelligent, courageous, and beautiful. The kind of woman who attracted him. And that was the ultimate problem. He didn't want to be attracted to her. Not that way. Physical attraction was all right, because it was limited to a few rolls in the hay with both their going separate ways in the end. But to be drawn to a woman for any deeper reason would be disastrous.

Steve hacked viciously at a vine, the blade of his machete severing it with ruthless efficiency. He didn't need to be involved with anyone. To have someone be important to him. Allowing anyone into his life only precluded happiness. He should know that well enough. It never failed.

When he had a pile of leafy vines and moss that looked to be enough, he carried it back to the fire where Eden sat with her knees drawn up to her chest. Her arms were curved around her bent legs as if for protection. He didn't blame her. He'd done everything he could to scare her to death. She was probably contemplating a preference between the predators ranging through the jungle, and the one she'd just joined for dinner.

Catching a quick, surreptitious glance toward him from beneath her curved lashes only confirmed his suspicion.

Well, he should be happy now. He'd managed to shatter their earlier comradery.

He dumped the vines and moss on the ground near the fire. "Here. This will be more comfortable than sleeping on the ground. Spread a towel over your half of the pile for a bed. Use the other towel as protection against the worst of the insects."

She slanted him another quick glance. "There are only two towels. What will you use?"

"I don't need one." He shrugged. "A little more green wood will make enough smoke to keep the worst of the pests away from us. I'm used to them anyway."

Rising, she muttered, "I don't see how. I'm not certain I could ever get used to so many insects."

"You can get used to anything you have to. God knows, I've done it often enough."

She didn't say anything to that, but bent to plump up a pile of vines and moss into a bed. One leg of the loose trousers had been ripped almost to the waist, and she'd tied it in a kind of knot at her knee that still provided ample glimpses of bare thigh each time she moved. He indulged himself in a brief fantasy before shifting his gaze elsewhere. No point in borrowing trouble. Hadn't he done enough damage for the night? The barriers should be firmly in place by now.

After spreading one of the towels over the cushioning moss, Eden straightened with a pleased smile. "There. That looks comfy enough. As cozy as my own room at home."

"I shudder to think of your former circumstances, then," he muttered. A few swift motions arranged his own bedding by the fire, as far away from Eden as possible. He could hear her moving about, the rustling of leaves, moss, and vines as she settled herself for the night. With the fire between them, it was much easier to contemplate the flames instead of the woman.

Damn good thing, he thought in the next instant when

she began to remove her boots. Even through the flickering flames he could see an alluring amount of bare leg as she crossed one over the other to unlace her footwear. He tore his gaze away and focused on the towering black structure looming behind them. A temple, of course. Even beneath the thick shroud of vines he could detect the unmistakable rise of shallow steps that would lead to the very top. He'd seen a lot of them in the jungle, ancient edifices with detailed carvings and tunnels that often held a king's ransom in precious jade and gold. Not that he was about to tell that to Eden. No, she'd pester him to reveal their locations, and he certainly didn't want a lot of Americans down here rambling about. There was always the chance he would be recognized.

Steve rolled onto his back and stared up at the patches of sky visible through tight-laced branches. A three-quarter moon was high overhead, silvering the night. In the distance, a tanager gave a startled whistle and was joined by a brief, rasping chorus of frog-throated toucans. A few monkeys joined in, a high-pitched chattering of sleepy protests that quickly died down. Even in the jungle there were residents annoyed by loud neighbors.

Leaves shifted and rustled high overhead, and the sharp tang of smoke from the fire filled the air. Unfortunately, the smoke didn't help him much when it came to the insects. He'd chosen to sit upwind of the fire. But, he was more accustomed to the biting. Besides, he didn't want to hear her whine about insect bites.

"Steve?" came the soft voice from across the fire, and he tensed.

"Yeah?"

"Good night."

He closed his eyes. "Good night." Good Lord. With two words she could blast a devastating hole in the barriers he'd erected. A simple, soft-voiced "Good night" and he felt his resolve crumbling like limestone walls. God, he was weak.

Why did he have to keep remembering how she'd looked atop that rock today? Ivory skin, pink pearl and smooth, damp from the water, and a fall of angel-pale hair in long, curling drifts . . .

Botticelli. That was it. The name of the artist who had created *Birth of Venus*. Yeah. Those Italians knew how to bring the female form alive with a few dabs of paint and an empty canvas.

With the real thing only a few feet away beyond a stack of burning logs, he was burning alive with frustration. What was it his father had once told him—? Be careful what you wish for because you might get it. That was it. He still hadn't learned. He was still burning wishes.

What he should be envisioning was a way to get her away from her newfound interests and back to his camp without too much difficulty. When she'd looked at the glyphs he'd recognized that gleam in her eyes for what it was—trouble. And he sure didn't need that.

No, what he needed was to rid himself of her at the first opportunity. Merída was out of the question, but so was Tulum, where the Cruzob were so hostile to whites. If he could manage to get her south to Ambergris Cay where James Blake could help out, that might work. Blake knew him, and wouldn't betray him. Trouble was, Ambergris Cay was a hell of a lot farther away than Tulum. The farther he went from the safety of the remote rain forest, the more he risked.

But the alternative involved keeping her. And that involved certain risks as well. So, was it riskier taking her down the coast, or having her close enough to ruin him? It was like choosing between a crocodile-infested swamp or a pit full of jaguars.

Rubbing his eyes with the heels of his hands, he smothered a groan of disgust at his predicament. Maybe he should invoke the name of Itzamná again and make another wish.

This one could hardly have any worse consequences than his last impulsive request.

A piercing scream brought him bolt upright. Before he could determine the source of the sound, he was struck forcibly with a warm, heavy weight. It straddled him so quickly that he half-fell back off his bed. An instant later, he recognized Eden.

Wrapping her arms and legs around him like a baby monkey, she half-sobbed, "S-s-something is in bed with me . . . !"

"No," he said firmly, "you have that backward. Something is in bed with me."

She was shaking. He could feel the tremors ripple through her body, and at almost the same time, he realized that she was wearing little more than her chemise. Long, bare legs straddled his waist, her thighs pressed against his lower ribs.

Lord, these challenges . . .

"Eden, for Chrissake—"

"No, I mean it . . . there's something in my bed."

"Why do I feel like one of the three bears?" he muttered. "All right, Goldilocks. I'll get up and see what it is." She didn't move, so he slid his hands up her arms to grasp her elbows. Her grip tightened. "I can't get up until you let go," he said in what he hoped was a reasonable tone that did not betray his growing arousal pressed so close to her soft body.

Bending her head so that her hair brushed against his jaw, she shuddered. He could feel her warmth, and it was all he could do not to put his arms around her shaking body and draw her even closer. He clenched his teeth.

Her breasts were pressed against his bare chest. He could feel the stiff pressure of her nipples against his skin even through the thin muslin of her chemise. It was hardly helping things to have her next to him like this. Damn the woman. Did she somehow know what he had been thinking? Because if she had, she would certainly know that this close a proximity was liable to have him putty in her hands before long.

"Get *off* me," he said through clenched teeth, and she tilted back her head to look up at him with wide, frightened eyes. A shiver trembled through her quaking limbs.

He could hold back no longer. He didn't care what was in her bed, or what had scared her, or why she had ended up in his lap. She was here, all warm and soft and needy, and it ignited every male instinct he had been doing his best to smother.

Tangling one hand in the hair at the back of her neck, he held her still and kissed her. To his vague surprise, she didn't react with shock. It was as if she'd known what he would do. His mouth closed hard on hers, harshly tender and demanding. Then her lips parted, opening for his tongue, and he was lost.

Six

It was the dream that was to blame. Since the night of the massacre, it haunted her. Even half-awake, she'd felt the coils of terror closing tightly around her, and then the brush of something against her bare leg had catapulted her from the bed toward Steve. Blind with driving fear, her only thought had been to reach safety.

And despite his determined efforts to frighten her with his broad hints of villainy, Steve represented safety. She didn't know whether to believe all he'd said, or whether he was only building walls between them for reasons of his own.

In the dark terror, it didn't matter.

She clung to him with trembling arms as he kissed her. Awash with unfamiliar sensations, still quivering inside from the dream, her head tilted slowly back under the pressure of his mouth. He kissed her parted lips, his tongue stealing inside and igniting a fire in the pit of her stomach. She moaned softly, helplessly. When Steve's lips moved to her eyes, her cheek, then her throat before claiming her mouth again, she shuddered.

"Damn you," he said against her parted lips, the words more of a groan than a curse. "Damn you."

There was an urgency in the way he shifted to pull her closer to him, his hands moving down to cup her hips and drag her body up to his. Eden didn't resist when he held her there; his breath was hot against the side of her neck, and she discovered that the tiny fire in the pit of her stomach had grown into a raging blaze.

Her bare thighs scraped against the leather belt around his waist as she arched closer. With a kind of helpless motion, her hands moved to his shoulders. She could feel him shudder beneath her splayed fingers, a slight tremor of muscle that betrayed his reaction. A hoarse mutter escaped him, and his teeth raked against the sensitive skin of her throat.

Everything around them swirled out of focus, and she was conscious only of his heated breath against her skin, the pounding of blood through her veins, and the sweep of his hands down over her shoulders to the rise of her breasts. His palms moved to caress them, fingers and thumbs grazing the muslin-covered nipples. She arched into his hands, feeling the world slip away.

His touch escalated her breathing, so that she felt as if she were drinking in heated air, liquid and hot and so consuming that she was aflame with it. Fear had been replaced by something even more suffocating. And dangerous.

Slowly drawing away the edge of her bodice, Steve's fingers slipped inside the thin muslin to explore the shape of her breasts. Cool night air whispered over her bare skin, and she shuddered at the exquisite contrast of heat and cold.

"Damn," he said again "This is crazy . . ."

When he pushed her abruptly away, she gave a disappointed protest. Her hands fell away from him. Then he was pulling her hard against him again, a rough embrace that trapped her hands between them. Beneath the curve of her palm, she could feel the steady, hard thud of his heart. Its rapid beat echoed her own, wild and tempestuous and dangerous. Too dangerous. Her fingers curled into his bare skin, and from somewhere deep inside, she found the strength to push him slightly away.

Steve let out a harsh breath that tickled the side of her face and shifted her hair. His chest rose and fell erratically, as if he were having trouble breathing. His voice was a rough growl.

"I'll check out your bed, Goldilocks. You wait here."

Eden swayed slightly when he set her on her feet and moved away. She pulled her chemise back up to cover herself, and watched as he strode to her bed and bent to investigate. He stripped away the towels and shook them, then turned to glance at her. He pointed to the ground.

"Scorpion. Curious, I guess, but fairly harmless."

"Scorpion . . . ?"

"He wouldn't have hurt you unless you rolled over on him. The bite isn't too bad. He looks more vicious than he really is." He paused, then caught her gaze and added softly, "Unlike me."

"You don't have to keep saying things like that," she said irritably, and crossed her arms over her chest against a sudden chill. "I am well aware that you want me to believe you are the worst villain on earth. All right. I believe it. Now what?"

Steve blinked, and she had the impression he was more surprised than anything. What did he expect? Maybe she had some reservations about him, but she wasn't so bad a judge of character that she couldn't recognize some decency in him too. After all, he hadn't done anything *too* bad. Except go off and leave her. And try to frighten her half to death. . . . She sighed.

"Hell," Steve snarled, "I don't know. You jumped into my bed, remember. You tell me."

"I was frightened," she said defensively. She shivered, increasingly aware that she was standing there barely-clad while he glowered at her. Perhaps it hadn't been such a good idea to remove her outer garments before lying down. At the time—in light of his obvious efforts to keep her at arm's length—it had seemed preferable to sleeping in soiled, ripped garments. Now she knew better.

"Are you still frightened?" he snapped. "If not, you

should be. I'm not feeling particularly generous right now, and if you keep standing there without any clothes, I'm liable to do just what I've wanted to do since you rolled down that damned hill and landed at my feet. Do I need to explain to you in detail what that is, or do you think you can figure it out on your own?"

Oh no. She knew exactly what he wanted. Even if she hadn't suspected it before, the truth was in front of her in the form of a man with blazing gold eyes and tight pants that revealed his arousal. It didn't help to realize that she was struggling against a similar reaction.

Drawing in a shaky breath, she said with as much dignity as she could muster, "I shall go back to bed now. Thank you for your assistance. And for being such a gentleman."

"Any time, Goldilocks." He bent and swept up the towels from the ground to toss them on her mossy mattress. "But next time," he said when she walked toward him, "don't go climbing all over me unless you mean it. I'm not a gentleman. And I won't make any promises I may not be able to keep."

Still holding her arms across her chest—and achingly aware that her legs were bare and covered with goose-flesh—she walked past him to her bed. The heat of his gaze was almost as scorching as her burning curiosity as to what might have happened if he hadn't been such a gentleman.

Morning came with a subtle change of noises. The nocturnal creatures found their holes or burrows, while the daytime inhabitants gave noisy greetings to the sun. A flock of chachalacas that looked more like the turkeys Eden knew, cried raucously. Their high-pitched squeaks sounding remarkably similar to someone yelling, "Knock it off, knock it off!" was answered by a gruff, lower-toned, "Keep it up, keep it up!"

Steve was already awake. Truth be told, he'd been awake

for a while. It wasn't easy to sleep when all he could think about was what might have happened—if he hadn't been such a damned *gentleman*.

Smothering a curse, he rose and moved to stoke up the fire with fresh wood. He glanced at Eden. She was asleep, the towel covering her revealing the fact that she'd decided to wear the shirt and trousers again. Prudent, if a little late.

Now the barriers were once again in place, though not as firm as they had been. It occurred to him that in the past twenty-four hours, he had undergone some vast revisions in his thinking. The pendulum had swung back and forth with amazing rapidity, from desire to denial and back. Denial was, of course, the most sensible direction to take. Anything else would only complicate matters.

By the time Eden awoke, Steve had a little fire going and leftover turkey laid out on the same rock they'd used the night before. A few pieces of fresh fruit lay next to the meat, and he didn't look at her when he said, "Breakfast is served."

She looked at him with shy wariness, a flicker of her long lashes and a glance that skittered away as quickly as she dared. He understood. After all, she had definitely responded last night, and unless she was a coward or a liar or both, she'd have to acknowledge it at least to herself. It was that response that had almost been too much, her open mouth and the silky feel of her bare breasts beneath his hands . . .

Steve rose abruptly. No point in dwelling on it now. If he had any sense, he'd get rid of her quickly. Any way he could. Or he was going to end up making one of those mistakes that could cost him his freedom. Or his life.

"When you're through eating," he said, as he slung his rifle over one shoulder, "we'll head back to my camp."

Eden looked up. "I want to look at the glyphs a little more closely first, please. It's very important to me."

"It's not to me."

She put on her boots, and then finished lacing them before saying firmly, "I won't take long."

He bent to scoop up a portion of turkey meat and an orange, then stuck his machete into his belt loop. "Take all the time you want. I'll see you later."

"Steve . . ." Lurching to her feet, Eden gave him an imploring look. She gestured toward the spire of vines and vegetation. "It could be an important find."

"And what will you do if it is? You have no equipment. No paper or pen and ink—nothing but stubborn persistence. You don't even know where you are, for Chrissake. How do you think you'll be able to document this find?"

She stared at him. "I don't suppose you'd help."

"You suppose correctly. I have no intention of being any part of more expeditions into an area that has already seen too many deaths. Haven't you had enough? What has to happen before you realize it's too dangerous?"

"I do realize the danger." She drew in a deep breath. "But I also realize the significance of these discoveries."

"You're a lunatic." Steve turned on his heel. "I thought I was supposed to be the crazy one. Explore away, Mrs. Miller. If you decide to be sensible, I'll leave a trail of bread crumbs to my camp for you to follow."

"Very funny." She came after him and caught him by the sleeve, holding tightly. "I realize that I'm not prepared now, but if you would just *think* about bringing me back once I have the proper equipment, I can promise that it will be very profitable for you."

"Just for thinking about it?" he mocked. "How generous of you."

"Must you be so sarcastic? You know very well what I mean."

"And you heard me tell you that I want no part of it. It's quiet and peaceful out here. No one knows I'm here except for a few natives who leave me alone. That's the way I intend to keep it. If I'd known there was an American expedition anywhere nearby, I might have massacred them myself." He saw her face go pale, but ignored it. "Once civilization discovers this place, it won't be the same. They'll turn the rain forest into nothing but fields, destroy whatever animals they can find, and ravage the countryside with all the efficiency and humanity of Genghis Khan. No, thank you, Mrs. Miller, I'll have no part of that. You go back to the States and tell whoever will listen that the jungle is a wild, dangerous place. Tell them to stay home, not to come here. Let these temples and their secrets stay hidden. Once they're found, this will all be changed forever."

He reached down and uncurled the fingers she had tucked into his sleeve. She gave a surrendering shrug of her shoulders and shake of her head.

"All right. I can see that you feel strongly about this. And I can't promise that it wouldn't happen just as you say. Still—" She cast a long look toward the stone and vine obelisk straining toward the sky. "It seems a shame to deny such beauty and skill the recognition it deserves."

"Obviously you haven't had your illusions shattered for you lately," he muttered.

"Oh, haven't I? What makes you think you have a monopoly on shattered illusions? I've had my share."

Steve gave her a dark look. "Breaking a fingernail doesn't count."

Eden put her hands on her hips and glared up at him with so fierce an expression he took a wary step back. He hadn't forgotten the way she'd brandished a knife at him.

"Do you think I'm some hothouse flower?" she demanded. "If I was, I certainly wouldn't be here. I'd be home drinking tea in my parlor with vapid friends instead of out here in the jungle drinking coconut milk with a man barely above the level of a wild beast."

A flash of fury spurred him into grabbing her by the arm and jerking her close. "Well, it's about damn time you recognized your situation. Now a word of advice—be careful of prodding the tiger. You may not like the results."

When he released her, she rubbed her wrist for a moment

before looking up at him. "I meant what I said. I'm not a frail, fragile flower that wilts at the first sign of a storm. Maybe I don't know as much about living out here as you do, but I could learn if had to. And I could live in primitive conditions for as long as I felt it necessary. You seem to have this preconceived notion that I'm accustomed to silks and demitasse cups. You're wrong. Once I lived very well. I could do so now, if I chose. But spending my days painting watercolors of flowers and pastoral scenes did not appeal to me. I've spent a few years in the field with my husband, and I can assure you that I know all I need to know about survival. Colin was not a man to pamper a woman. If I survived, it was because I learned to adapt. Something you, obviously, have not yet managed."

"You're wrong. Survival is my strongest virtue."

"I wasn't talking about survival. I was talking about adapting. In case you don't know, those species that haven't learned how to adapt are now extinct."

"Then maybe they should be extinct." He looked up and past her at the vine-shrouded tower. "There's a season for all things. Like the ancient Mayans. The Mayans who still live here have adapted to other ways. They survive, if you want to call it that. Once the Mayans ruled this land. Now they serve it. Do you call that survival? I don't. It's not even adapting. It's surrender."

"Oh. And you equate surrender with extinction."

Dragging his gaze back to Eden, Steve stared at her for a long moment. "Yeah. I guess I do. Lee surrendered at Appomattox. Now the old South is dead. It's virtually extinct. Just like the ancient Mayan priests and temples."

Eden gestured to the carvings behind them. "But they're still here. Monuments to a past time and people. Perhaps the temples will never be as they once were, but why allow them to be forgotten? Why allow history to fade into obscurity?"

"Because it can't be brought back." He drew in a ragged breath as images flitted through his mind, visions he'd just as soon forget. "Leave it alone, will you? Let the dead rest. It's taken me a long time, but I've learned to do it."

"Have you? Somehow, I think not."

Steve jerked his gaze back to her. The anger had faded from her eyes. He managed a careless shrug. "Think what you want. I don't have any interest in trying to convince you differently. And I don't have any interest in hanging around here any longer. I'm leaving."

As he turned away, she said, "Let me gather what's left of my clothes and I'll go with you."

It should have felt like a victory. She'd given up the argument and the notion of further exploration. So why did he have this inescapable feeling that he'd lost? And that it wasn't over?

On the walk back to his camp, Steve found himself glancing at her often. She was quiet, apparently lost in thought. He didn't trust that for a minute. Not with her. In the short time since she'd tumbled down a hill to his feet, he'd come to recognize that Eden Miller was not a woman who gave up easily. If she were, she would never have managed to survive two weeks alone in the jungle. No, she had something on her mind. He didn't trust her silent acceptance for an instant.

They arrived at his camp in early afternoon. It was quiet, with no sign that anyone had come while they'd been gone. Steve slung the water gourds he'd retrieved to a lopped-off tree limb that served as a peg, then ducked into the hut. The mosquito netting still lay in a gauzy pile on the floor, waiting to be rehung. He shoved it aside with his foot, looking for a specific basket.

Finding it in a corner, he retrieved it and went back outside. Eden was seated on the camp stool near the dead fire, looking at him with a narrowed gaze. She looked about as friendly as a barracuda. He ignored her. Later, he'd deal with that particular problem. Now, he was trying to solve a more immediate one.

"What are you doing?" she finally asked.

Steve looked up from the rope webbing he held. "This is a hammock. Tonight, I intend to sleep in my own hut. There's no reason why either one of us should be uncomfortable."

"Oh." She looked uncertain. "Which bed do I get?"

He turned his attention back to the webbing, which was tangled and needed repair in places. "We can always arm-wrestle for first choice." He knotted a frayed strand, then tested it for strength. It parted immediately, and he began to work the strands of hemp into another knot. "Or draw cards, if you feel lucky." He looked up at her when she remained silent.

She was sitting with her elbows resting on her knees, pale hair framing a frowning face as she watched him. "You choose," she said after a moment. "It's your hut and your beds."

"How kind of you to acknowledge that fact. Should I point out that you are an uninvited guest, or would that be straining the boundaries of hospitality?"

"Definitely straining the boundaries. But understandable if one considers the circumstances." She paused, then added with a faint smile, "I really do appreciate your kindness."

"Yeah, I can tell."

"I didn't say I agreed with your opinion regarding the Mayan temples. That's an entirely different matter. But that doesn't mean I'm insensitive to your views. I just don't share them."

He tested the knot again, and this time it held. "How nice. Now hold this end." When strung out full-length, the hammock swung with gentle invitation and no sign of weakness. He smiled as he examined it. "Good. A few blankets and it will be comfortable enough for a while."

"Steve . . ."

When he looked up, she was staring past him with a strange expression. He followed her gaze, half-turning.

Slowly, he released his end of the hammock. It fell into the
dirt with a soft plop. A quick glance was enough to show
him that his rifle was out of reach, still leaning up against
the tree where he'd left it. He took a deep breath, silently
willing Eden not to scream or get hysterical. It would probably get them killed.

One of the armed men standing at the edge of the clearing stepped forward and pointed toward Eden. Rattling
loudly in Yucatec—a native language Steve had no trouble
understanding—he made several gestures that were instantly recognizable.

Holding up one hand palm out, Steve said sharply in a
mixture of Yucatec and Spanish, "No, she is with me."

The man hesitated, whether trying to sort out Steve's
faulty use of the language or considering his next move,
Steve wasn't certain. Anyway, he wasn't about to leave anything to chance.

Bending in a sudden motion, he swept up a handful of
dirt from the forest floor and let it slowly cascade from his
palm in a thin stream that drifted on the wind. "Ik," he
said loudly. The man's eyes grew large and he gave Steve
an uncertain glance. When he said something to the two
men behind him, Steve rose to his feet and waved an arm
in the air to indicate the sky. "Itzamná." Digging his thumb
into his chest, he added, "Balam."

"El Jaguar?"

Steve nodded shortly and folded his arms over his chest.
Eden hadn't moved, and he spared a moment's gratitude for
that. She probably thought he was crazy, and he certainly
hoped the men watching him so closely thought so, too.
His refusal to speak their language was probably confusing
them. These natives didn't look like ones he'd met before.
Maybe they were just curious. Since they'd made no overtly
threatening moves, he was beginning to think that might be
the case. The three stood beneath the flowering canopy of
a pinkwing tree, just watching him and Eden.

After several tense moments passed, Steve pointed to an object in one of the native's hands and asked in Spanish, *"Qué haces? Qué hay?"*

"Agua potable." Slowly, the native lifted his arm, and Steve saw that he carried a jug. He relaxed slightly. Maybe they just wanted water and would go. He stepped back, indicating the calabash gourds hanging from the tree limb. Then he crossed his arms over his chest and waited. After a brief consultation, two of the three men came forward, one with the jug, the other warily regarding Steve and Eden.

She sidled closer to Steve, moving slowly and cautiously. "What do they want?"

"Water. I think."

"Are they friendly?"

"I'm not asking them to dinner, if that's what you mean." He kept his voice low, regarding the men impassively.

"Steve," she whispered against his shoulder, "shall I try to get the rifle?"

"Only if you're ready to die. These guys probably know more places to get water than the birds. They want to check us out, see what we'll do. I think they're just curious but I don't want to take any chances. Stand still."

"Don't they think you're crazy?"

"I sincerely hope so. Or that I'm on a divine mission from the gods."

"Are they the Cruz—"

"Shut up," he cut in before she could finish. Eden subsided into silence, and he focused on the natives. They were garbed in loose cotton garments, and the swords they carried looked old but deadly. It didn't make him feel any better to realize that the man waiting beneath the tree held a rifle in one hand. He couldn't have told Eden if they were Cruzob or not. He didn't think so, but he'd been wrong before.

When they'd filled their jug, one of the men turned toward Steve. Speaking in Yucatec and halting Spanish, he asked if this was the man known as *El Jaguar* who was an *ah-pulyaah*.

Hesitating only briefly, Steve replied that some liked to call him so. This reply was greeted with a quick, whispered consultation, then the spokesman turned gravely to Steve and pointed at Eden. "And the woman—is she your woman?"

Nonplussed, Steve shrugged. "Sí. Why?"

"We were told there was a woman with hair of sunlight and eyes like the sky. It was whispered that *El Jaguar* had found her."

Steve's eyes narrowed, and his voice was a rough growl when he asked why that would matter.

"To us, it does not matter," was the enigmatic reply. The native studied Steve for a moment, then Eden before he finally nodded and wished him a good day in obvious farewell.

Steve replied in kind, then offered them *tzamna* and *uah* for their journey. After politely declining the offer of black beans and tortillas, the three men took their leave in the same quiet way they had arrived.

Frowning, Steve gazed after them while Eden gave a huge sigh of relief and sank to the ground. He glanced down at her. "You seem to spend half your life falling down," he observed.

Ignoring that, she asked, "What did they want? Why were they here?"

"Water, and I don't know." He shrugged. "Odd. I figured they would either kill us or expect hospitality. They did neither. I think they're looking for someone." He crouched down and cupped Eden's chin in his palm. She looked at him with wide, startled eyes of gentian blue. Rubbing his thumb over one corner of her soft mouth, he murmured, "I think they're looking for you, Goldilocks."

Seven

"Me," she sputtered, "why m-me?"

"Why do you think?" His thumb caressed the line of her upper lip, then brushed over the curve of her bottom lip before he dropped his hand and rose to his feet. "If the others in your expedition were known to be murdered and you were the only woman, don't you think the ones who murdered them would eventually realize the only female in the group was missing?"

Shuddering, she hugged her knees to her chest. It wasn't over. The others were dead, now they wanted her dead. If she stayed here, they'd be back. Now they knew where she was.

Slowly, she rose to her feet, brushing leaves and dirt from the seat of her trousers. "Should I leave now or in the morning? don't know which would be best—"

"Don't be stupid." Steve sounded irritable, and she gave him a surprised glance.

"I thought you were anxious for me to leave anyway. Now you have the perfect excuse to get rid of me." She turned to look into the jungle where the men had disappeared. "They know I'm here. They'll come back. And they may kill you, too."

"This is probably the safest place you can be right now. Damn it." He raked a hand through his hair, giving her an exasperated look. "Did you hear what he asked me?"

"I couldn't understand a word of any of you were saying."

"He asked if I was an *ah-pulyaah*. That's a practitioner of black magic. I wonder . . . I know." He grinned suddenly. "A few years ago when I got into a tight spot and was trying to convince some of the natives that I had the special powers of a *h-men,* I did some loud praying to Chac for rain. The rains were late, and the natives were worried they wouldn't get their corn planted on time. Damned if I no sooner finished the ceremony than it started raining. It rained. And it rained. They were pleased at first." He shook his head, the grin fading. "Then it kept on raining. Poured down in torrents. It ruined the crops, caused floods, and the run-offs were torrential."

Appalled, Eden asked in a faint voice, "Then what did you do?"

"I waited until they came to me. They asked if I would pray for the rains to ease, since my prayers had brought them. Of course, I had to pretend to be reluctant, not wanting to insult Chac, the Rain God who had answered my prayer. Finally, I agreed to intercede for them after a suitable interval of time."

She gave him a skeptical stare. "And I suppose the rain stopped."

"It would have sooner or later anyway." He shrugged. "I was just lucky. Anyway, I reminded our visitors that I am in the habit of consulting with Ik, the god of the wind, and Itzamná, the Lord of Life, and am also known by some as Balam."

"Jaguar."

He favored her with a faint smile. "You remembered."

"I heard them say *El Jaguar.*" Eden looked down at her folded hands and drew in a deep breath. She didn't know how much of his ridiculous story to believe, but he didn't seem especially worried. Of course, it wasn't his life that was in danger. It was hers. If he found it more prudent to hand her over to angry natives, would he? It wasn't a question she felt ready to have answered.

"Come on, Goldilocks," Steve was saying as he held out a hand to her, "let's fix the hammock. Then we'll worry about tomorrow."

His casual attitude concerned her. Perhaps it should have been reassuring. If he wasn't too worried about being butchered in his sleep, why should she worry?

Still, as they sat companionably before the fire that night while night birds murmured in the treetops and an occasional screech erupted, she felt increasingly apprehensive. Steve certainly was being nonchalant. Too nonchalant. It was unsettling. There was a distinct indifference to his mood that set her slightly on edge. It was as if he was trying too hard to convince her that there was no danger. Yes. That was it.

But she didn't believe him.

A nighthawk's low, trilling call echoed through the treetops, drifting down through the tight-laced canopy overhead and causing Eden to shiver. Steve seemed not to hear it. He sat reading near the light of a lantern. Their evening meal of fresh fruit, leftover turkey, and hot corn tortillas had been eaten before dusk. Eden had used a small amount of their water supply to wash dishes and herself. Now she sat restlessly, the silence nurturing her growing doubt.

Glancing up from where she sat near the fire on a woven mat, she asked, "But if the Indians here think you're crazy, why would they come near your hut at all?"

Steve didn't look up from the book he was reading. Light from the lantern hung from a tree branch above him spread over his dark head and the pages of his book. An owl whistled with a low, staccato sound. "I told you. Curious. That's all."

"Really." She frowned down at the slender twig she held between her hands, testing its flexibility by bending it back and forth several times. "Then they aren't as impressed with your supposed powers as you assumed."

Turning a page, he shrugged, a casual lift of broad shoulders beneath his cotton shirt. He took a sip of bourbon from a tin cup before saying, "Maybe they're just not worried about being drowned in a flash flood right now. Don't think about it."

The stick strained in her hands. "It's difficult not to think about it. If they return, they'll be wanting to kill me, not you."

He looked up then, his amber gaze slightly narrowed beneath the thick brush of his lashes. "Do you think I'd just stand there and let them?"

"I don't know. Would you? You aren't exactly thrilled that I'm here."

"True. But that doesn't mean I condone murdering women. Or that I'd stand by like a stone and allow it to happen."

She bent the slender stick until it broke in two with a brittle pop. "I wish I was as sure of that as you seem to be . . ."

His book closed with a loud snap and he surged to his feet. "If I wanted to be rid of you, Goldilocks, I know of more ways to do it than you can imagine. Don't tempt me."

Eden stared at him. There was an air of barely controlled violence about him, as if he held himself in check with an effort. His voice was soft, almost a purr, but there was a savage note in it that made her realize she'd provoked him almost to his limit. Perversely, she wanted to see how much farther she could go.

Leaning back against the rough bark of the tree behind her, she eyed him for a long, deliberate moment. A drift of smoke curled toward her, sharp and acrid on the night air.

She smiled and said softly, "Really, you certainly do brag a lot. My guess is, your bark is much worse than your bite."

There was a flash of incredulous fury in his eyes, a quick explosion of light that he hid with a lazy downward drift of his lashes. He smiled, but the slow curve of his lips over white teeth was more feral than amused.

"Maybe you're right. Care to find out?"

Her throat tightened. "I don't know what you mean."

His face lost the faint trace of sardonic humor that was all that softened it. "Oh, I think you do." He moved toward her, a smooth stride that suddenly reminded her of a jaguar. "I think you know very well what I mean, little girl."

Before she could react, he'd reached down to grasp her by the wrists and pull her to her feet. He held her despite her effort to retreat, his arms hard around her squirming body. Slightly breathless, she forced herself to go still and quiet, tilting her head back to look up at him.

"All right. We've both proved a point. You can release me now."

"You're right about one thing—we've both proved a point. You wanted to see how far you could push me. So now you know. Don't you want to see what happens next?"

"No." She pushed against his chest, but he was immovable. She felt a flicker of fear at the growing realization that she had gone too far. She took a deep, calming breath. "You're right. I wanted to know how far I could push you. Now that I know, I won't do it again."

"Ah, little girl, it's not that easy. There's a big drawback to teasing the tiger. Once you've got his attention, you've got to decide what to do with him."

"These stupid metaphors you use—" She strained against his broad chest, but it was like pushing at a wall of stone. He held her easily. She was trapped in the vise of his arms. "Steve. Let me go."

"I will." His dark head bent, and his words were a soft growl. "When I'm ready."

Before she could reply or react, his steely fingers lifted her chin with a firm grip. Despite her frayed nerves and the threat of danger, a pulse in her throat began to hammer. There was something elemental about the way he held her, a ruthless stripping away of pretense that left her bare. She wanted to protest, to resist, but her legs were weak and her breath was locked in her lungs.

When his mouth took hers, claiming it with a fierce urgency that made her think of the night before, she pressed her lips tightly together.

"Open for me," he muttered against her closed lips, and slid his thumb up to press against the corner of her mouth. His hand cradled her jaw, gently forcing her mouth open to let his tongue slip inside with a warm, probing exploration. He tasted of bourbon, warm and intoxicating. His arms tightened around her.

A slow, steady ache throbbed low in her stomach. She felt as if she were moving through warm water, her limbs heavy and sluggish, her mind hazy as if drugged. His hand shifted to slide down the bare skin of her throat, slipping beneath the open collar of her blouse to tug at the lace of her chemise. Dimly realizing what he intended, she tried to twist away, but he held her more tightly with his other arm around her back.

"Oh, no," he said softly when she wrenched her mouth free. "You started this, and you're not going anywhere. Not yet."

"Steve, please," she whimpered against a rising surge of apprehension, but he ignored her.

His hand splayed across her bare back, searing into her skin as his fingers trailed along the curve of her spine up to her shoulder, then around to cup her breast in his rough palm. She shivered. His thumb and finger closed around the hard nub of her nipple and she cried out. He only pulled her even closer against him.

Digging her hands into the taut muscle of his upper arms, she tried to push him away. The cotton material of his shirt bunched beneath her fingers, but he didn't budge. Another whimper formed in her throat. She shouldn't have teased him. He was right. She wasn't ready for this, wasn't prepared for what might happen next.

"Steve . . ."

"Hush," he said roughly, and bent to lift her into his arms. He carried her toward the hut with long strides, then ducked inside.

She had a blurred view of the interior as he knelt on the mattress and lay her atop it. The lantern outside was behind him, while darkness filled the hut with soft, velvety shadows. From deep black to soft gray, the shifting, melting images of furnishings and light blended together.

"Steve," she said again, her voice little more than a husky whisper, but he leaned forward when she tried to sit up and pressed her back into the rough wool of a blanket spread over the mattress.

Circling her wrists with his fingers, he drew her arms up and over her head. Most of his weight was supported on his hands as he settled against her. Fitting his body to hers, he rocked his hips into the cradle of her thighs. She could feel his hardness pressing against her. Unbidden, the image of him as she'd seen him in the pool flashed through her mind—heavy and fully aroused. She struggled to banish the memory, but it didn't help when he dragged his body against hers in a slow, aching stroke.

His face was dark, a silhouette against the light behind him. He held her, coming closer until his breath was hot against the bare skin just above the edge of her chemise. His tongue flickered out, damp and burning, wetting the muslin and making her moan softly. When his teeth closed gently around a nipple, she found herself arching toward him.

He pulled aside the muslin with one hand and began to trace imaginary paths around the swollen nipple with his tongue. Eden shuddered as his mouth moved from one breast to the other. The flame between her thighs grew higher and hotter, and she could hardly breathe. Her world had narrowed to the feel of his hands and his mouth on her skin, focusing on the aching need his touch provoked.

When Steve's weight grew heavier atop her, she dimly realized that he was untying the rope that held up her loose trousers. Then they were gone. With the cool air against her bare thighs, a semblance of sanity returned in a rush.

Shoving hard against him with the heels of her hands, she attempted to twist away, but he caught her wrists again.

"Easy, Goldilocks," he muttered as he transferred both her wrists to one of his hands. His head was bent, concentrating on what his free hand was doing, and she saw only the top of his head. With a fierce effort, she twisted one of her hands free and grabbed a handful of his hair.

When she yanked hard, he gave a startled yelp and quickly grabbed her arm. "Let go, dammit."

"Don't . . . do that," she managed to get out, and saw his mouth curve into a faint smile.

"You say one thing but do another, Goldilocks. You weren't saying no a minute ago."

A hot flush burned her cheeks. He was right. She still burned with an aching need that left her weak and trembling, but she was not at all certain she was ready for this. The image of him swimming in the sacred pool returned with aching clarity, and she drew in a deep, shaky breath. There was a searing promise in the memory of him as he'd looked then, dark and strong and powerfully male.

His eyes narrowed. Even in the dim shadows of the hut, she could see their hot glitter. Slowly, his head bent to claim her mouth, and she felt her resolve weaken.

He kissed her until she was quivering again, his tongue plundered the hot recess of her mouth with skillful strokes that left her clinging to him as if drowning. His hand shifted to move along the sensitive skin of her inner thigh, making her jerk in response.

"Easy," he said against her mouth, and his lips stopped her weak protests. He kissed her fiercely, until he had her reduced to quivering helplessness. Pulling aside the final cloth barrier, he slipped his hand between her legs, fingers brushing against the tight curls there. She shuddered again, but couldn't stop the treacherous arching of her body against his.

Steve breathed softly against her cheek, a warm murmur of reassurance. Then his hand moved from between her legs, and he undid the buttons of his pants with quick, deft motions. Part of her desire-hazed brain knew she should protest, but the irrational part—the part that was responding to him—urged her closer. Delicious sensations were shivering through her, making her forget everything but the driving need to seek an end to the exquisite torment inside.

It was only when she felt him hard against her, hot and insistent, that she realized there would be no stopping now. And truthfully, she didn't want to. Why should she refuse the sweet promise of release that he was offering? Nothing was certain in this life, and certainly not the promise of tomorrow. She'd seen that, and this was here and this was now, and she could barely think for the raging need inside her.

Steve lifted himself over her, his knees spreading her thighs, and then there was no time to think of anything but the sweetness of surrender. His head was bent, the curve of his shoulders a strong outline against the light, the slow slide of his body into hers a welcome intrusion. She cried out, and he bent quickly to cover her mouth with his, tongue jabbing inside to duel with hers until she grew comfortable with the feel of his body inside her.

Clutching at his broad back as he moved over her, she strained upward, wanting him even closer. He moved with deep, hard thrusts, creating a rising tension that made her moan. She was overwhelmed with a driving, taut need that seemed to swell and swell until she thought she could no longer bear it.

His breath came harshly through his teeth, and he surged

against her with motions that took her higher and higher until everything around her faded into nothing. There was only this moment, this man inside her, and his breath hot against her cheek while his hands cupped her hips and lifted her into his hard thrusts.

The tension stretched until it became intolerable, until she thought she would explode. Then, with a hoarse, guttural groan, Steve buried himself deeply, and she felt the first drowning waves of release convulse her. She couldn't stop, couldn't breathe, couldn't do more than lift herself into his embrace as he took her up and over the edge into oblivion. The world tilted and veered sharply away, while she clung to Steve with tears streaking her face.

Vaguely, she realized that her heartbeat was slowing at last, and that Steve still held her in his arms. He nuzzled the side of her face with his lips, then rose and released the mosquito netting so that it fell around them. He returned to her side and pulled her into the curve of his body, his arms holding her tightly.

"Go to sleep, Goldilocks," he said softly against her ear. "You'll be safe."

She believed him. Somehow, despite the coils of fear that had haunted her for weeks, despite the threat of the Indians who had come to their camp today, she believed him.

Outside the hut, the soft quiet of the rain forest closed around them. It was a dark, shrouded peace like that inside the sanctuary of a cathedral. Steve's arms enfolded her with more than physical warmth—there was an immutable sense of security in being with him. He'd fallen asleep with his arms still around her, and she could feel the measured rise and fall of his chest.

Nothing had ever prepared her for the intensity of what had just happened, and Eden thought drowsily that perhaps she had found paradise after all.

* * *

Balam came in the night, a stealthy, familiar intrusion. Steve heard the soft pad of his paws in the dirt, then the faint snuffling sound of curiosity he made when he discovered Eden curled beneath the netting. He put out a reassuring hand, and the jaguar purred with a loud, rasping rattle low in his throat.

Satisfied that everything was secure, the jaguar made a cursory inspection of the hut, then flopped down on a woven mat beneath the empty hammock. Steve detected the slightly metallic scent of fresh blood, and knew that Balam's hunt had been successful.

Beside him, Eden stirred slightly. Her bare leg brushed against him and his stomach clenched in reaction. With his arms still around her, he tightened his embrace. His palm cupped her breast in a light hold, fingers caressing its weight with teasing strokes until her nipple grew hard. Her low moan mimicked Balam's feline purr. It took him a moment to realize that she was still asleep, her body unconsciously responding to his touch. His hand drifted lower, to the soft tangle of curls between her legs. She felt warm, her curves so soft and rousingly female that his body responded in a rising surge. He closed his eyes. Damn. Well, this was what he'd wanted, wasn't it? A warm, willing woman?

Now he had one. Despite his earlier pleasure, he couldn't help feeling a prick of regret. Things hadn't been easy before. Now, they could go either way. He had no idea how she'd act when she woke up. And he had no idea how he would react when she did.

His reactions were too volatile where she was concerned. Too uncertain. *Damn.* He didn't know what he wanted. If he had any sense, he'd get her out of here. She was dangerous to him. A threat to the ordered familiarity of his existence. There was a sameness about his days that was safe. Secure. The only way for him to survive was to leave everything that was reminiscent of his former life behind him. He knew better than to get involved with anyone, especially a woman. It meant trouble.

No, he was much better off living alone, with only a jaguar for companionship.

As if sensing the direction of his thoughts, Balam looked toward him and made a long, rolling sound in the back of his throat. The jaguar equivalent of contentment. It was close and dark inside the hut. The only light came from the dying fire outside, which cast uneven, vague shadows. Yet even in the faint light, Steve could see the dilated golden moon of Balam's eyes, wide-open and dark-sheened. Ever vigilant, even in repose.

It reminded him that he should not relax his guard, either.

But when he glanced again at Eden, his throat tightened with reluctant admiration. Beneath her outer fragility, she was tough as nine-penny nails. She'd survived a massacre that had widowed her, hidden alone in the jungle for two weeks, and now ended up in his bed. How would she handle this? He probably should have stopped once he'd proven his point, but he hadn't. The challenge in her eyes and words had been more than he needed to set the spark to dry tinder. He'd be damned if he'd apologize or act sorry about it. And she damn well better not expect it either.

Releasing her, he rolled over and tried to focus his mind on something other than the raging need of his body. It was a long time before he fell asleep, and then it was more restless than restful.

Rising before the first light threaded through the tight-knit canopy of trees overhead, Steve had a fire going and beans and coffee heating when Eden awoke. He heard her sleepy mumble, then the sharp intake of her breath when she saw Balam. He waited for her reaction, and was faintly surprised when she didn't scream. Apparently, she'd decided to accept the jaguar's presence.

After a few minutes she emerged from the hut wearing only the loose shirt and trousers. The frayed hem of one leg flapped around her slender thigh as she moved toward him.

"Your jaguar is back," she said, taking the cup of coffee he held out to her.

"He showed up a few hours before dawn. Want some beans and tortillas?"

Eden sat down on the camp stool near the fire and brushed back a dangling strand of her pale hair. She smiled softly, her quick glance at him rather shy. "Yes, that would be nice. I didn't expect to find a chef cooking for me this morning."

"Yeah, well don't get too used to it. About the only thing I have any experience cooking is army fare." He caught himself and said nothing more, but she noticed and quickly seized upon the bit of information.

"Army fare. Were you in the army long?"

"Long enough to know I didn't like it. Here. Black beans inside a corn tortilla. I put some chilies in it for seasoning, so it might be a little spicy."

She ate daintily, holding the hot coil of tortilla in both hands to keep it from falling apart. It didn't help. The beans dribbled out and landed on the plate in her lap, and Steve leaned forward to show her how to eat it.

"Like this—fold up the bottom, then hold it at the seam. Yeah, like that. It gets easier the more you eat."

"I hope so," she said around a mouthful of beans. Her tongue flicked out to catch a bean at the corner of her lips. "It's delicious. Spicy. I didn't know either side of the American army served beans and tortillas."

Steve didn't look at her as she set the lid back on the pot which was hung over the fire. "Me either," he said shortly. "Can't speak for the Yankees, but most of the Confederacy felt damned lucky to get anything to eat."

"Yes, so I understand." Eden finished her meal in silence, then sat back with her tin cup of coffee. Steve tried not to look at her too closely. She didn't appear to be the least ill at ease, while he suddenly felt awkward and strange.

It was vaguely amusing, he supposed sourly, that she was dealing with last night better than he was. He found it difficult to look at her, and even more difficult not to. She looked relaxed sitting on the stool and leaning back against the slender trunk of a guava tree. Her pale hair fell in loose curls around her face and over her shoulders, and her eyes were a soft, sated blue that made his throat tighten.

After finishing his third tortilla, he emptied the scraps on a wooden platter and carried them a short distance from the camp. When he returned, Eden was washing the last dish. She looked up at him with a faint smile.

"I can at least be useful. Is there anything else I can do?"

Oh yes . . .

Aloud he said, "Nothing I can think of right now. Unless you want to mend your trousers. It's attractive, but might be a bit dangerous if you catch the loose part on a limb."

She peered down at her trouser leg and nodded. "You're right. I assume you have a sewing basket in the hut."

"I try to be prepared."

She laughed. "So I've noticed. All right. I'll repair them."

While Eden sewed up the long rip in her trousers, Steve found chores away from the camp. Leaving his rifle behind, he reassured her that he would be within shouting distance. He cut some firewood, and did some cursory scouting about to see if the Indians had returned. There was no sign of them.

On his way back to the hut in the clearing, he saw the first line of ants. Quickening his pace, he reached camp before the long columns of insects, and flung the load of firewood to the ground.

"Come on," he said to Eden, startling her when he grasped her by one arm to pull her to her feet. "Get inside the hut."

"What—but why?"

"Don't stop to ask questions, just do it."

Once they were inside the hut, he reached up over the front opening and unfurled the length of netting tied over it. With a few quick twists, he had it cascading down to cover the opening.

"Hand me some of those baskets," he said without taking the time to look at Eden. "Where's Balam?"

"Gone. Which baskets?"

"Any of them will do. I just need something to hold down this netting . . . yeah, that'll do."

"Would you mind telling me why we're doing this?"

"Army ants," he answered as he checked the walls to be certain none of the mud daubing had recently fallen out. "Any deserters might find their way in here, and it stings like hell when they bite."

"Army ants? Are they dangerous?"

"Not singly. In a group, they're damned aggressive little bastards."

As he finished, he heard the distinctive rustle of approaching insects through the decaying leaves on the forest floor. He motioned for Eden to come to the front. "Look. Out there. See the bushes move? It's not the wind causing that. It's ants."

The rustling grew louder and then the ants appeared, a live river of half-inch to inch-long creatures moving forward at a swift pace. Traveling several ants wide, the advancing battalions of army ants swarmed over the forest floor in a seething tide.

"Oh my God," Eden breathed, and he could feel her kneel on the floor of the hut next to him. "Will they try to get in here?"

"Probably not. They're searching for food. When they find what they want, they'll carry it back to their colony a piece at a time. It's just best not to get in their way. They've been known to kill small animals, and even injure larger ones. I'd rather be safe than sorry."

She made a strangled sound, and he half-turned to look at her. One hand was at her throat, and she was shaking her head.

"Are you certain they can't get in here?"

"No. But I don't think they'll try hard. I dump food scraps a bit away from here, and this is one of the reasons why. If they're foraging, they'll find tasty tidbits there, not here."

The rustling grew louder, and there was a soft, humming vibration as the ant colony swarmed past in a glistening tide. A few ventured to the edge of the hut, but as he'd predicted, moved past fairly swiftly. In minutes, the last battalion of tiny soldiers could be seen at the rear, and then the ants were gone.

Eden turned to look at him, her eyes wide and blue. "It's positively dangerous out here."

He grinned. "Yeah, a real jungle. I'm surprised you didn't think of that before you came."

"It was hardly my idea, though I admit that I was excited at the prospect of discovering ancient temples. And it was much better than being left behind again."

He studied her face. There was a lot about her husband she wasn't saying, and the picture he'd formed in his mind of the deceased man was anything but favorable. Maybe that was why she'd exhibited very little grief about his actual death, moreso over the way he'd died. Normal, he supposed. He looked away.

"Did Colin leave you behind a lot?"

"It depended on the circumstances." She hesitated, then said softly, "And on how much of my money he needed to fund his little excursions."

"Ah." He'd been right. Colin Miller had been anything but a perfect husband. After a moment of silence, he asked, "So why did you marry him?"

She looked startled. "Why—it was arranged by my grandparents. I had no choice, really. But that doesn't mean that I didn't want to marry him." She gave a shaky laugh. "I was so young and lonely. My grandparents tried, I suppose, but it must have been hard for them to raise a ten-year-old child after my parents died of fever. They were going to rectify the terrible mistake my father had made by marrying below him, you see. They felt they'd been lenient with him, which was why he was so headstrong and stubborn that he would marry my mother—a woman of no class or consequence."

Her mouth twisted bitterly, and Steve felt an unexpected pang of sympathy. "So you married Colin when they told you to."

She nodded. "Yes. But don't think I hated the notion. I didn't. I fancied myself in love with him. Oh God, I was so young and foolish, so hungry for—he paid attention to me, you see. Brought me flowers, told me I was pretty. His family was acceptable, though Colin had a bit of a reputation for being wild. But *blood tells,* you know, and I think my grandparents believed Colin's bloodlines might negate the damage done by my father mixing his blood with my mother's. Oh, it sounds silly now, but I wanted to please them. I wanted, just *once,* for my grandparents to approve of something I'd done. To approve of me."

The last was said in a husky whisper, and Steve's throat tightened painfully. Rising to his feet, he began to fold up the netting. "Want to help me with this?"

When they had it furled and tied above the door again, he turned to look at Eden. She'd pulled back her hair into a loose braid, and stray tendrils clung to her cheeks and waved over her forehead. Perspiration flushed her cheeks. She looked hot—and very desirable. He turned away from her.

"I'm going shopping. Care to come along?"

Eden repeated, "Shopping?"

He grinned. "Yeah. That's what I call it. Actually, I take along some empty baskets, and see what I can find to eat. Only enough for a few days though. It spoils quickly in this heat."

"I'm amazed at the variety of fruit and vegetables growing wild here. How do you know what's good to eat and what isn't?"

"Experiments. Some experiments have turned out rather badly, so I've tried to rely on familiar plants. Or those the Indians use. I had a—friend—who taught me a lot when I first came here. Thul saved my life more than once, stopping me from eating something I shouldn't. Too bad—" He jerked to a halt. That was behind him. He looked up and met her gaze, shrugging at the question in her eyes. "Before the caste wars started, there was a banana plantation a few miles south. It's gone now, but some of the trees spread out and still bear fruit." He bent and picked up a basket to hand to her. "Let's see what we can find, Goldilocks."

As she took the basket, her hand grazed his, and she looked up with a quick upward sweep of her lashes that made him think of a startled doe. An unexpected wave of tenderness was as disturbing as it was surprising. He didn't want this. Didn't need this. She was vulnerable and touching and beautiful, and he could feel himself slipping closer and closer to that dangerous edge.

Eden. Her name meant beauty, delight, pleasure, paradise. Yeah, all of that—and trouble with a capital T.

Deliberately, he pulled his hand back, making his tone light and careless. "After you, my lady." No, he couldn't allow himself to respond on anything more than a physical level. He knew better than to get close to anyone. It would be too dangerous.

Eight

It was the dream again, coming in the night like rolling thunder and bolts of lightning to invade her sleep. Screams and shouts, dancing points of fire, flashing swords and machetes, and the driving urgency of numbing fear. Colin's face—pale and terrified—changing to sickening realization of approaching death.

In the dream haze he reached out to her, silently imploring, his hand lifted for her to help him. And she could not. If she stepped from the shrouding shadows of the mangrove tree, they would see her. And she would die, like others were dying with horrible screams and blood . . . so much blood, everywhere, staining the earth red. So she crouched in the musty, dark recesses of the stilted tree roots and watched him die.

Unable to move, unable to call out, she watched with wide, horrified eyes as a machete, the wicked blade glittering in the light of torches and blazing tents, descended to end Colin's life. Only then, as the blade sliced into him with a sickening sound, was she able to close her eyes, blotting out the sight of death. But she could still hear, and the sounds of slaughter would haunt her forever.

Moaning, she tried to evade the sounds, the clamor of men swollen with blood-lust. But it was so real, so vivid and terrifying that she could not escape, even by running as she had run that night, ignoring the tree branches slapping in her face, dragging at her clothes, tangling in her hair, slowing her down as she fled into the dark, pitiless night. And even when the din of death behind her grew fainter and fainter and faded away, she still ran. Panic-stricken, she ran this way and that, aimless and floundering, until light finally came and she took refuge in the hollowed-out trunk of a tree. It was there Paco found her, his round brown face solemn and mirroring his own horror.

She looked up with relief, but then screamed as the Indian boy's face changed, melting into a grotesque parody of death with lips drawn back from his teeth and his eyes wildly staring. She screamed, and screamed again, all the despair and horror she'd ever felt injected into the wail.

"Eden . . . Eden, dammit, wake up," a voice insisted, and this was not a voice of nightmares, but of security.

Slowly, clutching at something solid, she opened her eyes, as sobs racked her entire body.

Steve's face was barely visible in the shadows of the hut. "Wake up," he said again, more gently this time as their eyes met. "It's only a dream."

Her fingers dug into his upper arms, sliding slightly on the sweat-sheen of bare skin. "No . . . no, it was real." She took a deep breath to calm herself, but the old terror clung tenaciously, chilling her and making her body tremble. "I wanted to help," she forced out, battling the shreds of nightmare and guilt, "I did. But I couldn't. They would have killed me, too, and there was nothing I could have done . . . nothing. Oh God, Colin's dead. So many times I wished he'd die when he didn't, and when it finally came it was a judgment against me . . . I caused it all." Tears flowed, hot and steady, down her cheeks, seeping into her mouth and tasting of salt. "It's all my fault," she whispered, voice faltering, the breath harsh and quick and rattling her chest with racking sobs. "I wished him dead and now he is . . ."

Steve pulled her into his chest, pressing her face against the taut muscle and holding her head with his fingers tangled in her hair. "You didn't cause anyone's death," he said softly, his breath warm against her bare shoulder. "It was a massacre. I told you. A caste war. It's happened much too often. 'Cry havoc, and let slip the dogs of war,' Shakespeare wrote. That's what it is, Goldilocks. Havoc. Chaos, confusion, destruction. Chance. You survived. That's what you were supposed to do. You did nothing wrong, caused no one's death."

Curling her fingers into the smooth, warm span of skin on his chest, she said haltingly, "You don't understand. We argued. I told Colin that I wished he would die. He was so . . . I shouldn't say it now, I suppose. He's dead and it doesn't matter."

"Sweetheart, if death came to every man a woman wished would die, the world's population would be completely female," Steve said with a soft laugh. "It only means that you're human, and whatever he'd done to cause you distress was enough to make you lash out."

Closing her eyes, Eden drew in a shaky breath. Maybe he was right. If Colin hadn't died as he had, she would probably never have felt guilty about their final argument. But the massacre had come close on the heels of a raging disagreement that led her to lash out at him. And now he was dead and she could not take back her hasty words.

A long shudder quivered through her, and she huddled close to Steve for warmth. He bent his head and pressed warm lips against her cheek, brushing away her tears with his strong, warm hands.

"Don't cry, little girl," he murmured against her ear. His breath stirred a looping curl and tickled her skin, but the tears continued to flow. "Jesus, you're cold. Like wet marble—here, let me hold you close. That's right. Body heat's the best thing for a chill . . ."

In the close envelope of mosquito netting and darkness, Eden melted into his embrace with a sense of relief. Steve was there, as he had been for the past three weeks, strong and secure and comforting.

"Steve," she whispered softly, and his arms tightened to hold her even closer. She could feel the strong, steady thud of his heart against her cheek, and turned to press a kiss on his chest.

"Goldilocks. . . ." One hand curled under her chin and tilted her face upward. His other hand flexed, then slid down the curve of her spine to shift her into the hard angle of his legs and chest. It seemed natural to lift her face for his kiss, natural to open her thighs for him to slip inside. He moved gently against her at first, then with increasing power until she felt the rising crescendo build up to a fever-pitch. His body was creating exquisite friction inside hers, dragging her up and up until she was clutching at him with breathless anticipation. The aching need sharpened to a taut pressure that was almost pain, then exploded into blinding release and gasping heat. She cried out. Feeling strangely weighted and boneless at the same time, Eden held him close when he went suddenly still and tense in her arms. Groaning softly in her ear, Steve slowly relaxed, his arms still around her and his breathing growing gradually calm.

They slept then, and when she woke, it was almost light. No dreams jerked her awake this time, only the heavy pressure of Steve's body still resting on hers. She eased from under him, smiling when he sprawled atop the mattress in sleeping abandon. Pale dawn had begun to lighten the hut with strange shadows, silhouetting the trees outside into dark-laced shapes. The light bathed Steve's face in a colorless brush of harsh angles and solid planes. She resisted the urge to stroke the side of his face, contenting herself with watching him sleep. It didn't ease her any to realize that hers was the action of a woman in love.

Dear Lord, in the weeks she'd spent with him, had she managed to fall in love?

No. Not possible. It was frightening. It was exhilarating. It was incomprehensible. It was madness . . .

It couldn't have happened in such a short time. God, she was so confused. He kept her in turmoil, physical and mental. She found herself staring at him for no reason, then quickly looking away if he chanced to catch her. Could she have—?

No, no, it was just the artist's appreciation in her, the acknowledgment of a purity in line, form, and face. With his raven-black hair and shimmering gold eyes, set in a warm, sun-bronzed face of surprisingly refined angles and planes, he would be enough to inspire any artist. There were moments she'd amused herself by imagining a painting of him done in oils, the different shades of teak and umber she would use to produce various shadings of the hard ropes of muscles on his chest and stomach, the brushstrokes she'd use to create just the right flow of muscle into the symmetrical sweep of his arms where they tapered with masculine strength. The black of his hair would have to be highlighted with fine strokes of deep russet to mimic the way it gleamed in the sun, and his eyes—there she usually faltered. How could a mere mortal recreate the intense gold of his eyes without making them too yellow or too brown? There was a trick of light that made them dance with deviltry or glitter with anger, and she was not at all certain she could ever reproduce it. She'd have to work on that.

Yielding to the urge to touch him, she brushed her fingertips over his forehead to push back the fall of dark hair. His brows drew together in a faint frown, then smoothed. A rough bristle of beard darkened his face, making a whisking sound when she drew her fingers lightly over his jaw.

Moving her hand downward over the strong brown column of his throat to his chest, she marveled at the clean lines of his body, so sturdy and competent, and achingly male. Tiny dark hairs curled on his chest and made a darker line that arrowed down his belly, and she touched the mat lightly with one hand. It sprang back when she lifted her fingers, curling slightly around the tips.

"Greedy Goldilocks," he startled her by saying in a thick, sleepy voice. His hand moved to catch hers and hold it against his stomach, but when she looked up at his face he was smiling. The hard line of his mouth slanted upward, and his eyes glittered with a warm light that was growing very familiar.

Her face heated, but she matched his smile. "Are you complaining again?"

"About this?" His hand tightened around hers, pressing it harder against him. "I may be crazy, but I'm not stupid."

"Glad to hear it. I was getting pretty worried."

"Yeah," he muttered, pulling her slowly down, "I noticed how worried you were . . . oh yes, sweetheart, like that . . ."

Kissing him, his chest, then the rapid pulse beating in the hollow of his throat, Eden found herself soon lost in a haze of desire. It was utter madness, she thought dazedly, complete, utter madness to allow herself to lose sight of everything but nights with this man she didn't even really know. . . . A wave of searing heat washed over her, and her lips went soft beneath his searching mouth. There was something compelling about a man who could sweep her so effortlessly into passion. The touch of his mouth, his hands, the scalding heat of his tongue when he dragged it from her lips down her throat to her breasts, made her moan. Tremors shook her when his hand shifted to cup her breast. His fingers teased the tight bud of her nipple, igniting a fire between her legs.

His back was taut, hard, smooth beneath the grip of her clutching fingers. The heat and yearning for him spread throughout her body, burning everywhere they touched, making her ache.

"Steve, please," she whimpered, and he lifted his head to stare down at her with an enigmatic expression. Then he bent, kissing her throat, pushing back the damp curls of her hair and coiling it in his fist. Eden washed her tongue over the hot, bare skin at the muscled curve of his shoulder, and he groaned.

Then he took her, this time roughly, his body surging into hers with powerful thrusts that made the world careen around her in a dizzying spin. The explosion, when it came, left her quivering with aftershocks.

Light spangled the trees around their camp in flashes as Steve positioned the polished silver oval he was using as a mirror. He propped it atop a wooden crate and leaned it up against the trunk of a tree, peering into it with a scowl. Straddling another crate, he lathered his face and then picked up his razor. Slowly, he drew it down the side of his jaw in a smooth stroke, cursing softly when he felt a sudden sting.

"Cut yourself?" Eden asked. She came from the hut and sat across from him, elbows resting on her bent knees and her chin propped in the cup of a palm. He flicked her a quick glance, unwilling to be too distracted by her attention.

"No. I just like swearing."

"Ah." She smiled and added, "I didn't complain about your beard. I thought it rather—piratical."

"Piratical—ouch!" He glowered at the spreading pinkish stain blossoming into the thin layer of lather. "With this much blood, I'll have every carnivore within a ten-mile radius here before I'm finished," he muttered. "Or at least the vultures."

"Do they have those down here?"

"Winged, or two-legged?" he asked as he carefully eased the razor over his chin. "Both. Damn. I'm out of practice. My jaw will look like Balam's been chewing on it."

Eden absently wound a strand of her pale hair around one finger as she watched him. He shook a glob of lather free of the razor's blade, then glanced at her again.

"Don't you have something to do?"

She gave him a blinding smile. "No. I've done the dishes and swept out the hut, and even put on a pot of beans for dinner. I got bored with reading. All I have to do now is watch you."

"Hoping I'll cut my throat?" he muttered, and turned his attention back to the mirror. "You're out of luck if you think I'll leave behind any money."

For a moment she didn't say anything. Silence stretched between them. After a moment, she asked softly, "Have you always been this cynical?"

"No. Once I was as stupid as anyone else. Then I learned better." He rinsed the blade free of lather in a small tin bowl of water, and looked over at her. She was staring at him with wide blue eyes full of wary consideration. He looked back at his reflection in the mirror, and felt as if he were looking at a stranger.

A feeling of guilt washed over him. He didn't know why he said the things he did sometimes, except that he had an overwhelming need to keep her at a distance. If she got too close, she'd only be hurt. It was inevitable. Once she knew him for what he was, she'd suffer disillusion, and he didn't need to deal with that anymore. He'd had enough practice shattering illusions.

Eden rose to her feet in a graceful motion and pushed back a fall of pale hair from her eyes. "It doesn't matter,. you know."

He paused and turned to look at her. Overhead, a flurry of quarreling toucans scattered leaves and feathers, piercing the soft quiet of the forest with screeches. "What doesn't matter?"

"I don't care what's in your past. All that's important to me is here and now."

"Yeah? The only reason you can say that is because you don't know what's in my past. Just like I don't know what's in yours. Hell, you may have six kids at home for all I know . . ."

"No children. One husband—recently deceased—and two parents, long deceased. My grandparents died last year. I have no one who will miss me, no one who will care if I don't return. Except, perhaps, for the attorney who is in charge of my estate." She drew in a deep, shuddering breath. "So you see, we're two of a kind."

"Don't count on that, Goldilocks." He wiped the rest of the lather from his face with a scrap of towel and rose to his feet. "I'm afraid you'd be aghast at the company you're keeping."

"So just what did you do that's so terrible?" she countered. "Murder someone?"

He curved his mouth into a stiff smile. "Precisely." Her eyes dilated and her lower lip trembled slightly. His smile widened with sardonic humor. "There. That ought to teach you to think before you speak."

"Yes," she said, "you're right. But war doesn't count. I still hold to my original statement."

His brow lifted. "Do you? I confess I'm amazed. And a little shocked. I didn't know you kept such bad company on a regular basis."

"Why don't you stop beating around the bush and say what you mean outright?" Anger flashed in her eyes, shooting blue sparks at him. "Just say it—you don't want me to get any ideas about falling in love with you. Well, you certainly don't have to worry. There's a big difference between love and lust."

Steve didn't know if he was more angry or surprised. He tossed the towel near the half-empty basin and glared at her. "That's a hell of a way for a lady to talk."

"Now, there *you* go making assumptions. Who said I was a lady?"

Irritated, Steve deliberately raked her with a thorough stare from head to foot, letting his gaze focus wherever he liked until she began to fidget. A faint smile pressed at the corners of his mouth. "Maybe you're not a lady, after all.

But then, most men prefer a woman who's a Saturday night whore and Sunday morning saint. It makes life more interesting."

A flush rode the high rise of her cheekbones and made her eyes an even brighter blue. She tossed her hair, and a shaft of leaf-filtered sunlight lit the pale strands with gold. Crossing her arms over her chest, she said calmly, "You're trying to evade the issue. You say things for effect. I've noticed that. I'm not at all certain I believe you."

"Really?" Steve bent to scoop up the wash basin and towel. "Suit yourself, Goldilocks."

"Maybe I will." She took a deep breath, and favored him with one of those blinding smiles that always roused his deepest suspicions. "In fact, I've decided that since I'm here and you obviously have no intentions of taking me to a town any time soon, I might as well branch out on some excursions of my own. I intend to go back to the wall I found. That huge mound is probably the steps to a temple, and if I'm right, it could be the temple of the jaguar, which would be a wonderful discovery."

"It could be the last one you make, too." Steve dumped the water from the wash basin and dried it with the damp towel. "Don't you ever learn? Wasn't what happened last time enough for you?"

"Don't you see? It's because of what happened that I must go back. Richard, Colin, and the others shouldn't have died in vain. The discovery of the jaguar throne would be a memorial to them."

"It won't take away those feelings of guilt, Goldilocks." He cleaned the straight razor with brisk, efficient swipes of the towel, not looking at her. "You'll have to deal with those another way. What happened wasn't your fault, and the fact that you survived and they didn't is only an erratic twist of fate. I know. I've been to war, and a cannonball comes whistling down and the man next to you is gone in a roaring puff of smoke and bloody mist, while you're left standing there wearing what's left of him, but without a scratch. Fate. Chance. Divine mockery. Whatever you want to call it, you have no influence over it." He looked up, and saw that her face was pale and her mouth set into a taut line.

For a moment, his surroundings wavered, and he caught a blinding flash of memory, of a youth with pale hair and face, blood streaming from his mouth, his eyes open and horrified and disbelieving as he gazed down at what was left of his body below the waist. With a supreme effort of will, Steve wrenched his mind back to the present, to the sight and sound of the peaceful jungle and the beautiful woman staring at him with faintly puzzled eyes.

He sighed. "I hope you don't think I'll take you back there."

"Steve—"

"No. I won't even discuss it. Let it go, dammit. Stop while you're ahead. And still alive. Maybe you don't mind risking your life, but I'm not too fond of the notion. I like my head where it is right now—still attached to my neck. And relatively unbruised, though a mite bloodied at the moment."

"I see." She rose from her perch atop the wooden crate and smoothed her wrinkled cotton trousers with one hand in a gesture as elegant and practiced as if she were standing in a ballroom. "Is there anything I can say that will change your mind?" She looked up from beneath the sumptuous curve of her lashes, and he caught a flash of searing blue before she looked down again.

Smothering the insane urge to give in, he growled, "No. Nothing. Ah hell, Goldilocks. I know why you want to go back, but it's too dangerous. And it won't change the past, no matter what you think."

"Who said I'm trying to change the past?"

"Oh. Right. Those nightmares you have and the feelings

of guilt over something you couldn't control are just for entertainment. Christ. Don't you think I understand?"

"Do you?" She drew in a deep, shaky breath. "Do you know how it feels to be so helpless? I don't think so. You're the kind of man who is capable of fighting back. If you'd been there, you would have found a way to help them . . ."

"No, Eden, what I most likely would have done was save my own neck. It's a family trait, survival. Or cowardice, whichever you prefer. For God's sake, don't stand there looking at me like I'm some kind of damn hero. I'm not."

She met his gaze, chin lifted as she stared at him for a long moment. Then she said softly, "Yes, you are. I found the newspaper clippings about you in one of your books. You're Captain Steven Houston Ryan, a Civil War hero credited with saving the lives of over sixty men at a bridge in Georgia. Even the Yankees said you were courageous and daring—"

Fury flashed through him. He snatched at it and stuffed the swelling anger back down inside where it belonged. Taking a deep breath, he took a step toward her. His voice was admirably calm.

"Damn you for a little snoop. And not a very thorough one at that."

"What—" She swallowed suddenly, and he wondered if she could see the beast in him spring to life, the tiger that always lay sleeping just below the surface, waiting to be awakened. He took another deep breath and willed the tiger back to sleep, then listened grimly as she finished, "—do you mean?"

Steve shrugged. "If you'd pried a little bit more into my private life, you'd have found the articles that came later. Articles that tell how those sixty men I 'saved' died later, slow and painful, starving to death in a damn prison camp when it could have been quick and over with. Yeah, I was a real hero all right. Now leave it alone, will you?"

Eden drew in a deep, shuddering breath, and he knew

with resigned futility that she wouldn't leave it alone. She
shook her head. "I can't. You're feeling guilty for something
over which you had no control. That's not right. And it's
not right that you should blame yourself." She held out a
hand, eyes earnest and full of misguided fervor. "It's all
right, Steve. It wasn't your fault."

Steve closed his eyes to shut out the sight of her earnest
face staring at him as if he was a damned hero when he
knew better. The safe barriers he had managed to keep in
place for so long began to crack; he could feel them wavering. It wasn't right. He knew better.

Shaking his head, he said blindly, "You don't understand.
Those men—I rode with them. They were my friends."

"Yes, and Colin was my husband. Yet I'm alive and he's
not."

Steve opened his eyes and looked at her. He could feel
the walls shaking, those walls that shut out the memories
that came to him when he wanted to keep them away.

A flame flared inside him, reminding him. He smiled
faintly. "Yes. We're alive, you and I. We're survivors. I'm
not sure that's fair or right, but it's a fact. We're here and
they're dead."

Eden looked relieved. And pleased. She smiled at him.
"So you're not a murderer. Not really. It was as you said—
just fate."

"Oh, no, Goldilocks," he said, shaking his head. "Fate's
not always to blame. Sometimes it has help. My commanding officer, the fat, stupid bastard who didn't want to listen
to reason or humanity or anything else, paid for his indifference. It didn't matter to me that he was my commanding
officer. He sent my men to their deaths knowing what
would happen. And when I got my chance, I killed him for
it . . ."

Nine

"Did you think I was joking?" Steve asked coolly, and from somewhere she found the presence of mind to shake her head.

"No. I didn't think that. I just . . . just thought you were being modest."

"Modest. Christ. What a joke." He made a short, savage motion with one hand. "There's nothing heroic about leading men to their deaths, Goldilocks. Nothing. Modest? Oh no, just sickened by it all, by war and death and the vanity of old men who sit safely in their tents miles away from the battle and talk about sacrificing young men not even old enough to grow beards—yeah, I was real heroic. I did what was expected of me and some damn good men died for it."

"But—that's war."

Steve jerked his gaze from a distant point to her face, and she flinched from the blazing anger in his eyes. "Yes, I know all about war, Goldilocks. I believed in it. I believed in a lot of things back then. But it didn't change anything. Whether I believed in it or not didn't matter. Things change. I've changed."

Steve's mouth was turned downward in a sulky curve, his eyes sullen and half-hidden by his lashes. He looked as if he'd been insulted, and she didn't know whether to laugh or cry. Really. What did he expect? Admitting to murder—even one he felt was justified—was bad enough, considering the circumstances. But he wasn't even penitent. Not a shred of remorse had colored his telling of it, only a sort of grim satisfaction.

She couldn't understand that. Would never understand. How could murder—any murder—be justified?

"Is that why you're hiding out here in the middle of nowhere? Why you don't want anyone close by?"

Raking a hand through his hair, Steve shook his head. "I didn't always have a choice about my neighbors. The reasons don't matter. I'm here and I like my peace and quiet." His gaze lifted, thick lashes half-raised over the sulky gold eyes fixed on her face with narrow speculation. "I like you being here. But I won't tolerate anyone else, and I won't invite trouble by exploring the Mayan ruins. Any find will only bring in more people, and I told you I don't want that."

"So you just intend to stay out here alone in the jungle, decaying little by little until there's nothing left of you but an empty shell, is that it?"

"Sounds about right. Did you expect more?"

"Yes. I'm not usually wrong about people, and despite what you say, I think you're inherently decent." ·

"Christ."

He stared at her, and in the sunlight filtering down through the yellowish-pink blossoms of the pinkwing tree, she saw the quick flash of reaction in the muted gold of his eyes. He lowered his black lashes in a deliberate evasion and shrugged.

"Think what you want, Goldilocks, though I can't say I have a great deal of faith in your judgment of character. If you were married to a man you didn't have the foresight to know you would not like, why would your assessment of my character be any better?"

"That's not fair." She glared at him, her face heating with a mixture of hurt and resentment that he would be so cruel as to remind her of a midnight confession. "And I never said I didn't *like* Colin—"

"Oh no, a wife usually wishes her beloved husband to

an early grave. Don't look at me like that. I told you I understand, and I told you it wasn't your fault. But if you want me to stand here and swallow your high-minded prattle about what a great and noble man I am because you say so, you can forget it. We both know better. And no matter how wonderful we both may think I am, I still won't agree to guide you back to the ruins."

"Even with my limited perception, I believe I understand that," she managed to say coolly, silently damning his insolent smile and the knowing look he was giving her beneath the dark fringe of his lashes. "So tell me. What *do* you intend to do with me? Am I supposed to stay here with you forever?"

"God forbid." His gaze lingered on her flushed face before traveling downward in a slow scrutiny. "Not that I mind you being here right now. I rather enjoy our evenings together."

"That doesn't answer my question. Am I supposed to leave at first light tomorrow? What do you want me to do?"

He looked away, his bare chest rising and falling in an even motion as she watched him. For several long moments he didn't say anything, but stood looking out over the cleared area of his campsite with a distant light in his eyes. Eden's throat tightened. She didn't know what she wanted him to say—that he wanted her to stay with him, certainly, but what else? Vows of love? Of undying loyalty? Of—what?

"Eden."

She looked at him through a sudden blur of tears, heard the soft resignation in his voice as he moved toward her on silent, bare feet. He reached for her, arms pulling her to him.

"Damn," he said. "Damn. Must you make me say things I don't want to say? Things I don't want to feel?"

"I can't make you do anything," she mumbled against his chest, and felt his muscles tighten. His mouth brushed against her cheek, breathing heat in her ear.

"Right. You underestimate yourself, little girl. Or overestimate me. I don't know which." There was a pause, then he nuzzled the side of her neck and murmured against her skin, so soft she almost didn't hear the words, "Stay with me, Eden. Stay with me."

"I will," she heard herself promise, "I will."

He was insane, of course. He recognized that now, though he'd resisted the knowledge that hovered like a dark cloud above him longer than mortal man should endure. But now he'd gone and done it. He had asked her to stay. And worse—she'd said she would.

Oh yes, he was definitely insane. What had he been thinking of, to surrender to the pleading light in her eyes and say what she wanted to hear? It wasn't kindness. It was the ultimate cruelty and he had committed it. He knew better. It had been proven to him more than once that he always lost those he loved.

Steve skimmed the sharp edge of a knife blade over the piece of wood he held in his other hand, watching the mahogany strip curl away. Rich colors gleamed in the carving, deep red and lush golden brown, blending to form a beautiful pattern. He held it up after a few more careful strokes, only slightly satisfied with his creation. If this was a spoon, he was a toucan. He sighed. He'd never claimed to be good at this. But it should suffice, and that was what mattered most.

Still, when he gave it to Eden and saw her eyes light with pleasure, he felt vaguely foolish for attempting it.

"It's nothing," he muttered when she threw her arms around his neck and told him he was wonderful. "I just got tired of hearing you complain about eating with your fingers."

"Well, I won't have to complain now. A spoon—and look at how beautifully you carved a design in it. It's a . . . uh . . . bird, right?"

"Jaguar." He grimaced. "I had trouble with the fangs. Guess they look more like a bird's beak."

"No, no, I just wasn't holding it in the light—now I see. Of course. Balam. However did you do it?"

Shrugging, he muttered something about finding the fallen tree and hacking out a chunk of wood. "Nothing special. Just a spoon.

Eden glanced up at him from under the lush curve of her lashes, a faintly shy look in her eyes. He bent and brushed his lips against hers, thinking with a sigh that she was most fiercely seductive when she was uncertain of what to say or do.

"I shall treasure it always," she looked up at him and said, "mostly because you made it for me."

"It won't last that long," he said practically. "Although I think mahogany is a fairly hard wood and should last longer than most." He let his arm shift to lie across her shoulders, fingers spreading over the curve of her arm. Cotton bunched beneath his hand, loose-woven and soft from too many washings. She had a fetish about cleanliness, he'd discovered, and made him think of a bandit-faced raccoon at times. His arm dropped away from the casual embrace. "What do you say to another swim, Goldilocks?"

"It sounds like the perfect way to pass an afternoon." A smile curved her mouth upward, and mischievous lights danced in her eyes. "I think, however, you have ulterior motives."

"You wound me," he said in mock hurt. "I think only of your pleasure."

"Which is as it should be." Rising to her toes, she pressed a quick kiss on his jaw. "I have laundry I can do while we're there."

"Unnecessary. Just hang 'em on a bush and beat 'em clean. I had in mind a more pleasurable way to while away the day."

Laughing, she ducked into the hut to fill a basket with

dirty clothes, and he leaned back against a tree to wait. This couldn't go on forever. He felt as if he was racing time, trying to squeeze in all he could with her before the inevitable happened. One morning she would wake up and decide that playing Eve to his Adam just wasn't her cup of tea anymore. And then he would take her back to civilization and that would be that. Nothing was forever. Hadn't he learned that lesson well enough?

But this was here and this was now, and he intended to make the most of it. After all, he didn't really want forever anyway.

When they arrived at the cenote, Steve pulled her into the hushed shadows of the cave. It was much cooler inside, and the soft sound of the water in the rocks was soothing and peaceful.

"Forget the laundry," he said when she heaved the basket to the surface of a flat rock. "We'll do it later."

Kissing away her protests, he drew her with him down the damp rock trail to the water's edge. In moments, they were stripped and in the cool water of the pool, splashing one another like children. Water clogged her lashes and his, and dripped from their noses. Steve curved his arms around her waist and carried her with him into deeper water, ignoring her squeals of alarm. Spreading his legs, he balanced both feet on the bottom for support in the chest-high water.

"I've got you," he said, and laughed when she clung to him with all the fervor of a baby spider monkey. "You'll drown us both."

"Serve you right," she said against his ear. She wrapped her legs more tightly around him, and he felt the inevitable response.

Water-slick and aroused, he slid his arms under her hips and lifted her slightly, watching her eyes grow large when she realized his reaction. He gave her a wicked grin.

"See what you do to me?" he murmured.

"Um. Not bad—no! Don't do that . . ."

Ducking beneath the water, he lifted her so that the juncture of her thighs was level with his face. He felt her shudder when he touched the tip of his tongue to the tight nest of curls there, and even underwater, he could hear her shocked gasp. Her thighs clamped hard around his head, and he wrenched free.

"Trying to drown me?" he asked reproachfully when he surfaced.

"What do you think you were doing?"

He looked at her in faint surprise, then grinned. "Obviously something new for you. Never mind. I think you might like it."

Her cheeks were a hot pink, and the dripping fringe of her lashes blinked rapidly over her eyes. "You can't be serious," she sputtered, and he laughed and held her close.

"Goldilocks, I couldn't be more serious. But maybe it's too soon for that. How long did you say you were married?"

She stiffened slightly in his embrace, and he regretted bringing it up. Rubbing her face against the wet surface of his shoulder, she murmured, "Colin preferred—other partners."

He didn't pursue the subject. Apparently, the deceased Colin had not been a very faithful husband. No wonder she hadn't grieved too long about his death.

"Sorry, sweetheart. Here. Let me show you how to tread water. Even if you can't swim, you can stay afloat if you ever need to know how. I'm holding you up, so don't worry." Sliding his hands under her arms, he supported her weight while he instructed her how to move her arms and legs in the motions that would keep her head above water.

Sunlight filtered down through the hole above, warming the water and lighting the cave with a hazy glow. Reflections wavered on the rock walls and stalactites, shadows of light and dark looking almost like ancient spirits as he told her more about the Mayans who had revered the sacred cenotes.

"Sometimes they cut steps down into these wells to get

at the water, or if the rock walls washed away, they'd hang long ladders of hemp down into them. Near where you found the stelae, the lakes are more like lagoons. Here, these cenotes provide most of the water during the dry season."

"And the sacrifice of virgins you told me about? Did they really do that?"

"They held sacrifices, yes. It wasn't always virgins. Sometimes it was old men or women, even children. Gold and jade, silver—whatever might appease the gods."

"How do you know all this? I mean, did they leave behind written histories that you've managed to find?"

He hesitated, then shook his head, letting his palm drift down the gentle curve of her rib cage to the span of her waist. "No, no histories. Some of the Mayans speak Spanish, even a bit of English. I learned a few things from one of them. A friend."

Eden leaned back in his embrace and let her body float near the surface, supported by his grip. Her head nestled into the curve of his arm and shoulder, and she closed her eyes. Water dotted the smooth contours of her face, and her hair floated free like a silken web. Steve gazed with mute appreciation at the tips of her breasts peeking from beneath the water.

"I do see why you stay," she murmured. "It's peaceful here. And self-sufficient. My first impression was of a tropical paradise, but that was before everything bad happened." She drew in a shaky breath. "It's like being in the Garden of Eden before the serpent came along."

He smiled wryly. "Careful. The last time I had that thought, you ended up at my feet."

Tilting back her head, she opened one eye. "Complaining again?"

"Ah no, sweetheart. No complaints about that." His gaze drifted back to her breasts and the rosy buds barely breaking the surface of the water. He slipped one arm under her body to continue the support, while his free hand caressed her with light, teasing strokes. A soft sigh slipped from her. Still cupping her breast, his hand paused. A distant noise penetrated the hushed peace of the cenote, so faint he wasn't certain he had heard it. He waited, but could hear nothing other than the rhythm of his own breathing and the lapping of water at the rocky walls.

The constant ebb and flow of the water level with each cycle of rain and drought created erosion and unseen currents in the pool. Steep, vaulted limestone walls soared overhead to the apex where light poured in through the rough, grassy opening. The gentle motion and hazy sunlight lent a misty aura to the underground pool that was mysterious and compelling at the same time, and Steve wondered if Eden felt it with the same intensity that he did.

"Steve?" she murmured, a soft, lazy drawl in the quiet. "I really don't care about going back to that temple."

He pressed his lips against her damp forehead and smiled. "Not even if it's the one that has the jade and gold throne in the shape of a jaguar?"

Twisting, legs and arms flailing in the water with a loud splashing, she wriggled around to look at him with wide eyes. "Is it? Is that the temple rumored to have the jaguar throne? Have you seen it? Oh—! You beast."

Slicing the edge of her palm through the water, she sent up a geyser to drench his face and drown his laughter. Like a slippery eel, she twisted away from him with surprising agility, shoving her feet hard against the rock bottom of the pool to launch herself toward the rocky shelf where they'd left their clothes. Steve was right behind her, gauging the distance between them so that she had only a few moments of possible triumph before he caught her at the water's edge. His hand closed around her ankle as she clambered up and out of the water, holding tight.

She had to stop, and turned around on one foot to balance precariously, glaring down at him with mock anger. "You.

You let me think you knew where it was, when all you were doing was teasing me. I ought to drown you . . ."

"Think you can, Goldilocks?" He grinned up at her, admiring the view from this angle. "All I have to do is give a little tug, and you'll be sitting on the rock face to face with me. Or close to it. Not a bad idea, I think . . ."

When she squeaked with alarm, he heaved himself up and out of the water, then caught her behind the knees with both his hands to bring her safely down to his level. She fell forward and against him. Her hands dropped to his shoulders for balance, the angle bringing his face into the wet valley between her breasts. Just right, he thought with a sigh of pure pleasure, and took a small nibble.

"You have good reflexes," he mumbled against her left breast, and felt her shake with laughter. Her wet hair dripped over both of them in cool trickles, dribbling into his mouth and tasting of the agave soap he'd given her. Then she grabbed his ears and pulled hard. He yelped with surprise. "Ow!"

"I ought to pull them off. What if I hadn't caught myself in time?"

His hands were trapped in the bends of her calves and thighs, and he gave a helpless shrug. "I had faith in you."

She released his ears and stood up. Bending from the waist, she wrung the water from her hair then slicked it back from her face. Steve leaned on one elbow and watched in admiring silence. Their intimacy had loosened her from the bonds of shy modesty she'd first felt around him, and though still reserved, she was obviously more at ease. From time to time she would glance at him, then quickly avert her eyes as if still faintly shocked. He didn't push her. Complete ease would come in time.

"Come sit with me, little girl," he said when she moved to take up her shirt and pants, and he saw her hesitate at his words. He slid a hand out to the empty space beside him. "Please."

Leaning over, she scooped up a blanket she'd brought to wash and spread it over the hard surface of the rock, then sat gingerly on the nubby wool. With her legs drawn up to her chest and her arms around them, she rested her chin on her knees and smiled. "I'm here."

"So I see," he said appreciatively, and drew a lazy circle on the outside of her thigh with his finger. It was cool in the cave, and she gave a small shiver. He looked up at her and felt that damn lurch in his chest again, the one that pricked him a lot lately. "Cold?" was all he said, and she shook her head.

"No, it feels good after the heat outside. By the time we get back, we'll be hot and sticky again." She paused then asked, "Why didn't you build your hut closer to the cenote?"

Frowning, he toyed with the edge of the blanket, then ran a finger over her bare toes curled into the wool. "Too great a chance I'd have unwanted company, I guess. I tried to choose a spot few would find unless they stumbled over it." He smiled faintly. "Or fell into it."

"I was more lucky than I realized."

"Yeah. So was I." Irritated that he'd revealed too much, he shifted to sit beside her on the blanket. Taking her hand in his, he laced his fingers through hers, then cupped her chin in his other hand and kissed her gently on the mouth. Her head tilted back for his kiss, and he deepened it until they were both breathing heavily. Moving slowly down, dragging kisses from her open mouth over her throat to her breasts, he worked his way to the tiny indention in her belly. She gave a soft moan when he stuck his tongue into it, then gasped when he moved even lower.

"Steve . . . no—what are you doing?"

"Easy, Goldilocks," he murmured, gently parting her thighs. "I wouldn't hurt you. Don't you know that by now?"

"But . . . this is indecent."

"Not between us. Not unless you don't trust me." His hand found the sweet recess of her body, stroking it with

searing motions that made her arch helplessly toward him.
Her hands fluttered aimlessly at his shoulders, his head,
touching lightly then flitting away like pale butterflies.
Steve's thumb caressed her with skillful accuracy, until she
was writhing and gasping, her breath coming in quick, hard
pants. She pressed upward, thighs opening for him as he
trailed a line of kisses along the silken skin. When his
tongue followed the path of his hands, he heard her shocked,
wild cries echoing from the vaulted roof of the cave. He
tasted deeply, while she moaned and twisted and clutched
at his shoulders with raking hands. It wasn't until the growing sounds of frenzy in her throat coalesced into one, long
female strain of ecstasy that he paused, looking up to see
her collapse into a shuddering release. He smiled. "Now,
that wasn't so bad, was it?"

Still shuddering, Eden rolled to one side and looked at
him. Her chest rose and fell erratically as she drew in ragged
breaths. Beneath the curved, spiky fringe of her lashes, her
eyes were a hazy blue. She put out a hand and touched him
lightly on the cheek, her fingers trailing down his face to
his mouth. "No," she whispered. "That wasn't bad at all."

"Wait a minute," Steve said, as they drew close to the
hut. He put out a hand and Eden stopped, looking at him
curiously. Late afternoon shadows already darkened the forest, and they had hurried to get back before dark. They'd
stayed too long at the cenote, and barely made it back before the sun set.

"What's the matter?" she asked in a faint whisper, but
he gave a quick shake of his head to silence her.

A drift of smoke wafted toward him on the slight breeze,
coming from the direction of his hut. He heard nothing. Not
even the familiar chatter of birds. Shifting slightly, he
brought up his rifle and eased back the bolt. He felt Eden's
start of alarm, and gave her a quick, fierce glance. She stared

at him with wide eyes, but made no other sound. Silently, firmly, he pushed her behind him. He debated leaving her in the shadows of a tree trunk, but there was no guarantee that someone wasn't already watching them. She'd be safer with him, no matter the danger in their camp. He motioned for her to set down the basket of laundry and follow him.

Easing forward, Steve left the familiar path and walked carefully through the thick undergrowth to come up on the hill overlooking his hut. Roots formed snaking tangles, some worn bare by rain and wind and time, twisting around and around in treacherous coils across the ground and over the edge of the bluff. Below, he could see that a fire had been lit, casting orange and gray shadows. He knelt, and pulled Eden down with him.

Several men were outlined by the glare of the fire, and to his surprise, he recognized one of them as Yac, the Indian who had spoken with him in his camp the month before. Apparently, Eden recognized him as well. Stiffening, she leaned forward, peering down the hill and into the small clearing.

Steve turned his attention to the other two men with the Indians. They were white men, one older with a slight frame and balding head, the other younger and blond, moving with an awkward gait that indicated he was either lame or injured.

Strange. All his senses warned him that trouble was below, yet there was a casual air of waiting about the men that suggested they had not come as enemies. He frowned.

Beside him, Eden gave a soft, strangled cry. He whirled to look at her, and saw in the fading light that her face was deathly pale. Turning wide blue eyes to his, she said in a choked whisper, "Colin. It's Colin down there . . . Dear God, he's alive."

Ten

"Colin—how? You . . . you're alive. I thought—I mean, I saw you fall . . ." Eden stumbled to a halt, staring at her husband.

"Yes. I'm alive. Surprised? Or upset?" Colin's pale blue eyes shifted from Eden to Steve and back to Eden again. His mouth curved into a faint smile. "We've been waiting for you. We were beginning to think you weren't coming back here."

"No." Eden drew in a shaky breath, still trying to absorb all the implications of her husband's presence. Relief that he had survived mixed with piercing pangs of dismay. "We were—washing clothes." Aware that her shirt and trousers clung to her with noticeable damp patches, and that her hair was still wet from their swim, she avoided meeting Colin's suddenly sharp gaze.

"Really?" Colin drawled. "I can't tell that by the looks of you. Where are these clean clothes you've been so industriously washing?"

Eden's head snapped up and her eyes focused on her husband. He was leaning heavily on a sturdy stick; his garments were torn and filthy. His pale eyes regarded her closely, and narrowed with definite suspicion when he flicked a glance toward Steve. Eden cleared her throat to capture his attention.

"When we realized someone was here in our camp, I left the clothes a short distance away until we could be sure you weren't dangerous." Eden drew in a deep breath, her throat tightening. She should say she was glad he was alive, should acknowledge his narrow escape in some manner, but she couldn't force the meaningless words past the sudden lump in her throat. *Colin*. Alive. Now, after all that had transpired in the past few weeks of newfound happiness. . . . Dear God, how would she deal with this?

Fortunately, Steve stepped into the breach. "How did you two men survive the massacre and manage to find us?"

"Blind luck," Colin said slowly, and turned to look at Steve again. "I was wounded, and would have died if some natives had not come along fairly soon." Indicating the three men standing silently to one side, he added, "They have some knowledge of herbal medicine, appallingly primitive, but effective. They found you and brought us here. I don't suppose you have a few coins to give them for their trouble, Mister—?"

Ignoring the obvious invitation to give his name, Steve said shortly, "No. I don't." The rifle slid through his hands to rest butt-end against the ground, and he slid the three natives a quick glance. "They wouldn't know what to do with money anyway. Currency out here is useless. Simple courtesy usually does much better." Pivoting on his heel, Steve jerked up the rifle and stalked toward the natives. In a moment, the lyrical sound of their conversation drifted back, and Eden tore her gaze away from them.

The older man cleared his throat with a slight cough, and she moved to where Richard Allen sat on a stool by the fire. Kneeling down beside him, she smiled. "Richard, I'm so glad you're alive. Are you badly injured?"

"Not at last examination, though I did suffer some minor wounds in the horrific conflict. Worse, I lost my glasses. Although I did manage to save a machete and my portable shovel, of all the things to—" He put a gentle hand on her shoulder and managed a smile. "We were so worried about you, Eden. When the smoke cleared and these kind gentlemen found us, we searched and searched for you. Then we were told that you had not been taken prisoner as we'd begun to think, but had managed to find this camp." His eyes shifted to Steve, then back to her. "Once Colin was able to travel, they brought us to you."

"Well, I'm very glad to see you," she said softly, and put her hand over his. "I know it's been a dreadful time for you."

"Yes. Yes, it has," Richard said with only a trace of a quiver in his voice. "But it could have been worse. I think of our fallen friends, and the atrocities committed . . ."

His words trailed into silence, and Eden squeezed his hand. "It's over now. There's nothing we can do."

Colin took a halting step forward, and Eden turned to look up at him. A long scratch still marred one side of his face, though it was mostly healed now. Always so immaculate in his appearance with not a hair out of place, Colin looked filthy and disheveled and completely miserable. Sympathy prompted a smile from her, but his sneering words froze it on her face.

"It occurs to me to wonder, my sweet wife, how it is you managed to escape without any sign of injury. I don't seem to recall seeing you after the first attack." His mouth twisted into a familiar, mocking smile.

She stood up slowly, forcing herself to meet his narrowed gaze. "Are you complaining, Colin? Should I exhibit gory wounds, perhaps? Would you have preferred I died?"

He flushed with anger. "Don't be ridiculous. I merely wondered aloud how you managed to escape unscathed, that's all."

"I wouldn't say *unscathed,* Colin. I am still haunted by that night, and will most likely always be. I spent two weeks alone in the jungle, terrified, hungry, and wondering if each breath would be my last. No, I certainly would not say I escaped unscathed."

"How did you manage to find him?" Colin indicated

Steve with a short jab of his thumb. "Or did you already know where he was? You two seem pretty cozy for new acquaintances."

Eden stared at him, refusing to even glance toward Steve. Yes, this was the Colin she knew best—insufferable, suspicious, cruel. And to think, she'd once thought him the most handsome and honorable of men. God, what a long time ago that had been, and how naive and gullible she must have appeared.

"Really, Miller," Richard was protesting, and Eden glanced down at his unhappy face. "Don't be an ass. You should be rejoicing that she is alive and managed to find refuge. Don't badger the poor girl. Can't you see that she's been through a great deal as well?"

"Ever the champion of the weak, Richard," Colin mocked, but he moved a short distance away and perched clumsily on the broad stump of a ceiba tree. His leg stuck out at an awkward angle, and blood-stained bandages circled it from thigh to ankle.

Taking a deep breath, Eden shifted her gaze back to Richard. "Thank you," she said softly, "but I don't want you to feel you must protect me from him. I've discovered a lot about myself in the past few weeks, and I won't be bullied any longer."

Clearing his throat, Richard muttered, "You've always been a strong woman, Eden. But that doesn't mean I enjoy listening to him make an ass of himself."

She smiled wryly. "Neither do I. But I no longer feel powerless. I will not allow him to browbeat me."

"Good girl," Richard said with a faint smile. His eyes moved toward Steve who was still talking with the natives. "This man who has saved you—*El Jaguar* the natives called him—do you trust him?"

"Yes," she relied promptly. "With my life. Why?"

Richard shifted uneasily, and a shadow passed over his face before he turned his myopic gaze upward. Blinking to clear his vision, he shrugged slightly. "He seems to have quite a—fierce—reputation in this area, if my rusty Spanish is to be believed."

"What do you mean?" Eden glanced toward Steve, who seemed to be getting along well with the three men. Laughter drifted in the air, and a jug was being passed between them.

"Well," Richard said slowly, "I first heard about him in Merída. He's had quite a life, it seems. Wanted for murder in America, and for looting tombs and temples in Mexico. For a while, he was a slave."

Eden drew in a sharp breath. "What do you mean—a slave?"

Shrugging, Richard said, "Just that. It seems the Cruzob began to take slaves for their fields, and until he managed to escape, he was one of them. That's probably where he learned their customs. The natives who cared for us seem to think he's some sort of mystic, or medicine man who can call on the gods at will. Of course, rumors do get out of hand, but it's still a bit peculiar I think, don't you?"

Eden drew in a deep breath. She couldn't refute the rumors about Steve's past, or even his present. After all, she knew very little about him save for what he had told her— and the few clippings she had come across tucked between the pages of one of his books.

"Did the natives tell you all this?" she asked, and Richard shook his head.

"Oh no. Not all of it. The mystic part, yes. The other I heard about from the Mexican government. They've been searching for Steve Ryan for some time. Apparently, he's been accused of looting the temples here and selling artifacts out of the country. They get quite annoyed about that sort of thing, naturally enough."

Doubts skittered across her mind, but Eden ignored them. "I don't think Steve would steal artifacts. He doesn't even want people down here. It would destroy the rain forests, he said. If he was looting temples, don't you think there would be some evidence of that here? I've been here for over a month, and I've seen nothing to indicate that he's party to that."

"I hardly think he would allow anyone to know of it," Richard said dryly, "but I do trust your judgment of his character. If you believe in him, so shall I."

Eden bit her lower lip and glanced toward Colin. She recalled only too well Steve's caustic reminder that she apparently wasn't too skilled at judging men's character, or she wouldn't have married Colin. That was only partially true, but valid enough to leave her feeling vaguely uneasy. What if she were wrong about Steve? What if his protests about exploring Mayan ruins were only a smoke-screen? It didn't bear thinking about.

"Richard, does Colin know all that you just told me?"

Looking up at her, he said in surprise, "Yes. Of course. Why?"

"No reason. I just—you know how he gets. If he steps on Steve's toes, there will be an argument."

"Dear Lord, I hope not. The natives who brought us here will take us no farther. They are unwilling to take us to a town, and would agree only to find *El Jaguar* for us."

Eden sighed. "If Colin irritates Steve, I'm afraid we may all find ourselves abandoned to our own devices out here. Unless you two have managed to find a map, we need him to guide us to safety. There are still hostile Indians in the jungle who would be only too glad to finish what they started."

Richard frowned. "You know, I've been thinking about that. The night of the massacre—I could swear I heard some of our assailants speaking English."

She stared down at him. "But that's impossible. They were Indians. The Cruzob, Steve thinks, who are involved in a nasty caste war in the Yucatán."

"Yes, yes, I know about the Cruzob. And it was chaotic that night. All the guns firing, the swords and machetes and our tents burning—yes, I suppose I could be mistaken. It's just that I was so certain for a time . . ." He paused and looked up at her. "Were there any other survivors that you know of?"

"Only Paco. He found me hiding in a tree trunk, but he's dead now."

"Ah, I remember Paco. A rather quiet young native boy. How did he die?"

"I'm not sure. A crocodile, I think. We hid in some trees near a swamp, and in the night I heard a splash and a scream. I was so terrified—I couldn't even call for him, and I didn't hear him scream again. When it was daylight, I came down from the tree and looked for him, but found only a shred of the shirt he'd been wearing." She shuddered. "It had blood on it."

"Poor child," Richard murmured, and put out a hand to catch her by the wrist. "You have, indeed, suffered greatly. I hope that soon our ordeal will be ended. We shall see how quickly Colin can travel, so that Mister Ryan will lead us to safety."

It was, Eden thought bleakly, the best solution. Now that Colin was alive, she would have to make a decision. He was her husband, and despite what had transpired between her and Steve, she was duty-bound to remain with Colin. A feeling of guilt knifed through her that had nothing to do with the feelings she'd had before. She'd been unfaithful. Never, even when faced with Colin's most flagrant infidelities, had she been tempted to do the same. But—and this was the worst of all—if Steve wanted her, she would fly to him in an instant, Colin or not.

Closing her eyes, Eden tried not to think about the days that lay before her in a long stretch of empty misery.

* * *

"Hell no, I'm not giving up my bed," Steve snapped. "If you want to give him yours, fine."

"But Steve, he's injured."

Eden met his gaze for only a brief instant before glancing away again. He wasn't surprised. She had not been able to look directly at him since they'd come down the hill and joined her husband. It was infuriating. He felt like smashing something, in particular, Colin Miller. The insufferable boor. He sat with his injured leg outstretched snapping orders at Eden as if she were a servant instead of his wife. She had already brought him water, food, a pillow for his leg, and even a book. Now she was supposed to arrange a comfortable bed for him.

Shrugging, Steve said, "That's not my problem. If you want to let him have the hammock, that's up to you."

The hammock, empty and dusty from disuse, still swayed in one corner of the hut. It looked as if it would get some use now. Well, he'd prayed for a temporary woman, and it seemed that was what he'd gotten. Eden Miller had been a miraculous but brief sojourn in his life. Now it was time to face reality again.

"Really," Colin turned to say with a petulant frown, "that is hardly very generous of you. Do you intend that my wife should sleep out here on the ground?"

"No. She can have the hammock and you can sleep out here."

"But I'm injured, my good man," Colin protested, gesturing toward his leg. "You can't expect me to be comfortable on a few blankets out here, while you—"

"Take the hammock, Colin," Eden said quickly. "I'll be perfectly comfortable out here, with a little insect repellent. Besides, it will give Richard and me a good opportunity to talk. Won't it, Richard?"

Richard glanced up with a smile. "I'm truly looking forward to it, Eden. I saw the most marvelous things on our unfortunate trek through the jungle."

Eden glanced at Colin—who was glowering balefully at Steve—and ran a hand through her hair in a nervous gesture. "So did I. I discovered a stela with glyphs that still had traces of paint on them, and the carved face of a jaguar—"

"Where?" Richard demanded immediately. "A jaguar, you say? It could be part of the temple we've been seeking—"

"Forget it." Steve's cold tone drew Richard and Eden's instant attention, as he'd intended it to. "If I guide you folks anywhere, it will be to a town."

"Now see here, man," Richard began to protest, "a find like that could be invaluable."

"I don't give a damn. As soon as Miller's leg mends, I'll take you as close to a town as I can, and that's as far as I'll go." He flashed a furious glance at Eden for even bringing up the stelae she'd found. "After that you can do what you damn well please."

"My, what a surly individual," Steve heard Colin mutter as he pivoted on his heel to walk away. "I'll certainly be glad to get out of here."

Richard Allen had apparently forgotten anything but Eden's discovery, and was peppering her with questions. Steve snatched up his Winchester and stalked into the night. They could work out what they liked. He needed to blow off some of his bad mood on someone or something. If he had to remain in camp much longer, he'd end up sending them all packing. Except for Eden, maybe. Which showed the extent of his idiocy. If he had any sense, she would be the first to go.

A full moon rose above the tops of the trees, glittering like ice in the black night sky. Vines snatched at his clothes as he strode away from the clearing with quick, angry steps. Insects swarmed around him, and he swore softly, belatedly remembering that he hadn't used any of the ointment as he usually did. All he'd been able to think about was Eden. And Colin. *Jesus.* Just the thought of her being with that foppish whiner made him feel crazy and sick inside, made him want to—he drew in a deep breath. No. Not again. He'd sworn no woman would ever turn him inside out again.

Slinging his rifle to a downward position in the crook of his arm, he began to run, feet instinctively finding the path in the dark. The Indians who had brought Richard and Colin to him had told him what had happened, how they had found the men not far from the ruins of their camp. Smoke from the burning tents had drawn them there, that and curiosity. Colin had been unconscious, Richard in shock, he supposed.

Yac, the leader of the group, had informed him with a frown that the older man had been sitting near Colin's prostrate form without moving, as if waiting for death. Men did that, Steve knew, having seen it happen even in the midst of a battle. He'd seen men sit with tears streaming down their faces, or just blank stares, while around them bullets flew and cannonballs crashed, and they just sat there like stone statues. Shock and fear, he supposed, made each man react differently.

Slowing his pace, Steve panted for breath. Moonlight silvered the ground, black shadows shifting as clouds passed overhead. Wind made the leaves of a ceiba tree rustle in the wind, and the silk pods rattled in solid clicks against the trunk. The sweet, heady fragrance of moonflowers twining up a host tree lent spice to the night, their pale blossoms white against the dark bark. It was beautiful out here. And peaceful. And he had the inescapable feeling that it was all about to change.

Steve leaned back against a tree, crushing a spill of flowers under his shoulder. His head tilted, scraping the rough bark almost painfully. He welcomed it as a distraction, anything to ease the building tension inside of him.

His palms were damp with sweat, and he slid the rifle down to rest against his leg. The barrel was cool and slick, familiar in the curl of his hand. A pauraque gave its hoarse, plaintive *purwe'eeeeer* whistle in the trees overhead, the cry soft and lilting. Other birds hooted softly in reply, then grew quiet. This was not the natural quiet, but a tense, waiting silence that filled the forest with strange apprehension. Steve waited, senses alert, straining to hear and see in the tropical night.

He knew the moment it came, treading noiselessly on the forest floor, huge padded paws confident and stealthy. His fingers coiled around the gun barrel and slowly drew it upward, just in case. Keeping his movements slow, he eased back the lever on the rifle. In the distance, a shadow flitted beneath a patch of moonlight, so quick he wasn't certain if it was actually there.

Then he knew that it was there, as he heard a low, rumbling snarl. He caught a quick glimpse of two golden eyes reflecting moonlight, then the unmistakable growl of triumph. A flash of yellow moved with leonine grace, then sprang. Bringing up his rifle in a swift, familiar motion, he pulled the trigger. The sound of the shot echoed through the still night like thunder, the quick, bright flash of percussion a flaming stab in the dark.

There was a crashing thud and anguished roar, then a loud rustling of leaves and snapping of twigs and limbs. Steve waited a few minutes, then cautiously moved forward. The warning shot had been only meant to scare it away. He'd hoped to miss. But when he knelt to investigate a tiny glitter on a fallen limb, he knew that he had not missed. Huge drops of blood smeared the limb and fallen leaves. He must have winged it, and now there was a wounded jaguar roaming the forest. Damn. He stood up, wiping the blood on his pants, eyes searching through the night shadows. He certainly didn't want to run into it on the way back.

When he finally returned to camp, Eden rushed toward him, eyes wide with fear. "Steve. Are you all right? I heard a shot—dear God, there's blood on you . . ."

"It's not mine." He gripped her hard around the wrist, having seen the way Colin Miller watched them with narrowed eyes. "A jaguar thought I'd be a tasty midnight snack, that's all," he said, digging his thumb into her skin until she looked up at him.

She blinked, her dilated eyes slowly regaining focus under the pressure of his harsh grip. "Oh. I thought—the shot. It made me think of the night we were attacked."

Easing his grip, he managed a smile. She was so close he could have caressed the frown lines away from around her eyes and on each side of her mouth, but he knew better than to offer any kind of physical comfort. If he touched her that way, he might not let her go, husband or not.

"Sorry. It couldn't be helped," he said, and took a backward step away from her. "I only wanted to scare it away."

She glanced around, looking slightly embarrassed. Pushing the loose hair from her eyes, she laughed awkwardly. "Well, this is a day for excitement, I suppose. I'm exhausted."

As she walked back to the others, Steve glanced toward Colin Miller. He was still sprawled in front of the fire. A lantern above his head gleamed brightly, revealing the narrowed eyes and taut set of his mouth. Suspicion was evident in every line of his features.

Richard Allen spoke up. "Did you shoot the beast?"

"Yeah, I'm afraid I did. It's not dead, though. I only winged it."

"Wonderful," Colin sneered. "Now we've got a wounded jaguar roaming the forest. How humane of you."

"Colin," Eden protested softly, "don't say things like that. Steve would never endanger anyone, or shoot a jaguar unless it was necessary. He respects the wild creatures of the forest."

"Doesn't that sound cozy," Colin muttered, his pale gaze swinging from Eden back to Steve. "You even defend him."

"No one has to defend me, Miller," Steve said, cutting across Eden's protest. "I don't have to answer to you. This is my camp. If you don't like the accommodations, you're free to leave at any time."

"Really." Colin reached out to grasp Eden by the hand, tugging her toward him with a steady pull. "And my wife? Is she free to go with me?"

"Colin—" Eden tried to pull her hand away, but he held it firmly, sliding his other hand up her leg to her hip. He let it lie there, his palm flat upon the swell of her hip, fingers idly ruffling the material of her loose trousers. After her first attempt to pull away, Eden remained still, but her eyes flew to Steve's face begging him not to interfere.

"Don't be ridiculous, Colin," Richard put in quickly. "You have become overtaxed with all the day's stress and are leaping to wild conclusions." He stood up and moved toward Colin as if to stand between him and Steve, then turned to give Steve an apologetic smile. "Forgive him, Mr. Ryan. It's been quite a trying time for both of us. For all of us."

"There's nothing to forgive," Steve said abruptly. "Miller can think what he damn well pleases."

"I don't need your permission for that," Colin said softly.

Turning on him, Steve felt his mild dislike of Colin Miller burgeon into a more active emotion. His eyes narrowed. These men represented trouble in more than one way. If the natives that had found them revealed where they'd taken them, the Cruzob might very likely come looking for them. And if Miller recuperated too slowly, Steve himself might very well be willing to give them to the Cruzob without a twinge of guilt. It could be a dangerous situation. He should be concentrating upon that.

Instead, he was focusing upon his growing hatred of Colin Miller, and the proprietary way he glanced at Eden. She was his wife. He was making that very clear to everyone, particularly Steve. As if he could forget for a moment that Eden belonged to someone else.

Eleven

It was still dark when Eden was roused from a fitful sleep by a faint sound. Suddenly alert, she lay still and tense, listening. For a moment, all she could hear was the familiar night noises of chirping insects and night birds. Then it came again, the soft rasp of uneven breathing. She turned her head slowly, blinking as she strained to see Richard. He lay asleep, a dark, blanket-clad mound barely lit by the glow from the dying embers in the fire.

When she tilted her head back slightly, she caught a glimpse of golden eyes, wide and unblinking. She stared into the shadows, focusing on the darkened silhouette until she could distinguish it from its surroundings. Her heart lurched. A jaguar. Was it Balam or the animal Steve had wounded? She suppressed an urge to call out with an effort. If it was not Balam, her cries could certainly provoke an attack by a wounded, dangerous jaguar. For long, tense moments, she lay watching, fearing to make any sudden moves.

Then the shadow moved, making no noise, gliding lithely toward the hut. It must be Balam. No other animal would go into the hut with such sure, purposeful strides.

Eden sat up in her blankets and debated calling out to Steve. He would immediately recognize Balam, of course, but Colin lay asleep in the hammock. She wasn't as certain about Balam's friendliness as Steve was, and if Colin made any sudden, threatening moves . . .

All speculation ended in the next instant, when she heard

a loud yelp, a snarling cough, and a string of oaths that she recognized as belonging to Steve. Untangling her legs from the clinging folds of blankets, Eden lurched from her bed and toward the hut.

It was still quite dark, and she stumbled over something on the way, limping the final steps to the open entrance of the hut. She could barely make out the forms of struggling men. Panting curses filled the air, adding to the chaos. Eden screamed when a sudden shot shattered the night. A blinding flash of light punctuated the dark, followed by more angry curses and a jaguar's snarling cough.

"Steve. My God—are you all right?"

The sounds of the fierce struggle ebbed, and then there was the scratching sound of a match being struck and a tiny flare that caught and burned steadily. Holding up the oil lantern so that it lit one side of his face, Steve gave her a furious glance.

"I'm fine. This damn fool almost shot Balam." With another contemptuous glance at Colin, he tossed his rifle behind him to the netting shrouded mattress.

The light grew brighter as Steve fiddled with the knob on the oil lantern. Colin was sprawled on the floor beneath the hammock, eyes wide with fear and anger. In one corner, Balam crouched as if ready to spring at any moment, his fangs bared in a snarl and his gold eyes dark and dilated. Steve made a soothing motion with one hand, and the huge cat crept forward, keeping a wary eye on Colin as he stretched out his head for Steve's touch.

"How the hell was I to know it was some kind of pet?" Colin snapped from the floor. He rubbed at his jaw with one hand. His gaze remained focused on the jaguar as if afraid it would spring upon him at any moment. "And in case you're interested, my sweet little wife, I'm just fine."

Eden flushed. "I can see that, Colin."

"Yes, so you say." Edging cautiously to a sitting position,

Colin pulled his injured leg beneath him. "Hold your pet, Ryan, so I can get up."

"No need to hold him. Just move slow and easy and don't try to shoot him and he'll leave you alone."

"For all I knew, it was the animal you wounded earlier. You could have warned me, you know," Colin muttered sullenly as he eased himself up.

"I didn't think about it."

"Didn't think about it. Good God, man, I could have been killed . . ."

"Balam was in more danger from a trigger-happy fool than you were from him," Steve shot back. "You could have killed him or me, waving the damn rifle around like an idiot."

"Too bad I didn't." Colin's eyes narrowed to glittering slits and he took a limping step forward. "Or were you hoping maybe that the jaguar would kill me in my sleep? That would have made it pretty convenient for you, from the looks of things around here."

"Colin," Eden protested, "don't say things like that."

"Why not?" He turned toward her. "Do you think me blind or stupid? You've been alone with this man for some time now. And you come back from a cozy little tryst in the jungle all dirty and sweaty like some street whore—"

"Enough." Steve took a menacing step forward, one hand bunched into a fist. "Shut your mouth or I'll shut it for you."

"No. Don't." Eden flung herself between them, both arms outspread to keep them apart. She shot a glance toward Steve. His face was set into a hard, tight expression that she'd begun to recognize. Beneath the flat of the hand she had pressed against his chest, she could feel the rapid slam of his heart. A pulse in his throat beat hard and fast, and his muscles were taut with strain. "Don't," she repeated in a pleading whisper that drew his eyes from Colin to her.

There was a flash of frustration mixed with the fury in his eyes. He didn't yield, but he didn't press forward, either.

He let her hold him at bay. Now, if only Colin would be sensible and keep his mouth shut, she might be able to calm them both down.

"What's going on?" Richard asked from right behind Eden, and she turned to him, grateful for the interruption.

"Richard. It's—"

"Nothing," Colin interrupted. "I didn't know about his pet, and I'm afraid he took me by surprise in the night. That's all."

When Richard slanted an inquiring glance toward Steve, he gave a short nod. "Yeah, that's right. It was just a misunderstanding."

Nodding slowly, Richard eyed the jaguar at Steve's side. "I see. A most remarkable animal, Mr. Ryan. *Panthera onca.* Quite unusual to see a black one. The rosettes yellow jaguars have are still there, only as a variation in texture instead of actual spots. A fine specimen, indeed."

"Yeah. He is." Steve fondled Balam's ears, and was rewarded with a loud, rasping rattle that passed for a purr. The jaguar rubbed his muzzle against Steve's leg in the same manner as a house cat, eyes half-closed with pleasure.

Some of the tension eased, and Eden took a relieved breath. Richard's calm remarks were just what was needed. Her arms lowered and she managed a stiff smile. "Balam was the first stray Steve took in, from what I understand."

Steve looked up at her with a faint smile. "Yeah, but he was a lot tamer than you and not nearly as much trouble."

"Flatterer."

Clearing his throat, Richard said mildly, "Now that we know we are not about to be mauled by a wild animal, do you suppose we could get some sleep? This is the first night in some time that I've felt secure enough to sleep without one eye open."

Colin took a step backward, reaching behind him for the swaying hammock. "I could certainly use some rest," he muttered, and flashed a narrowed glance at Steve. "I'm not too sure about sleeping with both eyes closed, though."

Steve shrugged. "Suit yourself, Miller. I don't give a damn how well you sleep."

"Now gentlemen," Richard said with a serious expression, "I certainly hope you don't intend to continue this feud into the night. It smacks of juvenile theatrics."

"There's no feud." Steve moved to the mattress and held up the netting. Balam sauntered with sinuous grace into the sleeping area and stretched out like a gigantic fur throw. Yawning hugely, the jaguar began to clean the pads between his claws with rasping strokes of his tongue, ignoring those who watched him with mixed emotions.

It was hard for Eden to contain her amusement, particularly when she saw the wary fear in Colin's eyes as he regarded the cat, or the grim relish in Steve's gaze as he regarded Colin. They were like two dogs battling for the same territory, she decided, caught between exasperation and growing anxiety. A clash was inevitable, unless she managed to get Colin away from here before it happened.

Apparently, she discovered when she and Richard went back to their blankets by the fire, it would not be as soon as she'd hoped.

"You know," Richard said softly, kneeling beside her in the soft light from the glowing embers, "I cannot leave this area until I have found the temple of the jaguar."

"Richard . . . but you know what happened . . . it's too dangerous to try it again."

"I agree. We shouldn't proceed as we did before. We were foolish, and I depended upon Colin's knowledge of men and weapons too greatly, it seems. This time, I think the solution would be to have someone familiar with the area guide us. A handful of people are much less likely to attract attention or pose a threat. No, hear me out," he said quickly when she started to protest. "While in the Indian camp, I was able to glean certain facts. *El Jaguar*—Steve

Ryan—he knows this area like the back of his hand. The Indians trust him, and even the hostile bands leave him alone because they consider him capable of communing with their gods. We must persuade Ryan to guide us back to our original campsite. Perhaps enough of our supplies are left that we can finish what we began. And then we can search for the temple of the jaguar. I'm convinced it's in the area where you found the stelae."

"He won't do it." Eden shook her head. "I tried to get him to take me back, but he refused. He said he doesn't want men down here prowling around."

Richard looked crestfallen for a moment, then lifted his head to gaze directly into her eyes. Even in the dim light she could see his hope. "You can convince him, Eden."

Shaking her head, Eden murmured, "No, no I can't. It will only make him angry if I try."

"You have a weapon no one else has, though," Richard said softly, and put a hand atop hers where it lay on the blanket. "Colin is not the only one who's noticed the way Ryan looks at you. Wait a minute—I'm not offering any judgment. Nor do I want to hear denials or confessions. I'm just stating a fact. Think about it for a while before you decide. It will be several days before Colin is up to making a distant trek anyway. And that includes back to Merída." He patted her hand. "Just think about it, Eden. Promise?"

"I . . . I promise to think about it. But that's all. And I already know what his answer will be if I do bring it up."

Richard smiled. "I have the utmost faith in you. All of the important archaeological information we could gather depends upon your success, you know. And you'll succeed. I know you will."

When he'd gone back to his blankets, leaving Eden alone with her thoughts and the familiar night noises, she had the sinking feeling that Steve might very well end up hating her.

* * *

Steve jerked his gaze back from Eden to the rifle he was cleaning. It was a mistake to look at her, a mistake to watch Colin Miller put a hand on her, a mistake to let the slow fires burn inside him. Three days had passed since the unexpected arrival of her husband; since then the first spark of enmity had exploded into full-blown dislike. It was vaguely surprising that he felt that way. Not completely unexpected, perhaps, but surprising that he felt as strongly as he did about Colin Miller.

Keeping his eyes on the small bottle of oil and the glistening bore of the Winchester's barrel, Steve tried to ignore the couple sitting in front of his hut. Eden, with pale hair falling about her shoulders in a careless spill of sun-touched gold, graceful and slim and oh so tempting—and Colin, ever-watchful, pale eyes following his every step, especially when he spoke with Eden. Damn him. When would Miller's leg heal so he could get rid of them?

"Excuse me," Richard interrupted, and Steve glanced up at him. "I don't wish to bother you, but I thought we might chat a bit if you don't mind."

Shrugging, Steve indicated a wooden crate standing one end up. Richard dragged it close and seated himself. He watched silently for a moment as Steve reassembled the rifle, then cleared his throat.

"I understand that you are familiar with this area."

"Familiar enough." Steve didn't glance up. He smoothed the oiled rag down over the gleaming wooden rifle stock.

"In your explorations, perhaps you've seen some mysterious mounds. A few stone carvings here and there."

"Perhaps." Breaking open the rifle, he slid shells into the empty magazine, then closed it with a solid click and looked up at Richard. "If you're hinting that I play guide, forget it. I have no intention of taking you anywhere but to the coast where you can catch a ship back to the States."

Richard looked down at his clasped hands for a moment. "I didn't ask you to guide us to any ruins, but I don't see the reason for such violent objections to doing so, if I were to ask."

Amazed, Steve shook his head. "Don't see a reason for my objections? You've got a short memory, then. I guess having most of your expedition massacred has escaped your mind. Well, it hasn't escaped mine." He stood up. "Forget it. There's nothing you could offer me that would make me change my mind. If you want to explore ruins, go right ahead. Just leave me out."

Rising, Richard held a hand out palm up. "Mister Ryan, there's no need to be angry with me. I didn't ask you to guide us anywhere. I was merely making conversation."

"Then why do I have this nagging feeling that if I'd said I'd show you the ruins, you'd have leaped at it?"

A wry smile twisted Richard's mouth. "Because you must sense what a fanatic I am when it comes to Mayan ruins. Yes, of course I would leap at the opportunity to go back. After all, that is the reason I came down here, the reason I'm still determined to continue my quest as soon as possible." He laughed. "I'm not sensible when it comes to this subject. But I'm certain that there are things you feel very passionate about as well."

"I'm sure there are." Steve kept his eyes on Richard Allen despite the temptation to glance at Eden. "But that doesn't mean I'm stupid enough to risk my life for them."

"Ah. Then perhaps I was wrong about you, Mister Ryan. I had thought you a man of intellect and passion, a man who would be capable of accomplishing anything he desired."

"Did you." Steve shook his head. "Guess you can't always be right."

"Perhaps not."

Richard continued to look at him thoughtfully, and there was something in his eyes that made Steve wary. An assessment, maybe, as if he knew more than he was telling.

Steve knew Allen had heard the rumors about him, and he had a damn good idea where he had heard them.

Cradling the rifle barrel-down in the crook of his arm, Steve asked, "Where did your expedition buy supplies before beginning the trek inland?"

There was a brief pause before he answered, "Mérida. Why do you ask?"

"No reason. Just curious. Tulum is the closest town from where we are, but I'd say San Gervasio on Cozumel Island was safer. What do you think?"

"Definitely. I'm not at all certain of Tulum's stability at the moment, what with the native uprisings and the Cruzob raging so wildly about the area." Richard frowned. "It was thought they would stay close to the Caribbean coast and not come so far inland. But, I should have paid more attention to the warnings, I suppose."

"Yeah, I'd say so. It would have saved some lives. As well as a lot of grief."

"Don't remind me." Richard glanced toward Eden and Colin. "But at least we know Eden is safe now. We were so distressed at first, then, when we didn't find her body . . ."

"So you did go back to look for her?"

"Of course." Richard sounded affronted that Steve would even ask that question. "Although Colin was not exactly in his right mind, I was able to conduct a thorough search. By night, of course, when I was fairly certain I wouldn't be seen. We were only in the forest a day and a night before the Indians found us. I was quite surprised that they were so solicitous. At first, I feared we would be slain."

"Not all Indians have joined the Cruzob cult. Although, that doesn't mean they're delighted we're here. I think they'd just as soon be left in peace."

"You know, they seem totally unaware of the value of these abandoned temples. I actually saw one ruined temple being used as a sort of residence. People live in it, oblivious to the significance of their surroundings."

"They've lived like that for hundreds of years. Why change now?"

"I find it illuminating. It must be how it was a thousand years ago, temple atop temple, city atop city—just as in the Holy Land, where recent discoveries have made men famous throughout the world, not just in archaeological papers." Drawing in a deep breath, Richard added softly, "I could be as famous as John Lloyd Stephens, who discovered the temples of Chichén Itzá and others, were I to make such a discovery here."

"Ah, so this isn't just about exploring history. There's a more personal goal in mind."

"Hardly, Mr. Ryan. My discovery would enlighten the entire world, not just the world of science. Think of it. Just thirty-two years ago, Stephens came to explore the Yucatán. While here, he made many important finds, among them the ruined city of Chichén Itzá—and a small jaguar throne. It is rumored," he said softly, "that there is another jaguar throne that once belonged to a great ruler in a huge city. This throne is quite large and made entirely of gold and jade, sitting in a throne room filled with jade masks, gold cups, silver jewelry—all extremely precious and valuable. I had a copy of a very rare grammar published in 1746 by a Franciscan Father, Pedro Beltrán, and it would help to unravel the mystery of the ancient writings as few volumes could do. Unfortunately, my copy was destroyed in our recent mishap. So you see, it is imperative that I find these lost ruins. I am indebted to those who have gone before me, and committed to restoring their legacies. I do this not for myself, but for the world."

"That's not how it sounds to me."

"No? How does it sound to you, pray tell?"

"It sounds to me, Mr. Allen, as if your main objective is to be known as the man who made the most important discovery of our time. You want your name in headlines, you'd like to be fêted around the world by dignitaries and illuminaries of every country. You don't really give a damn about what you discover down here, as long as it will make you famous. Am I far off the mark?"

Stiffening, Richard Allen stared at him frostily. "I find your remarks offensive, and quite far from the truth, sir."

"Sorry about that. I just tell it the way I see it."

"Do you. If your aim is to make enemies, you certainly do have an efficient method of accomplishing that goal."

"Oh, are you my enemy now?" Steve shrugged. "I don't like being taken for a fool, or being manipulated. You may think you are quite clever at manipulation, but I've gone up against the best. You, Mr. Allen, are a rank amateur."

Pivoting on his heel, Steve strode away. He could feel Richard Allen's gaze boring into his back, and Eden's, too. No doubt she'd heard part of their conversation. He hadn't tried to keep his voice down, or hide anything. He didn't care if she heard. In fact, it would probably be to his advantage. Damn, if he didn't resent being taken as a naive idiot too gullible to recognize duplicity when he heard it.

Next, would come the big guns. Eden would try to talk him into guiding them to Mayan ruins. He'd heard the conversation between Eden and Richard that first night, and it made him furious. Furious that either of them would think of using her, and furious that both apparently knew how he felt about her. He couldn't have been the only one to overhear. Colin lay in the curve of the hammock only a few feet from him, and unless he was stone deaf, he had to have heard at least part of it. And he'd made no protest, no comment, which could only mean that he was a part of the plan. Damn them. Damn them all.

Eden's attempt to coax him into agreeing came at dusk two days later, when she joined him on the hill overlooking camp.

"Steve?" Eden appeared just behind him where he sat alone with his thoughts and a cup of bourbon. He was watching an emerald-throated hummingbird sip nectar from the pale petals of an orchid growing on the side of a tree, and he didn't move or acknowledge her arrival. She hesitated when he didn't reply, then put a hand on his shoulder.

His fist clenched around the tin cup. "I heard you. Won't your husband be looking for you?"

Ignoring that, she asked, "May I sit down with you for a few minutes?"

"Not if a jealous husband is going to come barreling around a jacaranda bush with my loaded rifle in his hands." He took another sip of bourbon, relishing the way it burned down his throat. The hummingbird drifted to another blossom higher up, tiny wings whirring in a blur of motion.

Eden sat beside him and crossed her legs. "You have your rifle with you," she pointed out.

"So I do. How clever of you to notice." He poured more bourbon into his cup, then recorked the bottle. Holding up the cup, he turned to look at her. "To your health, Mrs. Miller."

Her face tightened, but she didn't say anything as he took another swallow. He could feel her eyes on him, large and blue and full of questions, and he wanted to toss away the bourbon and take her with him, away from camp and away from Colin Miller. But he couldn't, of course. She belonged to Miller.

He took another sip of bourbon before she said softly, "I thought Colin was dead, Steve. I saw him fall."

"Yeah. So you said. Good thing he survived. Now you two can go merrily on your way."

Eden frowned and looked down at her hands. "Is that what you want? For us all to leave?"

"Since when did what I want enter into the picture? Hell, you and your archaeologist buddy have got my next month all figured out, haven't you? I'm to guide you to the ruins so Richard can be famous and lord it over all his cronies, and I guess you'll just share in the limelight and fame and money the best you can. Or do you get half? Forgive me if I'm not up on all the finer points of the scheme."

She had the grace to flush, her chin lifting as she met his gaze with steady eyes. "All right. So Richard wanted me to coax you into leading us to the ruins. I admit that. But I told him you wouldn't agree."

"How foresighted of you. At least you were delicate enough to wait a few days before bringing this up, but then, I guess you wanted to be certain Colin's leg is healing. Did you also tell your friend how close you and I were before your husband had the bad taste to show up here alive?"

"You're not being fair, Steve."

"Not being fair?" He lowered his tin cup and stared at her. She'd braided her hair again, but small tendrils had escaped the plaits to frame her face in tiny, endearing wisps. He wanted to reach out and brush them away from her cheeks, caress her soft skin and kiss her . . . "I'm being *very* fair," he muttered, looking down into his cup again. "Your precious Colin has been here five days and I haven't killed him yet. How much fairer can I be? By the way, has he always been such a lazy whiner or is this a new trait he's cultivated?"

Eden sighed. "No, he's always been a bit of a spoiled baby. His injuries have only intensified his tendencies toward complaining."

"How charming. And to think I almost missed the display."

"Steve—"

"Dammit," he snarled, unable to stop himself, "what do you want from me? I won't make à decision for you. It's up to you. If you're too cowardly to choose, don't expect me to be gallant enough to step in and do it for you. And I won't take you to those ruins, or the temple of the jaguar, or whatever it is you want. It's not safe. I want you out of here. As quickly as possible. I'll get you to the coast, and you can take the next ship to the States. But I won't," he bit out through clenched teeth, "stick around to watch you and your husband play parlor games. Have you got that?"

Shaking, Eden made a small sound like a muffled sob, bending her head so that he couldn't see her face. Steve stared at the top of her head, the pale strands of hair mixed with darker ones, soft and silky to the touch. Her shoulders shook slightly, and he groaned. Damn. He didn't need this. Didn't need her tears or her pleas, or any of the emotions she provoked in him. He needed peace. Not the kind of peace he'd found in her arms, but the kind he'd had before.

"Eden." He touched her lightly on her crown, then slid his hand beneath her chin to tilt her face upward. A tear slipped down her face to the corner of her mouth, and he brushed it away with his thumb. It seemed so natural to kiss her, to taste the salty residue of her tears on his lips. A strand of her hair clung to his mouth like silk thread, and he pulled it away. "Eden. God. We can't do this. You're married. We have to forget what happened between us . . ."

More tears slid from beneath the curved wings of her lashes, sliding over her cheeks. "I know . . . I know. Maybe this is my penance for wishing Colin dead. I thought it was his death that was my punishment, but this—dear God, what am I saying?"

She lifted her anguished eyes to his, and he was lost. It didn't matter where they were or who she was or who he was. All that mattered was here and now. Shoving his fingers into her loosened hair, he pressed a kiss against the vulnerable skin beneath her earlobe. She shivered, and moved her head lower, kissing his throat. Breathing heat on the bare skin where his shirt wasn't buttoned, she lifted her face and he found himself kissing her deeply, his tongue exploring her mouth in fervent thrusts. His hands pulled her tight against him, so that he could feel the firm crush of her breasts against his chest, and he groaned as he brought up his hand to caress the soft temptation. She shuddered beneath his touch, straining toward him, her mouth open and seeking, her hands sliding over his back to urge him even closer.

Breath coming in quick, hard gulps of air, he tried to regain control, tried to remember that what they were doing was wrong. But the frayed threads of logic wavered and drifted away when she put his hand beneath her blouse and his palm grazed the rigid tip of her breast. Sitting back on his heels, Steve dragged her into him so that her thighs were on each side of his, his body hard against hers. Eden responded with a surge of excitement, but her faint, throaty cries that sounded like the cooing of a dove somehow brought an edge of reality to the moment.

From somewhere amidst the collapse of all his good intentions, he found the strength to push her away, slowly and gently, and regretfully. She blinked, lips parted and bruised from his kisses, her eyes wet with tears.

"Steve," she whispered, and he shook his head.

"You know we can't. You'd never forgive yourself or me. Not now. Now that we know he's alive."

"God." She fell against him, breathing deeply, wetting his shirt with her tears. "You're right," she said, the words muffled by his shirt. "As usual."

"Damn, I hate being right so much."

She laughed softly through her tears and sat up sniffing. "I suppose you think I'm horrible."

"I always have, Goldilocks." He smiled. "Use my shirt to wipe your face, then go back to camp before anyone misses you. I think I'm going to stay out here a while."

She hesitated, then wiped her face and stood up. "What can we do, Steve? What about us?"

He turned to look up at her. "What about us? You're married. It's your choice. I can't ask you to choose between your husband and me. I've no right to do that. You make the choice."

"But . . . but if I did choose, and it was you—what would happen then?"

"I don't know, Goldilocks. I can only answer that when you make the choice." He paused, then asked softly, as if the answer didn't matter, "What do you want?"

Twisting her hands together, she stood silently for a long time, while the evening breeze lifted soft tendrils of her hair and blew it in a golden web across her face. A large flock of brilliant parakeets took wing overhead, filling the darkening sky with color and sound. She looked up with anguished eyes. "I'm married to Colin, but—I'm not sure what I should do . . ."

Steve studied her and saw the raw indecision in her eyes. Damn. She really didn't know. It was no choice then. He looked away from her, focusing on the vivid blue blossoms clustered on the spire of a jacaranda bush.

After a moment, Eden said softly, "Guide us to the temple of the jaguar. Give me more time. I . . . I don't know what's best. Maybe Richard and Colin will go back to the States without me. Then I could stay with you for a while."

Dangerous options, Steve thought, much too dangerous to even consider. A choice without commitment was always dangerous. He'd made enough of them in his life. He ought to know.

Shifting his eyes to the spilled cup of bourbon in the grass, he said softly, "What makes you think I want you to stay?"

Eden didn't answer. She stood there a fraction of a moment longer, then turned and walked away. Steve stared into the lush green vegetation of the jungle without really seeing the slender, closed blossoms of the morning glory, or the pale, snowy buds of moonflowers slowly beginning to open to the night. None of it registered, not the beauty nor the wildness. Nothing penetrated the bitter haze of his disappointment.

Twelve

She'd really made a fool of herself, Eden thought bitterly. Stepping carefully over a tree root slithering across her path, she made her way around a thick clump of bushes and into camp. Colin and Richard sat in front of the fire talking in low tones, and she acknowledged them with a brief nod as she passed. It was difficult to keep from crying. But she couldn't let them see, couldn't let them know what a fool she'd made of herself.

It was her own fault. She was a coward. Why hadn't she drummed up the courage to say what she really felt? Why had she hesitated? Yes, she was still married to Colin. But the marriage was a sham. Had been a sham for a long time, and they both knew it. It had only been convenience that had kept her with him these past years, that and fear. Oh yes, she was truly a coward. Instead of telling Steve that she didn't want to go with Colin, she had babbled on about what-ifs. Her entire life had been composed of what-ifs. Apparently, Steve had no patience with hesitation. Not that she blamed him in a way, but he could have at least given her the opportunity to feel her way slowly.

His quick acceptance had been too revealing. All his talk about wanting her to stay had been just that—talk. He hadn't meant it. Not really. She'd offered him a way out and he'd taken it. Why was she so surprised? Hadn't he warned her?

Yes, but I didn't want to believe him . . .

To forestall possible questions from Colin or Richard, she retrieved a book from the hut and curled up with it as if she were reading, though her mind was focused on anything but the printed words.

It was some time before Steve returned to camp, and though she was well aware of his return, Eden did her best to ignore him. Head bent, she continued staring at the pages of the book she was pretending to read. She had no idea what it was about. Over and over, like a church bell tolling in a quiet village on Sunday morning, Steve's rejection of her sounded in her head.

What makes you think I want you to stay?

Night shadows had lengthened, and the lantern over her head began to flicker and fade. She barely noticed. The pages of the book were blurred anyway. She didn't look up until she heard Colin speak to Steve as he passed by. Colin's tone of voice was its usual sarcastic drawl, but it was his words that grabbed her attention.

"You know, Ryan, it has occurred to me," Colin was saying, "that your whereabouts would be of great interest to the Merída authorities."

Disaster. Eden let the book fall from her lap to the ground and stared at her husband. Whatever was Colin thinking, to try and provoke Steve? Why didn't Richard say something, try and stop Colin from saying anything else?

But though Steve had turned around and was looking at Colin with a lifted brow, he offered no comment. Apparently, Colin took this as permission to continue; he rose from his place by the fire and took several limping steps toward Steve.

"It might be very . . . inconvenient . . . for you if that happened, don't you think, Ryan? I mean, since you are wanted for the crimes of looting their temples, it would stand to reason that Mexican officials would be very pleased to have you in their hands."

After a moment of taut silence, Steve drawled with obvious amusement, "And who would turn me in, Miller? You? I don't think you have the guts."

Colin flushed, and took an angry step closer. "Don't bet on that. I might surprise you."

"Surprise me? You'd amaze me. Hell, you can't even find your way to water, much less Merída. How do you intend to inform the authorities?" Steve looked from Colin to Richard and back. "Or maybe you just remembered that you know the way out of here after all . . ." His eyes narrowed, glittering dangerously in the pale light. "I get the feeling that you know a lot more than you pretend to, and I don't like it."

"Now wait a minute," Colin said quickly, "I didn't say I really would turn you in. It wouldn't be profitable. But I do have a suggestion—guide us to the temple of the jaguar. No one has to know who you are, or anything else about you. Certainly, after your generosity of guiding us where we need to go, none of us would—"

"What the hell do you take me for?" Steve cut in with a contemptuous snarl. "A complete fool? Even if I knew where the damn temple was, once I did what you wanted you'd turn on me. I know your type, Miller. I've dealt with too many of 'em not to recognize a snake in the grass when I see one. Guide yourself. I'll be damned if I will." He pivoted on his heel, then halted and turned back to Colin. "And tell whoever you want where I am. By the time they get here, I'll be gone. Then I'll hunt you down and put a bullet in you for your trouble."

"Now see here, Mr. Ryan," Richard spoke up at last as he rose to his feet, "Colin didn't mean anything. He may speak out of turn and a little hastily, but it's only because we're both so adamant about finding this jaguar throne we've heard so much about. It tends to make us a bit desperate at times. Surely you can understand that."

"What I understand is I don't like listening to stupid threats. As far as I'm concerned, you could wander the jungle for the rest of your life. But for the lady's sake, I'll take you to a road leading to town. After that, you're on your own."

Tension vibrated between the men, and Eden realized she'd risen to her feet. She looked from Steve to Colin. Her heart sank when she saw Colin's pale eyes narrow into a look that was only too familiar. She wasn't surprised to hear him say softly to Steve, "All right. Don't bother with us. I think I can find my way back well enough without you. But before I go, I intend to search for the temple of the jaguar."

"Go ahead." Steve's shrug was full of contempt. "Though I doubt you'll find it. Or survive the search, for that matter."

"Maybe not, but I refuse to give up too easily." Colin smiled slightly. "We should find it, with Eden to guide us."

"Eden?" Steve took a step forward. The thick bristle of his lashes half-lowered over his eyes as he glanced from Colin to her, then back. "You can't be serious. What makes you think she could find it for you?"

"She stumbled across a stela with jaguar glyphs. It is situated near some lakes, and our research indicates that as the most likely spot for the ruined city we seek. Richard and I have discussed it, and we think this is the key to what we've been searching for. At any rate, we intend to give it a try."

Stunned, Eden stared at Colin. He was serious. His jaw was set in that stubborn square of determination that she'd confronted on more than one occasion. It would take a miracle to sway him from his course—or a complete disaster.

"Colin," she said faintly, "I don't know how to get back to where I saw the stelae. It was quite a ways from here, and I was lost . . . you really have no idea what you're asking of me."

"You can find it." Colin wasn't looking at her—he was watching Steve. "It may take a little trial and error, but I'm sure you can find it if you try hard enough, Eden. At any rate, I've no intention of leaving you behind. You're my wife. You'll go where I go."

Steve looked down at his feet for a moment. He shifted his rifle from one hand to the other, then looked up at Colin. "Do you have supplies, Miller? Shovels, axes, machetes, anything to explore with if you do find it? No? No food, no tents, no blankets or medicines—what the hell do you think you'll do in the jungle without those kind of necessities? You're not exactly the type of man who can live off the land. I doubt you could find water if it was six feet from you. You'd probably eat poinsettia berries, or sit on a log next to a fer-de-lance." He laughed harshly. "I've played poker before. You're bluffing. Go ahead. Look for the damn temple on your own. When I see the vultures circling overhead, I'll come bury what's left of you if I'm in the mood to be that charitable."

Giving Eden a swift, furious glance, Steve spun on his heel and ducked into his hut. In a moment, the netting over the door cascaded down to bar the entrance. It was a silent method of warning them to stay out, she supposed.

She turned to Colin. "Now you've made him mad. Have you gone crazy, or do you just enjoy picking fights with the only guide we have available?"

"I meant what I said." Colin's mouth twisted when she just stared at him. "You've been there. Try hard enough, and you can remember the way."

"Colin, don't be ridiculous. I was lost. I told you that. I have no idea which way to go, and besides, even if I did, he's right. We have no supplies, no tools. How would you go about digging if we did somehow manage to find our way there?"

"Richard has a machete and his portable spade with him."

"How foresighted." Incredulity gave way to rising anger.

"And if we are attacked, do we wave the machete or the spade at our assailants, pray tell?"

"Eden, if we are attacked," Colin said, in a soft, mocking voice, "it will hardly matter what kind of weapons we have. It didn't the last time, when we had all sorts of supplies and guns. I hardly think it would matter if it should happen again."

"You're mad," she said after a moment. "Stark, raving mad. Your injury has obviously unhinged you." She turned to Richard, who had been silently listening. "Talk to him. Tell him how insane this scheme is, Richard."

Richard looked down at the ground. For a long moment, he said nothing, then he looked up at Eden with a faint, wry smile. "I am afraid I have to say this may be our only chance to find the temple of the jaguar, my dear. And even though it is a slim chance at best, it is better than none. I do not want to go back without having exhausted every opportunity—"

Taking a step backward, Eden said in a choked voice, "You are both mad. I won't go with you. I refuse. Leave if you must, but I have no intention of being a party to this insanity—"

Moving faster than she'd thought possible with his injury, Colin surged forward and caught her by the wrist. His thumb dug painfully into the tendons until she gasped. "Oh, yes, my sweet little wife, you most certainly will go with us. In fact, you will be our guide. You have no choice. If you refuse, I will be most certain to notify the authorities about your friend's criminal activities—and his location. Once they know for certain he is here, it will be quite easy for them to find him, I assure you. So think about it. Think about your choice, Eden."

Releasing her with a contemptuous shove, Colin stared at her with hot, narrowed eyes while she rubbed at her wrist. He wouldn't do it. Steve was right. And even if he did it wouldn't matter. Steve would move before they could find him. No, Colin wouldn't dare. Would he?

"Think about it," Colin said again, softly, the threat hanging in the air like thick smoke.

Eden tried to tell herself that Steve was right. It was only a bluff. Once Colin realized he couldn't maneuver Steve into taking them to the stelae near the swamps, he'd give up. He'd have to. It was too crazy to even consider.

It didn't occur to her until she was rolled up in her blankets in front of the fire to sleep, that Steve had never tried to deny Colin's accusations about looting. He'd made no denial, no comment. He hadn't even seemed surprised to hear them. . . . *Gold and jade bring handsome profits in foreign markets* he'd said to her. God, there was so much she didn't know about him, so much he'd never said. Not once had he mentioned that he'd been a slave of the Cruzob, not once. Maybe it was all a lie. What she'd thought he felt, the way he looked at her, a fallen angel with wide eyes full of lies . . .

Narrowing his eyes, Steve stared at Colin. "It won't work, Miller. I ain't buying your trick. Go ahead."

Colin Miller stared back at him, a faint smile touching the corners of his mouth. "It's no trick. We're leaving this morning. If you would be obliging enough to give us a few supplies, I'll sign a promissory note to repay you as soon as feasible."

Steve leaned back against the trunk of a guava tree. "Keep your damn promissory note. Take what you need. Within reason." He didn't dare look at Eden. She stood to one side apart from the group, her hair clubbed back in a kind of loose braid and her expression unhappy. Served her right. She should have taken a stand, told Colin that she wouldn't go. But maybe she was as greedy as the others.

He wouldn't be a damn bit surprised. Not anymore. Not at much of anything.

Pushing away from the tree, he reached up and yanked down one of the fruits dangling from a branch. It was small, barely filling the palm of his hand, and not yet ripe. He suppressed the urge to throw it at Colin, but stood there tossing it up and down as if it was a child's ball.

"I have a stipulation, Miller—Eden chooses what to take."

Colin shrugged. "No problem. I imagine she has a pretty good idea of what we may need."

"Yeah, I'm sure she does." Steve glanced toward her. "Take one of the calabash gourds to carry water. There are beans and some fruit. And a jar of ground cornmeal. You can take some of that if you know how to use it. Don't forget antiseptic and insect ointment. And a few blankets as well."

Colin seemed faintly surprised, but covered it with a careless shrug. "Awful good of you, old man. I didn't expect your generosity."

No, I bet you didn't.

Aloud, Steve said, "I have plenty. And I know where to get more. But I can't spare any of my weapons. You'll just have to rely on Richard's machete in case of trouble."

After a brief hesitation, Colin nodded. "I can't say trouble is unexpected, but I don't think even a rifle would help us if it came like it did last time."

"No. If the Cruzob find you, the only thing that would help would be a bullet for each of you." Steve stared at him coldly, finding grim satisfaction in the rapid paling of Miller's face. "Do Eden a favor if that happens—kill her quick, before they can. If you don't, what can happen next may be too horrible to say."

With that dire pronouncement hanging in the air, Steve let the guava fruit fall to the ground with a solid splat. As he went past, he stepped on it, and heard the satisfying crack of it beneath his boot. That warning should give the smug Miller something to think about. Maybe he'd decide he wasn't so brave after all.

"Steve."

Eden's voice stopped him. He turned to face her, then wished he hadn't. There was appeal in her wide blue eyes, in the slight quiver of her lips and the one hand she held out as if a supplicant. "Don't," he said softly, the one word meant only for her ears.

Her hand dropped and she took a deep breath. "You— you've been very kind. I . . . we . . . appreciate all you've done for us."

His mouth twisted. "Do you? I find that debatable, but I won't be so rude as to contradict a lady."

She smiled faintly. "Thank you."

A perverse inner demon compelled him to try one more time. Two steps took him close to her. "Do you intend to go along with this?" He indicated Colin and Richard with a short jab of his hand. "This search for a mythical temple is liable to end badly. It's not safe. Have you listened to *any*thing I've said?"

"I've heard it all." She took a deep breath, hands twisting in front of her. She looked down at them. "But I have no choice."

"There are always choices," he said softly. "You just need the courage to make the right one."

Her eyes flashed up to him, shadowed beneath the lush curve of her lashes. "Sometimes it's not the choice I thought I wanted that's the right one . . ."

He stepped back, his voice flat. "You're right. Go ahead. I hope you find what you're looking for."

Her chin lifted slightly, and there was a defiant lilt to her voice when she said, "So do I. And perhaps this time I won't make another mistake."

He didn't have to ask what she meant. Her pointed gaze was evidence enough. He walked away, not looking back at her, not meeting her eyes again even when she walked out of his camp with Colin and Richard. Bitterness clogged his throat when he watched them leave, filing through the thick vegetation with all the defiant bravado of mutineers marooned on a desert isle. Idiots. He should have at least stopped Eden. Miller and Allen could be as stupid as they liked, but it was obvious to him that Eden's overactive conscience had forced her into joining their little suicide mission. Or so he wanted to believe. It was hard justifying the notion that she'd gone because she preferred being with Colin . . .

He sat by his fire for a while, staring into the flames. It was quiet. Deserted. The silence seemed to press down on him with a stifling oppression. Even the normal racket of the birds sounded muffled, as if drifting down through layers of clouds. Or guilt. Hell. He should be glad he had his camp to himself again. No more drying clothes hanging from tree limbs like tattered flags, slapping at him when he came upon them unawares. No more female clutter in the hut when he tried to find one of his books. No one to worry about but himself. Food for one. Drink for one. Space for one.

Unwillingly, he allowed his gaze to drift to the hut and the netting shrouded mattress. The past four nights had been oddly lonely without her. Knowing she was only a few yards away hadn't helped. Nothing had helped. The sharp-eyed, sharp-faced Colin Miller had occupied the hut like a eunuch, determined that neither Steve nor Eden would get past without his knowing it.

Not that either of them had tried.

Rising to his feet, Steve decided to go for a swim. Maybe that would help. He had taken only a few steps when he knew that it wouldn't help. Nothing would help. The cenote would only bring back the memory of his last time there with Eden.

He sure didn't want to think about that. Couldn't think about that. Not without forgetting he had any sense and going after her. And that would never do. Even if he went after her, she still belonged to another man. Damn. He'd given her an opportunity to choose, and she had.

He fetched his bottle of bourbon from the cache. Then he sat down on an up-ended crate and propped a foot against a tree trunk. The pungent scent of sour mash stung his eyes and nose as he poured a liberal amount into a tin cup and began to sip. Maybe he shouldn't have said what he had to Eden on the hill. But what was he supposed to do? She was married, for chrissake, and neither one of them could escape that fact. Before, when they'd thought Colin dead, there had been only each other to think about. And that had been enough. Time didn't matter that much.

But now, now that things had changed, he'd have to accept the inevitable. Tension coiled inside him like a spring. He took another sip of bourbon, letting it burn his throat with a sweet familiarity. Even at best, the jungle was unpredictable. Dangerous. Barring the two-legged predators, there were still the natural predators that awaited the unwary. He hadn't really expected Richard Allen to be quite so foolish as to undertake such a journey without proper provisions or a guide. He'd obviously underestimated the other man's determination. Or overestimated his intelligence. Whichever, it was Eden's safety that still concerned him. Damn. She'd made her choice. Why should he keep worrying about it?

Steve took another sip of bourbon. He'd let a lot of chores go undone the past few days. Now that he had time, he'd get around to them. It was time to plant a few rows of corn in the tiny plot of cleared ground where he usually played farmer, time to make his usual rounds to gather fruit and vegetables, dry some seeds for planting and eating. Yeah, he had a lot to do. It was time to get back to his old routine, the everyday things he'd done before Eden had come rolling down that damned hill.

Too bad he didn't feel like doing a damned one of them.

* * *

Pausing, Eden searched the anonymous blend of brilliant green leaves and dripping Spanish moss. She looked up, wincing slightly at the piercing brightness of the sun weaving through the branches overhead. It was past noon, if she was any judge of time. Which she usually wasn't. Not that it mattered.

"Well?" Colin demanded testily. "Are we going the right way?"

"How the devil should I know?" she snapped. "I told you I wasn't sure. I'm no guide. I know we're on the right path to the cenote, because I've been this way a few times and I think I can recognize some of these landmarks. It was . . . somewhere in here that I fell off the path. There's a sort of flat, elevated path like a road or something on the other side of a ravine—"

"A road?" Richard's eyes lit with interest. "Do you mean a *sacbe* by any chance?"

She shrugged. "I have no idea. It's sort of wide, and I seem to recall a lot of stones lining the banks."

"A *sacbe* is an ancient road built by the Mayans," Richard explained. "Often, from what I understand, these roads led from one ceremonial temple to another. Or to different cities. The writings of Brasseur give that as a possible explanation."

"Brasseur. He was one of the first to see these Mayan temples, wasn't he?"

"Oh no. Brasseur revolutionized the study of Mayan language and codes. John Lloyd Stephens and his artist Frederick Catherwood, who did beautiful depictions of actual glyphs, were among the first to see them. Stephens wrote about his early explorations. I had brought with me my copies of *Incidents of Travel in Central America, Chiapas, and Yucatán,* but, unfortunately, both volumes were destroyed when we were attacked. Ah, they are invaluable

to true Mayan scholars. After Stephens died in 1852, Brasseur discovered another codex, and is making great head-
way in the translation of the glyphs."

"So I understand." Eden's attention turned back to the
blur of vegetation as Richard rambled on to Colin. It didn't
really matter which way she chose. It would all be guesswork. And anyway, even if they did manage to stumble
across the temple, it was unlikely they'd be able to excavate
anything of note. Their tools were few and crude, nothing
like the sophisticated equipment they'd arrived in the Yucatán with. That was moldering in the jungle, no doubt, or
being used as decoration in Indian huts.

"Blast it, Eden," Colin snapped impatiently, *"think.
You're not trying. Can't you remember anything?"*

She flashed him a resentful glance. Oh yes. She remembered a lot. But nothing he'd want to hear. She pressed her
lips tightly together and swung an arm upward.

"There. That way. Down this hill and up the other. We
should find the roadway Richard claims the Mayans built."

"Not claims," Richard corrected as he bent to lift the
bundle of supplies. "They did build it. You'll see. I'll prove
all this, and one day my writings will be known the world
over."

It occurred to Eden as they cautiously made their way
down the vine-tangled side of a gully, that Steve had been
right in more ways than one. Richard was obsessed. Colin
was a whining brat. And she was too cowardly to do what
she really wanted to do. She deserved this fate. She should
have made a choice while she'd still had the option. But
she'd waited, and now it was too late. Too late for everything.

Her throat ached with suppressed anguish. Steve's narrow
stare when he'd demanded to know if she intended to go
with them still haunted her. She'd courted the brief, wild
hope that he wanted her to stay, but his flat assurance that
he hoped she'd find what she was looking for had been

evidence enough that he did not want her there. With Colin listening so closely, she'd tried to tell Steve that she'd made the wrong choice, but he did not seem to care. And so she'd gone, unable to look at him again, unable to fathom how everything had gone so wrong.

Sudden tears blinded her, so that she stumbled and Richard helped her up the rock-studded slope. He tactfully averted his gaze from her tears, and she was grateful for his diplomacy.

To her surprise, when they climbed to the other side, after hacking a path through vines so thick it was like a woven mat beneath their feet, there was a roadway of sorts. Stones covered with vines and bushes could still be seen, and the smooth, flat surface of the road could be discerned as well. It was overgrown, but visible.

"Yes," she said, panting from the climb, "I think this is it. It looks the same."

Her clothes were damp and sticky from the heat and humidity, and her hair clung in moist tangles to her cheeks and the back of her neck. It was uncomfortable, and she sat down on a fallen log to rebraid her hair. Absorbed, she was startled from her task by Colin's sudden shove. The heel of his hand hit her hard on the shoulder, tumbling her from the log.

Falling backward, she gasped with outrage as she scrambled to her feet. "What are you—"

"Don't move."

There was something in his voice that stopped her. Colin's white, tight-lipped face caught her attention, and she stood still. From one corner of her eye, she could see a blur of movement, then Richard stepped forward with a quick slice of the machete. It flashed up and down, and she saw a coiling body fly through the air. A snake.

Swallowing hard, Eden waited until Colin and Richard made certain it was dead, then let reaction set in. Trembling, she collapsed on the ground and breathed deeply. It took several moments before she could speak.

"I should know better than to sit down on a log without looking first," she said hoarsely. "Colin—thank you. You probably saved my life."

For a moment as he looked at her and smiled, she thought of the man she'd first fallen in love with, that idealistic youth who had captured her imagination as a young girl. There was still a trace of that in him, maybe hidden so deeply he didn't even know it was there. The years had slowly covered it, just as the jungle growth had hidden ancient temples.

"No problem, princess," Colin said softly, and grinned at her. "All in a day's work."

"Well," Richard said briskly, wiping clean the blade of his machete, "shall we continue? I'd like to be at the site before dark if we can find it. You did say it only took you a few hours to walk back to your camp from the site?"

Eden rose to her feet, brushing leaves from the seat of her trousers. "Yes. But Steve knew where we were going, remember. I have only a faulty memory and a prayer to get us there."

"Save your prayers," Colin muttered, eyeing the jungle around them. "We may need all of them for bigger things before long."

It was not the most comforting of sentiments, but Eden found that she heartily agreed with it.

Near dark they still hadn't found the stelae, and Eden was exhausted. She slumped to her knees, careless of the damp earth beneath her, shivering as the setting sun took with it a lot of the day's heat. Colin came to kneel beside her.

"Where is it?" he asked softly. He put a hand on her shoulder as if to comfort her, but his fingers dug into her skin with painful intensity. "You have to remember . . ."

"Colin," she protested, "that hurts."

"Don't start whining," he snarled. "We have to find it. Do you hear me? We must find that temple, and by God, you better not be deliberately misleading us."

Brushing away his hand, she surged to her feet, angry and tired and still filled with grief over Steve. It left her temper raw and unstable, and she lashed out at him.

"Damn you, Colin Miller, I swear even if I knew where it was this moment I wouldn't tell you. What do you think I've been doing all day? No, don't bother to answer. I don't care what you think. Or you either," she snapped when Richard stepped forward. "Both of you are selfish and inconsiderate, and this is insane. Do you hear me? Insane. I think you're mad, or so obsessed you don't care if it costs your life . . . just stay away from me."

Swirling away when Colin took a step toward her, she fled. It didn't matter how far she went, or even where, just so she had a few minutes alone, a few minutes to herself without both of them hovering like avenging angels of hell.

"Eden," Colin bellowed, but she ignored him. His limp would keep him from following too close, and she'd have a few moments of freedom before they caught up to her.

In the near dark, she didn't see the twisting root of a tree snaking across the path until it was too late. She tripped, and flung out both hands to catch herself. Painfully slamming one knee into the ground, one of her arms caught on the thick root, while the other smacked against a rough surface. She lay there a moment, breathless from the impact.

After several moments, she pushed herself to a sitting position, wincing at the stinging cuts on her scraped palm. Faint light still hovered above, though it was dark and shadowed on the ground. Eden tilted back her head and held up her hand to view the cuts, squinting to see in the fading light.

A dark obelisk rose just ahead of her, silhouetted against the setting sun. Tilting back her head, she saw what she'd not seen before—the looming hump of a mountain covered with vines and trees. And stones. Her heart lurched. She'd found it. Not just the stelae, but the dirt-crusted mountain of a temple buried beneath a thousand years of forest growth . . .

With trembling hands, she reached out to touch the stela that she'd uncovered that day with Steve. Her hands brushed away clinging vines, new and green and curling over the structure as if determined to reclaim it. Now, in the fading light, she saw it again. Dark and dangerous, she could just see the bared fangs and snarling face of the stone jaguar. She turned to call out, but didn't. Colin and Richard stood still a few yards away, apparently having seen it for themselves. "We found it," Richard said with a note of awe in his voice. "This has to be it—the temple of the jaguar."

Thirteen

It was vague at first, more an instinct than anything definite that warned him. Steve frowned and sat up in his blankets by the fire. Flames leaped and glowered, casting tall shadows across the trees and the entrance of his hut. The haunting hoot of an owl drifted down through the canopy of tree limbs and leaves, followed by the low, trilling call of a nighthawk. For some reason, the familiar bird calls set his teeth on edge.

His rifle lay close by, and he reached for it. Pulling it to him, he cradled the Winchester .44 in one arm. He drew one leg up under him, damning himself for falling asleep without the usual precautions.

Another bird call sounded in the night, then faded away into sudden silence. It was the silence that could be the most unnerving, the sudden absence of sound in a forest that always teemed with noise and soft mutterings.

Someone was out there. An alien presence lurked in the trees beyond his camp. He could feel them watching him. The feeling was different than when he felt the presence of an animal nearby. This intruder was human—and cautious.

Steve felt the tiger deep inside him come alive, waking and stretching, unsheathing its claws. It was familiar, exhilarating. He knew someone was watching him, was waiting for him to make a mistake, or leave himself open for attack.

Deliberately, Steve yawned and stretched, then slid down

in the blankets again as if going back to sleep. This time
the rifle was across his belly beneath the blankets, loaded
and ready. If his instincts were right, whoever was trying
to sneak up on him was about to get a big surprise.

Time slipped slowly by. Moonlight shimmered in wavering patches of light and shadow. Light had grown dim and
misty before he heard the unmistakable snap of a twig beneath a stealthy foot. His hand eased the blanket down
slightly so it wouldn't catch on the rifle barrel when he
brought it up. Whoever was creeping up on him wasn't very
used to stalking prey, that was for certain. Or didn't care
if he was heard. The sharp pop of a dead limb underfoot
was almost as loud as a pistol shot. Steve watched carefully
from beneath his lashes.

Two shadows appeared at the far edge of his camp, moving slowly toward him. Then they stopped suddenly, as if
caught on something. Steve waited, eyes narrowed intently.

Another shadow appeared, swift as quicksilver, an ebony
flash against darker shades of trees and night. *Damn.* Steve
recognized the low, snarling cough, followed by high-
pitched screams from the intruders. Balam.

Lurching to his feet, Steve moved toward the frenzied
activity, faintly astonished to hear what sounded like the cries
of a child. "Balam . . . back," he ordered, straining to see in
the dark. It took a moment to differentiate one shadow from
another, and he saw that the jaguar was straddling a wrig-
gling form. Light bounced off the metallic barrel of a pistol,
and he moved forward to put a restraining foot on the arm
that held it.

"Get him off me, señor," came the hoarse, breathless cry
in faulty Spanish." Get him off, *por favor . . ."*

"He's not exactly a trained pet," Steve drawled, "but I'll
do what I can." It took a moment of gentle coaxing before
the jaguar was persuaded to relinquish his prey, and by then
Steve saw that a young boy accompanied the fallen man.
Pointing his rifle at the moaning man in silent warning,

Steve bent and removed the pistol from his hand. Then he glanced at the boy. He looked to be no more than ten or twelve, with the flat Indian features of a native. Frozen in obvious terror, the boy was staring at the jaguar with wide eyes. When Balam released the man on the ground and moved to Steve's side, the boy seemed to recover from his stupor. He looked up at Steve.

"El Jaguar—it is you, sí?"

Steve stuck the pistol into the waist of his pants, then put a hand on Balam's head. He continued to hold his rifle on the man on the ground. "Sí. What do you want here? And why come in the night like enemies, if you know me?"

"We were . . . afraid." The boy glanced around, shivering. "You are alone?"

"What do you want? Oh no, amigo," he said, prodding the man on the ground with the rifle barrel when he started to rise, "you'll answer some questions before I let you up. What are you doing sneaking up on me?"

It was the boy who answered, his voice slightly steadier now. "We were afraid. You are rumored to be protected by the gods, and we did not wish to offend them."

"So you decided to sneak up on me in the night? That may not offend the gods, but it sure as hell offends me."

Finally the man on the ground spoke, his voice sounding disgusted. "He's a bloody American. Are you certain this is the right man, Paco?"

Steve's eyes narrowed, his gaze whipping back to the boy. "Paco? I've heard that name before."

Eden's voice came back to him them, shivering as she related the horror she'd been through; he remembered how she'd said the native boy with her had disappeared, presumably killed by a crocodile. Was this the same Paco?

"El Jaguar," Paco was saying, "I need you to help me find someone lost in the jungle. A blonde woman. It is said that you will know where to find her." His eyes moved to

the jaguar, and he shifted uneasily from one foot to the other.

Losing interest in the conversation since he'd been deprived of his prey, Balam turned and padded into the night, moving noiselessly over dead leaves. Both the boy and the jaguar's intended victim relaxed slightly

"And if I do?" Steve asked after a moment. "Why do you want to find her?"

"Because," Paco replied, gesturing to the man still on the ground, "she must be returned to her husband."

Steve's mouth curled into a sardonic smile. "Is that right. I think we all need to sit down in front of my fire and have a little chat, gentlemen." He stepped back and made a motion with the rifle. "After you."

"You're not Colin Miller." Stretching out one leg, Steve eyed the man in front of him. Of medium height and light hair, with a pale coloring that no amount of exposure to the sun would darken, there was an air of condescension about the man that grated on his nerves. A bandage was now wrapped around his upper arm where Balam's claws had dug deeply, but other than that, the man was unharmed. And oddly unruffled by the incident.

Shrugging, he said in an impeccable English accent, "I don't know quite what to say, old chap. You're right. I am John Carter. Forgive the lie, but I hoped that you would be more agreeable if you thought she was my wife."

"Why would that make any difference?"

"A grieving husband and all that rot. It was a shot in the dark and it didn't work. No harm done." John Carter returned his stare without flinching. "I'm a bit desperate to find her."

"There seems to be a lot of that going around," Steve muttered. He still didn't quite believe Carter. It sounded too pat, too convenient. "So what makes you think I might know where this Eden Miller is?"

"I deduce you already know the answer to that." Carter's brow lifted slightly. "Paco saw her alive after the . . . unfortunate event. Some of the natives who aren't determined to kill all white men say they heard the moon goddess had come down to take *El Jaguar* as her lover."

Steve considered that. It sounded like one of the tales that might be repeated. Ixchel, the moon goddess—wife of the sun and patroness of fertility, weaving and medicine— also took varied partners on earth, according to Mayan myth. How perfect.

Shrugging, he said, "And from that you decided that Eden Miller was here with me?"

Carter sat back and regarded him for a long moment. "It stands to reason. This moon goddess the natives claim to have seen with *El Jaguar* is said to have the pale hair and skin of the moon, and eyes the color of the sky. You are the one known as *El Jaguar*." He sat forward again, eyes narrowed and intense. "So where is the moon goddess?"

"Obviously, she isn't here."

"I can see that."

"Look," Steve said after a moment, losing patience with the polite verbal fencing, "I don't have any intention of telling you anything. You're lying through your teeth, and I don't trust you."

Carter looked somewhat nonplussed, but managed a smile that was more of a grimace. "Well, you do believe in being blunt, I see. Very well. I shall endeavor to be just as blunt—Eden Miller is the only survivor of an American expedition funded by a major museum. I wish to know more about these discoveries our young native friend has mentioned, and the fact that Eden is alive and aware of their findings is invaluable."

"Your concern for her welfare is commendable," Steve said dryly, and was rewarded with an angry flush from Carter. "I suppose next you'll want me to believe that you came out here all alone to find and rescue Mrs. Miller for purely humanitarian reasons. I don't buy either explanation, Carter." He stood up, still holding the rifle barrel loosely in one hand.

Carter stood up, too, facing Steve. "I see that you are a man who must be told the entire truth. Very well. There are several rival factions searching for the temple of the jaguar. Some are more—shall we say determined?—than others. This determination to be the sole discoverer of such a rare and valuable find leads to a certain ruthlessness on the part of some contingents." He paused, then said slowly, "It is my belief, that if we do not safeguard Mrs. Miller, she will be captured and ultimately murdered for her knowledge. It is imperative that we take immediate precautions, or there are those in this area who will not be quite so *humanitarian* as I am."

There was a ring of truth to his words, and Steve studied the other man for a long moment. Paco sat silently, his head lowered, hands dangling between his knees.

"Paco," Steve said softly, asking in rapid Spanish, "Are there more men like him in the jungle? Do they all search for her as well?"

"Sí," Paco said, flicking a glance toward Carter before he added, "She is not safe. I liked her. She was kind to me, and spoke gently—I would not wish to see her harmed, señor."

Steve frowned. A trilling chatter of birds heralded the approach of dawn. The fire had burned down to sullen embers and gray ash. He didn't like this. He didn't like it at all. The jungle that had seemed vast and empty save for natives and wildlife, now teemed with ruthless explorers all searching for the same thing. And Eden was the one who held the key. He looked up at Carter. Apparently, he was unaware that Colin Miller and Richard Allen had also survived. And that they were just as determined to find this hidden temple. Interesting.

"If I help you find her," he said at last, "what guarantee do I have that you aren't likely to kill her? I'm not sure I like the idea of being a party to murder."

A faint smile curved Carter's mouth. Reaching inside his coat pocket, he drew out a small card and held it out. Steve took it. *Metropolitan Museum and Archaeological Association* was inscribed on the square of vellum. *Sir John Worthington Carter, London.* He looked up at Carter and gave it back.

"Impressive. What's that supposed to mean to me?"

"The Millers were sent here by my establishment. I am responsible for their welfare. And for the discoveries they have made, of course.

"Ah, that clears up one of my questions, anyway—your basic reason for being here. I seem to recall that the Metropolitan museum is in America. And you said the Millers are American, not English."

"So true. Look here, old chap, enough equivocating. It is my funding that supports the Metropolitan, and it is at my behest the Millers came to the Yucatán."

"Yeah? Not a very smart choice. Why not Chiapas instead? Or even British Honduras? There are plenty of ruins in both places. Hell, everywhere you see a small mound in this damn country there's a temple under it. You had to know how dangerous it is down here, with the Cruzob raging around slaughtering any white man they see."

Carter studied him silently for a moment, obviously carefully weighing what he'd say. Then he shrugged with a faint smile. "In those places, there are other explorers. Other men sifting through artifacts. My goal is much grander—I seek what few men dare to search for—the mythical jaguar throne. It is a quest, you understand. And I was fortunate enough to find men who share my vision."

"Share your stupidity, you mean." Steve shook his head.

"You should never have sent Eden Miller here. And you shouldn't have bothered finding me. I like it right where I am."

"Mr. Ryan, I chose to come to you unaccompanied, save for this young boy who is the only remaining witness to Eden Miller's survival. I feel the weight of responsibility quite fully, and since I was not here at the beginning to ensure my expedition's safety, I also feel responsible for their fates. Do be a good man, and tell me what you know before it's too late."

Despite his misgivings, Steve recognized the urgency in Carter's tone. It seemed that Eden was in more danger from these civilized men than she was from the perils of the jungle.

Slowly, he said, "She's not here, but she's not alone."

Carter's brow lifted. "Not alone? Where is the woman if she's not here. I was told—"

"She wasn't the only one to survive the massacre, Carter." Steve almost smiled at the expression of incredulity that passed over the Englishman's face, and his obvious agitation.

"Not the only—but who—I mean, good God, man. I wasn't told that there were others who survived."

"Richard Allen and Colin Miller." This time, the amazement on Carter's face was almost ludicrous.

"But how . . . marvelous. Of course, I'm delighted to hear it. Aren't you, Paco? Three of them survived—They were here then?"

"For a while. They've gone."

"But where? I find it difficult to believe that I have missed them, or that no one told me of their survival."

"Maybe your sources aren't as good as you think." Steve shrugged. "If you leave at first light, you ought to be able to find them."

"Yes. Of course. Which way did they go? Back to Merida?"

"No. They're headed east." He smiled faintly, adding, "To the temple of the jaguar."

Carter's pale eyes bulged. "The temple—I must find them. It is imperative that I do so. You will take me there tomorrow, and I will pay you quite handsomely."

"I don't need your money. I'll tell you the same thing I told them—if you want to find the temple, do it yourself."

"Then I infer that they aren't certain of its location?"

"Apparently not." Steve eyed him closely. He could almost see the wheels turning in Carter's head. It would be funny if it weren't so damn irritating. He didn't like the fact that a lot of men were searching for this jaguar throne. There was a tendency to be vicious even among the best men, and it didn't bode well for Eden that she was caught in the middle. No, not well at all.

"Now look here," Carter was saying, "they could be in grave danger. We must find them before it's too late."

"What the hell are you talking about?"

"I told you—other factions. There are other expeditions out here searching for the same temple, all intent upon finding the jaguar throne. If we do not find them first, they may be killed . . ."

Dusk cast pale shadows, making it too dark to see in the looming shadow of the temple. Eden walked the short distance to the fire and sank wearily to the ground. When she raked a hand through her hair, sharp pains shot through her palm. She turned her hands over to stare ruefully at her palms. Blisters were forming. Every muscle in her body ached—some she hadn't even known she had. Too bad Steve had donated two shovels. She could have done without all the digging and scraping, though the excitement of possible discoveries was hard to ignore.

"Another glyph," Richard called out, and she looked toward the mound. Holes pocked its surface now, and some of the choking vines had been cleared away. Part of the way up, probably two feet above her head, Colin had uncovered the stone head of a jaguar. It looked to be part of a doorway, perhaps the upper corner. In the years since the temple had been erected, a lot of dirt had accumulated, raising the level of the temple to an even greater height. When one climbed to the top, there was an impressive view of the surrounding jungle. It was the tallest structure in the area, and though it had taken the better part of a day, they had all scaled the heights and stood atop the summit. From there, it had been easy to see other mounds as well as the lakes below. There were dozens of other mounds, all smaller, but all apparently temples and buildings. Richard was in his element. He'd pointed out the roads that could still be seen from this height, all leading to buildings or from the ruined city, pointing to the evidence that once this had been an important hub of Mayan civilization.

It was difficult to detect that now, Eden thought, looking at the vine- and tree-covered mounds. If not for the evidence of stone steps leading upward, she would have thought the temple a hundred foot hill. She imagined that once it was entirely cleared of surrounding vegetation, the temple would be massive in size. But now it was difficult to tell just where the building gave way to jungle growth.

Carefully scraping away rubble and vines, Richard and Colin had managed to uncover some exciting artifacts. A huge stela with intricately carved glyphs had been found lying on the ground, broken in several places but with the ancient inscriptions still legible. Ecstatic, Richard had managed to carefully scrape away years of mold and dirt to reveal a huge carving of what appeared to be a nobleman standing atop two conquered slaves. An invaluable find, he'd declared. And inside the mound, tunnels had been unearthed to reveal promising objects. Masks of jade, pottery shards, and several items of gold and silver jewelry had been added to a growing pile of discoveries. Yes, this site had proven to be a veritable trove of exciting findings, evidence of a past civilization.

"What is there to eat?" Colin asked, flopping down beside her. Sweat streaked his face and matted his blond hair into dark tangles. He swiped one hand over his cheek, leaving behind a smear of dirt.

"Fruit," she replied coolly. "And water."

"Is that all?"

"I don't recall your being especially worried about food when you insisted we set out without proper provisions, Colin." Eden dug into one of the burlap sacks of supplies and brought out a bruised banana that was almost mush. "We've been here several weeks, and our provisions are almost gone. If you eat too much tonight, there will be no breakfast."

Colin scowled. "Don't be so uppity. We found the temple, didn't we? That ought to be enough to show you that we were right in persisting."

"It hasn't gone anywhere in a thousand years. I doubt it would have moved if we'd done the sensible thing and gone for supplies first."

"No," Richard said, joining them and accepting without comment Eden's silent offer of a banana, "but others might have made the discovery before us. Now, it shall be recorded that our expedition was the first." He grinned, and there was a jubilant light in his eyes that Eden found impossible to ignore.

Shaking her head, she smiled. "I suppose I can't argue with success, but what if we hadn't found it? What are the odds of us stumbling across this temple, after all. Look how long we were out here before we found the other, smaller ruin, and it turned out not to be what we were seeking, after all."

"But we were in the right vicinity." Richard swallowed the last of his banana and carefully folded the peel. "Our original camp is only a mile or two away from here, by my estimate."

Eden tried to ignore the sudden stab of fear that news gave her. "Only a mile or two—? But if we're that close, shouldn't we worry about another attack?"

"Attack is possible anywhere in this cursed state, according to Steve Ryan," Colin muttered. "Look at it this way—there are only a few of us now, and we're much less noticeable than our entire noisy expedition was. And less of a threat, I would think. After all, what can just three people do?"

"My point exactly." Eden drew in a deep breath, unable to keep from surveying their surroundings more closely. With fading light, the trees were dark against the pale reds and pinks of the sunset, and the grating calls of the toucans in the area suddenly sounded sinister instead of familiar. She shivered. "What could we do against another assault?"

"Eden." Richard put a hand on her arm and smiled. "Don't think of the worst. Think of the best. And besides, Colin and I discussed it, and tomorrow he intends to make the trek back to our former camp and retrieve some of our supplies. All that are still there and usable, anyway. We must have them in order to proceed with the excavation."

"Madness." Eden shook her head, unable to keep her hands from trembling. "I have a bad feeling about this, Richard. I keep thinking, and remembering—"

"Don't. It will change nothing. Focus on what will be ours when we return with the greatest finds yet discovered by man—the secrets of the Mayans unlocked for all to see."

"Give me another piece of fruit," Colin said, ignoring her recent admonition. "I'm hungry now. Besides, I'll get more tomorrow when I go back to our old camp."

"It's been two months. I doubt there's anything worthwhile left there, Colin."

When Eden gave him an orange, he let his hand close around hers, holding tight when she would have pulled away. She looked up at him, startled and uneasy at the expression on his face.

"Sweet little wife—ever prudent with food as well as everything else."

She jerked her hand free. "I don't know what you're talking about."

"I'm sure you don't." Colin dug into the orange with his thumb and began to strip away the peel with quick, jerky motions. "Never mind. It doesn't matter. What does matter is the fact that we'll all be rich beyond our wildest dreams. Once we dig deep enough and start itemizing all our finds, I'll bet we have a fabulous treasure trove on our hands."

Richard frowned. "Not this again. We seem to have had this argument before, Colin. None of these recovered artifacts are to be viewed as treasure. These are antiquities. They are to be carefully preserved for study and knowledge, not wealth."

Snorting, Colin said, "Yeah, right. I didn't come all this way and risk my life—and almost get killed—just to hand over everything to a bunch of dried-up old archaeologists. You forget, Allen, that my money is involved in this project as well as others."

"No, I haven't forgotten that." Richard flicked Eden a quick glance that let her know he was well aware exactly whose money had funded their part in the expedition, but he was wise enough not to confront Colin about it. Instead, he assumed a conciliatory air. "And you're absolutely correct to remind me of that fact, of course. But I was under the impression that you were as committed to the study of the Mayans as the rest of us."

"Oh, I am. As long as it's profitable." Colin popped the last segment of orange into his mouth and said, "I have my own investors to satisfy, you know."

Stiffening, Richard asked carefully, "What do you mean, your *own investors?*"

"Just what I said. There are some important men waiting

to see what we discover down here, investors with enough money to buy all of the Yucatán if they wanted."

Eden's throat tightened. The implications were obvious, and she remembered the cause of the argument she'd had with Colin the night of the massacre. It had been over this very thing, his dragging unknown private investors into what was supposed to be a project funded by a reputable museum. She'd found through the years that Colin had a bad habit of dealing with unscrupulous men, men who stopped at nothing to collect valuable art objects for their private collections.

Obviously, Richard had the same concerns. Surging to his feet, he stared at Colin with palpable fury. "You driveling idiot," he said softly. "Do you have any idea what you have done? Just who are these important investors?"

Colin scowled. "Their identity doesn't matter. I know who they are. They have nothing to do with your portion of the find, Richard, so don't go getting all sanctimonious on me. I share in this too, remember."

"Dear God, you are so short-sighted, so voracious and blind, that you cannot even see the danger you may have created with your greediness."

"You're overreacting, Richard." Colin's dry tone conveyed his contempt. "As usual. Just stick to what you do best—digging in the dirt. I'll handle the business end."

"And what of the Metropolitan? What of their vested interests, may I ask?"

Colin shrugged. "I didn't sign anything with them."

"You accepted their money, for heaven's sake, and promised to abide by the standards of our agreement—"

"In writing?" Colin's smile was bland. "No, I signed nothing with the Metropolitan. As my sweet little wife will be more than happy to corroborate."

Eden drew in a deep breath and met Richard's incredulous stare. "It's true. That was why—well, one of the reasons—why we argued the night of the massacre. You remember. You tried to pour oil on the troubled waters before we all went to bed that night."

Richard sat down abruptly. "Yes," he said stonily. "I do recall that night well." He drew in a deep breath. "I see. This certainly does complicate matters."

"Oh, I don't think so," Colin disagreed. "We just have our own agendas, that's all, Richard." He gave a light shrug. "I need the money. My former investments have not—awkwardly enough—been profitable. I fear that I've overspent, and my wife's inheritance is gone." He smiled at Eden's angry gasp. "Not to worry, my dear. Our portion of what we find will more than replenish your inheritance. Once we've managed to recover enough Mayan art, we'll divide it all up fairly. Simple enough, don't you think?"

"No," Richard said softly, "it's not quite that simple." He stared at Colin for a long moment, then glanced at Eden. "No, not that simple at all. Well. What's done is done. Nothing can be changed right now, I suppose. We'll just have to deal with it when the time comes."

Eden had the inescapable feeling that Richard was even more disturbed than he was willing to reveal, though his distress was certainly evident. He raked a hand over the sparse hairs of his head as if to smooth them, and managed a weak smile of reassurance for her. She looked down at her hands, and realized that she'd gripped them together so tightly two of the blisters had burst. Damn. What was it Steve had told her about being careful of infections in the damp heat of the rain forest?

She rose to her feet and moved to the packs filled with their meager supplies. Somewhere in the jumble, she seemed to recall a small bottle of antiseptic. She'd included it at the last moment, Steve's dire warnings echoing in her head. She'd tried to recall the little things he'd told her, like the warnings about mosquitoes at dawn and dusk, and keeping an eye out for vampire bats, and scorpions that liked to crawl into warm places, and the snakes that hid under fallen logs and flat rocks. But it was difficult to remember everything, as all the little dangers and details were so alien to her. Why had she ever thought she could manage to adapt to the jungle? It had seemed easy with Steve only because he made it look easy. She should have known better.

Blinking away the sudden tears that stung her eyes, she found the antiseptic and used a clean strip of cloth to dab it onto the burst blisters on her palms. Too bad she hadn't thought to bring along some of Steve's bourbon as well. She could use it right now, if only to bolster her courage.

She felt so alone, abandoned and lost—this was worse than the day she'd lost Steve on the path, because then she'd known that he would come for her. Steve would never have allowed anything to happen to her. If he was here, she wouldn't be so frightened, or hungry, or even thirsty.

Steve was adept at finding food, snatching edibles seemingly from the air—as he had done the coconuts. If she closed her eyes, she could see him as he'd looked that night, amber eyes narrowed and light-tricked, glittering at her from beneath the thick brush of his lashes as he'd laughed and said, "Native wine. I do hope it's properly chilled . . ."

She'd tried to find green coconuts, but the only ones she'd seen at all had been high up in towering trees, still firmly attached and not likely to fall at her feet. There was water, but only a little, and she hadn't wanted to travel alone to the lake to fetch more. The memory of Paco and the crocodiles she'd seen still made her shudder.

She swallowed the sudden lump in her throat. She shouldn't even think of Steve. What had been between them had been brief and doomed from the beginning. After a while, she would have realized that he was entirely unsuitable for her. He'd made it plain he intended to stay in the Yucatán, and she could not visualize spending the rest of her life in the jungle. And not even the softer memories of their nights—laughing at some silly tale he invented to amuse her, listening to him read from one of his interminable volumes of history, or the hazy hours beneath the mosquito netting in his arms—could dismiss the reality of him. There were too many unanswered questions about his life. At least with Colin, she knew the worst. And better the devil she knew than the devil she didn't . . .

Glancing over her shoulder, Eden gazed at the huge, brooding structure still shrouded by trees and vines. An air of mystery and haunting secrecy surrounded it, woven into the very earth that covered it, as if deliberately buried by time and ancient Mayan priests. She wondered what those Mayans would think of modern men who wanted to plunder their temples and tombs, wondered if they would be displeased by the intruders.

She shivered at the thoughts, and rose to her feet. She was letting her imagination run away. After all, this was what she had journeyed so far to do: uncover the secrets of the ages, to present them to all who would appreciate them.

And that she intended to do, despite Colin's schemes. At the first opportunity, she would discuss with Richard how to circumvent Colin's greed. There had to be a way. His avarice would end up their undoing if he wasn't stopped. Her money was gone, and she could do nothing about that. But she could stop him from looting priceless treasures.

It was faintly surprising to discover how little she cared that her money was gone, only the manner in which it had been spent. Damn him. And damn Steve Ryan for his greed as well. If she had her way, neither one of them would profit from these temples. In fact it would be the perfect vindication, for her and Richard to return to the Metropolitan with the jaguar throne that so many men sought for personal profit . . .

Fourteen

Winding through giant, buttressed tree roots, Steve paused in the dark shadows of a mangrove to watch and wait. A motmot bird perched on an overhead limb called in soft, velvety tones. The low-pitched *oot* sounded plaintive and wistful. Other than the whisper of leaves rustling in the wind, he heard nothing else.

He was vaguely surprised. There was no sign of Richard Allen, Colin Miller, or Eden. He knew they'd come this way, because he'd seen evidence of their passage. What caught his curiosity was their absence from the ruins. He'd expected to see Richard feverishly attacking the hill of dirt with spade and blade, and Eden patiently carting away loads of soil while Colin supervised. But here he was, almost in the shadow of the damn thing, and there was no sign of them. He shifted uneasily.

Maybe he'd miscalculated. He'd been sure they had found it. After all, he'd followed their tracks long enough to be certain they were going in the right direction that first day—despite his vows not to care what happened to them. They'd been within sight of it when he'd turned back. How the hell had they missed it? Anything was possible.

It wasn't long before Carter and Paco caught up with him, and he shrugged at the Englishman's inquiring glance. "Not here. Maybe they gave up already."

"Not bloody likely," Carter said with a disbelieving snort. "I know Richard Allen. The man is obsessed. He survived a massacre that killed almost everyone else, didn't he? He'll dig with his hands if he has to. He's that kind of dedicated man."

"Foolish sounds more accurate." Steve rubbed a hand over his jaw. He needed a shave. Dropping his hand, he slanted a glance at Paco. The boy didn't quite meet it, but let his eyes slip away. There was something about the youth that didn't quite measure up, but he couldn't decide what it was. Paco was reticent and shy by nature, but Steve had the nagging impression that he was hiding something.

"All right," he said aloud, "you two wait here, and I'll go take a look around."

"Oh no." Carter stepped forward. "I'll be right with you."

"I don't need a damn nursemaid, Carter," Steve growled, and saw a flash of surprise in the other man's eyes.

Then Carter smiled. "I've noticed that. You're still angry because I followed you, I perceive. Well, I must admit that you are quite an excellent guide, swift and accurate and all that rot, and I am certainly not going back to wait at your camp."

"Fine. Then you can make yourself useful." He turned and pointed. "See if there is any evidence of their digging. I'm going to look around the other side of this damn thing."

"Right-ho, old chap." Carter eyed the huge mound of dirt. "Bloody hell, it must be over a hundred feet high. I believe this time they've found it, all right. Don't you?"

"How the hell would I know." Steve shrugged. "I'm not up on all my archaeological history."

"Yes, well, neither am I. But you can safely wager that Allen is up to date on all of it. The man is a pure genius when it comes to locating important finds . . . although, his first dig was not quite on the mark. Actually it was only a few miles from here, I believe, if my calculations are correct."

"How do you know that?"

Carter's brow lifted again, and he said with obvious amusement, "I made it my business to know all I could when I arrived here. And of course, I had ways of getting information from time to time. How do you think I knew which area they'd been working in? It wasn't a random guess, old chap."

Steve looked from Carter's bland expression to Paco's averted face. "How does he fit into all of this?"

"Paco? He's just a native needing money for his family." Carter turned to Paco and said something Steve couldn't quite hear, and the boy nodded. Then he flashed a glance at Steve before turning to run into the brush.

"I believe you've scared him off, El Jaguar," Carter said dryly. "You shouldn't be so fierce to these poor natives."

Steve ignored that. "Just how much do you know, Carter?"

Shrugging, the Englishman met his gaze with a steady stare. "I know all I need to, I suppose. Except the location of the jaguar throne, of course."

"Of course. That's where Allen comes in handy."

"Right-ho. I'm convinced he is closer to finding the throne than any man has been since the days of the ancient Mayans." His eyes narrowed slightly. "Or p'raps I should amend that to closer than any man will admit to being."

For a moment, Steve didn't say anything. Then he gave a careless shrug. "If it wasn't for the missing lady, I wouldn't care if the damn throne was ever found."

"You haven't ever been tempted to, say, remove a few items of value from temples you've come across in your stay down here? I find it difficult to believe you could resist."

"I don't give a damn what you believe. You know, Carter, you have too many quick answers to suit me. I find it hard to believe that you came to the Yucatán by yourself to join Allen and the others."

"Oh, I never said I arrived here by myself. I'm not that

intrepid. No, I brought a full contingent with me, but I felt it best to accompany Paco on my own."

Steve's irritation grew. "It occurs to me to wonder why you even bothered looking for Eden if you already know where their first camp was located."

"Why, I told you the reason. I could not allow her to wander the jungle alone once I discovered that she'd survived the massacre. It wouldn't be humane."

"Or safe for you." Steve smiled when Carter blinked. "I'm beginning to understand how you archaeologist fellows think. It's not just discovering rare finds that's important, it's the timing of it. If Eden had managed to find this jaguar throne and told someone else about it, then your efforts are void, right? No, don't bother to answer. I know I'm right. I listened to Richard Allen spout the same kind of idiocy. Well, I'll tell you this—when I find Eden Miller, I intend to get her out of here. The rest of you can fight it out over the damn throne and temple, or whatever else you may find."

Shrugging, Carter said, "Don't grow so agitated, my good man. Once you find their little group, all will be well. I have sent young Paco back to his village for the rest of my expedition, and we can commence our dig."

"It ain't quite that easy, Carter." Steve shouldered his rifle and glanced at the mountain of stone and dirt jutting up from the forest floor. "I'm going to take a look and see if I can find 'em. Now do us both a favor and disappear while I'm gone."

Carter laughed softly. "Not a chance, old chap. Not a chance."

Something was definitely wrong here, Steve decided. Carter was too glib. If he knew where their first camp was, why was he bothering to look for Eden? Not for humanitarian reasons. And not just because she might know important details of the dig. Now that Carter knew Allen and Miller had survived the attack as well, he didn't need Eden.

Circling around the mound, he came up to it from another direction. From this angle, he could see evidence of some intense digging. A few holes pocked the mound here and there, and vines had been scraped away to reveal the stone head of a jaguar. Its fangs were bared in an eternal snarl, sightless eyes staring down the centuries.

Steve crouched down beneath the shelter of a dwarf palm's broad leaves, eyes narrowed. He didn't like this. Didn't like it at all. Something was wrong. Missing. Out of place. Where the hell were they?

He slid one hand down the carved stock of his Winchester, adjusting it between his knees. His other hand was curled around the cool barrel of the weapon, fingers moving restlessly up and down. Too many possibilities came to mind. There was no indication they'd left quickly, so he didn't know what to make of the partial excavation's desertion.

Uneasy, Steve finally rose from under the palm. He needed to find out what had happened. Maybe there was no sign of danger, but there was no point in taking chances where Eden was concerned. Allen and Miller could take all the chances they wanted, but he'd be damned if he'd let 'em risk her.

It didn't take long to find their tracks in the soft dirt of the rain forest floor. Three sets of prints were readily visible. He stood up and looked in the direction they'd gone, and understanding dawned. The dumb bastards. If Carter was right, their original site was ahead just a mile or two. Surely, they wouldn't have been stupid enough to go back there.

But yes, of course they would. Allen would want any tools that had been left behind. Damn—if they didn't get lost, they'd be blind lucky to make it back without running into serious trouble.

John Carter did not seem very surprised by Steve's suspicion when he went to look for the other man. He looked up from a dirt-crusted object he'd found and nodded slowly.

"Yes, that would be the logical thing, I imagine, to go back for their equipment."

"Logical—" Steve shook his head. "It always amazes me how little respect amateurs have for the jungle."

"This is a rain forest, Mr. Ryan." Carter looked amused. "Oh I know about all the dangers, of course, hostiles and predatory animals and all that, but don't you think you're exaggerating the perils?"

"Am I?" Steve swung around to face him, eyes narrowing. "I think maybe you're underestimating them, Carter. We have guns, remember. They have a machete and a couple of shovels. And even if they had rifles, I don't think it would do them any good when it came down to it."

"It is my understanding that Mr. Miller is well acquainted with the use of firearms." Carter regarded him thoughtfully. "He fought in your recent civil strife, I believe."

Steve's mouth tightened. "Get this straight—" He took two steps forward, until he was staring down at Carter. "When it comes to survival out here, it doesn't matter where you come from or what you once did. What matters is what you can do now. Try to remember that."

"I shall endeavor most ardently to remember that at all times. And you?"

"I've never forgotten it for a moment."

"Excellent." Carter's smile was bland. "Then we shall get along famously, I expect."

"I expect not." Steve eyed him narrowly. "You don't seem very concerned about them now for a man who showed so much concern about Eden Miller a day or two ago."

"Now that I know there are three survivors, I admit I feel a bit better about the entire episode. Granted, the deaths of so many are depressing, but the three principals of the expedition have survived."

"Yeah, I imagine that will look better on paper." The

bastard. He was as cold-blooded as Richard Allen. All any of them could think of was the damn temple.

"Ah, I can see that you disapprove, sir. I am quite sorry for that. But one must keep one's perspective in matters of this sort."

The uneasy feeling that had pervaded since John Carter had arrived in his camp grew stronger. If Steve hadn't been worried about Eden, he would never have left. Carter's involvement and tales of rival expeditions was alarming enough. But add to that the unpredictable element of the Cruzob, and it was a deadly mixture.

"I'm going after them," Steve said abruptly. "You stay here in case they return by a different route. Besides, you can prowl around your precious ruins to your heart's content."

"Jolly good suggestion, old chap. May I have my pistol back? Just in case."

Sliding it from his belt, Steve handed it to him. "Don't waste bullets. You may need 'em."

Carter gave him a quick, frowning glance. "I certainly hope not."

Not bothering to reply, Steve set out after Eden and the others. This had begun to be more a wild goose chase than a rescue mission, and he was already weary of it. If it was up to him, he would drag Eden back to his camp—forcibly if necessary—and let the others rummage around in the ruins until they got damn sick and tired of it. Or found what they wanted and left the Yucatán.

But it wasn't up to him. It wasn't really even up to Eden.

Something wet hit the back of his hand as he trudged along the obvious trail they'd left behind, and he slanted a glance skyward. Rain. It wouldn't be long until the rainy season would arrive. That would force a halt to any major excavations, unless Richard Allen knew a way to work in mud six feet deep.

Steve wasn't surprised when he heard a soft, gentle hiss

overhead. It was rain, invisible but audible, hitting the tree leaves high above. The noise steadily grew louder, working up to a dull roar as he followed the trail. He didn't bother to hurry. It was damn near impossible to outrun rain, and it was only a matter of time before it penetrated the thick canopy of leaves. Steve kept going, trudging through thick undergrowth and the murmur of birds overhead.

Toucans leaped from branch to branch, wings folded and voices grating alarms at the intruder below. Noisy little beasts, but an excellent harbinger of trouble. The hiss of rain was much louder now, some of it piercing the natural umbrella of leaves to patter softly against the ground. Broad leaves shuddered at the impact, and crystalline drops slid along the sharp edges of high grass and the sleek coils of vines.

As more rain fell, the musty growth underfoot grew slick. He almost slipped going up a steep incline, and caught hold of a slender vine coiling down. That brought a shower of accumulated rain down on his head, as the upper portion of the vine dumped the moisture from leaf-cups. He glanced up at the sky, and muttered a curse. He'd better find some shelter fairly quickly to wait this out, unless he relished spending the rest of the day in drenched clothes.

The muffled roar grew louder and the shadows in the forest much deeper when he saw a deep gully cut into the hill just ahead. It was manmade, slashing up the towering pyramid in a straight, raw line. Looters had been here. At the end of the gully, he could see the pale block of stone that signified some sort of chamber. It would have to do.

Rain spattered down faster, and he made the final leap down into the gully to duck under the stone chamber just as the clouds opened. Crouching down, he wiped a hand over his face and stared out from the comparatively dry chamber. The dark forest had abruptly changed to a world of silver-white mist, shimmering and loud. The storm obliterated any other noise, and that was the strangest of all—no birds could be heard, or monkeys chattering overhead. It was a silence filled with only the roaring sound of the rainfall. It permeated everything—the smell of fresh rain soaking into the earth and plants, the feel of moisture that penetrated even into his little shelter, and the sight of nothing but that bright curtain.

Then it was over as quickly as it had begun. And there was only the sound of water dripping from leaves to spatter on the ground, and the rustle of plant life slowly lifting back up as the pressure of rainfall was released. Birds began to call again, and he saw a brilliant blue butterfly shaking its large wings beneath the broad leaf of a fern. Monkeys screeched in the high branches of the trees, and the rain forest brushed aside the rejuvenating shower and came back to life.

Steve glanced around him at the stone walls of the chamber. He could see faint traces of painted figures in different poses, and made out the form of a huge bird with spread wings. Tiny specks of red, blue, and green paint still flecked the walls. It always humbled him, these vivid reminders of a long ago age and art, the forgotten moments in time. Shifting his feet to stand up, he felt something beneath his boot and bent to retrieve it.

A large piece of crusted pottery jutted up from the ground, and he brushed away some of the dirt with his hand. Traces of carved figures could barely be seen beneath the accumulated dirt, but one of them he recognized as a male dancer in jaguar-skin headdress and trousers, impersonating *Ah Cup Cacap,* the god of the underworld. Part of a drinking vessel, maybe. Just a small shard, worth little to anyone but the creator. And to archaeologists, of course, that fanatical group dedicated to delving into secrets. He put it in his pocket. Eden would probably be delighted with it.

This wasn't the first Mayan memento he'd found, and he doubted if it would be the last. If Richard had his way, he'd be neck deep in artifacts and treasures of the past before long.

Steve stepped out of the chamber and drew a deep breath. The rain had only made it more humid, and he saw shimmering heat waves wafting up from the ground in places where the sun could reach. It was like a sweat bath, and if he had any sense he'd forget this idiocy and wait for them to come back to the temple of the jaguar. Nothing would happen to her. He was just being overprotective . . . God. It had happened. He was thinking of Eden as if she were important to him.

Huddled beneath a large portion of scorched canvas tent that had survived the fire, Eden peered out at the rain. She could barely see farther than a foot or two; everything was blurred by the pounding downpour. Richard and Colin had taken shelter beneath a stone overhang. There wasn't much left of their supplies: A few shovels with charred handles, some tins of food, scattered books and notations that were largely ruined by the humidity, and one pistol that had apparently been overlooked.

The most grisly discovery had been the bodies left behind. Some of them had been desecrated by wild animals, bones scattered haphazardly over the area. Richard and Colin had buried what they could, scratching graves in the shallow soil with the shovels and covering the sites with flat stones to prevent them from being dug up by other scavengers.

Shuddering, Eden tried not to think about it. Just returning to the site had been harrowing enough. She expected at any moment to hear the frenzied screams of assailants descending upon them, though she supposed there was some truth to Colin's insistence that the natives would not expect them to return.

"They think we are all dead, so I hardly expect another attack, Eden. Use your head."

She'd glared at him, pointing out that there were those in the rain forest who knew of their survival, and it was always possible that they'd look for them. Richard had agreed with this last, though he thought it unlikely.

"We're not a great threat anymore. But it is true that as long as some people know of our survival, we're not entirely safe."

It was hardly a comforting thought. Eden wiped at a trickle of rain that found its way under the stretch of canvas. Her hair clung in damp wisps to her face and neck, and she shifted uncomfortably. The rain was completely unexpected. Though she knew the rainy season was not far off, she'd not thought it would arrive so early. It made it even more imperative that they quickly get back to the digging. The time away from the mound to retrieve the few supplies they'd found was hardly worth it, in her opinion, but Richard did not agree. The tinned food alone was a fortunate discovery.

The resounding roar of rain ended as quickly as it had begun, and the world beyond her patch of tent cleared. Eden blinked in surprise. The dripping of rain from leaves and branches was the only evidence of the storm. That, and the musty scent of wet earth and wood.

Slowly, she emerged from the canvas cocoon and stood up to stretch her cramped muscles. A few yards away, Richard and Colin left the shelter of the stone buttresses. This find had been disappointing in that it was not what they sought, but on a level of elemental discovery, it was evidence of ancient habitation. A small temple, perhaps, or even just a residence.

"I believe," Richard said, turning to study the dwelling, "that it must have been some kind of small temple. Most of the natives probably lived as they do today, in palapa huts. But, in light of the approaching rainy season, we must abandon this discovery in order to excavate all we can of the temple of the jaguar."

"You're certain we found it?" Eden asked.

Richard nodded. "It is my belief that we have. All those carved jaguars, and did you see the relief that I uncovered right before we left? I'm anxious to uncover it further, for I believe that we must be at the right place. If we're able to dig deep enough and long enough, I am convinced that we shall find the throne we seek."

"I hope so." Eden didn't look at Colin. She still hadn't forgiven him for his abominable behavior. He'd been rude and brutal, and no matter what excuse he tried to give, it was unforgivable.

Colin sat down on a log after giving it a kick to rouse any hidden creatures. "We need to start back now that we have all we can scavenge from here. I don't want to leave the temple unguarded for too long."

"Unguarded?" Richard turned to him. "Unguarded from whom?"

Colin scowled. "Anyone who chances by, Richard. For God's sake, you don't think we're the only ones searching for this damn throne, do you? I told you—"

"I know. Your investors." Richard's scorn was evident. "If they expect you to share your interests with them, why would they bother coming here at all? Don't they trust you?"

Waving a hand impatiently, Colin said, "Not just them, Richard. You know as well as I do that after that piece came out in the English journal about that French fellow's investigations and his belief that this throne was still here, nearly everyone who read it will be prowling around. I don't want to lose our advantage, that's all."

Eden turned to look at him. There was something Colin was not saying. She could tell. She knew him well enough to sense when he was hiding something, though she rarely discovered what it was until he was ready to tell her. How like him. He'd probably endangered all of them with some wild, improbable scheme.

"What have you done, Colin?" she asked with a sigh. "I know you've planned something. I can tell. I can always tell."

Colin's eyes narrowed. "Do you think if I *had* done something I'd tell you about it? Hardly likely, under the circumstances, my sweet."

"And what circumstances are those, Colin?"

"I think you know." He sneered at her, lip curling up with obvious contempt. "I'd have to be blind not to have known what was going on back in that camp. You and Ryan were a bit too cozy. Don't bother denying it. Even Richard knew what was going on, though he's much too polite to admit it."

Richard gave him a harsh look. "You've always been an ass, Miller, but particularly so now. If I'd had my way, you'd never have been included on this expedition. And I swear, I have no idea why Sir John allowed you to come along."

Amused, Colin drawled, "Because of my wife's money, of course. Why do you think? And I do have a reputation for being thorough when it comes to excavations, though I don't have your impressive credentials."

"You don't have any credentials," Richard said hotly.

"Enough." Eden took a deep breath. "None of this matters right now. Can't we co-exist in peace? At least until we find the throne? If the rainy season catches us before we've completed our search, we'll have to wait six months to try again."

"I have no intention of allowing a little rain to stop me," Richard said with obvious astonishment.

Eden stared at him. "But Steve said it's nearly impossible to travel during the rainy season. Any road would be impassable at best, quagmires at worst."

"Perhaps for him, but I won't need to travel about if I'm excavating, my dear." Richard smiled. "There's food enough to sustain us for a while, and we can add to our meager supplies with fresh fruit. You've been invaluable in that respect, though I am also fairly knowledgeable about some of the native fruits and vegetables. Now come. We must gather up what we can and return. Let's take all the pieces of canvas tent we can find. They may come in handy."

Faced with such obdurate determination, Eden had little choice but to accede. Besides, she was hopeful that the throne would be found quickly. Then she would go. She would find a way to leave whether Richard and Colin wanted to or not. She couldn't stand the thought of remaining there, being so close to Steve when it was impossible to be with him. And it didn't matter what he'd done. She'd grown increasingly aware that she couldn't remain married to Colin.

Before, when there had been no one else, she'd been able to overlook Colin's character. That was no longer possible now. Maybe it wasn't fair, but when she compared Colin to Steve, she knew she would never again be able to accept her husband for what he was. Whether she liked it or not, her life had changed forever.

"So," Colin said softly, coming to take her by the arm, "you think I've planned something devious. You have such great faith in me. I'm honored."

Eden tried to jerk away, but Colin's fingers dug into her arm above the elbow, holding her fast. She glared up at him. "Let me go, Colin. It doesn't matter what I think."

"Ah, you're absolutely correct. It doesn't matter what you think." His grip tightened. "But it does matter what you do. And if you think I'll sit idly by while you dream about another man, you're sadly mistaken."

"I don't know what you're talking about."

"Oh, I think you do. Remember, you're married to me, Eden. Perhaps it was a bit inconvenient of me not to die, but there you have it. I'm alive, and I'm still your husband whether you like it or not."

She tried to pull away again, but he held her painfully close. His face was set and angry, and for the first time, she was afraid of him. "Colin—let go of my arm," she said, as calmly as she could. "You're hurting me."

"Good. At least I have some kind of reaction from you. If anger or pain is all I can get, I'll take it."

"Try to recall some of the other reactions you've gotten from me," she said coldly. "Do you think I've forgotten all the times you didn't come home at night? All the whispers and laughter I endured because of you? I haven't. I remember it all. After a while, it didn't matter anymore. I didn't care who you were with or why. Or who you spent my money on . . ."

"Really. Too bad I don't feel the same way. You're my wife. Maybe you enjoyed playing around with this *El Jaguar* for a while, but it's over now." He caught her by the other arm and pulled her up against him. "I'm through sharing."

"You're mad—" She shoved hard against him with the heels of her hands, and his grip loosened. Taking immediate advantage, Eden brought the heel of her foot down on Colin's instep. She was rewarded with a howl of pain and her release, and she took several steps backward. "Don't come near me again," she warned when he looked up at her.

Colin took two steps toward her, his face creased with lines of fury. "You bitch. I'll do what I damn well please—" He lunged for her and she screamed as he caught her around the waist with both arms, slamming her to the ground.

Twisting, Eden clawed at him in a desperate attempt to push him off. Colin rose to his knees, straddling her. When he doubled up a fist, she threw her arms up to protect her face. The blow caught her on the side of the head, and light exploded in front of her eyes. Dimly, as if from a great distance, she could hear Richard shouting something. Then there was a loud sound, like a shot, followed by more shouts.

Dazed, she slowly became aware that Colin was no longer astride her, and that she could move. She started to rise, desperate to escape, but something was holding her down, not harshly, but firmly, and she struggled against it.

"Eden," came a familiar voice, "it's all right. Be still a minute—Christ. You're bleeding."

As her vision cleared, she looked up. A face swam over her, vague at first, then became clear. Steve. He was frowning. She wanted to say something, but her lips wouldn't form words. It sounded as if all the birds in Mexico were in the trees, their chattering growing louder and louder, drowning out whatever it was Steve was saying. She could see his mouth moving, knew he was talking to her, but couldn't decipher a single syllable. Then she closed her eyes and darkness settled over her.

Fifteen

"You bastard."

Colin stumbled backward, holding his bleeding mouth. "If you shoot me, you'll hang. Richard will be witness against you—"

"If I was going to shoot you, you'd already be dead, Miller." Steve fought the urge to do just that. He took a deep breath, not daring to look at the tempting gleam of his rifle. Colin's battered face would have to suffice for now. He glanced at Richard, who was tending Eden. "How is she?"

"She'll be fine. Probably just fainted from stress as well as exhaustion." Richard looked toward Colin with a frown. "You shouldn't have hit her, Colin."

Wiping at his bloody mouth with the back of one hand, Colin slid a wary glance at Steve and shrugged. "She's my wife."

"That doesn't mean you can hit her any time you feel like it," Richard pointed out.

"But it's all right for Ryan to hit me, I suppose."

Steve cocked a brow. "You're big enough to fight back. Come on. Man to man—I'll be glad to oblige you."

"Yeah, you'd like that. I'm still crippled from being attacked by natives. It would hardly be a fair fight."

"And you think hitting a woman is fair?"

"I think my wife is none of your business," Colin retorted. "And you know what I mean by that."

"Touch her again like that, and I'll kill you whether it's my business or not," Steve said softly.

"With your reputation, I'm sure you don't make idle threats," Colin sneered. "I stand chastised and warned."

Steve lifted a brow in amusement. "You're wrong. I make all kinds of threats, from idle to extravagant. Some of them I actually keep. It's up to you to guess which ones are which."

Steve held Colin's gaze until he looked down at the ground. The pistol shot had gone wild, buzzing past Steve's head much too close for comfort. If Richard hadn't pulled him off, he might very well have killed Colin Miller with his bare hands. He'd seen him knock Eden down and hit her. When he'd heard Steve's shout, Miller had been dumb enough to pull a pistol—Steve didn't know where the hell Miller had gotten it, but he took it away before giving him a well-deserved beating. Not that it helped Eden, but he certainly felt better.

Eden moaned, and Steve glanced down at her. Richard had placed a wet cloth on her forehead and one on her throat, and it seemed to be bringing her around. When he looked up again, Colin had backed farther away. His split lip had begun to swell, and his left eye to discolor. A cut on his eyebrow still bled.

"She's my wife, Ryan," he repeated belligerently.

"Like I said, that doesn't mean you can hit her. I'd advise you not to try it again. When I'm around, anyway."

Colin nodded tightly. Then he spun on his heel and stalked to the shade of the partially unearthed temple, where he crouched down to wait.

"You cannot interfere between a man and his wife, Mr. Ryan," Richard said softly. He glanced up. "Though I must say, I am not sorry that you gave Colin a taste of his own treatment."

"Neither am I. How's she doing?"

"She's coming around slowly. But she'll be fine, I'm certain." He gave a slight cough. "If I may suggest, it might be best if you keep your distance from her."

Steve's mouth tightened, but Richard was right. He nodded. "All right. Do you know a man named John Carter?"

Richard looked startled. "Sir John? Why yes, of course. Why do you ask?"

"He's here."

"Here? Do you mean in the Yucatán?"

"Yeah. He's waiting on us to return to the temple—"

Richard surged to his feet. "He promised he'd wait. Damn him . . ."

"Wait a minute. Aren't you partners with him?"

Waving a hand impatiently, Richard said, "Yes, yes, in a manner of speaking. But I shan't allow him to share in the discovery. It's mine, do you understand? *Mine.*"

"I thought Carter funded your expedition."

"He did. Partially. But the credit for what is found is given to the man who discovers it. I will not share with Sir John. He's not even a proper archaeologist. He's only—well, never mind. I shall take that up with him shortly. He's waiting for us, you say?"

Shaking his head, Steve muttered, "Yeah. He thinks more highly of you than you do of him, it seems. He's convinced you've found the right place." Steve glanced at Colin and back to Richard. "Look, is Eden going to be all right? If I leave her with you after I've taken you back, I don't want to worry that you've let anything happen to her."

"Heaven forbid. She'll be fine. You just bring out the worst in Colin, I'm afraid."

"I wasn't even here when he decided to hit her," Steve pointed out. "If he does it again, I meant what I said. I'll kill him."

"As I have said, you cannot interfere between a husband and wife. Let them work it out, Mr. Ryan."

Steve still wasn't satisfied. It would be Eden's choice whether she stayed or went, once she woke up. But when

Eden regained consciousness and sat up, holding her head, she wouldn't let him near her. She looked up at him, then away, and he wondered bitterly if she still hated him. She'd certainly acted like it before leaving his camp, and in a way, he couldn't blame her. But she'd made her own choice, and if she expected him to be happy about it, she could forget it.

Eden insisted that she was able to walk, and they set out for the temple. To make it easier on all of them, Steve walked ahead, cutting a path with his machete where the underground was too thick. Sandwiched between Richard and Colin, who was bringing up the rear, Eden had very little to say. Steve could hear snatches of her conversation with Richard, who was trying a bit too hard to keep up a running dialogue.

"I say, Eden, John Carter is waiting for us up ahead."

"Is he."

Richard cleared his throat. "Yes. According to Mr. Ryan, he showed up yesterday and insisted upon finding us at once. Worried about our safety, I suspect."

"Probably so."

Steve hacked at a clustering palm with the edge of the machete. She didn't seem surprised to hear that Carter had come to the Yucatán. Maybe she'd been expecting him. He was beginning to think they all had hidden agendas. Richard certainly didn't bother to hide his obsession with the temple of the jaguar, and Miller had made it obvious he was in it for the money and not the archaeological importance. But underneath both of the men's outward intentions, he suspected even more ulterior motives. And Eden? She was a complete mystery, and he found himself wondering just what was in all this for her. Not the satisfaction of discovery. Just before Colin's sudden appearance, she'd told him that she didn't care about the temple of the jaguar. He couldn't imagine another motive for her determined stay.

Dammit, he couldn't imagine why she didn't want to stay,

either. She should. She should have stayed in his camp with him, told Colin Miller to go to the devil and flaunted convention for once in her life. It wouldn't have killed her.

But her going had killed something inside both of them, whether she wanted to acknowledge it or not. It had slain the growing trust in one another that had slowly been nurtured by time and the elements. He'd thought—fool that he was—that perhaps she cared for him a little bit. And it had made him retreat at first, before he'd realized that maybe he cared a bit for her as well. But that had come too late. The awareness that she meant more to him than a warm body in the night had struck him that last afternoon in the cenote, when he'd held her to him and listened to her soft cries.

Maybe he should have followed his first instincts and told her how he felt, but experience had taught him to go slowly. Things didn't happen that fast, not things that really mattered. If it was serious and lasting, time would tell.

And time had, though it wasn't the way he wanted it.

Steve slanted a glance upward, noting the position of the sun in the sky. They'd reach Carter before dark. He'd stay the night, then go back to his camp first thing in the morning. There was no reason for him to stay longer. He could wash his hands of all of them.

"Mr. Ryan," Richard Allen said, and Steve realized that it was the second time he'd spoken. He halted and turned to face him. Indicating Eden with a wave of his hand, Richard said, "She needs to rest, I fear. Could we have a brief respite from our trek?"

"Not if we want to get back by dark." Steve flicked a glance at Eden, noting her pale face and trembling hands. With a faintly defiant stare, she tucked her hands into her armpits as if to hide their shaking. His mouth curled in a slight smile at her grim determination. He stepped forward and shoved his rifle into Richard Allen's startled grasp. "Take this. I'll carry her."

"Now see here," Colin began, bristling with anger.

"You want to carry her?" Steve challenged. "We need to get back before dark. I don't mind traveling at night by myself, but one of you three is bound to fall or get lost, and I don't have the time or the patience to deal with it. I don't give a damn who carries her, but one of us is going to do it. So hurry up and decide, because we're burning daylight standing here talking about it."

After a moment of thick silence, Colin gave a brief jerk of his head. "You carry her. You must know I'm unable to do so."

Steve didn't bother to agree. He turned to Eden, who was staring up at him with consternation. "I can walk," she began, but he ignored her.

"It will be easier on me if you climb on my back. That way I can still use my hands. Hurry up."

He turned his back to her, and after a short hesitation, she moved forward and put her hands on his shoulders. He bent slightly and caught her beneath the knees, lifting her to his back. As she straddled him, he brought his arms to the front while her legs dangled on each side, resting on his forearms.

"Ready?" he asked, and felt her warm breath against the side of his neck.

"Yes. I'm quite comfortable. And you?"

"Like carrying a baby. Just hold on and we'll be there before you know it."

With her arms circling his neck and her legs astride him, Steve was reminded of similar positions under different circumstances. He wondered if she thought of that, or if she had forgotten everything that had happened between them. The fragile strength of her grip and the touch of her breasts against his back was a kind of pleasant torture, even with Colin Miller glaring at them. Oddly, he felt a kind of pity laced with his contempt for Colin. Not pity that he was injured, or that he knew Steve had made love to his wife—

this pity was for his failure as a man. And as a decent human being.

Maybe he could accept Eden's rejection of him, her choice of Colin instead of a man she didn't really know.

And really, what had he expected? That life would be fair?

He knew better. The war had taught him a lot, but what had come after had taught him the most. It was hard to think of that now, hard to remember all the events that had led up to this place, this moment in time. Especially when a harsh reminder of all the things he'd held and lost now clung to his back.

"Am I hurting you?" Eden murmured against his ear, and he realized he must have made some kind of sound. He drew in a deep breath to smother the words he wanted to say.

"No," he said tersely.

"Steve, if I'm too heavy—"

"Forget it." He shifted her slightly, and felt the scrape of her breasts against his back through their thin shirts. Another reminder. Christ. It should be obvious to anyone that he enjoyed misery and self-torture. Wasn't this proof of it?

She'd clasped her hands in front of him, and they nudged against his throat with every step he took. Every step made him even more achingly aware of the pressure of her against him, the sweet torment of her body pressed into his, and the soft touch of her unbound hair against his cheek when she turned her head. His jaw clenched, tightening so painfully against the urge to hold her even closer that it was a grateful distraction.

Maybe if he hadn't been concentrating so fiercely on his own misery he would have noticed earlier, but he didn't. It was one long, anonymous blend of brush-crowded jungle and the tantalizing heat of Eden's body next to his that numbed him to the awareness of his surroundings. It was his own fault, really, that he didn't see the danger until it was upon them.

The first indication he had was the sudden absence of sound, the short, abortive squawk of a parrot followed by nothing. Just the rasping sound of his breath and the beat of his heart in his ears as he wallowed in misery and memories. It took several precious moments to sink in, but finally his head jerked up and he came to an abrupt stop.

Eden's arms tightened around his neck. "What is it?"

"Be still."

"I say, Mr. Ryan," Richard protested, "why are we stopping now?"

Steve didn't answer. He couldn't have told them what was the matter, yet all his instincts warned him of danger. He released Eden, allowing her to slide to the ground so he could reach for his rifle.

As she slid from his back, he could feel tension in the air. It was all around him, vague whispers in the thick underbrush, the scent of danger rife. It could just be the wind, but he knew it wasn't. The familiar weight of his machete was at one side, hung from his belt beside a knife. Colin's empty pistol was useless.

"Steve," Eden whispered, "what is it?"

"Stand behind me." As she obeyed, face pale with sudden fear, he felt the concerted gathering of forces around them. "Hand me my rifle, Richard."

Not looking at the other man, he held out his hand, but Richard was slow and clumsy. He dropped the weapon, hands shaking with fear as he bent to retrieve it, and Steve swore softly.

"Damn it, give me the rifle . . ."

"Steve!"

His head jerked around at Eden's soft cry. A shimmy of leaves was the first warning. Then it came, high-pitched shouts and whoops, the fierce rustling of trees and bushes and the sudden appearance of armed men surrounding them. Eden screamed.

For an instant, Steve stared at the wicked blades and determined faces. Then he exploded into action.

It all happened so fast, it was a blur. Eden was aware of numbing fear, flashing light from uplifted blades, and of Steve, moving so quickly that he reminded her of Balam. Lithe and silent and deadly, his machete was a blink of light that disappeared and reappeared with blinding rapidity.

Vaguely, as if in a dream, she knew that Richard was fumbling with the rifle, and that Colin was on his knees in the dirt and leaves of the path, sprawled as if struck down by lightning. She couldn't move, could only stand in frozen horror.

She couldn't see Steve's face, but saw the muscles in his back strain beneath the thin material of his shirt. Damp patches spread on his back as he turned, and a tunnel of light skittered up the sharp edge of the machete blade as he brought it down in a wide arc. For an instant, she saw a strange face beyond Steve. It was contorted with blood bubbling from the mouth, dark eyes wide and faintly astonished. Then the man crumpled forward, to be replaced by another. Steve's machete flashed again, wicked and lethal, and the next man vanished beneath the flurry of steel.

One and then another, they seemed to be everywhere, pouring from the trees and sky to descend upon them. The noise was loud, slamming against her ears in indistinguishable tumult. A wavering sound like a triumphant scream rose high in the air to penetrate the haze of chaos. It seemed to shock some of the natives into momentary paralysis, jerking them to a halt. The sound continued, eerie and frightening and vaguely familiar. Then she caught a glimpse of Steve's face as he turned.

It was the devil's face she saw—a slash of black brows,

white teeth gleaming behind snarling lips, cat-gold eyes glittering with a savage light of destruction. With a shock, she realized it was Steve making that inhuman sound, the undulating howl that seemed to well up from deep inside him. It hit her then, where she had heard that wild cry—jubilant Confederate soldiers pursuing the enemy or just galloping down the middle of the street had yelled like that, the renowned Rebel yell that had been known to send the enemy running. It was a blood-curdling sound, and apparently it had the same effect on these natives as it had on the Yankees. There was a haze of other faces around Steve, expressions briefly frozen in horror before melting into a blur of violent reaction.

Steve shouted something at her, but it made no sense. Nothing did. This was all madness and movement, a whir of confusion that tumbled around her with frightening rapidity. Her breath came quickly, and she had to concentrate to keep from fainting. It was so bloody—blood was everywhere, staining the loose cotton garments of the enemies, glistening on the ground and bright green leaves of plants around them. Shouts and screams, all of them unintelligible to her, assaulted her ears, adding to the confusion. It was her nightmare again, wavering between reality and the dream-world.

Time shifted, and when she could focus again, it had grown quiet. Men lay on the ground, some groaning; others still. Several men formed a wary half-circle around Steve, just out of his reach. He stood with a machete in one hand and his knife in the other, chest rising and falling with exertion.

Steve said something to them, a low, growling comment that produced quick replies just as fierce-sounding. Eden fought a wave of dizziness. She swallowed hard. Heat pressed down with growing intensity, and her head throbbed painfully. Steve looked like an avenging angel, and it was obvious whatever he'd said to the men was insulting. They scowled fiercely, and one of them gestured with his blade and said something that made Steve laugh.

It was not a pleasant sound, that laughter. Steve didn't look at all concerned, only slightly breathless as he stood there with his weapons raised and waiting. A thin trickle of blood slid down his left arm and stained his shirt sleeve. A faint, feral smile curled his lips. Beneath the shadowed curve of his lashes, the waiting glitter of a cornered tiger lurked in his eyes. His chest rose and fell; there was an air of calm certainty about him that seemed to frighten the men surrounding him.

There was another brief spurt of conversation among the natives. They seemed more cautious now, and as she surveyed the bodies strewn on the narrow path Eden could understand it. Another volley of dialogue in that strange language flowed back and forth between Steve and the natives, until finally one of them made a short, sharp motion with his hand. Steve shook his head.

Eden stared at the man who stepped forward. His smooth brown face was broad and flat, curiously unlined by age. But it was his eyes that held her, velvety soft and dark beneath thick, straight lashes, looking at her as if able to see into her soul. Eden shivered, and the man's full lips curved into the slightest of smiles. He turned and said something to Steve, who shook his head violently.

Her throat tightened. The conversation was about her. What could they want? Her heart beat faster. She was dimly aware of Richard behind her, the muffled noise he made when two of the natives stepped forward again with a menacing gesture. Colin still knelt in the path on his knees, and she could hear the ragged, frightened rhythm of his sobbing breaths.

It was Richard who drummed up enough courage to ask, "What do they want with us?"

Steve kept his gaze on the apparent leader, shrugging. "We are considered trespassers."

"I gathered that much—will they allow us to pass in peace?"

A heartbeat passed before Steve said softly, "No."

Eden's head whirled. Her knees were trembling, and she did not know how much longer she could remain standing. It took an immense effort to keep from collapsing to the ground, but she sensed that it would only create more problems if she gave in to the weakness.

"Oh God," Colin said in a wheezing half-sob, "can't you reason with them?"

Without turning around, Steve said, "These men are Holcanes, warriors sent to bring back slaves for sacrifice. You won't be killed right now. Stand up like a man if you want to be treated as one. They have no respect for men who grovel like dogs on the ground."

Stumbling to his feet, Colin managed to stand up without swaying too badly. He was whimpering with fear. Eden couldn't look at him. It was difficult enough to retain her own composure; she couldn't watch Colin's collapse.

She glanced around them, and counted at least sixteen armed men on the path and in the bushes. There were seven dead on the ground. The spokesman said something else to Steve, who gave a shrug of his shoulders and short reply.

"What do they intend to do with us?" she asked at last, and Steve flicked her a grim glance.

"We have been invited to accompany them to their village. It doesn't look like we have much of a choice."

Eden took a deep breath. The nightmare grew worse with each passing moment. She remembered Steve's remark that first night, and how he'd said the Cruzob took white prisoners as slaves. But these men had been sent to bring back slaves for sacrifice—was that to be their fate?

Several of the natives came closer, two of them jerking Colin roughly to his feet when he collapsed again and gripping him by the hair to hold him up. A harsh laugh made her wince, but when she looked at Steve he seemed not to even notice what they were doing to Colin. His eyes were narrowed and a hot, glittering gold, and focused on the spokesman with grim ferocity.

The native gestured to Eden, scowling when Steve said something sharp in that strange language. Despite his scowl, there was a gleam of admiration in the man's eyes when he gave a short, reluctant nod. Some of the tension in Steve eased, and he reached back with his hand for Eden without taking his eyes from the man or lowering his weapons.

"Stay calm and close to me," he said shortly, and Eden could not stop the sudden jerk of her hand away from his. He turned to look at her with narrowed eyes, and she could not meet them.

"You . . . all the blood on you," was all she could say, faintly, almost an apology for her instinctive rejection of his touch. She heard him draw in a sharp breath. But she couldn't help it. There was blood on his arms, his hands, drenching his clothes. Little of it was his; she had dim memories of the crimson splashes, the torrent of scarlet blood that spouted wherever his machete touched.

"Stay beside me," he said again, but did not try to touch her. She nodded, and fell into step beside him. The others followed, all of them surrounded by the quiet, brown natives with spears and machetes.

Eden struggled to remain calm, hoping that once they assured these natives they meant them no harm, they'd be released. But it was hard to reconcile that hope with the reality that swamped them as they were forced to march along a narrow path through the jungle surrounded by warriors armed with sharp blades and grim determination. No one had taken away Steve's knife or machete, but the rifle was now in the possession of the native leader.

It was hardly comforting to realize that they treated Steve with respect, not when they reached the native village just after dark and were immediately encircled by more armed men, all jabbering in that strange, guttural language. Eden tried not to show her fear, tried to be calm and composed like Steve, but it was growing increasingly difficult. She had a vague impression of a large collection of thatched-roof huts, camp fires, and women in bright, multi-colored woven skirts. She kept her gaze trained on Steve at first, unwilling to look too closely at those around them.

And then, when she dared look beyond Steve to the village surroundings, she saw the chilling evidence that they were not the first white captives to be brought here. As if drawn by a magnet, her gaze went directly to the center of the village. A severed head adorned a long pole, lips drawn back in a grimace, light brown hair flowing over sightless blue eyes. It looked as if it had been there several weeks. Eden's stomach lurched, and she heard Colin's choking cry as they recognized a former member of their expedition.

Sixteen

Steve gazed impassively at Colin sprawled on the floor of the hut beside Richard. How could he sleep? The man had disgraced himself by falling to the ground and retching, but there was no help for that now. Now in the growing light of approaching dawn, Steve weighed their chances of survival. It didn't look good. At the moment, all that kept them from certain death was the native superstition that it was bad fortune to kill one precious to the gods. He'd even been allowed to keep his knife, though they had been adamant about taking the machete from him. Not that he blamed them.

For a short time, back there in the jungle, he'd felt the old fury take hold of him. It was as if the tiger that always slumbered deep inside had been awakened, taking possession of his body in order to slaughter without respite or remorse. And he had enjoyed it. That was the odd part of it, and in a way, frightening. He should be repulsed. But when it came on him as it had, there was no thought of humanity or sanity. There was pleasure in the mindless thrust and parry of weapons, in seeing the enemy fall before him.

However, he hadn't been able to look directly at Eden, afraid he would see his own reflection in her eyes, view the horror he became when faced with danger. He'd caught a glimpse of it, of her instinctive rejection at the blood on him, and could understand it. She slept beside him now, her body curled against his—warm, solid, and alive. It was that warmth and presence that kept him from becoming the tiger. He shied away from seeing himself in her eyes, seeing the beast that he knew was his real nature.

Maybe that was why they called him *El Jaguar*. Not because of Balam. Because of native intuition that had divined his real nature, the essence of him, of what he became once the tiger awoke. He didn't like that part of him, but couldn't deny it. It haunted him, had haunted him since the war. Even then, the men in his command had sensed it. Though they joked about it, about how he could get them through anything, there was an uneasiness to their laughter, as if they didn't quite understand it or feel quite comfortable with him. And he'd always understood. He felt the same way. And after—after the war, he'd thought if he left it all behind, came to where there were no people and no fighting, he could avoid the beast. But he'd brought it with him.

Beside him, Eden stirred in her sleep, and he put a hand on her shoulder. She had the dreams, too, though not like his. Not like the ones he'd had the first two years he'd been down here, the ones that jerked him from sleep and persisted into the days, making him crouch under trees and bushes lying in wait for an enemy that never came. The few who had crossed his path those first years had never lived to regret it. He'd learned a few things about living with the tiger since then.

"Do you have to keep touching my wife?"

Colin's petulant voice snared Steve's attention. He smiled. "What do you think they have planned, Miller?" he asked, ignoring the question. Tilting his head toward the open door of the hut, he said softly, "A village this size has lots of corn fields to be worked. Henequen, too. Now that the Mayans have caught on to the white man's penchant for slaves, they've smartened up and gotten their own. You look a little skinny, though. Maybe they'll just sacrifice you instead of make you work their fields."

Colin blanched, looking even paler beneath his bruises. "Shut up."

"Have you ever thought about what it's like to be a slave? Odd, but I never did. We fought a war about slaves, and I still never saw the other side of it. Not until I came down here." He tilted his head back against the wall and stared up at the bare beams of the thatched roof. "It never looked so bad . . . we never had any slaves ourselves, but I knew men who did. They seemed happy. Well-fed. Clothed. It never occurred to me how it would feel to be . . . owned."

Silence fell, and after a moment Colin said, "You sound as if you're speaking from personal experience."

Steve's head jerked forward, and he narrowed a harsh stare at Colin. "I'd rather die than be a slave."

"You know what, Ryan?" Colin said softly, "I think there's a lot you're not saying—"

"You're right. But don't let common sense stop you from speaking your mind. Go ahead. I've still got my knife. When I get tired of listening to you, I know how to make you keep quiet."

Colin stared at him for a moment. One eye was nearly swollen shut, the other badly bruised. He shrugged, drawing up one leg to rest his arm on his knee. "We owned slaves. Until my father realized it wasn't politically expedient. Then he freed them."

"Politically expedient. Guess that's as good a reason as any to set men free." Steve looked down at his hands. They were clenched into fists in his lap. He slowly uncurled them, and spread his hands on his thighs.

"But you," Colin said suddenly, "never even owned slaves. Why did you fight for slave owners?"

"I fought for states' rights. Not slave owners. Not even the slaves. I believed that America was a free country, and men should have the right to choose their own way of life."

"Well you see what that got you," Colin said, and Steve nodded.

"Yeah. I see what that got me. I hope to hell I've learned something since then. Maybe it's not *politically expedient,* but I still think men should have the freedom to live in peace. It just seems like I'm the only one with that opinion." He rubbed his hands down his thighs and looked up at Colin. "Take these people here. They're simple. They have their own set of rules, their own religious beliefs. We may not like 'em, but they have 'em just the same."

Colin gave a hollow laugh. "Apparently chief among those beliefs is the line of thinking that decrees human sacrifice. Are you saying that's right?"

"No. But they don't think we're right to come down here and plunder their lost cities and take away their treasure, either. All I'm saying is, there are two sides to every issue. Sometimes both of them are right."

"You're crazy." Colin shook his head. "Richard was right. You are completely insane."

Steve grinned. "Yeah. Try not to forget that."

Colin gave him a strange look, then turned his battered face away. Looking past Colin, Steve watched the light grow brighter through the open door of the hut. Though there were no bars or visible barriers, he knew well enough that they were being closely watched. Escape would be damn near impossible.

Drawing up one leg, Steve rested his wrist atop his knee. He let his head lean back against the wall behind him, while he kept his other hand on Eden. She'd be safe. He'd do what he could to keep her alive.

Outside, he could hear the early morning sounds of life: faint, clucking squawks of chickens, the rhythmic slapping of corn meal dough into flattened tortillas, and the buzzing rasp of machetes being sharpened. The tang of cooking beans filled the air. If not for their circumstances, it would have been a simple domestic start to the day.

Several minutes passed, and finally Colin dredged up enough courage to ask, "Do you think they'll kill us all?"

"Maybe." Steve squinted at the light growing stronger through the cracks of the palapa hut. "Maybe not, if I can think of a way to get us out of this."

Colin snorted. "I thought you were the all-powerful, invincible *El Jaguar.* Your reputation is supposed to scare off your enemies throughout all the Yucatán . . . why doesn't it work on these natives?"

Steve regarded him silently for a moment. Then he shrugged, glancing down at the still-sleeping Eden. "Ask 'em yourself if you're that curious."

"Don't they know who you are?"

This time Steve gave him a cold, hard stare. "Anyone ever tell you that you're an idiot, Miller?"

Bridling, Colin snapped, "What do you mean by that?"

"Sweet Jesus, I can't believe that you'd not know. It should be obvious to a monkey that they either don't know or don't care, or do know and don't care—figure it out. If my damned reputation as some sort of god would work on these people, would I be sitting here in a hot, mosquito-infested hut with a babbling idiot?"

Colin's mouth tightened. "Maybe. Or maybe they've decided you'd make a nice sacrifice, being a god and all."

"Maybe." Steve's mouth twisted in sardonic humor. "You better hope not. I'm the only one here who seems to know how to use a gun or sword."

Colin colored and looked away. Time passed in a slow crawl of buzzing insects and vague, mysterious sounds. Colin slanted another glance at the open door of the hut. "Why aren't they guarding us?"

"They are, Miller. Make no mistake about that. Try and get out that door and see how far across the compound you get before you resemble a pin cushion."

"I can't stand this." Colin sat up suddenly. His throat worked convulsively. "The waiting. Not knowing."

Steve watched him warily. Hysteria wouldn't help. Especially from a man. "Richard said you were in the war,

Miller. You ought to know how this works. Waiting is what most soldiers do. Wait for orders, wait for food, wait for the next fight—you should be used to this. Don't fall apart now."

"War." Colin's laugh was brittle. "Yeah, I was in the war. A clerk in the home office doesn't see much action, though." He glanced at Eden. "I used to write home, tell her how hard it was, the fighting and deplorable conditions. And it was. But not for me. My father had influence, you see, and I made officer without ever seeing a battle." He drew in a shaky breath, then looked up at Steve as if seeing him for the first time. Then some of his bravado returned, and he shrugged. "As a Union lieutenant, I was appointed aide to a general on Sherman's staff. We never left Washington. The best food, best accommodations that could be had were ours. All official, of course."

"Must have been nice." Steve shifted slightly, easing his shoulders to a more comfortable spot on the wall of woven tree limbs. What was he supposed to say? Maybe it wasn't Miller's fault that he'd never seen action, and really, it didn't matter. Standing in a muddy ditch to shoot and be shot at wasn't exactly his idea of a great way to spend a few years. And he'd endured worse since then. Maybe if he'd spent the war dining out with a general, he'd be just as pompous as Colin Miller.

"Yes," Colin was saying, "I suppose it was better than starving in the trenches."

Steve's mouth tightened, and he stuffed the sudden flashing memory of whistling cannonballs and jarring explosions into the deepest recesses of his mind. "Yeah," he said, "chicken with a general would taste much better than hot lead and mud with foot soldiers."

"Do you think they'll feed us?"

Squashing the surge of impatience that flooded him, Steve managed a careless shrug. "Depends on how quick they intend to get rid of us, I guess."

He was only faintly gratified by Colin's rapid paling. The insufferable ass. Motivated by greed for one thing or the other, it seemed. Used to living well; no doubt once the war had reduced his circumstances, he'd grown used to living well on his wife's money. It explained some of his greed, Steve supposed. Had to be rather embarrassing and galling to live on a woman's money, no matter how legally binding their relationship. Maybe that was part of the reason Miller was so blindly intent upon making a fortune with the improbable discovery of lost treasure. Of course, taking a decent job would probably never occur to him. Not someone of Colin's nature, who depended upon daddy to get him out of doing his duty during wartime.

"Glad to see you two getting along," Richard Allen remarked as he sat up and wiped a hand over his face. "Wretchedly hot already, don't you think?"

"It won't get any cooler," Steve said, meeting Richard's gaze. There was only a quick flick of his eyes toward Steve's hand resting on Eden to indicate he'd even noticed it; apparently he thought it best to ignore the silent statement of change. If Colin could not protect her, at least Steve might have a chance.

Or so Steve thought. Hell, he knew he had the best chance of getting them through this, but the devil of the thing was, he had no idea how he'd manage it. However, he couldn't let them know that, of course. Miller was likely to break down in a weeping fit that would so surely disgust their captors they could all end up dead. No, he had to brazen this thing out.

Stretching out his legs until they reached halfway across the small hut, Steve said mildly, "If they bring us something to eat, it's a good sign. Whatever happens, stay calm and watchful until we figure out how to proceed."

Richard nodded silently, and Colin just stared at him. Steve glanced down, frowning a little as Eden began to stir. He resisted the urge to stroke back a long curling strand of her pale hair. She'd slept deeply. That was good. He could have used a little sleep himself, but hadn't dared. It had been a long night.

In light of everything, he wasn't too surprised when Eden awoke and moved away from him, her quick, startled glance as telling as her crab-like scoot across the dirt floor of the hut.

"I . . . I must have slept after all," she murmured, eyes skimming over him and then away, as skittish as a butterfly. "I didn't think I'd be able to sleep."

Steve shrugged. "It's good for you."

Across the room Colin seemed to give himself a mental shake and sat up a little straighter. "We were . . . talking."

Eden didn't look surprised, but pushed back the hair from her eyes with a faint smile. "Good. I hope you figured out some way to leave here with our skins intact."

It wasn't quite what he'd expected her to say, and Steve grinned. She wasn't as jittery today as she'd been last night. That was a good sign, too. Hysterics always got on his nerves.

"We were hoping," he drawled, "that you would have an idea."

She looked at him then, a direct stare from eyes as wide as blue saucers. "As a matter of fact, I think I do." In a quick, breathless voice, as if afraid he'd laugh or interrupt her before she was through, she said, "What would happen if you predicted dire fates for them if they killed us? Would they believe you? I mean, one of them did call you *El Jaguar,* didn't he?"

"Jesus, you do believe in fairy tales, don't you." Steve frowned. "To be honest, I'm not sure it'd work, Goldilocks. They obviously weren't too impressed with my reputation or they wouldn't have stuck me in this hut with the rest of you. I don't think they'd take me too seriously if I told them they'd have a plague of locusts or painful boils should they be unwise enough to use us for target practice."

"You made it rain," Eden pointed out, "and you obviously have done other things to make them call you *El Jaguar* and leave you alone all this time. Do something. Make it rain. Make it not rain. Have a frothing fit."

"Hell, I could make it rain frogs while having a frothing fit and that wouldn't be any guarantee they'd let us go. Most likely, they'd amuse themselves for a while before—" He stopped, grimacing. No point in going into graphic detail. The head on the pole should be example enough of what was possible.

"What about John Carter?" Richard asked suddenly. "Do you suppose he could help us?"

Steve picked up a small stick from the ground and dug it idly into the dirt for a moment. "I thought of that. Even if he knew where we were, I doubt he could do anything. He brought a crew with him, he said, but I never saw 'em. Except for Paco, he was alone."

"Paco . . ."

Eden's sharp echo brought up his head. "Yeah. Seems he didn't get eaten by a crocodile after all."

She stared at him with obvious disbelief. "But I heard . . . I saw the blood on what was left of his torn shirt. Where was he?"

Shrugging, he muttered, "Ask him next time you see him."

She put a hand over her face. "None of this makes any sense. It doesn't fit. There are too many pieces that don't quite fall into place." She looked up, and her eyes met Steve's. "There is something odd going on, and I don't know what it is."

"The fact that we're huddled in a damn palapa hut waiting to be executed isn't odd enough for you?" Steve asked mildly. "You're definitely a challenge to entertain."

"Don't be funny. You know what I mean." Her gaze was intense and narrowed, and he looked away with a shrug.

"Back to the present situation, if you please. Maybe your idea isn't so far-fetched after all."

"It has possibilities," Richard said slowly, "if you think we can actually arrange some kind of trick."

"Whatever we do, it has to be good." Steve's mouth tightened grimly. "We'll only have one chance."

No one had a response to that. It was too close to the truth to be debated or ignored.

Eden stared glumly into the small turtle shell bowl. "What is this stuff?"

Barely glancing at her, Steve said, "Zacá. Try it. It's pretty good."

She hesitated a moment longer, then tilted the bowl. It was grainy and sweet and watery, but not bad at all. She looked up in surprise. "It tastes a little like grits."

"It should." Steve drained the rest of his meal and wiped his mouth on his sleeve. "It's cornmeal stirred into water and mixed with honey. I would have preferred *balché,* but guess I shouldn't be so picky."

"I'm not certain I want to know what bal-kay is." Eden sipped more of the sweet-tasting zacá, staring at him over the rim of her bowl.

Steve looked up at her with the faint devil's grin that always made her wary. "It's an acquired taste, but dulls the edges as effectively as sour mash. *Balché* is a liquor made of fermented honey and the bark of a tree. Has quite a kick."

"I should have known." She finished her bowl of zacá and set it down on the dirt floor. Since seeing Steve fight their attackers, she didn't know how to react to him. Now she knew what he'd been saying to her that day so long ago; she'd seen the way he fought, as viciously as any madman, as if he were someone other than the lazily mocking man she'd first thought him. Beneath the thin veneer of civility lurked a man capable of extreme violence. Now, she could finally believe that he had calmly and deliberately murdered a man. If it fit his sense of justice, he would do it without a qualm.

Batting at a tiny swarm of minute insects in front of her face, Eden said practically, "Since they've fed us, they must intend to allow us to live a while longer."

Steve gave her an appreciative glance. "You were paying attention. I thought you were asleep."

"Not the entire time." She looked down at her feet, and saw that her boot laces were untied again. The thin strings were close to rotting away in places. Soon, she would have no laces at all to keep her boots on her feet. When she'd finished lacing them, she asked, "What should we do now?"

"Wait." Steve shrugged impatiently when she glared at him. "I don't know what you expect. Heroics? Sorry. I'm fresh out of 'em. Feel free to do whatever you think might work, however. I prefer to wait and see which direction this is going."

Richard asked hesitantly, "Are you certain that is wise? Shouldn't we have some kind of plan?"

"Certainly." Steve waved a careless hand. "Plan away."

Eden glanced at Colin. He'd been strangely quiet since the native had come in bearing bowls of food. Not questioning what had been brought or what would be done, he'd simply drunk his portion and sat quietly. She directed her question to him.

"What do you think we should do, Colin?"

He looked up from contemplating his feet. "Whatever Ryan thinks, I suppose. He seems to know more about this than any of us."

Help from an unexpected source, Eden thought wryly. Steve must be pleased. She glanced at him, and saw his brows lower in a faint frown. Maybe not.

"There are," Steve said after a moment, "several options. The first and most logical—though not very appealing—is that they will kill us outright. Second choice could be to use us as slaves. Since they haven't killed us yet, and are obviously going to keep us alive a while longer, they might still be considering that option."

"You said several," Richard pointed out. "That was only two."

"Right. There's always the option of using us as entertainment." He paused, then said softly, "We better pray for number two."

Eden shuddered. Colin made a soft sound of distress, and Richard's face paled several shades. Only Steve seemed unaffected, but when he flicked her a quick glance, she saw the strain in his eyes. Oddly, it made her feel slightly better.

"Do you think there's a chance of escape?"

"Yeah, slim as the hair on a gnat's as—leg," he said with a slight shrug. "I have a feeling they'll let us know what they've decided before too long. For the moment, our main worry is surviving the heat."

As time passed, it grew even more stifling in the hut. The buzz of insects was constant, while outside, they could hear the murmur of conversation. Occasionally Steve would catch a word or two that he thought was relative to their situation, and he'd pass it on to them. Most of it was curiosity about their captives, but once or twice even Eden caught the words *El Jaguar.*

It was late afternoon before Steve turned to look directly at her. "Sorry about this, Goldilocks."

"It's not your fault." She shrugged and glanced at Colin and Richard, who were dozing on the bare dirt floor. "We should have stayed with you. Perhaps none of this would have happened if we'd taken your advice and gone home."

"A little late to think of that now." He grinned when she flashed him an irate look. "Try to remember that next time."

"If there is a next time," she whispered past the sudden lump in her throat.

Steve sobered, and there was a grim set to his mouth. "I

damn well intend for there to be an opportunity to hold this over your head, that's for sure. Listen." He moved closer to her, and she felt the warmth emanating from his body. "This will sound bad, but hear me out. I've still got my knife. If it looks like the worst, do you want me to . . . to let you take the easy way out?"

Her heart thudded. He was offering her a quick death over whatever might happen. That meant he wasn't at all certain they would get out of this. She felt faint. She tried to force words from her dry lips, but the ones she knew she should say wouldn't come.

Shaking her head, she finally croaked, "No. Whatever may happen, I'll face it."

Steve smiled faintly. "Good girl. You'll survive. I always said you were a survivor, didn't I?" He inclined his head toward Colin. "I think he's already given up. He's liable to be a problem if we do figure a way out of this."

She drew in a shaky breath. "We'll have to help him the best way we can."

Steve stared at her from beneath the thick bristle of his lashes. "Is that what you want?"

"I could never live with anything else."

After a moment, he nodded. "Yeah. You're right. I've been thinking. I was able to glean a little bit of information from their conversations all day, and it seems that they're planning some sort of religious festival."

Eden's heart dropped. Her mouth went dry and she tried to control the sudden trembling of her hands. Steve put one of his hands over hers. He drew in a deep breath that contradicted his reassurance.

"It may not he that bad. And I think your idea will come in very handy."

"My idea?

He grinned. "Yeah. As high priest and master practitioner of black magic, I hope to convince them to let me conduct a ceremony. I've been paying attention to their conversations. It seems that the rains haven't come to their fields yet, and they're concerned about their corn crops. It rained the other day, remember? With any luck, it will rain here in a day or two."

"What if they don't want you to make it rain?" She chewed her bottom lip, eyes searching his face. "Any other ideas?"

He smiled. "As a matter of fact—yes. It has come to my attention that you are a goddess. That could come in handy."

She stared at him blankly. "What are you talking about now?"

"Ixchel. The Moon Goddess. Takes mortal lovers at times—" he slid a sly glance toward the sleeping Colin. "But is known to be rather fickle." Reaching out, he lifted a curling lock of her hair in his fist and held it for a moment, rubbing it between his fingers with an intensity that made her heart lurch. His hand brushed against her cheek, warm and familiar. She closed her eyes, not wanting to remember things that were past—lost to her now. Maybe forever.

"Eden." His soft voice opened her eyes. "Sweetheart, listen to me. Carter said there's a rumor among some of the natives that you're the moon goddess come to earth. We might be able to use that to our advantage. Think you can play the part?"

She wet her lips with her tongue, staring at him. Nothing daunted him—but she was a coward. She'd discovered that on the jungle path the day before, when all chaos had broken loose around her and she'd only been able to stand in paralyzed fear and watch while Steve surged into action. It was Steve who had saved them from certain death in the jungle. Now he was all that stood between them and disaster.

"I'll do what I can," she said, the words dredged up from

deep inside her, halting and hopeful and frightened all at the same time. "But I don't know if I can . . ."

"Sweetheart, you can do anything you set your mind to. I've seen you. You're a survivor, remember? You survived two weeks alone in an inhospitable land. You survived me." His mouth curled in a crooked smile. "You'll survive this. I know you will."

She managed an answering smile. "Just tell me what to do."

Drawing her to him, heedless of Colin or Richard or any other distraction, Steve pushed his hand into her hair to hold her head to his mouth. He said softly against her hair, "I will. But the rest will be up to you. It doesn't look good right now. There are a lot of varying factors. I have a feeling that you are our T.O.H."

She tilted her head to look up at him. "T.O.H.?"

"Yeah—ticket outa here."

Seventeen

"It's too crazy to work," Colin said irritably. His hand shook as he pushed it through his hair in a nervous gesture. He bit his lip, shook his head again, and repeated, "Too crazy."

"Got a better idea?" Steve challenged. When there was no reply, he turned his attention back to Eden. "All right. I'm going to try everything else, but it may come down to one option. Do you think you can do it?"

She was shaking, too, her hands quivering as she clenched them in her lap, but her mouth was set in a determined line. "Yes. I can do it."

"Good girl." He slashed a quick look at Richard, who was staring down at his feet. "I'm going to suggest a ceremony to bring rain, using our moon goddess here. I'll try to distract them as long as possible. You two keep watch. If a chance to escape comes, it will be up to you to get Colin out of here as quickly as possible, Richard. He still can't run all that well."

Richard looked up and smiled faintly. "We'll manage. You provide the distraction, and we'll do the rest."

"I still say it won't work." Colin's voice rose slightly, and Steve clamped a hard hand on his wrist until he gasped.

"Shut up, Miller. If you want to die here, fine. But the rest of us are going to get out alive."

"All right," Colin said after a minute. "I'll try."

Steve released him. There was always a weak link in

every plan, and Colin was theirs. If the man botched things, he'd kill him before the natives could do it.

Rising to his feet, Steve gave Eden another encouraging smile and said, "Don't forget what I told you. Stay calm; show no fear; be watchful. I'll do the rest."

It might not work, but he'd be damned if he'd sit by and wait for the worst. And it was worth a chance. It was the old demon again, the sleeping tiger that prodded him into taking risks, but this time, he was being more cautious. This time, there was a far greater risk, for it involved Eden.

Keeping that in mind, Steve wasn't as brazen as he might have been when he demanded to speak to the village h-men. He knew the natives would not respect anything but boldness, but he tempered it with civility when he made his demand. He was relieved when the village h-men agreed to speak with this man called *El Jaguar.*

Seated before his hut, a neat palapa structure with the familiar steep thatched roof, the h-men, or Maya priest who served the old gods, gravely inclined his head in greeting when Steve was escorted to him.

"I am told," he said in faultless Spanish, "that you wish to speak with me."

"This is so." Steve made a gesture of respect, and the priest indicated that he sit down on a woven mat facing him. Steve sat, crossing his legs and resting his hands in his lap.

"You are the one called *El Jaguar.* This was not known when the Holcanes first came upon you. But I have heard of you," the old man said gravely.

"And I of you." Steve matched his gravity. "All have heard of the powerful h-men who walked across the fiery stones without harm, oh Lord of the Sun. Your wisdom has spread across the land like a feathered cloak, touching all who hear of you with awe."

"Indeed." The old man stared at him. Dark eyes set in a face of timeless wrinkles and age gazed at Steve as if focusing on another plane of time. He nodded slightly. "As has your fame spread as a mighty warrior chief. You are favored by the gods, Nacom."

The last caught Steve by surprise, but he kept his face expressionless. "I am honored that you know of me, Yum Kin."

Facing the elderly man, Steve waited politely for the ritual small talk to end. When the subtle signal came for him to discuss the reason for this conversation, he did so without delay.

"The corn withers in the fields without rain. The gods told of your difficulties, and sent me to your aid."

Yum Kin, Lord of the Sun, let his eyes focus upon Steve. He could read nothing in the bottomless black depths, and waited. All the odds were on the h-man's side, of course, and this was only a desperate ploy to buy some time and possibly their lives. The old Maya priest would know this. Would he be insulted that this upstart—this foreign devil who had slain men of the village—claimed to have been sent by his ancient gods?

After a lengthy pause, Yum Kin said, "It has been said that you have brought the rains before. Chac listened to you then. But there is no certainty he would do so now."

"If I make the proper preparations, oh wise and powerful Lord of the Sun, the God of Rain will heed my requests. He has smiled upon me before. Would you allow me to offer my services?"

There was another lengthy pause before the old man said slowly, "Someone in the village has displeased Chac, for he has not heeded my prayers or the sacrifices we made. The decision has been made to offer a blood sacrifice to appease the gods."

Steve did not allow his face to reflect the concern that remark gave him. He shrugged lightly. "A wise decision. You have chosen an animal for this sacrifice?"

Yum Kin shook his head. "No. It has been decided to choose from among you."

"Perhaps the blood of a captive is not necessary."

"We have no other choice now. Our decision has been made."

Damn. Steve looked down, then asked as if the answer did not matter, "Who have you chosen?"

"It has been said that perhaps the gods would be pleased with the sacrifice of a woman—"

"No. Women are weak. I offer myself as a sacrifice." Steve met the old man's eyes steadily. "I am *El Jaguar,* and would be the best choice for a sacrifice."

Shaking his head, Yum Kin said, "We have already chosen. It would not be wise to risk Chac's anger by sacrificing one as special to him as *El Jaguar.* The woman with hair of sunlight is to be given. It is an honor for her still-beating heart to be offered to Chac."

The tiger inside sprang to life with bared teeth to defend Eden, but Steve held it at bay with an effort. Not now. He had to think, could not risk losing even the smallest advantage. After the briefest hesitation, he said, "But if you displease Father Chac even more by sending one blessed by him to Metnal for the god of the underworld, the crops may dry up and turn to dust."

Yum Kin considered that gravely for several moments. His dark eyes narrowed slightly. "The woman is special to Chac?"

"Yes. It is said she is Ixchel, the Moon Goddess. Perhaps you have heard that she has come to earth and taken a lover. It is known by many that she chose *El Jaguar* for a partner. Would you risk offending Father Chac by choosing one god over the other?"

"It is difficult," Yum Kin said after a moment. "But there is no proof that she is Ixchel. There must be a sacrifice."

"I will give you proof," Steve said, his mind leaping from one possibility to the next. "I can give a demonstration of her powers."

Shaking his head, Yum Kin said, "We will test her with

fire or water. If she is not the Moon Goddess, she will be given to Ah Chhuy Kak, the god of sacrifice."

"Let me arrange it," Steve said quickly. "I will intercede for you. If Chac is displeased, it will be with me and not you."

There was a brief pause, then Yum Kin inclined his head. "You shall have the honor of testing the Moon Goddess. But if you are not successful, mighty warrior chief, we shall take that as a sign that Chac requires the ultimate sacrifice—your still beating heart that represents life."

Steve bowed his head in agreement. "I will be successful, Yum Kin. For I will prove to you that she is the Moon Goddess, Ixchel, by offering her to Ah Cantzicnal, the god of the water. He will give her back, so as not to deny Chac."

A faint light flickered in the old man's eyes, flaring quickly before he lowered his eyelids. "Perhaps I misjudged you. To offer such a prize and take such a risk, one must be certain of success."

It wasn't a comforting thought, but there was little choice. If he succeeded, all would be well. And if he failed—he only hoped Eden survived to forgive him for it one day.

Terrified, Eden endured the preparations silently. She had been bathed by several women of the village, and her long hair had been brushed dry until it hung in soft waves down her back. Brilliant scarlet flowers were entwined in a circlet atop her crown, and she'd been dressed in a long, white cotton robe that hung in graceful folds to her bare feet. One of the women had solemnly fastened a heavy jade and gold necklace around her throat, and it hung as a weighty reminder of what was to come.

It had been two days, and she'd seen Steve only once since he had been granted an audience with the village priest. He'd returned and stood silently as she was summoned to her feet by two armed men. When she was escorted past him, he'd murmured, "Keep your hands and feet moving." But that was all. No instructions about what role she was to perform as the goddess, nothing but those terse words. It was perplexing. Just as mysterious and distressing, she had been taken from their hut to another and she'd seen none of the other captives since. She had no idea exactly what was to happen, and could only trust that Steve would be successful in whatever he was trying to do.

Chattering in their soft language, some of the women gazed at her with shy smiles, offering her tempting morsels of food and more of the zacá. She ate sparingly, her appetite having fled as tension mounted. Fretfully, she wondered how Colin and Richard were faring, and if Steve had been able to reassure them. It would be nice to know what was happening. The uncertainty was more terrifying than anything else.

There was an air of purposeful determination to the women with her as they furiously worked, making massive quantities of tortillas. Puzzled, Eden could only wonder as to the significance of the corn tortillas placed in stacks of thirteen, then cemented with dough and wrapped in broad green leaves. She'd seen a pit outside, a huge ditch covered with logs and piled high with stones atop the logs. Chickens had been killed, plucked, and cleaned, then plunged into buckets of water over several fires. The enticing aroma filled the air.

It was nerve-racking, knowing these were preparations for some kind of ceremony in which she was obviously to take part, yet not knowing what that part would be. She wished Steve had been able to tell her. And she hoped—prayed—that these were his preparations, and not those of the villagers.

But when she was led from the small hut as the sun broke over the eastern sky, Eden began to long for the safety of ignorance. Her heart beat furiously, and her mouth and throat were dry as she was ceremoniously led forward. Familiar jungle noises greeted her, the raucous cries of toucans in the trees mixing with the soft murmurs of the villagers. Her feet stirred up small clouds of dust as she walked slowly across the central court nestled in the midst of thatched-roof huts. She had a vague impression of pigs, chickens, and turkeys rambling among the huts, and a tall beehive in the center of the village. She tried to keep her chin up and her eyes straight ahead, repeating over and over the first instructions that Steve had given her: "Stay calm; show no fear; be watchful." And finally, the inexplicable—"Keep your hands and feet moving."

It wasn't easy. Especially when she had no idea exactly what would happen. She kept her shoulders rigid, her chin lifted, and as the lines of silent villagers parted, she saw at the end of the columns a large altar with Steve standing in front of it.

Relief flooded her. Perhaps he'd managed to succeed. There was no sign of Colin or Richard yet, but Steve must have arranged something for them. She spared a brief prayer for all of them, then focused on Steve.

He was dressed still in the same clothing, though his shirt and pants looked much cleaner. He waited silently, watching her as she approached the altar. A huge cross had been erected behind it, and wooden bowls were lined on the altar. When she was within a few feet of him, he made a motion with his hand, and she was taken to one side, away from the altar and the ceremony.

Vaguely surprised, she looked around her, and saw that only men remained in front of the altar. She was taken to a hut not far away, where more women prepared the leaf-wrapped corn tortillas for baking. Another wait, while the women behaved deferentially toward her, as if she was, indeed, the Moon Goddess she pretended to be. It occurred to Eden to wonder what they would do if she commanded them to leave her, but suspected that it would only create problems. No, she would wait. She would trust Steve.

* * *

"Bring the *tutiwah*," Steve said, "and the boiled chickens for the sacrifice."

While men went to remove the loaves of tortillas and dough wrapped in the leaves of the *bob* tree and baked in huge ovens, Steve brought out the glass globe he'd requested from Yum Kin. Called a *zaztún*, meaning clear stone, it was small and clear and possessed high ceremonial significance. If he'd had his own, it would have made a better impression.

The men returned with the tutiwah and chickens, and Steve ordered the thirteen bowls—one for each Lord of the Day—filled with zacá to be passed among the men of the congregation. No women were allowed which, of course, made this easier. After piling the loaves of tutiwah and boiled chickens atop the altar, Steve dipped the zaztún into a bowl of balché. For the past two days, he'd fasted, drinking copious amounts of balché to improve the visions he was supposed to have. Feeling a little dizzy, he lifted the zaztún high to each point of the compass, staring through it as he addressed the altar.

"Oh Clouds," he intoned, "come now to bring the gift of life to this village, I implore of you . . . Oh Lord of Rain, Father Chac, we offer this bread and this meat as a gift for your blessing . . . let the rain fall upon these fields where they toil for survival . . . let life begin for them again . . . Oh Clouds, heed my orders to give rain to their fields. I have the power of Itzamná, the Lord of Life, as my benefactor, and We command this of you . . . With my power, and the power of the Lord of the Sun, Yum Kin, We order you to shower the fields with rain, to bring life to humanity . . . The Moon Goddess, Ixchel, gives of herself to you, Father Chac, so that these people may live . . . send now the rain that will wet the fields and make the corn grow and We shall send you Ixchel's blessing."

Not a bad performance, Steve thought, and it seemed to have had a powerful effect on the congregation. Of course, rain would have an even better effect. Well, he'd delayed as long as he dared.

Lowering the zaztún, he motioned for Eden to be brought from the nearby hut. He saw her confusion, the way she looked to him for comfort, and he nodded slightly. He hoped she didn't lose her nerve. It wouldn't look very good for the Moon Goddess to shriek and fight over a small thing like being sacrificed, when she was supposed to be immortal. Too bad he hadn't been able to explain her role to her, but he hoped she had enough sense to follow his lead. It would be crucial.

Heading the procession, Steve walked slowly along the path to the village's sacred cenote. Eden was behind him, flanked by two men, the hem of her long cotton robe dragging in the dirt of the path. He frowned. Too bad there wasn't a way around that robe, but it would create problems if he'd suggested changing the ancient tradition. So he had to go with the familiar, not daring to alter too much of the ritual. He thanked his lucky stars that he'd attended a few of these ceremonies, or he would have had a devil of a time knowing what to do. The curious blend of ancient and Christian rituals could leave a man floundering for the proper protocol in this land.

When they reached the edge of the cenote, he turned to Eden. She looked up at him, her wide blue eyes registering trust. He almost winced. There was nothing for it, however. This might be their only chance. He'd had nothing more impressive to offer, once he realized that Yum Kin had commanded the village's awe and respect by walking on fire. He could hardly top that unless he learned to fly, and that was damned unlikely. And this certainly beat watching them cut out Eden's heart . . .

Here goes everything, he thought, and held up the zaztún to the sky. The sun was higher now, and he intended to drag out the ceremony as long as he dared. It would give Eden less time to endure what was coming.

"O Clouds," he chanted loudly, "We offered a sacrifice so that you will send down the rain. Now we offer Ah Cantzicnal the moon goddess in the name of Chac, so that he may decide our fate . . ."

Now he lowered his gaze and looked directly at Eden, and saw the hope in her eyes slowly replaced by horror as realization sunk in. He could not risk warning her directly, so said softly, "Remember the words you were told, Ixchel, and life will be renewed . . ."

Eden's lips moved soundlessly, and her gaze was stricken. But she didn't whimper or plead, only kept her chin lifted high. He fought the sudden impulse to weep for her touching courage, and the unfamiliar emotion shocked him.

His voice was rough and hoarse when he said, "As the goddess lives, so shall Father Chac reward us with rain."

It was the only way he knew to tell her not to surrender, and he hoped she understood. Stepping back to the edge of the cenote, Steve held up a hand to stop the men flanking Eden.

"It is my privilege to offer Ah Cantzicnal this greatest gift," he said, and the men released her and stepped back.

Steve grasped her by the arms, taking her to the very edge of the cenote. Fifty feet below, murky water filled the limestone pit, looking opaque and serene in the bright light of the sun beating down on the small clearing. It was already growing hot, yet he could feel Eden shiver as he held her briefly against him. Her back was to him, the soft brush of her hair a fragrant caress against his cheek, and he dared whisper in her ear, "Keep your hands and feet moving," before he pushed her over the edge.

Eighteen

Water closed over her head like a shroud. Eden choked on the chalky taste as it filled her nose and mouth, and she clawed her way to the surface, gasping for air. Tears mixed with the water streaming from her eyes and nose. Her vision was blurred, and all she could see was the anonymous blend of limestone walls around her. Far above, light filled the air.

Her heart pounded, pumping blood so fast and furiously that it was all she could hear for several moments. She was going to drown . . . she couldn't swim, and Steve knew it. Her hands slapped futilely at the water, sending up more geysers as she sank like a rock. Desperately, she made her way to the surface again, gasping for air. Steve—damn him. He knew she couldn't swim. Was this his idea of saving her?—or saving himself?

Damn him! But as she struggled, his last words came back to her. As if pulled by invisible strings, her hands and feet began moving in the pattern he'd taught her that day in the cenote. Was that what he'd meant? *Keep your hands and feet moving. . . .* Amazingly, she stayed afloat. The wet cotton clung to her legs as she moved them, but it was light, and she was able to pull it up so that it floated around her instead of dragging her down.

Blinking water from her lashes, she saw the circlet of bright flowers she'd worn on her head bob on the water's surface. They floated past, attracting the attention of a butterfly that came with brilliant gold and brown wings to light upon one of the fragile blossoms. Eden tried to focus on the flowers and butterfly instead of her tiring muscles. She wished she had wings and could flutter up as effortlessly as the butterfly when it tired of the flower ring.

It was deathly quiet in the pool. No air stirred. Nothing moved but her, her arms and legs constantly displacing water to keep her afloat. It grew hotter and hotter. She managed to move to the shadows at one side of the cenote, out of the sun beating mercilessly down. The water was warm, murky, but surprisingly buoyant. When she grew tired of treading water, she floated until the weight of her garments began to drag her down. Then she started the motions again that would keep her afloat, the movements of her arms and legs through the water.

The shadows at the side grew shorter and shorter, and so did her hope. She would drown here. She couldn't keep up the movements much longer. Her muscles ached, and when she tried to slant a glance upward, all she saw was the bright, blinding glare of the sun. Sobs threatened to steal away the precious air in her lungs, and she sucked in a deep breath to hold them back. She would not cry, would not give in to despair. There must be a reason for this, must be a reason Steve had pushed her into the sacred cenote. She just couldn't figure out what it could be.

After a while, she began to think of death as a friend. It would be a relief to cease the struggle, to slip beneath the surface of the water and surrender to the inevitable. Why did she even continue the fight? Foolish, really. What would she have if she did survive? A lifetime of regrets. She'd briefly tasted love with Steve, but that had ended much too quickly. There was only Colin left for her, and she had made that choice herself.

Would she ever forget Steve's face that evening, watching her so closely, his eyes narrowed and wary as he waited for her answer? And she had been too cowardly to say what she really wanted, to tell him that she loved him. It had been easier to waver back and forth between them, easier to cling to the safety of a loveless marriage than to take a chance that he did not love her back. Cowards deserved to die. And she was a coward.

Eden felt reality slipping away from her, as she yielded to the heat and the water and time. It would be so easy to give up. To surrender to the inevitable. Yet even now, when she knew it was hopeless, there was a stubborn part of her that could not admit defeat, could not let go of life.

She drifted, cotton gown flowing around her waist, the sun searing her face and making her eyes close against the glare. It was directly overhead now, pitiless and bright and painful. In the heavy silence that closed out the world beyond the cenote, she heard the faintest rattle. A rock, perhaps, from above. She remembered Steve taking her to the sacred cenote that first day, and the birds battling atop a limestone ledge and sending showers of rock hurtling below. Perhaps they were pelting her with rocks from above to kill her. She was the sacrifice. Fitting. Her life for theirs. But why hadn't Steve told her? Saved her? Why?

Eden.

She heard her name, and wondered vaguely if her mind was playing tricks on her. A sailor had once told her that just before drowning, one's life flashed before their eyes. She must be drowning. The struggle was almost over . . .

"Eden. Dammit, look up here."

The words jerked her eyes open again, and she peered up.

"Give me your hand—I can't hang here all day waiting for you to decide when to come out of your bath . . ."

There was a slight quiver in his voice, but when she looked up into Steve's face, she saw only grim determination. He was just a few feet from her, seemingly hanging in mid-air. His voice was pleading now, soft and urgent.

"Sweetheart—give me your hand. Let me help you."

Slowly, with the last of her strength, she held up her hand. He grasped it firmly, his strength flowing into her as he pulled her from the water and into his arms. Clasping her hands behind his neck, she clung to him while they swayed on the flimsy rope ladder suspended above the water.

"Just hold on," Steve said against her ear, "and I'll do all the work. You're safe now. It worked . . . it worked, my brave goddess. All you have to do now is behave like a goddess."

It didn't seem very difficult, in light of what she'd just endured.

Eden frowned. "I still don't understand."

Sighing, Steve said softly, "There wasn't much of a choice. It was either let them cut out your still beating heart or drown you. Of the two, you had a better chance in the cenote."

Seated on the floor of a hut, she looked up at him. Her hair was still slightly damp, lying in curls over her shoulders and the clean cotton robe she'd been given. She made him think of a small bird with ruffled feathers fluffed out to dry in the sun.

He smiled wryly. "Trust me, Goldilocks, I wouldn't have let you drown."

Her eyes were frankly disbelieving, and she turned her head slightly. "How do I know that? For all I know, you would have been safe either way. If I was sacrificed, your reputation was safe, and if I managed to stay afloat long enough, then you could have me declared a god."

"If I had that much damn influence over these people, I sure as hell wouldn't have risked my neck on such a flimsy chance as you staying afloat." He raked a hand through his hair with exasperation. He couldn't really blame her, he guessed. It looked pretty bad from her point of view. After all, she had risked the most. If it had been him flung into a deep pit of water with little explanation, maybe he'd be a bit put out as well.

This time her glance was like a poison dart, ice-blue and full of venom. "Risked *your* neck? And just how did you do that? Stand too close to the edge when you pushed me over?"

"Tsk, tsk. Such a vicious creature when you're still wet. Give me a little credit, Goldilocks. I never left the cenote. I was right there the entire time. You did excellently. I wanted to lower the ladder earlier, but these things are performed on a rigid schedule, it seems. They frowned on my going after you until the sun was directly overhead."

"You have my sympathy."

"At least you're still alive to hate me," he said quietly, and she turned her face away again.

"No thanks to you."

He let that pass. She wasn't in the mood to listen, it seemed. And maybe she was right. Maybe he could have thought of something else. Or at least given her an option. But things moved so quickly sometimes, and the choice could be gone almost as soon as it was offered. He'd lived to regret hesitation before now. He probably would again.

"Where," she asked after a few more minutes of stiff silence, "are Richard and Colin?"

"Nestled cozily in their hut, I imagine. Still under guard, of course."

She looked at him again, a narrowed glance from blue eyes hazy with anger and shadows. "Why are they still under guard? Aren't we safe now?"

He gave a regretful shake of his head. "You misunderstand the situation. *You* are safe. You were sacrificed to the gods and lived. These people can't swim, y'see, and so anyone who can stay afloat for several hours earns their deepest respect and awe."

Her brow lifted. "This is utter madness. All that, and we still aren't to be set free?"

"We're alive," he pointed out. "That gives us a chance. Try and see the silver lining, Goldilocks. And while you're at it, pray for rain. That may save all of us."

She made a strangled sound, shaking her head. "I can't believe it. After everything, we're in exactly the same situation as before."

"No," he said quietly, "not quite. You're a goddess now. Ixchel, the Moon Goddess of birth, fertility, medicine, and weaving—you have some influence. That's all-important here."

"I can't see that it's helped you any." She gave him another dark look. "You're *El Jaguar,* who calls down rain and thunder and lightning bolts, who slays men with a single stroke, and yet you can't walk out of here."

Steve didn't say anything for a moment. He was still weighing their options, still trying to figure out a way to manage it all. And she was right about one thing—he couldn't walk out. Not yet. Not if he wanted to please Eden, and oddly enough, he'd discovered he wanted that very much. This wasn't just about saving her, this was about being what she thought he was. Or had thought he was until he'd pushed her over the edge of the cenote. Her opinion of him had taken a drastic turn for the worse, it seemed, but there was still a chance to change that.

Of course, if it was up to him, they would already be gone. However, it would mean leaving Colin and Richard and he knew she would never allow that. Not willingly. And he wasn't about to tell her any more than he had to, on the off chance that he had to leave them behind after all. He'd try to save them, but if it came down to a choice between Eden and the others—he'd do what had to be done. He just wouldn't tell her there had ever been that option.

"Chicken?" he said after a moment, and smiled when she gave him an incredulous stare. He indicated the table with a nod of his head. "Boiled, but tasty. The bread is good, too. Tutiwah, they call it."

Eden glanced at the small table of food. "I watched the women prepare it."

She looked up at him, then around at their surroundings. Steve watched, wondering when the obvious would occur to her. It took a few minutes as she surveyed the walls of loosely-woven sticks, the high thatched roof, and the scant pieces of furniture. A small wooden table squatted against one wall, and several low benches were scattered on the hard-packed dirt floor. There was a drum of water and a gourd dipper, a few brightly colored woven mats, and a large hammock swinging from a solid beam. Hardened clay formed a fire pit, and a metal grill had been slung over it for cooking purposes. Homey and cozy. Peaceful.

"Where," she asked after a moment, "are you going to stay?" He smiled as she slowly turned to look at him. "Here?"

"Well," he said, "they already think we're partners. The rumors, you see. It's expected that we—the Moon Goddess and *El Jaguar* . . . it wasn't my idea, Goldilocks, though I damn sure don't intend to apologize for it."

"Ixchel—goddess of fertility, you said." Her face colored. "Damn you, Steve Ryan."

"It's not like we haven't already been together. Besides, according to legend, the Moon Goddess is wife of the sun and consorts with other gods, just like the moon crosses paths with the sun and stars and planets. If not for me, you might have ended up spending the night with Yum Kin, Lord of the Sun."

"I might have been better off," she spat, and he glared at her.

"Is that the thanks I get for saving your life?"

"Saving—you tried to drown me. All you care about is yourself. I just happened to be convenient."

Damn her. He should have known she'd act like this. His

jaw hurt, and he realized he was clenching his teeth too tightly to keep from saying what he shouldn't.

He took a deep breath and said calmly, "You're right. I don't like to get wet. I'm a selfish bastard."

"I'm glad we finally agree on something." She turned her head again, staring out the cracks in the walls of the hut. A slight breeze drifted through at last, easing some of the stifling heat.

He ought to leave her, he thought. He really should. She didn't believe in him anyway, and that damned cowardly husband of hers would love to have the chance to put a bullet in his back. The entire situation had gotten completely out of hand, and if he'd any decent sense of self-preservation, he would have made a deal with Yum Kin for the lot of 'em and gone on his way.

But he hadn't. And now here he was, embroiled in it up to his neck and unlikely to wriggle out now without a great deal of trouble.

Keeping silent—partly out of bad temper, but mostly out of that belated sense of survival that he'd recently rediscovered—Steve sat quietly on the woven mat he'd chosen as a seat and watched the light fade outside. A breeze had picked up and was sifting through the ventilated walls to cool off the hut. That was a good sign.

Eden still sat huddled in the voluminous white cotton robe, knees drawn up to her chest and her face averted. In the pale light, her hair took on the sheen of metallic gold threads. He wanted to touch it, to pull her to him and hold her in his arms, to tell her he had no intention of allowing anyone to hurt her.

But he couldn't. He didn't have that right. And she didn't want him to, anyway. He should be furious that she apparently thought he'd let her drown, but he wasn't. He could understand it.

Damn, he was tired. He hadn't rested except for scant snatches of sleep in days. If he allowed himself the luxury, he'd probably commandeer the hammock and sleep for the next week.

Pressing the heels of his hands into his eyes until he saw flashes of light behind the closed lids, Steve kept from yielding to sleep by sheer force of will. He didn't dare risk sleeping until he knew they were safe, until he was certain that nothing would happen to Eden. Damn her.

The tantalizing aroma of cooking food drifted on the wind into the hut, and he stirred at last. "Kabaxbuul," he said aloud, and Eden turned to look at him, a darker shadow against the pale light from outside.

"What?"

"Kabaxbuul." He jabbed a thumb toward the door of the hut. "It's the heaviest meal of the day, eaten at dusk. Usually black beans, and quite tasty."

She studied him for a moment, her eyes a faint gleam in the shadows. "How do you know so much?"

"When I first came to the Yucatán, I met up with a young man who invited me to his home. He wasn't part of the Cruzob, and had never seen a white man before." He smiled faintly. "We discovered common interests, I suppose you could say."

"Which were?" she asked tartly.

"Living without strife." He shrugged when she just stared at him. "Sounds silly to some, perhaps, but it was important to me at the time. Still is."

After a short silence, she asked, "So where is he now? This friend of yours. Do you still see him?"

"No." Steve drew in a deep breath. "He was killed a few years back."

"Oh." Silence, then she said softly, "I'm sorry."

"Yeah. So was I. Ah Thul was a good man, with a sense of humor and a fat little wife and baby. I felt at home there, oddly enough, more so than I'd ever felt in Texas."

Another silence fell, then Eden asked hesitantly, "Were you ever married?"

Steve bent his head to stare at the floor. Long shadows had crept inside, with only slices of light from campfires outside flickering in the hut. "No," he said after a moment. "Not quite."

"Not quite? That sounds undecided."

"Oh, it was quite decisive. Not my choice. Hers. But that was a long time ago, and I never think about it now."

Eden moved, a shift of white cotton in the gray shadows. He could feel her looking at him and wondered what she was thinking. Probably what a bastard he was. That seemed to be her favorite topic of the moment. At least she was talking to him. That was a change from a little earlier. Maybe it would keep him awake. He thought about it, about Eden, and all the events that had brought both of them to the Yucatán.

Without turning his head he said softly, "Your grandparents would be very proud of you, I think." He heard the sharp intake of her breath.

Then she asked in a faintly quivering voice, "Do you think so?"

"Yes. You're very brave. What you did today was more than most people could have done. I know they would be proud of you. And if it means anything, I'm proud of you, too."

Silence fell again, stretching into the soft dusk. Eden didn't move or speak for a long time, just sat staring into space. Then he heard the soft rustle of her garments as she shifted position.

"Steve?"

He turned toward her again, and was surprised when she got up and came to where he sat with his back against the wall. She knelt beside him, and he could see the shadowed curves of her face. His throat tightened. He never knew what she might say or do, this wildly unpredictable female who had managed to thoroughly disrupt his life in so very short a time. He gave her a wary look.

"What do you want?"

"Why do you think I want something? I think perhaps I've misjudged you, that's all. About some things, anyway."

"Yeah. Maybe." He slanted her a speculative glance. "You do seem to have turned my life upside down."

"Me?" She pushed a length of fair hair from her eyes and sat down beside him with her legs crossed. "Why do you say that?"

He smiled faintly. "Just two months ago I was rubbing along quite peacefully, the only excitement in my life coming when Balam managed to bring home a very nasty-tempered kinkajou he obviously intended to save for a midnight snack. The kinkajou—all bristling fur and sharp teeth—had other ideas, and the row grew to a terrific squabble that did a great deal of damage to my hut before I could get them both out with a minimum of danger to myself. Balam sulked for hours about the loss of the kinkajou, that disappeared with angry squalls and in a high dudgeon. Have you ever tried to console a sullen jaguar? Don't. They're very unappreciative."

She laughed. "Rather like me, I suppose you mean."

"Well, yes." He smiled when she cuffed him lightly on the arm with her fist. "Are we friends again, Goldilocks?"

"We always were." She sighed. "I was terrified. I wish you had let me know what you intended to do."

"I wish I could have. But it was impossible, not without alerting them that it might all be a masquerade." He frowned slightly. "Odd, but they've managed to blend a mix of Christian beliefs with ancient rituals that still baffles me at times. It's just not so easy to point out their mistakes or inconsistencies when I'm surrounded by armed men and someone's head on a pole—" He grimaced. "Sorry. Forgot you knew him."

"Yes." She shuddered. "Len Howell was one of the men on our expedition. I hope he didn't suffer."

Steve chose not to reply to that. Instead, he reached out

to draw her close to him, and closed his eyes when she didn't resist. He held her for a few minutes, cradled in the curve of his arm and shoulder. It was moments like these that made it all worthwhile to him. It wasn't exactly a comforting thought, but he'd begun to strongly suspect that he might be in way over his head with this particular female.

How else could he explain all he'd done? It wouldn't have mattered what John Carter said to induce him to leave his camp; if he hadn't been so damn worried about Eden, he would have stayed where he was and the expedition be damned. He didn't give a fig for the jaguar throne, or pieces of jade, or enough gold to fill a cargo ship. It was peace he craved, peace and the fusion of spirit it brought with it. And it occurred to him as he held Eden in the light clasp of his arm, that it was the peace he felt now, with her next to him, when all around them everything else was going to hell in a handbasket.

He held her for a long time, enveloped in peace and the soft feel of her body next to his. She didn't try to move away, and seemed content to lie there next to him. This was what he'd missed most after Colin had come, this silent intimacy. It was reassuring, comforting after the storm of passion had passed. Lying with her in his arms, listening to the sound of her breathing and the feel of her skin like velvet beneath his hand—it had been the only civilized thing he'd missed.

Dragging a hand down the curve of his chest, Eden turned into him and tilted her face up to his. "Steve, do you think we'll be able to escape?"

A faint smile touched the corners of his mouth. He'd been thinking of how good she felt, and she'd been thinking of escape. Which only went to show what a sentimental sap he'd become. He gave her a brief squeeze, then disengaged himself from her arms.

"If it rains, they may let us all go. Gratitude and all that.

I'll just have to convince them they're exceedingly grateful."

She frowned. "There's something you're not telling me. What is it?"

"Turned mind-reader on me after that swim, Goldilocks? I've told you all I know. All you need to know. It's simply guesswork from here on out. Yum Kin may decide we're too much competition for him and send us on our way at first light. Or he might be pleased that he has someone else to share the blame if it doesn't rain." He shrugged. "Either one would be all right with me."

He stood up before she could ask more questions. "Come on, Moon Goddess. I have a feeling we're going to need our rest. If you promise not to molest me, I'll share the hammock with you."

She laughed, but gave him an uncertain glance. He was glad it was dark and shadowed in the hut, so she wouldn't see how he really felt. But when they were finally in the hammock—after several abortive tries when the swag of hemp tried to disgorge them—he wondered if he shouldn't have taken a mat on the floor. Holding her like this, her lithe body pressed so close to his, was pure torture. He'd never be able to give her back to Colin Miller.

And he didn't know how he'd keep from having to do it.

Nineteen

A low, rumbling sound woke her. Eden lay still, trying to adjust to her surroundings. Heat enveloped the hut, making the inside close and stifling. It was pitch dark, and the warmth at her back was Steve. He held her loosely, and his chest rose and fell with a familiar, comforting rhythm. His arm lay over her in a casual caress, reminding her of their nights in his hut. She closed her eyes against the painful memory.

The sound came again, this time louder and more distinct. Her eyes widened. Thunder. It was thunder making that sound, the growling roll that promised rain. The breeze had grown cooler, keeping insects away as well as making the humidity bearable.

Turning slightly, she shook Steve. "Listen," she whispered when he came awake with abrupt alertness, sitting up so quickly he almost dumped them from the hammock. "I think it's going to rain."

Another low roll filled the night, closely followed by a crack of lightning that briefly illuminated the hut and Steve's face. A faint smile curled his mouth. Bracing himself with an arm on each edge of the hammock, he stilled its wild motion.

"About time. I think we're saved, Goldilocks."

She gripped him. "Are we? Oh God, Steve—it's a miracle. You did it."

Pulling her to him, he held her hard against his chest,

so that she could feel the steady beat of his heart against her cheek. "Yeah," he said softly, "I did, didn't I? Must be better than I thought. I wonder if I do have a connection with ole Chac after all." He nuzzled her hair with his mouth and laughed. "Of course, your performance was the clincher. I don't think anyone has actually survived the leap into the sacred cenote in Yum Kin's time, so you truly deserve the goddess title."

"Yes." She put a hand against his chest, fingers spreading over the bare skin where his shirt was open. "I suppose I do. Now that I'm a goddess and you're a god, what happens next?"

"Depends on how much it rains and how grateful they are. I think we'll be on our way tomorrow. Back to the temple and Carter. He's probably wondering where the devil we are by now."

Eden took a deep breath. Tomorrow. Tomorrow they would be Mrs. Eden Miller and Steve Ryan again, not *El Jaguar* and Ixchel. Tomorrow, she would have to give him up.

No. I can't—not without one last night—not without holding him one last time . . .

She didn't say anything when he rose and moved to the clay fire pit, stirring sullen embers into a small glow. Light spread softly around the hut, faint and soft as he came back to the hammock and lowered himself gingerly into the knotted hemp swag. The action rolled him toward her, and he braced himself with one hand against the edge.

"Steve—" Shy, slightly breathless at her own daring after all that had happened, all she'd said and felt and done, she put her hand flat on his chest and looked up at him. "Make love to me again. Please."

Silence fell, broken only by the rolling rumble of thunder and the sound of his heavy breathing. He shifted, and the hammock creaked a protest.

"Goldilocks . . ."

He sounded puzzled, strained, and she wondered if she had dared too much. Didn't he want her? Had she read more into his holding of her than there really was? She started to withdraw, but he put his hand over hers, holding it to his chest.

"God, sweetheart. I want to. You know I do." Spreading his hand on the back of her head, he drew her to him to press a kiss on her forehead. "But we can't."

It was not exactly the response she had envisioned, and Eden's face flamed. She'd made a mistake. She should never have yielded to the temptation. It was wrong. She was married. That would always stand between them.

"You . . . you're right," she choked out. "I don't know what I was thinking . . . it's just that it's all been so terrifying, and you were the only one who was strong and determined . . . I'm sorry."

"Sorry. *Sorry*—God. No, dammit, don't ever be sorry." His voice sounded suddenly fierce, almost savage, and his hands shifted to curl around her arms and hold her tightly. She could feel him looking at her in the shadows, feel the intensity of his gaze boring into her—golden cat-eyes in the dark. "Don't ever be sorry for what happened between us, do you hear? It wasn't wrong. It was—it was the best thing that's ever happened to me, and I'll be damned if I'll be sorry for it."

She began to sob then, softly at first, as emotions buffeted her from all sides. It was wicked. She knew it was. But she wished Colin weren't between them. Not that he was dead, just that he would vanish. Like a puff of smoke. But reality intruded, and she knew that he would always be there, between them as solidly as a stone wall.

"Don't cry," Steve said tightly, his voice caught between a groan and frustration. "I can't stand to hear you cry—ah, please sweetheart. No more tears. It's raining. Do you hear it? We'll be fine now . . ."

Lightning cracked, illuminating the small interior of the

hut with a brilliant flash. Eden lifted her face to his and saw in that split second of brilliance the bitter slant of his mouth and the half-lowered curve of his lashes. She recognized the distress in his eyes.

"Jesus," he said, with another groan, heartfelt and sounding as if it were torn from his soul. "I must have lost my mind . . . this may be our last time together. I don't want to be a noble bastard and do what's right. I want to be myself—as selfish and despicable as always. Yes. I want you—I want to put myself inside you and hold you in my arms until we're both too weak to walk. But you don't belong to me. You don't. Do you hear me?"

"You're right," she said with a sob, "it's all wrong. We . . . we shouldn't . . ."

Then it didn't matter what he said or she said, or what either of them had done or felt. Firmly, almost roughly, he was pulling her to him, his mouth hard and hot on hers, his tongue invading her open lips with searing thrusts. Eden felt reality sway out of reach with the same wild motions as the hammock, and she clutched at the rope sides with both hands while Steve moved over her.

Thunder rolled outside, and the crash of lightning lit the sky and the hut with shimmering brightness. It was close inside, the air still holding traces of warmth in the musty breezes that slipped through the cracks in the walls. The flash of light illuminated him, the sharp angles and shadowed planes, the fierce glitter in his tawny eyes. She cupped a hand on each side of his face, her fingers tracing the harsh outline of his mouth and grazing the rough stubble of beard on his jaw.

"God, Eden," Steve muttered thickly. His arms tightened around her trembling body, one hand slipping up her arm to tangle in the heavy weight of her hair, fanning it over her shoulders. The pressing need to bury her face into the curve of his neck and shoulder was irresistible.

It was frightening—the power he had over her. Slowly,

as if he tried to resist and lost, Steve's mouth claimed hers again, whirling her from despair into hope. She felt as if she was drowning again, sinking deeper and deeper into the cenote, submerged in the overwhelming waves of desire. Nothing else mattered; she was oblivious to everything but the driving, primitive need to couple with this man.

Swinging wildly, the hammock shifted balance as they moved. Steve swore softly under his breath and lifted his head. Shivering, she clung to him with fierce tenacity, hands moving to pull his head back down, aching for his kisses with a hunger that seemed infinite.

"Wait, love," he said in a half-groan. "Wait . . ."

Why was he waiting? Why did he want to wait when he could be kissing her, could be making love to her. . . . Eden buried her face against the rapid pulse at the base of his throat and felt the thundering beat that matched her own. It would be the last time. There was a precious quality to this moment, for after tonight, she would go back to her world, and he to his. There would be no tomorrows for them, nothing but long years ahead of her without Steve.

Aching with the bittersweet clarity of premonition, Eden had no intention of allowing anything to come between them now. She clung to him, kissing him even while he sat up and pulled her with him, swinging his legs over the side of the hammock.

"We're liable," he said softly, "to end up being dumped on the floor. Here. Come with me."

She rose with him, silent and compliant as he spread cotton blankets atop a few of the woven mats, then gestured for her to join him. She came to where he still knelt on the floor on one knee and looked down at him, at his dark head and uplifted face, a shadowy blur in the night.

Bending her head with a slight smile, she shivered as he moved to face her, both legs spread, knees pressing into the thick pallet of mats and blankets. His hands touched her ankles, slipping up her calves beneath the hem of her long

robe, fingers soft and exploring. She shivered. Bunching
the robe in his fists, Steve gathered it slowly upward, holding it against her hips. Sighing, Eden lay her palms lightly
on his dark head. She moved beneath his searching hands,
shuddering at the reactions he provoked.

It felt so familiar, so right for him to be doing this,
drowning out all the pain and guilt . . . there would be no
intrusions between them tonight. Only love.

Steve sat back on his heels and looked up at her, the
hem of her robe still clutched in his fists. A faint smile
touched the corners of his mouth as he gazed up at her, his
face a hellish cast of shadow and light and the devil's own
dreams in his gold eyes.

"I've dreamed of this, y'know," he said softly, shaping
his palms over her calves and up to her knees. "Touching
you like this. Holding you again. Kissing you . . . here."

She drew in a sharp breath when he leaned forward to
graze the sensitive skin of her upper thigh with his lips.
The gown moved upward, a slow slide of cotton against her
trembling skin. Cool air washed over her, making her legs
tremble, causing her to clutch at him with faint, fluttering
movements. A quick, rapid tumult began in her belly, low
and insistent.

Steve's mouth moved to the inner skin of her thighs, then
upward to the cleft between. His tongue was warm, heated
velvet, washing over her and making her moan. Sensation
shot through her in scalding arrows.

"Steve . . ." Breathless, needy, and hopeful, her voice
trembled. Her fingers curled in his thick black hair and held
him.

A wordless sound was her reply as he slid his hands up
over the bare skin of her legs to her buttocks and pulled
her closer to him, holding her hard against his seeking
tongue. The tantalizing rhythm made her squirm with torment, and her breath came hard and ragged. Even with the
noise of the storm outside, she bit her lower lip to keep

from crying out as he brought her to the brink of release, kissing and caressing until her knees buckled and she fell forward with her hands braced on his shoulders.

He rose to his feet, taking the robe with him as he did, tossing it aside to fall in a snowy puddle on the floor. Then he pulled her against him, and the exquisite sensation of her tender breasts against his skin and shirt made her shudder. Cupping them in his palms, he bent to kiss her again, letting his thumbs rake over her swollen nipples in arousing provocation.

Moaning, Eden's head fell back under the onslaught of his mouth, and she arched into his embrace. With her belly pressed against him, she could feel the hard nudge of his arousal. Moving her hips in silent invitation, she slid a hand down to caress him, fingers shaping the solid outline beneath his trousers.

Steve's groan was muffled against her mouth, and he muttered, "Let's get rid of these damned clothes, shall we? It's positively uncivilized . . ."

She helped him, casting a shy glance up at his face as she tugged away his shirt and helped unbutton his pants. Long black eyelashes shadowed his eyes as he looked down, and when she touched him lightly, running her fingertips up the rigid shaft straining toward her, he shuddered.

Steve's murmur of pleasure ignited a fiery response in her, and when his clothes were gone and he came to her, kneeling over her on the thick pallet, she opened her thighs in aching expectation. He moved over her, his body sliding between her legs without entering, slipping against the moisture. Her breath came faster, and her arms curled around his body to hold him.

Bending, Steve's mouth scoured the sensitive slope of her throat and shoulder, his weight driving her deeper into the blankets. She clutched at him wildly. His breath was hot against her skin. The agonizing thrust and drag of him between her thighs swept her to a fever-pitch of excitement, and she tugged at him with both her hands, urging him closer, urging him to move inside her.

She arched her hips, flexing into the strokes, needing to feel him deep inside. But he held back, his body raking against her in tantalizing thrusts, stopping short of penetration. Eden tilted her hips for his next thrust.

"Steve," she whimpered softly, "please . . ."

His shoulders were damp, slippery beneath her clutching fingers as he shifted slightly. His voice was thick, words muffled by her hair.

"Not . . . yet."

Frustration made her arch toward him again as he thrust forward, so that he came against her moist entrance with a hard, sweet pressure. "God," he said roughly, panting. Then he sat back on his bent legs, staring down at her, his face intent in the soft light. Deliberately, slowly, he pulled her over his folded thighs until he was brushing against her. Then he dragged his male hardness over her, over the throbbing cleft between her thighs, making her gasp. He rubbed her center with slow, luxurious strokes, sliding over her quivering flesh with rhythmic thrusts of his body. Her hands grasped handfuls of air, opening and closing as he moved against her, bringing her again to that brink of release. With his shoulders shaking with strain and his breath coming hard and fast between his clenched teeth, Steve gave a long, convulsive shudder.

Twisting under him, Eden tried to draw him closer, pull him to her and inside, but he held back. He glanced up at her, a sulky drift of lashes over his eyes. But he wouldn't slip inside her, wouldn't yield to the silent urging of her body. And then it didn't matter, because that teasing friction swept her up and over the edge and into shattering release. She cried out, body shuddering with explosive tremors, and then he was pulling back and moving over her, his weight driving them deeply into the blankets.

Holding her against him, he shoved roughly against her

belly, his hard male shape hot and heavy. Then he shuddered, a long groan in her ear, his body jerking in tight spasms as he held her hard against him. Eden lay still, panting for breath, not quite certain what had happened.

A soft moan deep in his throat curled past her ear, and she turned her face slightly to touch him. After a moment, he shifted to look at her, his eyes sleepy. A faint, bitter smile curled his mouth.

"I'm not certain of the fine line between actually committing adultery and thinking about it, but this is too damn close to call."

When he rolled to his back, she managed a smile. "I was right, you know."

His dark brow arched questioningly. "Yeah? About what?"

Trailing a finger down the curling damp line of hairs on his chest, she murmured, "You really are a hero."

He caught her hand, his voice soft and faintly puzzled. "You say the damndest things, Goldilocks."

"Yes." Her smile wavered slightly, and she looked up at his face, at the sweet, beautiful curve of his lashes and the sensual lines of his mouth, the masculine planes and angles that formed the man she loved. "I do, don't I."

It rained all night. Morning came with steaming heat and only fitful sunshine. More clouds were banked overhead, sullen and gray and threatening rain. Steve accepted the adulation of the villagers with solemn composure. All he wanted was out of here. And damned quick.

After negotiating with Yum Kin for the release of the other two captives, Steve wondered crossly why he had bothered. Colin Miller was petulant and ungrateful, and all Richard could think about was getting back to the damned temple and his precious jaguar throne.

Irritated beyond belief, Steve stood with crossed arms

and waited for the two men to depart the hut. You'd think they'd be damn glad to leave, but Colin was whining about his boots not fitting, and Richard had found a most "fascinating piece of Mayan pottery" that he was trying to coax out of its present owner's possession.

"Leave the damned thing," Steve snapped finally, and when Richard shot him a startled glance, he added, "I know where you can get a lot of that stuff, if that's what's causing the delay."

"You do?" Richard's eyes widened hopefully. "Excellent. Nearby, I hope. Ah, I shall be the most celebrated man to return from the Yucatán."

"If you don't hurry, you won't return at all. They're not too thrilled to see you two leave. I had to do some fancy negotiating to get you released, so let's go before they change their minds. It might stop raining. Or it might rain so hard they'll want me to stop it. That would entail another sacrifice, and at this point, you two are high on my list of expendable people."

"I'm sure you don't have Eden on that list," Colin muttered, and met Steve's quick, hard glance with defiance. "I don't know where she spent the last few nights. But it wasn't here. And I've a good notion who was with her."

"Then keep it to yourself. I sure as hell don't want to hear it, and neither does she." Steve's mouth twisted. He shouldn't have bothered turning himself inside out to keep from committing adultery—technically, anyway. Colin wouldn't have appreciated his efforts at all. But he hadn't done it for him. He'd done it for Eden, even when he wanted her so bad it hurt. But he wasn't about to be the cause of more pain for her, or more feelings of guilt. There was enough of that going around without adding to it.

Besides, he had other things to worry about that were a lot more important than Colin's ruffled feathers. Troubling questions had come up in his last conversation with Yum Kin—now he wanted some answers. Not just from Richard and Colin, but from John Carter. It was troubling that Yum Kin seemed to think the captives had been sent to him for sacrifice—not by the gods, but by one of their own. That bothered him. A lot. But when he'd pressed the village h-men for more details, the old man had been obstinately silent on the subject. Not a good sign.

It was as if, Steve thought irritably, the entire damn jungle was in on some gigantic conspiracy. Everyone had their own agendas, their own motives, and he was the only one he knew of that just wanted to live in peace.

"Get moving," he snapped when Richard and Colin were finally ready. "It looks like rain again." He stalked across the central court without looking back. They could follow or not. He was tired of pampering them. And he wasn't quite certain how he would react when he saw Eden again. Coward that he was, he'd left the hut before she awoke, not wanting to face her quite yet. He wondered if she would be aloof and pretend last night had never happened, or whether she would incite Colin with some sort of inflammatory word or action. She was, he'd discovered previously, very unpredictable.

Eden was waiting outside the hut where they'd spent the night, dressed once more in her former garments, the loose shirt and trousers. The only difference was a pair of sandals instead of boots, and he gave her a quizzical glance.

She grimaced. "My boot laces finally broke beyond repair. I would have used a length of twine, but one of the women insisted I accept the gift of her sandals. She called them *eexanab*, or something like that."

Steve smiled slightly. "Xanab—*ix-a-nab* in this part of the country. Other regions use the X at the front of the word like *eesh*. All right. Ready to go?"

She nodded; "More than ready. I've been given gifts according to my new status as goddess, so I'm afraid we have some baggage to carry."

He held out his hand. "I'll carry it."

Eden bent to pick up a square bundle, a blanket wrapped around several items. As she handed it to him, their hands briefly touched and she colored slightly, averting her face. Just as well. He didn't need to worry about goading Colin Miller any more than necessary. There had been murder in his eyes earlier, and that always presented a nasty situation.

Weighing the bundle, he said lightly, "Got the village treasure in here, Goldilocks?"

She flashed him a faint smile and shook her head. "No. Just gifts. For bringing rain, I suppose, though I tried to tell them that it was you who managed that particular miracle."

"Oh, no, you survived the trial by water. You're lucky they still think you're Ixchel instead of Ah Itzam. Being a goddess is a sight more pleasing than being a water witch."

"Let's just go," she said in a pleading tone, "before I learn something else I'd rather not know."

He grinned, glancing over his shoulder. "As soon as— here they come now. Pay attention to what I say and do, and I'll try to get us out of here quickly."

There was another exchange of words with Yum Kin before they left, and Steve had the unmistakable impression that the village h-men was as glad for them to go as they were glad to be going. A rival priest probably wasn't too good for his business, and having the moon goddess descend upon the village could certainly complicate matters.

Still, as they finally took their leave, escorted from the village along a narrow path through the forest, Steve couldn't shake the uneasy feeling that the danger wasn't behind them yet. He didn't know what it was, some chance word or glance, even just a vague nuance of some kind, but he didn't feel safe. Not yet.

Their escort took them several miles from the village before turning back, and Steve paused to get his bearings. He should be more familiar with this area. He'd spent time here a few years earlier, when Ah Thul Uuc had still been alive. Ah Thul—translated to Seven Rabbit—had been the closest thing to a friend he'd had in the Yucatán; other than Balam, which didn't quite count. It was Ah Thul Uuc who had taught him how to survive, which plants to eat and which to avoid like the plague, and it had been Ah Thul Uuc who had saved his life more than once.

"Which way now?" Colin asked impatiently. "Or do you know?"

Steve turned to look at him. "You can take off in any direction you like if you're not happy with the way I'm guiding us."

Colin looked away, his mouth twisted in a scowl. "No, you're better than nothing. It's just that it's hot standing here without moving, and the insects are a damned nuisance."

"Then let's go."

Twenty

Moonlight silvered the air and tops of the trees, but barely pierced the thick foliage to illuminate the ground high atop the hill. Steve put out a hand to stop the group and they waited, their breathing sounding loud in the smothering silence. People moved below, at the base of a towering hulk that was black against the lighter sky.

Eden shivered. In the pale, ghostly light, she saw the definite outlines of a temple, now cleared of trees and some of the brush that had obscured it for centuries. Fires dotted the ground, lighting a cluster of tents that sprouted like pale mushrooms. If not for that, she would have thought she was viewing the temple as it must have looked many years before.

She looked toward Steve. He still waited, not moving, his face a stark silhouette against the pale light shimmering around them. If nothing else, she had learned to trust his instincts. She remained quiet, waiting for him to move forward.

Several minutes passed, while overhead a faint breeze blew leaves in a whispering rush, and the sleepy murmurs of birds drifted groundward. Insects hummed loudly.

"What the devil are you waiting for?" Colin finally asked in an impatient whisper. "It's John Carter down there."

"I don't know." Steve took a deep breath, shoulder muscles tense beneath his cotton shirt. "I don't like it. There's something . . . wrong."

Richard had come to the edge of the hill opposite the temple, and he peered down into the camp over Steve's shoulder. "It looks quiet, Mr. Ryan. I don't see anything unusual, except that it appears Sir John has brought along a large entourage." His tone was disapproving when he muttered, "He didn't have to do that. I'm quite capable of heading the excavation on my own. I did not request help."

Ignoring Richard, Eden watched Steve. He was squinting at the campfires and temple with a taut expression. Heat and humidity had plastered his dark hair to his neck. In the faint light, his eyes glittered. "I don't like it," he repeated.

"Well I don't intend to stand up here all night waiting until you decide you *do* like it," Colin snapped. "We can see they're our men down there. It's Sir John. What do you think he'll do—kill us? I refuse to skulk in the bushes slapping at mosquitoes and slowly dying of thirst while you hem and haw." He turned to go down the slope toward the temple.

"Colin," Eden said, "don't go. Wait. I know it looks safe, but be certain first."

Colin turned, his face a pale blur in the moonlight. "This is ridiculous. Ryan just wants to show off. To impress you with what a marvelous guide he is. If he was that damned good, we'd never have ended up staying a week in a village waiting to be beheaded like poor Len Howell."

"You're not being fair. It wasn't Steve's fault we were taken captive. And he got us out alive, didn't he? Don't be so impatient, Colin."

He glared at her. "Do you think I don't know what's going on between you two? I do. I'm not stupid. Maybe I'm not in a position to do anything about it right now, but—"

"Shut up."

Soft and menacing, Steve's order made Colin stiffen. He shot a quick, hostile glance toward Steve, then said tightly,

"I don't have to listen to you. I'm going down there. Eden. You come with me. Eden. *Eden,* are you coming?"

"I . . . I'll be down in a minute."

His eyes narrowed and he flicked a glance at Steve before saying to her, "Fine. When you get tired of playing games out here, I expect you to join me."

Pivoting on his heel, Colin stalked away, disappearing through the thick brush crowding the slope. Steve didn't say anything, but turned back to stare down the hill. Eden hesitated. Maybe she should follow Colin. He was probably right. John Carter would hardly kill members of his own expedition.

Richard cleared his throat after several moments passed in silence. "I say, it does seem quite safe down there. Those aren't natives we're dealing with. I respect your knowledge and intuition, but perhaps the recent events have put you a bit too much on edge."

Raking a hand over his face, Steve muttered with a faintly embarrassed shrug, "Yeah, maybe you're right. I don't know what it is. Sometimes . . . sometimes I just get these feelings." He turned, and moonlight touched his face with a silvery mist. Shadows darkened his eyes. He lifted his shoulders again, and his voice was uncertain. "It's just . . . a feeling. That's all."

Eden put her hand on his arm, and he gave a quick, violent start. She applied pressure and said soothingly, "After everything that's happened, it's a wonder we're not all spooked. I certainly am."

He nodded, but there was a wary tension in his eyes that lingered behind the outward compliance. "Yeah," he said again. "I guess you're right."

When she turned to look down below, all was quiet and normal. Smoke curled up from fires, and people moved about easily. No sign of danger. No sign of a threat. A snatch of song drifted on the thick night air. Toucans shrilled familiar rasping croaks like frogs in the trees.

Richard coughed politely, and said, "I think I'll join my colleagues now."

Steve didn't look at him. "Be careful. Warn 'em you're coming in."

"Yes. Yes, Of course. That would be wise, I'm certain. Well. Well. Uh, Eden? Are you—"

"Yes. In a few minutes. I think I'll wait here a moment or two longer." She managed a faint smile. "Tell Colin I'll be with him shortly. After all that's happened, I doubt he can be much more angry."

"True." Richard hesitated, then gave an embarrassed cough and said, "See you shortly, then."

Eden didn't watch him leave. She kept her gaze on Steve, still staring tensely down into the camp.

"Why do you think it's unsafe?" she asked when Richard had gone. He turned to look at her.

"I told you, I don't know. It's nothing definite, you see, no open threat. But there's been trouble in the area, so many attacks—to go in at night, without warning, is inviting danger. If it was me, I'd have a defense ready—I'd be expecting trouble. After all that's happened . . . I should never have let you go with them in the first place." He sounded fretful now, and half-angry. "I knew it was stupid. All that damned talk of the temple and throne and everyone looking for it— but you wouldn't listen. Wouldn't make a choice. Wouldn't even look at me. What was I supposed to do? You're married to another man. I have no right. No right to stop you, no right to hold you—but I couldn't let you wander around the jungle with half the world looking for you. Christ."

He raked a hand through his hair, looking miserable in the bleak light. Eden stared at him helplessly. Her throat tightened against a surge of emotion. He'd never said it, but he must care for her. Beneath the sardonic mockery and light words he used to cover his feelings, he cared. She smiled slightly. Too late. Always too late for her. It had been too late when she'd met him, but she hadn't known that. And she was glad, fiercely glad that she'd not known Colin was still alive. Because then she would not have felt free to fall in love. And even though it was painful to lose him, to have lived her life without ever having known Steve would have been even worse.

She put a hand on his arm. "Steve, let's not go down there just yet. Let's stay here."

Shifting position, he moved to look down at her. Some of the tension in him eased; she could feel the slight relaxing of the muscles in his forearm. He took a deep breath and nodded.

"Yeah. We'll . . . stay here a while."

He looked around, rather absently, as if searching for something, and Eden tugged at her blanket-wrapped bundle. "We can sit on this, if you like. It's just my clothes. And the few things I was given by some of the women."

"A few things, huh. Nothing sharp, I hope."

She laughed. "Not that I know about. Of course, I didn't really look at most of it. I was in a hurry to leave."

"Yeah, so was I." Moonlight winked over him in silvery flashes, making long shadows across his face. They sat in silence for a long time. When he looked up at her again, Eden could see uncertainty in his eyes. "It's all too—easy," he said suddenly. "Don't you see? We were ambushed back there on the path. They knew we would be there. Yum Kin told me they'd been warned of our coming, that we would be suitable sacrifices. Four intruders, white strangers in their land, would meet the same fate as your friend Len Howell. But when they found out who we were—at least according to the myths—they were unpleasantly surprised. If not for religious superstition, our heads would be on poles or our bodies floating in the cenote—I think Yum Kin was just as shocked as me."

"But why?" she asked after a moment. "Who would want to see us dead other than the Cruzob? And if it was the Cruzob, wouldn't they have already come after us?"

"Yeah." He looked down at the machete he held in his hand like a sword. His chest lifted in a baffled sigh. "Yeah. You're right. I'm just being overly suspicious."

Eden leaned forward to offer some word of comfort to him. But then there was a loud shout, followed by a pop. Steve's head jerked up, and his grip tightened on the machete. He surged to his feet and stepped forward, staring intently down the slope to the camp. There was another shout, this time more of a cry, and he swore softly.

When she turned to look down the hill, Steve grabbed her by the elbow and pulled her away. "No—don't look. No time for that—come on."

"But what was that noise?" It was a question she already knew the answer to, but she couldn't help asking anyway. It was too monstrous to imagine, that John Carter would open fire on members of his own expedition. "Steve, there must be some kind of mistake," she managed to gasp as he pulled her with him through a tangle of brush. She couldn't see in front of her and was following him blindly. There didn't seem to be a path, only green darkness surrounding them, swallowing them up. Panting, she insisted, "It's all a mistake. We have to go back—to help them . . ."

Ignoring her, he kept going. He moved swiftly, hacking aside leafy barriers with efficient slices of the machete. It was steep, with the slope angling sharply downward. She stumbled once and he jerked her to her feet, barely pausing. Her breath was loud in her ears, vying with the thunder of her heartbeat. Birds shrilled protests, and underlying the familiar jungle noises were the faint sounds of human distress. Her side ached, pinching beneath her ribs with sharp stabs of pain. When she gasped out a plea to wait, he didn't reply, but bent to scoop her into his arms.

Steve's urgency was more terrifying than the jungle noises, than even not knowing what exactly had happened. She clung to him as if she were drowning. Everything was a blur; the hot night and sullen air, rasping, tortured breaths that she wasn't certain were hers or his—it all blended into one long nightmarish fog.

Gradually she became aware that they had stopped finally, that it was cool and quiet and musty-smelling. "Steve?" It was a faint whimper like a lost child in the dark. She couldn't see anything, not even her hand in front of her face.

"Yeah. I'm right here, Goldilocks. Just hold on a minute . . ."

After a brief scratching sound, there was a sulfuric flare, then a steady gleam. Steve's face came into focus, sharply shadowed from the glow of a lamp. She stared at him, then dared to look around. A gasp caught in the back of her throat. Fantastic figures loomed, dancing in eerie patterns over high walls. Serpents, jaguars, fantastic birds and humans writhed in various postures. Limestone crusted much of the mural. Her gaze shifted back to Steve's face, where a faint smile slanted his mouth.

"Pretty impressive, huh. I found this place a while back. As far as I know, no one else knows of its existence. Except maybe a few wandering Indians. And the little *toh.*"

She swallowed hard, and murmured, "Toe?"

His lashes flickered, dark shadows against his cheeks. "The motmot bird. They like to nest in the ruins. Fitting, I think."

Eden pushed herself to a sitting position, blinking at the steady glow of the lamp. Steve sat cross-legged across from her. It was obvious he'd been here before. Evidence of recent habitation was apparent by the mats they were sitting on and the various objects such as the lamp he'd placed in a small stone niche.

She shoved a hand through her hair. It hung limply in her eyes, damp and cluttered with leaves and bits of moss. She began to finger-comb her hair, idly, the act more for comfort than appearance. "Where are we?"

Steve hesitated, then shrugged. "It's an old temple. There

are a whole series of them here. Some accessible, most not. I used to come here sometimes to—think. Commune with the gods, sort of. It's quiet and peaceful. Like a confirmation of eternity."

Drawing in a deep breath, she summoned the courage to ask, "What happened back there? At the temple of the jaguar?"

There was another hesitation, then his eyes met hers, liquid gold and solemn. "They shot Colin."

The silence seemed to close in around her, soft and suffocating. She must not have heard him right. Shaking her head, she said, "That can't be true."

"It is." He was watching her carefully, face still and guarded. "I saw him go down."

"But—why?"

"Your guess is as good as mine. I didn't intend to stick around to find out. Those men didn't look to be in a chatty mood. If I haven't learned anything else, I *have* learned to mind my own business when it comes to grouchy men with guns."

"Colin, shot? It can't be. And Richard—dear God. Was he—?"

"I don't know. I didn't see him. All I saw was Colin."

"Is he . . . dead?"

"It didn't look good," Steve said carefully, and this time his eyes were looking past her, at a spot on the far wall. After a moment when she didn't say anything, he shifted his eyes to her face. "He could be alive."

"But you don't think so."

"No."

She drew in a deep breath, too exhausted and confused to examine her emotions. It was all so fantastic, so unimaginable, that after all they had been through, Colin could have been killed like that. Sorrow for what should have been brought tears to her eyes. She hadn't loved him, but his death was needless. To be killed by mistake like that. . . .

An alarming idea occurred to her. She looked up at Steve with a frown.

"It *was* a mistake, wasn't it?"

His eyes skittered away again, and he shrugged. "I wasn't down there. I don't know."

"But wasn't that John Carter down there? He's the man who hired us to come on this expedition, who—" She stopped. Colin had said he'd been dealing with other investors. Was it possible strangers were down there and had shot him? No, Richard had recognized Sir John. So had Colin. She closed her eyes. Her head hurt, her side still ached, and she was frightened. Shaking her head, she said blindly, "Things like this don't happen. Not after everything else. Not after a massacre . . . that horrible battle and all the blood . . . and almost drowning in that disgusting well." She opened her eyes.

"Things like this don't happen," she repeated hopefully. He didn't answer. Instead, he looked away, a highlighted silhouette as dark and mysterious as the painted figures on the temple wall.

"Steve?"

Sighing, he looked back at her and reached for her hand. "I don't have any answers. None that make sense, anyway."

"You knew—you didn't want to go down there. How did you know what would happen?"

"I didn't know. It was just a—feeling. Something was wrong, but I couldn't put it into words. It wasn't anything definite. Do you understand?"

He sounded almost pleading, and she nodded slowly. "I think so. Intuition. Instinct. Maybe they're the same thing. Maybe we should have waited to see what happened. It could all be a huge mistake. Like you said—coming in at night in a land where any stranger could be a threat . . ." She looked up when he made a strangled sound.

"No, we shouldn't have waited. It was too dangerous. Christ. All this damn conflict over a stupid throne that's not even there—" He jerked to a halt, then drew in a deep breath.

"How do you know," she asked slowly, "that the throne is not there?"

Shaking his head, he said wearily, "Because it's here." He waved a hand at the painted walls and lichened stones. "Right here where it's been for a thousand years."

Eden stared at him in the fitful light of the oil lamp. Her eyes were dark blue and wide, looking like bruises in her pale face. She gave a slight shake of her head. "Here?"

"Yeah." He grimaced at her disbelieving stare. "I found it a few years back. Idle exploring, you understand. I'd been hunting and kind of stumbled over this place. It looks like a hill from the outside, just like the one you call temple of the jaguar." He smiled faintly. "We were standing on it earlier, you know. It's opposite the other one . . . don't look at me like that. I told you from the start that I wasn't interested in finding any damn jaguar throne."

"But you knew . . . all this time, you knew" Her voice was accusing and slightly breathless. "When I think of all that could have been saved if you'd just told us—"

"All of what? What would have been saved?" He glared at her. "Nothing would have been saved. You'd still have come here, Carter would still have looked for you, and there would still be a lot of squabbling over who found what. I was trying to head it off, that's all."

"Why?"

"I told you, dammit. Why would I want dozens of expeditions down here crowding up the place? It's damned inconvenient as it is, with females rolling down hills and husbands showing up when they're supposed to be dead— Christ. I didn't mean that, Eden."

"Yes, you did." Rosy light flickered over her face, and he saw the shadows in her eyes. He shrugged.

"Yeah, but not the part about inconvenient females. You would never be inconvenient. Never."

Eden looked down at her hands clasped in her lap, fingers twining with nervous gestures. After several moments she looked up again, and his eyes narrowed at the expression on her face.

"Steve, I want some answers from you. The truth. No evasions."

"I'll have to hear the questions before I can promise that." When she just stared at him, he muttered, "All right. Fire away."

"Let's start at the beginning—why are you really here in the Yucatán?"

"I already told you. I came down to get away from everything. The disillusion of shattered lives after the war and all that noble stuff," he said mockingly. "Is that what you want to hear?"

"Is it the truth?"

"Basically." He shrugged. "Losing the war was bad enough. When I went home, I discovered my betrothed had married someone else. There. Is that detailed enough for you? Do you want to hear how bitter I was about it? Heartbroken? All that maudlin stuff that people love to hear when it happens to someone else?"

"I just want some honest answers. Reasons for some of the things you say and do—"

"Reasons." He stared at her. "Hell, if you're looking for logic, Goldilocks, you won't find it here. Not with me. I excel in illogic. Highest marks in my class."

She took a deep breath and settled her hands in her lap. "Are you looting the temples and selling artifacts to private collectors?"

"Christ." He should have suspected it, but it was still a bitter blow to hear how little she thought of him. "I don't have to ask where you heard that, I suppose."

"Actually, it was Richard who told me. He'd heard it from officials in Merída. Are you?"

"I don't think I'll answer that," he said coolly. "Next question."

She looked up. "You said you shot your commanding officer for sending men to their deaths. Is that true?"

He made a sound that was half-laugh, half-pain. She had to know it all. Damn her. Damn them all, every last one. It was hopeless, as he'd always known, but there it was. He had to own up to what he'd done eventually. He'd just been hoping for a different judge and jury.

Shrugging, he said, "It was a duel. Over a card game, as a matter of fact. He lost, and called me out." A grim smile curled his mouth as he remembered the moment with relish. "He was only half-right when he said I was cheating. I didn't have to, but I would have. I couldn't think of another way to get him mad enough to do something dumb enough to risk dying for. I plied him with enough good sour mash bourbon to cloud his judgment and let nature take its course. The hue and cry was deafening. Dueling, you see, is against the law, even for gentlemen in Texas. They call 'em gunfights now, unless one of the men is a three-star general. Even defeated generals have a great deal of prestige, it seems. So. That satisfy your curiosity?"

"Is that why you wouldn't take me to Merída? Because you're wanted for murder and looting?"

For a long moment, he didn't say anything. He listened to the heavy silence of the ancient temple and the soft sound of her breathing. He really should tell her the truth. It would serve her right. Why did she insist upon knowing everything? Uncovering all his past? If he didn't stop her, she would have him confessing to every dirty deed he'd done, including looking up Mary Ann Wright's skirt when he was ten years old and too curious for his own good.

Feeling maligned and quite sorry for himself, Steve said

slowly and deliberately, "Yes. I told you I'd be shot if they saw me, and it was the truth. Happy now?"

She looked stricken. "No," she whispered. "I was hoping—"

"That I'd say it wasn't true? That it's all a mistake? You should have realized by now that life has a charming way of making fools out of all of us." He stood up, running a hand through his hair and trying to sort out the reasons why he'd felt compelled to allow her to ask these questions. He'd known it would end badly. It always did. "Don't feel bad, Goldilocks. You're not the first person I've disillusioned with a confession." Shrugging bitterly, he turned to look at her, waiting for the disgust to show in her face. "My own father couldn't handle the truth. I won't blame you for feeling the same. Just don't turn up your toes on me like he did when he found out what a wicked fellow I am. It gets damned inconvenient to have to keep burying your mistakes."

"Steve—I don't know what you mean."

"Let me enlighten you—when the news about me and the general got out, my father keeled over. Bad heart, the doctor said, but everyone knew the truth. It was the shock of finding out his only son was a murderer. That's what did the old man in. So I left Texas, left the United States. I came here, where no one would know me and no one would care."

Drawing in a deep breath, he stared at a spot on the wall as the memories rushed in. More to himself than Eden, he mused, "I thought I could live alone. Hurt no one. But it didn't work out that way. There was Ah Thul—a simple man who saved my life. I should have been able to return the favor. Instead, I got him killed for his help. I didn't know, you see, didn't realize that when the Cruzob took me captive, they would hardly be pleased at any man who helped me escape. But Ah Thul didn't want to see me end my days working henequen fields. He came for me, got me away—and they took their revenge."

For a moment it was quiet, the silence pressing down on them like a blanket. Eden didn't speak, didn't ask any questions, and he was oddly grateful. He looked at her, at her pale face and the cloud of golden hair spreading over her shoulders. Like an angel. A goddess. His goddess, his angel.

"I was the one who found him," he said suddenly. "It was bad, what they'd done—I went berserk. For weeks after, I hid in the bushes, only coming out to kill. I burned two villages, took no prisoners—it was war. Then they left me alone. None of them would bother me. I don't know how or why—" He took a deep breath. "I'll never understand what happened. Later, when I could think about it without going mad, I sold some things I found in a temple and took the money to Ah Thul's widow. She had no man to look after her, you see, and he was dead because of me. Yes, I did loot the temples. But it wasn't for me. Not completely. I mean, I didn't use the money. Ah hell—it's the same thing. It was for me. Guilt. Blood money. Consolation for the death of a good man. But it didn't save my soul."

"Steve," Eden said finally, her voice soft in the murky light, "you were not to blame for Ah Thul's death. He was a man who made his own choices—just like you. Don't you see that?"

"But what kind of consolation prize is there for the death of a good man? None. Men like the general deserve to die. Complacent and swollen up with their own vanity, not caring what happens to the men who trusted them—but I did. And so help me, I'd do it again. If he was here, I'd shoot him again and know that I'd done the world a favor. It's only fair."

Twenty-one

"You have strange notions of what's fair," Eden said after several minutes of thick silence. Lamplight flickered in odd, distorted patterns over the temple walls. She shivered suddenly.

"Well?" he asked after a lengthy pause, his voice as sullen as his expression. "Have you decided my fate yet?"

She smiled faintly. "A life sentence."

"Unfair. I'd rather be executed. It's quicker and a lot less painful in the long run."

Eden studied his face. His features were darkly grim above the white blur of his cotton shirt; despite his light mockery, there was an air of fatal intensity about him. What was the matter? It was more than her prying into his past. He resented it, obviously, but there was more underlying his bitterness than that.

Looking down, she plucked idly at a leather strap on the sandals she'd been given. Maybe it was this land that provoked such intensity. Everything here was extreme. The heat. The rain. The choking green darkness that smothered ancient temples. The people. Yes. Maybe it was this land that made everything seem extravagant. Too much color, too much time, too much danger—just too much.

Steve sat down again, crossing his long legs at the ankle and leaning back against the wall. He made her think of a wary jaguar, all lean muscle and tension. He closed his eyes, but she could still feel the tension in him. It vibrated

just below the surface, that ever-present wariness that had
saved their lives more than once.

What was the matter with her? What did she want? He
wasn't perfect. He'd admitted it. He wasn't in the Yucatán
to hide from the past. He was here to hide from himself.
It was evident. And it struck her that, behind her outward
vows of being dedicated to preserving antiquities, it was
the real reason she'd wanted to come to Mexico as well.
To hide from her life, from what she'd become with Colin.
A coward. Too afraid to face the truth, the fact that she'd
made mistake upon mistake, one after the other until they'd
built up so high the wall of error threatened to crush her.
There had been nothing left for her in America, nothing
but Colin's schemes and embarrassing liaisons. Nothing to
hope for, nothing but long years of unhappiness.

Until she'd come to the land of the Maya.

Hope had blossomed for the first time in years, hope in
the form of a black-haired, golden-eyed adventurer. A fallen
angel with dark secrets. She remembered Steve's face when
he'd asked her to make a choice. There had been a wary
light in his eyes, as if he'd known what she would say. And
she hadn't disappointed him, had she? No, she'd been too
scared to take a chance, to make that leap into the unknown.
But she wasn't now. Not now, when everything else around
them was so uncertain. Now she knew.

"Steve," she said, softly, and his lashes lifted, a dark fringe
revealing golden eyes. "Steve—I'm sorry. For everything.
For my doubts, for being scared—you've saved my life more
than once. That's all you've done since I've met you, I think,
and I haven't shown you an ounce of appreciation. I'm grateful. Truly I am. I—I love you."

For a long moment, he sat there quietly staring at her.
There was nothing in his face to indicate his reaction, or
even that he'd heard her. Eden's throat tightened. She'd
waited too long.

His hand lifted slightly. "I don't need gratitude, Goldilocks. No charity work, please. I'll get you out of here alive. You don't need to say things you don't mean."

"I do mean it." She looked down at her twisting hands, unable to bear his steady scrutiny. "I knew it a long time ago, but—but I couldn't tell you. Not when I didn't know how you might—react."

"And now that we're hiding in the jungle and every breath might be our last, you figure this is a good time to tell me." He laughed softly. "No one can fault your logic, I suppose. Timing, maybe, but not your logic."

"I see." She tilted her chin slightly, pride coming to her defense. "You think I'm only saying this so you'll protect me. Or because we might die. Is that it?"

"It makes more sense than any other possibility," Steve drawled. "A few hours ago you were sticking with your husband. Now you're in love with me. Christ. What kind of idiot do you take me for?"

"Less gullible than I thought," she snapped, and was rewarded with a mocking grin. "Damn you."

The grin faded, and was replaced by the more familiar bitter twist of his mouth. "You're too late. I've been damned for longer than you know."

She closed her eyes, unwilling for him to see her misery. After a minute, she heard him move, heard the scrape of his boots on the stone floor of the temple. Then he touched her lightly on the shoulder, and there was real regret in his tone when he said, "It's always been too late for me. It's as if I have the touch of death. Everything I ever loved is gone. It vanishes, even when I don't want it to, when I want everything to be all right—" He took a deep breath, kneeling beside her as she opened her eyes to look at him, "I'll get you to safety, Goldilocks. You don't have to promise me anything or say anything. I wouldn't let anyone hurt you. Not any more. Last time I wasn't paying attention. I let them sneak up on us. This time, I'm ready for them. No one will hurt you."

His hand closed on her hair, firm and gentle, crushing her curls in his fist. She managed a smile. "It wasn't about being safe, Steve. I said it because I meant it."

"Eden . . ." Her name was a sigh. Soft and sibilant, his whisper came to her on the close, dank air of the temple. "Sweetheart, I swear I'll keep you safe this time . . ."

Something wet plopped onto the back of her hand, and she looked down in vague surprise. A tear. Warm and salty, they streamed down her face. Her throat hurt. Her head ached. Even the tiny stab of flame from the lamp hurt her eyes. She wanted to go to sleep, to lie down beside Steve as they had in his hut, with no worries, no fears, just each other. She didn't care if he kept her safe now. Not if it meant losing him.

"Just hold me," she whispered, and was gratified when he put an arm around her and pulled her against him. The steady beat of his heart beneath her cheek was familiar and soothing. Even his smell reassured her. She lay in his arms for what seemed like forever and yet it still wasn't long enough. When he shifted as if to release her, she gave a murmur of protest.

Bending, his mouth grazed her forehead. "It's only for a few minutes, love. I want to see how things are progressing outside. You wait here. Don't move. And don't be afraid. No one else has found this place in a thousand years."

"You won't take the lamp?" she asked anxiously, and he shook his head.

"No. I won't need it. I can find my way around these tunnels blindfolded. Good thing, in view of the fact that you want the lamp."

His attempt at humor was only slightly reassuring. Eden sat hunched into herself, arms across her chest, legs drawn up, as he gave her a smile and left. She watched him disappear, stepping into monster shadows that quickly swallowed him.

The imagery was not very comforting, and she determinedly swerved her focus elsewhere. Tilting her head back, she stared up at the darkened temple walls. Painted figures lined the walls, some of them almost life-size. Serpents coiled around dancers in jaguar skins; turtles and frogs decorated the huge mural. The temple was amazing. Richard would be delighted.

Richard. Colin. Were they both dead? Was either of them dead? She pressed the palm of her hand to her forehead. The expedition had been doomed from the beginning. A complete disaster. As far as she was concerned, the only good that had come from this venture had been Steve. And even that wasn't certain. Nothing was certain. Death could come in an instant, in the form of a snarling jaguar or the slice of a machete. Life was tenuous. Fragile. Undependable. She drew in a deep breath.

It was so quiet in the temple, so still. Nothing moved. Even the flame in the lamp had grown steady and unwavering. It was a solid ellipse of flame, the only light in a dark world. It was impossible for her not to make the comparison to Steve. He was the light in her world, whether he wanted to be or not.

Time crawled. It seemed like hours before Steve returned. He smelled of wind and danger. The light was back in his face, the one she'd seen that day in the jungle when they'd been surrounded by natives. He knelt in front of her, the tiger-glow in his eyes magnified by the oil lamp.

"Steve—" She paused and licked her suddenly dry lips. "What is it?"

"Anarchy. Total chaos. They're ripping at each other like a pack of jackals." He looked down, and she saw he held a rifle. His hand moved up the smooth wooden stock, expert and efficient as he broke it open to check the magazine. "I was able to grab a few weapons," he said in response to her quizzical look. "Here. Do you know how to shoot?"

Staring down at the pistol he thrust into her hands, Eden nodded slowly. "I know the basics. Load. Aim. Fire."

His laugh was a little strained, and she looked up at him again when he said, "That's about all you need to know. There's certainly not enough time for a complete course on the mechanics of firing small artillery. Careful—it's already loaded. It's a Colt so you'll have six shots, but it kicks. Try to brace yourself on something when you shoot."

"Steve." She drew in a shaky breath, unwilling for him to see how frightened she was. "Why do you think I'll have to shoot? What is going on out there? Are Richard and Colin all right?"

"I didn't see Colin. I saw Richard, and—he was alive." A frown dulled some of the excitement in his face. "I told you. All out war, Goldilocks. I knew there was something else behind all that archaeological blather."

"You're not making any sense—"

"Neither was Carter. I couldn't understand why he seemed to shift course in mid-stride. Now it makes more sense. No—don't get up. You're staying here."

She fought the urge to scream with frustration. As calmly as possible she said, "I have no intention of staying here unless you do, and I still don't know what you mean by Sir John shifting course."

"Yes you are, and what I mean is that Carter has no intention of listing what he finds in these temples unless it's in a sales catalog. He's a looter, sweetheart, plain and simple. A large-scale looter, but a looter just the same."

Eden stared at him blankly. "That's impossible. Why, he has excellent credentials, and he hired us to research and document the finds—"

"All a smokescreen." Steve wiped a dark stain from the barrel of the rifle he held, and Eden shuddered at the dark red smear it left on his shirt tail. She didn't need to ask to know what it was. With a grimace of distaste, she put the pistol on a rock ledge. Steve looked up at her and rested the rifle on his bent legs. "He hired Richard Allen because he was the most likely person to find the temple of the jaguar, and he hired you and Colin because he needed your money."

"My money——" She stared at him stupidly.

"Yeah. Your husband teamed up with Carter, not as a dedicated archaeologist or even an amateur, but as a looter. They intended to sell all they found. After getting rid of Richard and whoever else objected, of course."

Shaking her head, Eden said, "How do you know all this?"

Steve made a vague motion with one hand. "There are lots of temples in this area, and some of them have connecting tunnels. Most of the tunnels are clogged up with centuries worth of dirt and rubbish, but a few have been cleaned out by previous looters. It's like a rabbit warren or an ant hill under some of these mounds. Anyway, being the enterprising fellow I am, I got close enough to listen." He paused, and a savage glitter lit his eyes as he looked at her. "You realize, of course, that Carter has no intention of letting you or Allen leave the Yucatán alive. One word to the wrong person—and he knows he can count on either of you to chatter like a spider monkey—and he's in major trouble. There's more, Goldilocks, but I'm kinda in a hurry. You've got the gist of it now, haven't you?"

She nodded numbly, still not quite able to comprehend it all. Then it occurred to her that Richard was still in danger. Her gaze flew to Steve's face, but he was already shaking his head.

"Not a chance," he said softly. "I'm sorry for it, but I don't intend to rescue men who were too hardheaded to listen to me in the first place. My main priority is you."

Rising, she forced her legs to remain steady despite their alarming tendency to buckle. "I'm going with you. No, don't bother to argue. If you leave me here alone, I'll just try to follow you, and then probably get lost and wander forever in this maze. You have to take me with you."

He rose and looked down at her with a fierce scowl.

'Damn. You obviously have no notion of self-preservation at all."

"Obviously not." She lifted her chin defiantly when he narrowed his eyes at her. "And don't bother giving me that jaguar-glare, either. It won't work this time. I'm more afraid of staying than I am of going. And I know you can keep me safe."

"You're putting all your eggs in a basket with no bottom," he muttered with a resigned shrug. "But I can't take the chance you might try to follow me. It's not safe. You're not leaving me with much of a choice, I'm afraid."

When he glanced at her from beneath the dark brush of his lashes, Eden's throat tightened. She began to back away from the determined gleam in his eyes, the decision she could see he'd made.

"No, Steve. Don't. Please don't leave me here."

"Goldilocks—I have to. I'm sorry. I told you. I won't take any risks with you. This isn't a game. Those men are playing for high stakes, and they're out to eliminate any and all who might cause trouble."

She licked her dry lips, vaguely embarrassed to hear her voice come out in a faint whimper. "No . . . I promise I won't be any trouble . . ."

But Steve wasn't listening. He'd begun to shrug out of his shirt and tear it into long strips, occasionally glancing up at her as she stood in paralyzed apprehension. She began to back away, hands behind her against the wall, scraping her palms on the rough stones. "I'll never forgive you, Steve Ryan. Don't you do this to me . . . don't you do it . . ."

"At least you'll be alive to hate me," he said, and she was reminded of another time he'd said the same thing. She closed her eyes against the memory and the realization that he'd saved her then, too. She didn't want to be left behind in the dark.

She struggled against him, even as she knew it was futile. He caught her hands easily in one of his, holding her wrists while he looped strips of cloth around them. He tied it in a tight knot, then bent to bind her ankles together. While he worked, she said any and every thing she could think of to make him stop, but he ignored her worst curses and threats, as well as her sobbing promises.

When he was finished and she sat on the stone floor trussed like a Christmas goose, he knelt beside her. A faint smile curved his mouth when she consigned him to hell again. "Yes, I know you're mad. I don't blame you. But you'll be safe here. I'm leaving you the pistol, and by the time you get yourself untied, I'll be gone. If you want to try the tunnels, go ahead. Maybe I should warn you, though, that some of them wind back on themselves in a maze and I've run across more than one skeleton clogging a passage. Tell me you won't try it, and I'll leave you the lamp."

She pressed her lips tightly together, mad and tempted to tell him to take the lamp and be damned. But common sense and a fear of the dark unknown made her wiser. She nodded tersely. "All right."

His eyes narrowed slightly. "Ah no, Goldilocks. Your promise. Say it."

"I won't try to leave," she snapped. "Damn you."

"Good girl. I'll be back for you."

"And if you're not?"

She tilted her head to look up at him as he rose to his feet. He was quiet for a moment, then said, "If I'm not back in twenty-four hours, I won't be back. Then you can leave. Bear to your left. Remember that. Even when it looks like it's a dead-end. But you promised that you wouldn't try to come after me, and I expect you to keep your word."

"And just how am I supposed to know when twenty-four hours are up?" she demanded angrily. "This is insane. Untie me. Take me with you."

"No. I hope to be back by the time you manage to free yourself. Then you can say anything you want to me."

Before she could make another protest, he bent and kissed

1er hard on the mouth. Then he was gone, disappearing again 1nto the soft darkness beyond the lamp's glow. Eden put her 1ead back against the wall, fighting despair and fear. The 1ear, she realized, was more for Steve than herself.

Smoke hazed the air and stung his eyes. Steve knelt in 1he dirt and decaying leaves beneath a jacaranda bush and 1vaited. A shout went up from the direction of the temple. Γhey must have found the guards he'd killed. Pandemonium 1eigned in the camp, with men rushing back and forth in 1onfusion. A grim smile curled his mouth. Served 'em right.

They'd be looking for him now, of course. He was as 1nuch a danger to them as Eden and the other survivors of 1he first expedition. Not that he cared about his own danger. Γhe rush had come back to him, the familiar surge of ex-1ectation and calm that attended the tiger. It overpowered 1he strange frustration he'd felt at knowing Eden was leav-1ng him, knowing that she was going away with her husband 1nd he had no choice but to let her.

Even if Colin was dead—and he hadn't looked too lively 1vhen last he'd had seen him—there was no future for Steve 1vith Eden. He knew that now. For a time, he'd courted the 1vild hope that there would be, that he could lose himself 1n her and with her and the rest of the world would allow 1t. A foolish hope, of course. It was obvious to him now 1hat he wasn't meant to find peace. Not in this life. He was 1lmost thirty-five years old, and time was running out for 1im. All he could do now, his one contribution to the world, 1vould be to get Eden to safety. And he would do that even f it cost him his life.

Despite what he'd told her, he fully intended to get Rich-1rd Allen out of that camp. Richard could get Eden safely 1vay while he held the others at bay. If he didn't keep them 1usy, they'd remember Eden was still free. So he intended 1o see to it that they were too busy to look for her until she'd made it far enough away that they wouldn't find her. It was the only plan he'd been able to come up with, flimsy as it was. He didn't really have much faith in Richard's survival abilities. Or his willingness to go. But since Carter obviously meant to rid himself of any witnesses, Richard would surely see the sense in leaving. If nothing else, the fact that they'd tied him to a stump in the middle of the camp should be warning enough of what was to follow. Yeah, Richard would have no choice.

Damn Colin Miller. His greed had probably gotten them all into this. If he hadn't been so intent upon selling the treasure for personal gain, Richard could have made his discoveries, Carter would have quietly taken his share, and they would have all toddled happily away with the proceeds. But Colin had upset the apple cart by playing one man against the other and calling in rival investors to make a bidding war. Stupid of him. And it had cost him his life.

When the chaos below subsided a bit, Steve made his way closer. He had a plan of sorts, entailing great risk and a lot of noise, as did any plan worth its salt. But he had to have a distraction, something to draw as many away from his real purpose as he could.

Several of the tents were strung out along the perimeter of the camp. Men moved among them, their voices a low mutter that sounded uneasy. He grinned. So much the better. Let 'em sweat. It would only make it easier to throw them back into confusion again.

One tent stood apart from the others. He made his way toward it through the thick underbrush, ignoring the scratch of sharp leaves and the sting of insects on the bare skin of his chest and arms. His sweaty palms slipped along the smooth wood and metal of the rifle he carried. It felt like a steam bath pressing down on him, with the dark and humidity working to suffocate him. The summer rains would arrive soon, unless he missed his guess. The air was heavy with the promise of a storm.

Drawing to within an arm's length of the solitary tent, Steve paused to listen. Two men stood in front of it, talking in low tones that he couldn't quite decipher. Steve slipped his knife from his belt. He moved forward silently, and with quick, short moves, slit an opening in the canvas tent. When he stepped inside, he saw that he'd guessed right. It was the supply tent, piled high with wooden boxes and barrels. John Carter had spared no expense for this expedition, and obviously meant to stay until he'd gotten what he came for.

Moving silently among the crates and barrels, Steve found what he wanted off to one side. He knelt and pried up one edge of the crate to remove several rounds of ammunition. Then he found a small round keg of gunpowder. Using the tip of his knife, he dug a hole in a wooden stave, and shook loose powder along the canvas floor of the tent to the crate of ammunition. He made a tidy pile against the side of the crate, then sprinkled liberal amounts over the neatly stored bullets inside. Then he took a few quick moments to rummage through some of the supplies, slipping what he thought he might need into his pockets.

With the keg tucked under one arm, he made a trail from the crate to the slit in the wall, then outside. He had to hurry. If it rained before he managed to light the damned powder, this scheme would be useless.

Clouds scudded across the moon's surface; shadows flirted with light, making it difficult to see as Steve left a gunpowder path to the thick bushes behind the supply tent. Sweat poured down the sides of his face and into his eyes. He swiped an arm over his eyes to clear them, then knelt down.

It took three tries before he managed to ignite a spark and set it to the snaking trail of powder. Finally it sputtered, then sparkled with a faint hissing sound. Fizzing flame coiled along the ground, looking alive as it raced toward the tent. When it reached the wall and disappeared inside, Steve backed into the bushes again.

There wouldn't be much time after the explosion, and he needed to reach Richard before anyone figured out it was only a ruse. Time was critical. He had to get Richard away from his guards and back to Eden without anyone seeing him.

He made his way to a thick clump of bushes and waited in the shadow of a tree for the explosion. It came with a deafening roar, shaking the ground and sending up spears of flame and sparks into the sky. Beautiful, he thought with a grim smile as men shouted and raced toward the source. Flames spread quickly to a nearby tent, and several men ran toward the lake with buckets.

Now was his best chance, and he took it. Walking purposefully across the cleared stubble of the mound, he acted as if he belonged there. One man stumbled into him, and Steve shoved him toward the burning tent with a gruff order to hurry. The man never even glanced at him as he continued on.

But when Steve finally managed to make his way to the solitary stump where Richard was tied like a pack mule, he found him excessively uncooperative. Light reflected in the pale eyes turned up to him, and Richard shook his head.

"No," he refused bluntly, rubbing at his wrists to restore the circulation, "I can't leave here yet."

"Have you lost what little sense you had?" Steve grabbed him by the scruff of the neck, hauling him up by his shirt collar and swinging him around. "I don't have time for this idiocy."

Ignoring Richard's struggles, he dragged him through the dirt and toward the concealing line of brush that hadn't yet been mowed down in search of artifacts. The smaller man fought him furiously, but Steve had little trouble forcing him forward.

Once they reached the jungle beyond the camp, Steve shoved Richard up against the broad trunk of a tree, holding him upright with both hands. "What the hell is the matter with you? Do you want to die? Carter will kill you before he'll let you leave knowing what you do."

"You . . . don't know what . . . you're talking about," Richard got out in breathless grunts.

"The hell I don't. They shot Colin, didn't they? If he's not dead, he soon will be. And you will be too if you don't take my advice and get out of here. I want Eden taken to safety. You're the only one left I trust to do it. I'll try to keep Carter busy while you two get out of here the best way you can—"

Wrapping his fingers around Steve's wrists, Richard shoved hard at him, his face creased in lines of impotent fury. "You aren't listening—I said I'm not leaving. If you want Eden out of here, you take her. I'm not about to abandon this site to Sir John and his men so they can desecrate it—they're ruining it. Cutting slabs off stelae so clumsily they're being ruined . . ."

His voice faltered, unraveling into half-sobs as Steve stared at him incredulously. Opening his hands, he released Richard so quickly the man slid to the ground to land in a crumpled heap at the foot of the tree. Damn. This turn of events confirmed his worst suspicions. He found it incredibly absurd that Richard would deem the destruction of artifacts more important than his life.

Kneeling in front of Richard, he curled a hand around his throat like a vise. "Now listen to me, you dumb bastard. I don't give a good goddamn what happens to this temple or the mound or whatever else you may think is so important. I do care what happens to Eden. You're going to get her out of here, or so help me, I'll butcher you and leave you for the scavengers to find. Do you understand that?"

When Richard just stared at him in the hellish light from the fire and fitful moon, Steve swept up his other hand. Light flickered along the sharp blade of his knife in a deadly promise as he pressed the tip to Richard's throat.

"Which is it to be?" he asked softly, and finally Richard gave a barely perceptible nod of his head.

"I . . . I'll leave . . ."

"Good choice." Steve released the hand from Richard's throat, but kept the knife against his jaw as a reminder. "Pay close attention. If you mess up, I won't accept any excuses." Another nod revealed that he was listening, and Steve drew in a deep breath. He studied Richard for a moment, seeing the fear in his eyes and the taut set of his mouth. It was risky. Too risky. He didn't trust the man not to break down and become hysterical, but there was little other choice. Maybe he'd see the logic in living to discover other Mayan treasure.

"All right, Richard." He lowered the knife slowly. "Get Eden safely away from here, and once I manage to join you, I'll show you all the damn temples and glyphs you ever wanted to see. I know where the jaguar throne is, and I can tell you this much—it ain't where you're digging now."

Richard's eyes bulged. His lips worked soundlessly for a moment. "You know—you truly know the location?"

"Yeah. But I'm damned if I'll tell you where until you get her safely out of here. Understand?"

After a brief hesitation, Richard nodded. "But what if you're caught and killed?"

"Do what I tell you to do, and we'll make sure that doesn't happen, now won't we." Steve rose to his feet, slipping the knife back into his belt. He eyed Richard speculatively. He didn't like it. The old instincts were quivering with warning. Richard Allen wasn't quite sane when it came to Mayan temples and artifacts. He'd just proven that beyond any doubt. Still, Steve didn't have time to waste. Any minute now, they'd figure out that the explosion had been deliberate, and then they'd realize Richard was gone.

"Come on," he said, reaching down to haul Richard to his feet. "I'll take you to Eden."

Twenty-two

Rough stone grazed the palm and fingers of her left hand as Eden felt her way gingerly along the tunnel. The oil must be low in the lamp, for it had begun to flicker and sputter. She was terrified of being left alone in the dark, and when she had heard the muffled roar of an explosion, she'd abandoned any promises she'd made to Steve. If she had to stay in the dark and wait, she'd die of fright before anyone could find her.

Taking step by careful step, she made slow progress along the musty shaft. The air was close and warm around her, with no hint of a breeze to ease the heat. What was it Steve had said? Bear left. And something about a dead-end—oh, she should have paid closer attention to him. But she'd been too furious and frightened, with all her nerves on edge. It had been hard to focus on what he was saying when she was trembling with exhaustion and fear.

A slight noise caught her attention, and she jerked to a halt. It sounded as if there was someone else in the temple. Was that a footstep? Or only an echo from the mysterious explosion?

She stood motionless for several minutes, listening intently. No other noise disturbed the shrouding silence. There was only the harsh rasp of her breath and the rhythmic beat of blood in her ears. She took another cautious step, and a rock rolled under foot. The sandals were not as sturdy as her boots and easily slipped on the tunnel floor. Gasping, she flung out a hand to catch herself as she slid several feet. There was a clatter of rocks and a distant rumble. She came to a stop against something solid, and put out a hand to regain her balance. A sharp projection raked painfully across her palm and Eden jerked back her hand with a soft cry. She still held onto the lamp, and lifted it for a closer look. Then she took a startled step back.

Lamplight flickered over gleaming eyes and long fangs bared in a snarl, and she screamed in terror. She took two stumbling steps before she realized that it was some sort of statue. Feeling faintly foolish as her scream reverberated in the corbeled walls of the tunnel, Eden took a deep breath and touched the pistol stuck into the waist of her trousers for reassurance. It was still there, cold and solid against her bare skin.

Light wavered erratically, and she realized that the hand holding the lamp was shaking badly. She was panting, and her clothes clung to her skin in damp, clammy folds. It took several moments before she could summon the courage to lift the lamp high enough to look at the statue again, and then her heart leaped into her throat.

Gold dulled by centuries of neglect outlined the shape of a jaguar, standing over four feet high. Its head was lifted to form a sort of arm, and the animal's back was obviously meant to be the seat of a chair. The four legs were wide apart and sturdy, forming the legs to the chair, while the gilded tail curved down. She took a tentative step toward it and put out a hand. Beneath the dust and tumble of loose rocks she brushed away, it was cool and smooth. Jade. Gold. The jaguar throne that had lured so many to the Yucatán stood before her like a silent promise.

It was larger than she'd thought it would be. Amazingly, it was in excellent condition. So many artifacts that were found were in such deplorable condition, often unrecognizable, that she found it remarkable the throne looked as if an ancient Mayan king had only just risen from its wide, carved seat.

Trembling, Eden leaned back against the stone wall behind her. Surrounded by eons of time and mystery, she felt oddly connected. This was what enticed men to seek such treasures, to risk almost anything to make such discoveries. Until now, she'd not had the thrill of exploring on her own. Before, she'd always joined others after the first discovery had been made, digging and drawing and being part of a team. But this—even though she knew Steve was aware of its location, she felt as if the discovery were uniquely hers.

Steve. She held up the lamp, looking back the way she'd come. Panic flickered in her throat as she realized she'd lost her bearings. The slide, and then the discovery—which way had she come? Bear left, he'd said. She was certain that was correct. But was it left or right now? Was she turned around? Oh God, she was in the middle of a maze of twisting corridors and shafts in the bowels of the earth, and had no idea which way to go . . .

"How did you find this temple?" Richard Allen demanded, following close behind Steve. "Is this the temple of the jaguar? Where are we? My God, to be so close—hold the candle higher, I think I see something . . . I do. Dear God in heaven, it's a jade mask. Look at it . . . it's still intact—for God's sake, Ryan, will you wait a few minutes while I examine this?"

Losing patience, Steve spun around to face Richard. He brought up the barrel of his rifle and gestured menacingly. "We don't have time for this. The lamp is liable to run out of oil by the time I get you there if you keep dragging your feet. Come on. This will still be here later."

"Not if the others find it," Richard protested, but as Steve prodded him with the rifle, he reluctantly moved along.

When they reached the chamber where he'd left her,

Steve saw that it was dark. Damn. There should have been enough oil in the lamp. He lifted the candle high, stepping forward. He jerked to a halt, putting out an arm when Richard bumped into him.

"What is it?" Richard squeaked, and Steve gave an impatient shake of his head. The tiny flare of candlelight seemed puny in the overwhelming darkness around them. Damn her. She'd left the chamber. So much for keeping promises. But where was she now?

Sweat trickled down the sides of his face. Richard wheezed for air, the noise sounding overloud in the soft gloom around them. Steve waited, listening intently. After a moment, he started forward. He'd just have to start looking. The temple was honey combed with tunnels and shafts and deadends and sudden drop-offs. If she made a wrong step—he wrenched his mind away from that possibility. *Damn her,* he repeated, and didn't realize he'd spoken aloud until Richard asked anxiously what was wrong.

"Nothing, I hope." He quickened his pace, holding up the candle to shed light on the stone floor littered with centuries of dirt and rubbish. Every once in a while, he heard Richard make a small gasp of discovery, but he didn't bother turning around to see if he was close behind. Eden was his focus now, before she took a wrong turn and ended up at the bottom of a vertical shaft.

It wasn't until he rounded an angled corner and heard a faint sob that he realized he'd been holding his breath. He let it out slowly. Eden. He could barely make out her huddled form on the floor of a chamber just ahead. A faint smile curved his mouth. He recognized where he was, and knew what she must have found. There would be no getting Richard Allen away from it easily, and he cursed his rotten luck.

Too bad Eden had a penchant for independence. It would have been much better if she'd listened to him and stayed where he'd left her. But that would have been too much to hope for, and as he moved toward her and she looked up with a pale face streaked with tears, he felt some of his irritation fade.

"Steve—oh God, I thought I'd die here . . ." Lurching to her feet, she flung herself at him, arms going around him so hard that it carried him back several steps. The candle quivered, and he was barely able to hold it and his rifle as he tried to hold on to Eden.

"You were supposed to stay where I left you," he muttered, but his tone was more resigned than angry. "Don't you ever listen to me?"

Her face tilted up and she peered at him from beneath the tangled clump of her tear-clogged lashes. "I do. I swear I do, but I heard a noise—Richard. Oh, Richard, are you all right?"

But Richard Allen wasn't looking at Eden. Or Steve. His wide eyes were focused on the jaguar throne a few feet away. He seemed transfixed, mesmerized by the sight. Finally, almost reverently, he moved forward to gingerly touch the curved head of the throne. His fingers trailed over it lightly, through the dust and over the gilt and jade, tracing the outline of the eyes and snarling lips. Small noises came from his throat, none of them articulate.

When he looked up, there was a bright, clear light shining in his eyes. "It's . . . real. I had begun to think . . . after so many failures and disasters, I'd begun to think it was only a myth, like dragons and unicorns. But it's real. It's actually real. This outshines every other discovery I've made—I'll be famous for this. As famous as Brasseur. This may not be another codex, but it's as important. It validates the reign of a Mayan king no one before could prove existed. And I'm positive that once I search through this temple, I'll find other clues of equal importance. Possibly another codex like that of Bishop Landa's *Relación,* so that the glyphs and writings of the Maya can be translated. Maybe even another Rosetta Stone—"

"Hold on," Steve said. "You're getting ahead of yourself. There's a little matter of John Carter and about thirty men out there looking for our heads. I don't think this is the time to be planning excavations."

Richard blinked as if awakening from a dream. His hand ceased its constant stroking of the jaguar head, and his eyes narrowed slightly. "This changes everything—"

"The hell it does." Steve unfolded his arm from where it curved around Eden, shifting the rifle meaningfully. "It changes nothing. You two are getting out of here before Carter brings this whole place down around our ears. He brought enough powder and ammunition to start a full scale war, and I don't think he's going to give up easily."

Stiffening, Richard said, "That's not my problem. I cannot leave. Not now. Don't you see? Sir John has everything I need with him. For heaven's sake, he brought photography equipment with him, and plaster to make casts, and papier mâché—even a *camera lucida* to transfer images to paper accurately. No, I cannot leave now."

Steve swore softly. "I was afraid of this. Look—I don't care what you do after you get Eden safely out of here. You can come back and load everything onto mules for all I care. But you both need to get out of here now."

"No," Eden said clearly, and he slung her a quick, fierce glance. Her chin lifted with a familiar defiance, and she did not look away. "I won't leave, either. Not without you."

"Eden—Christ." He raked a hand through his hair in exasperation. "Don't you understand? I have to stay. I have to create a diversion, slow them down to give you time to escape. If you don't put some miles between you and them, they're liable to catch you. It's not safe, d'you hear me?"

"I hear you. It'd be hard not to, the way you're shouting at me. But I can't leave you behind."

"Great. Stay then. And we'll all end up dead because I'll be so busy trying to protect you that I won't be able to get away either."

She hesitated, and the appeal in her eyes made him want to say more than he should. He didn't. He waited in grim silence for the truth to penetrate. Finally, she nodded.

"Yes. I know that you will protect me." She sucked in a deep breath that sounded like a moan. "I can't allow that. Very well. I'll do what you ask. Only—only, please . . . don't take any unnecessary risks. I couldn't bear losing you."

"I'm not crazy about the idea either, Goldilocks." He leaned his rifle against a rock and reached for her, not caring what Richard thought, not caring about anything but holding her. She came willingly, sliding her arms around his waist and holding tight to him. He could feel the sharp pressure of the pistol he'd given her against his belly, and murmured into her hair, "This is the first time I've held a woman wearing a pistol, and it's a rather novel sensation. Don't forget to use it if you have to."

She laughed shakily, then drew back to look up at him. "Steve, you promise you'll be careful? That you'll catch up to us as quickly as possible?"

A faint smile pressed at the corners of his mouth, and he reached out to lift a long, curling strand of her hair in one hand. He held it between his fingers, letting it curl around his palm in a silky twist. "I promise. Now listen to me— you'll find the way out of here on a wide stretch of ground that looks like an ancient road. It is one, though a little rough in places. Follow it all the way. It leads to Chichén Itzá, about sixty miles north of here. There are men there who will help you get to Mérida. Tell them what has happened, all right?"

She nodded, and he pulled her into him again, putting his arms around her and holding her tightly. He could feel her tremble, the quiver of her muscles as she pressed her face into his bare chest. God. He couldn't delay any longer. He had to get her out of here, had to get her far away before Carter discovered the entrance to this temple. Regretfully, he pushed her away.

Glancing toward Richard, he began to warn him to travel

at night. But the faint metallic gleam of his rifle in Richard's hands stopped him. He went still and watchful.

Richard smiled tightly. "I see I have your full attention now. How gratifying. Sorry to put a damper on your plans, but I've no intention of leaving this temple behind for Sir John and his band of desecrators to butcher."

Keeping his eyes on the rifle, Steve said, "You'd rather be butchered instead? That's your other choice."

"No." Richard drew in a deep breath, and the rifle barrel wavered slightly. "I don't want that either. But if I make a deal with Sir John, he won't kill me like he did Colin. Colin was stupid. He wouldn't bargain. He insisted on the original arrangement and no compromises. It was idiotic, barging into an armed camp and demanding to be given a list of what had been found so he could determine his share. I've rarely seen such stupidity, and I can't say I'm sorry he's dead." His gaze flicked to Eden, who made a soft sound of distress. "Sorry, I know he was your husband, but I can't think you're all that disturbed over his demise."

"Richard—" Eden took a step forward and he swung the rifle in her direction.

"Don't. I won't be cheated. I've searched my entire life for a find this valuable, this rewarding, and I won't let anyone take it away from me. Not now. Not after I've been through so much—dear God, first the massacre, then losing all my equipment and the finds we'd made—then being ambushed again. I deserve this. Finding the temple of the jaguar is the greatest reward I can imagine. And here it is . . . the throne that was described in texts three hundred years old. Not since Bishop Diego de Landa wrote of it in the 1500s has it been seen."

He took a deep breath, and Steve shifted position slightly. If he could manage to get at it, Eden still had the pistol tucked into the waist of her loose trousers. He had to move slowly, because if Richard fired at this close range he was bound to strike Eden.

Richard's eyes narrowed. "I don't think I would do that, Mr. Ryan." He pumped the lever of the rifle. "I can hardly miss this close. Eden. Move away from him. Now. Yes, like that. Now hand me that pistol. Slowly, please, while Mr. Ryan takes three steps back. That's right—three long steps, if you please."

Not daring to rush him when he could so easily miss and hit Eden, Steve took the three steps back, swearing under his breath. He kept his eyes on the rifle, watching Richard's finger twitch nervously on the trigger. Damn. He should never have been so foolish as to put down the rifle, but he'd been intent on Eden and had never figured on Richard being daring enough to try anything like this. It seemed that he had underestimated the man's obsession with the jaguar throne.

Eden had the pistol in her hand and was staring oddly at Richard. She cleared her throat. "Richard. What do you intend to do?"

"I'm sorry, but I simply cannot allow him to interfere with my work any longer. From the beginning this man has stood between me and these important finds. Surely you can see that. He must be eliminated, or at the least, stopped from further interference. Give me the pistol, Eden. Give it to me, and I'll allow you two to leave. I can handle Sir John well enough, especially if I tell him how great a find I've discovered."

Steve's mouth twisted. "*You* have discovered? Is that the way it goes? Already, it's your discovery."

Drawing in a deep breath, Richard said impatiently, "If it was up to you, none of this would see the light of day. You've known about it all this time and never said a word. I suppose you meant to sell it yourself."

"If I had, I've had plenty of time to manage it," Steve drawled. He was stalling for time, trying to keep Richard's attention on him and not Eden. She hadn't handed over the pistol, and was still standing there staring at Richard with an intent expression. "Don't you think if I was going to loot these temples, this would have been one of the first prizes to go? Hell, I may not know much about the value of antiquities, but I'd have to be a complete idiot not to recognize that there are men out there who'd pay a fortune for something of this magnitude."

Richard frowned, shifting position slightly. The barrel of the rifle wavered, swerving between Steve and Eden. "All right. So you haven't looted this temple. It hardly matters now." He glanced at Eden. "Give me the pistol, or I'll shoot him now."

"Eden, once you hand him that pistol," Steve said quickly, "we're both dead. Look at him. Do you think he'll let us stand in his way now? He won't."

"Richard . . ." Eden's voice was soft, and pleading for reassurance. "Richard, you wouldn't do that would you?"

"Of course not. He's only trying to confuse you. Give me the pistol, Eden. I would never harm you."

"And Steve?"

"For God's sake, Eden, he's an adventurer. A murderer. You know the rumors. I realize you're fond of him, but he's trouble. He's caused nothing but trouble since we met him. Now *give me the pistol. . . ."*

"No." Eden brought up the pistol with both hands, holding it trained on Richard. "I won't. Put down the rifle. You don't have to take me anywhere, you don't have to leave here. You can go to Sir John and tell him anything you like. But first, we're going to get out of here. Steve and I are leaving. Do you understand?"

After a moment of tense silence, Steve said in an amused tone, "I believe what we have here is called a Mexican stand-off. Both sides fully armed and capable. I wonder who will blink first. You, Richard? If you shoot her, I'll rush you. And I'd like nothing better than to kill you with my bare hands. If you shoot me first, she'll shoot you. Either way, you're dead. So which is it? The lady or me?"

"Damn you both," Richard snarled, and the rifle barrel moved to center on Steve's chest. "You can see which I'll choose, Mr. Ryan—"

Even as Richard was pulling the trigger, Steve was diving to one side and pulling the knife from his belt in the same motion. The shattering roar of the rifle erupted just as he flung the knife forward.

Something hot struck him, knocking him backward, and then there was another shot. He heard it vaguely before the lamplit interior of the chamber wavered and receded into darkness.

Twenty-three

Deafening echoes reverberated in the chamber. It was instinct, unthinking reaction that made her pull the trigger. She saw the look of surprise on Richard's face, the widening of his eyes as he suddenly went limp. The rifle veered downward in a slow arc, then fell from his hands to the stone floor.

"You . . . you shot me," he whispered hoarsely. A trickle of blood seeped from his mouth, dripping to the shoulder of his white shirt. Slowly, he put a hand to his chest, resting his palm on the widening red blossom that stained it. He took a staggering step forward on faltering legs, then his muscles went slack and he dropped to his knees. His head wobbled on his neck as he turned his head toward the throne, putting out a hand as if to caress it before he pitched forward in a lifeless sprawl.

Eden let the still smoking pistol drop from her hands. It fell with a clatter. A harsh sob tore from her throat. She could feel the collapse of her muscles, the trembling that overwhelmed her, but it didn't matter. Nothing mattered but Steve.

Crying out, Eden lurched forward. Steve lay still, but his chest rose and fell with rasping breaths. A thin red line creased the side of his head, oozing blood. She examined him anxiously, checking his chest, arms, stomach, and even his back for sign of another wound. There was no evidence of another injury, nothing but the faint smear of blood over his right ear. It didn't even look very deep.

"Steve . . . Oh God." Hot tears welled up, filling her eyes and tumbling down her cheeks to fall onto his bare chest. She pulled his head into her lap, fingers shaking as she stroked back the dark strands of hair from his forehead. His eyes were closed, lashes making long shadows on his cheeks. Rocking him against her, she made soft, keening sounds of despair. He couldn't die. Not now. Not after everything they'd been through. Not after she'd discovered she loved him with all her heart and soul.

With trembling hands, she managed to tear a strip of cloth from her shirt, wishing she had something to clean the wound. She dabbed at it gingerly, while tears fell and her body heaved with racking sobs. The oil lamp flickered and sputtered with a hissing sound, and she looked up. The candle. He'd brought a candle with him—she went to find the only source of light, breathing a sigh of relief when her fingers grazed the wax candle stub where it had rolled under a rock.

Carefully, she relit the candle from the lamp and positioned it upright, then blew out the lamp to conserve the oil. She would alternate them as long as possible she went back to sit with Steve, holding his head tenderly in her lap. His chest rose and fell regularly, and when she felt his pulse, it was strong and steady. She made him as comfortable as possible, even covering him with the long tails of her shirt to keep him warm as he lay against her. Then she settled in to wait for Steve to wake.

Eden sat for a long time, not looking at Richard Allen's slowly stiffening body. A pool of blood congealed beneath him, dark on the stones. She had killed a man. She shuddered. Not just any man—a friend. He'd been a friend to her, and she'd killed him. But she'd had to. He'd shot at Steve in cold blood, without a moment's thought for anything but his precious jaguar throne. Her gaze drifted to the throne, to the lifeless eyes of jade and gilt, the lips frozen in a perpetual snarl, the catalyst for so much struggle and pain and death. She closed her eyes against overwhelming weariness and despair.

Beside her, Steve's body jerked, startling her eyes open. His muscles spasmed and one arm flung out to the side, hitting Eden. She gasped at the unexpected pain. Groaning, he rolled to his belly and pushed to his knees, balancing himself with a hand splayed on the floor. His arm quivered under the strain of his weight.

He went still, head down and dark hair wet with sweat and blood as he panted for breath. Then he looked up, eyes slowly focusing on her.

"Goldilocks," he muttered hoarsely. He reached up to touch the gash on his head, wincing. "Christ. He's a damn bad shot, I'll say that for him." A shudder went through him. His eyes shifted to where Richard lay sprawled on the floor, then moved back to her. He didn't say anything else, and gratitude mixed with Eden's rush of relief that he was alive and seemed all right.

Drawing a leg up under him, he sat for a moment, one knee on the floor, the other bent as if he were about to rise. But he didn't move, other than to crouch there, getting his bearings. After several moments passed, Eden asked softly, "How do you feel?"

"Like I've been shot." He grimaced. "My heads hurts, but other than that, I'm sound as a mule."

Eden wanted to weep with gratitude that he was his usual caustic and mocking self. In a faintly quivering voice she said, "I think you mean stubborn as a mule." She levered herself upward, pausing for a moment when her eyes were level with his. "Steve, what should we do now?"

He gave her a look of confusion. "Do?"

"Yes." She gestured to Richard, the throne, and the shadows beyond the chamber. "About—everything."

His eyes closed briefly, and a shiver went through him.

It was warm and stuffy in the temple chamber, but the bare
skin of his chest and arms was prickled with gooseflesh
and cool to the touch. Eden began to unbutton her shirt.
He needed something over him, and in absence of a blanket,
what was left of her shirt would have to do.

Steve looked up and frowned. "I don't think I'm up to
that yet, sweetheart, though if you insist, I'll give it my best
try."

"Don't be cheeky. You're injured and cold. You need
something to keep you warm."

Lowering himself back to the stones, Steve said shakily,
"I don't need your shirt, though some body heat might be
nice. Keep it on, Eden. If you don't, I might be tempted to
try something that would take all the energy I have left in
me."

"Now you're being stubborn." She slid the shirt off and
moved to wrap it around him. He grabbed it, his fist tangling in the cotton.

"I said no. I'll take Richard's."

"But he's—" She stopped, unable to form the proper
word. Her tongue balked at saying it.

"Dead." A faint wry smile curled his mouth. "I know.
But he won't miss it, and I have no intention of letting you
run around without your clothes. It's too tempting."

"I think you can resist, in light of all that's happened."
She pushed her arms back into the sleeves, irritated that he
wouldn't allow her to help him.

He looked up at her, his eyes gleaming with familiar
mockery. "I wasn't talking about me, though thank you for
recognizing my strength of character. Or lack of it."

"Then who—?"

"There are a lot of men out there who wouldn't mind
seeing a half-dressed female, y'know. Not that I plan on
running into any of them, mind, but just in case, it'd be
nice to know I won't have to stop and explain your penchant
for nudity." He closed his eyes as another shudder racked

his body. "Damn. Who'd have thought losing a little blood would make me feel like this?"

"Maybe we should stay here," Eden suggested. "You're weak, and it's dark. If we wait until tomorrow—"

"When it's daylight and they can see us better?" he cut in with a faint shake of his head. "No, Goldilocks. Since Plan A is now ruined, I'm afraid we have to go to Plan B."

"Which is?" she asked tartly when he rose to his feet and stood swaying for a moment. "Watching you faint?"

He put out a hand as if to catch himself, and his mouth twisted into a sulky grimace. "Lord, you're always nagging. If you can't think of anything nice to say . . ." His voice drifted into a whisper.

"Steve, please. Let's stay here for a while. You said they wouldn't be able to find us. We're safe."

Not answering, Steve walked to where Richard lay and bent beside him. Eden turned away as he rolled the dead man over on his back. She could hear him searching through Richard's pockets, and the rustle of cloth as he removed his shirt. There was a scraping sound, as if something was being dragged, and she shuddered. After a few minutes, Steve came to kneel in front of her. It took her a moment to gather the courage to look up at him.

Then she wished she hadn't. There was a queer, steady light in his eyes, muted gold beneath his shadowed lashes, making her heart lurch and the breath catch in her throat. He put a hand out to touch her gently on the cheek.

"You saved my life," he said softly. "I thought . . . it was my knife that got him. But it wasn't. It was you. I know it was hard for you, Goldilocks." His hand moved to curl into her hair, light and gentle and caressing. "Thank you."

Past the lump in her throat, she said, "It was only fair. You saved my life so many times." She ducked her head, unable to hold his steady gaze. "Isn't that what you wanted me to do?"

"Sweetheart—" Fingers shifting to curl under her chin, he lifted her face so that she had to look at him. "I was only bluffing Richard. I never thought you could shoot him. Not that I'm complaining, you understand. No, I'm the most grateful dog you'll ever see. I just wish—" He paused and drew in a ragged breath. "I just wish that you hadn't had to do that. I should have planned better, should have known what was most important to him. Ah, God. None of this should have happened. If I'd listened to my instincts, you'd never have left my camp in the first place."

"I didn't want to go," she said miserably, fighting the choking press of tears that threatened to spill down her cheeks. "I had hoped you'd want me to . . . stay."

There was a moment of silence, then he sighed heavily. "You were married. I couldn't choose for you. It was your decision. Not that I was happy when you chose to go with Colin, but I tried to understand."

Looking up at him, she whispered, "I thought you wanted me to go. You never said—"

"Christ. What could I say?" His fingers tightened almost imperceptibly on her chin. "I wanted you to know your own mind. You had to know without any doubts that it was me you wanted to be with . . ."

"It was always you, Steve. From the first day—it was always you."

Drawing her to him, Steve bent and kissed her, his lips warm on hers, stealing her breath and making her head light. She leaned into his embrace. In the murky gloom of the ancient chamber, she nourished the growing hope that all was not lost. Maybe there was a chance for them after all. Though he hadn't said the words, she knew he loved her.

When he drew back, his breath coming raggedly, she looked up at him. His hand was still tangled in her hair, resting on her shoulder against her neck, his fingers curled against the lower slope of her jaw. "Sweetheart," he murmured, "you were the answer to a prayer. I was just too hardheaded to admit it to myself. But now I know. Now I see what was missing from my life." He took another deep breath, smiling crookedly. "I thought it was fate. Bad luck. Destiny. All those things that happened to me, that led me to this place, sitting at the bottom of a damned hill offering prayers to ancient Mayan deities, they were just preparations for what was coming. Rite of passage, maybe, or lessons in self-discipline. Whatever it was, by the time you fell into my life, I thought I'd never find anyone so perfect. No, listen to me—you know I'm no saint. I never said I was. But there are things I've done that would make the devil blush for shame. I'm not proud of it, but that's the way it is. You know most of 'em, but there's a lot you don't . . ."

She put a finger over his mouth to still the flood of words. "I don't care, Steve. Whatever you've done is in the past. It's over. It can't be changed. The man I see now is brave and kind and generous. Life seems to have a way of offering difficult choices, and God knows, I've made my own share of blunders. I can't change mine any more than you can yours. All we can do is go on from here. As long as we're together, nothing else matters."

Steve pressed his forehead against hers and took a deep breath. "All right. All right—now we know where we stand. So all that's left to do is survive."

She laughed shakily. "Oh, is that all? I'm certain the two of us can manage that with no trouble."

His arms moved hard around her, holding tight. "We don't," he said softly, "have much of a choice."

Most of the flames had been extinguished. Only occasional sullen glimmers could still be seen pocking the ground. Steve motioned for Eden to join him in the shadowed recess of a tree, and she came to him, shivering with fear. He put a comforting hand on her shoulder. This wasn't

his best option. It wasn't even a decent option. But it was
the only option. And he didn't want to tell her that.

Slinging the rifle to his back, he carefully studied the
camp below them. Men still moved about; but slower now.
It was late, and after fighting fires and rescuing supplies,
they'd be tired and ready to rest. At least, that was what he
was counting on.

A flurry of toucans quarreled in the tree above them,
their voices lifted in rasping imitation of frogs croaking.
The night was still and warm, humidity already dampening
his shirt and making it cling to his back. Guards would be
stationed at intervals around the camp, watching for them.
At first light, a full-scale search would be launched, and
they needed to be far away by then.

He'd brought her from the temple through a series of
passages that angled sharply upward, emerging at a point
atop the mound that was almost completely covered with
brush. From here, he intended to make his way northward.
Their best chance lay in getting to civilization, or what
passed for it in the Yucatán. He'd set his sights on Merída.
That was where she'd be safe. And he had no intention of
stopping until he got her there.

"Is your pistol handy?" he asked without looking at her,
his gaze fixed on the scene below. He felt her shift slightly,
then murmur an affirmative reply. It didn't make him feel
much better, even knowing she was armed. There was so
much that could happen, so many variables that could crop
up at an instant's notice. The need to keep her safe made
him anxious, kept the tension churning inside. He had his
rifle, another pistol, two knives, and a machete with him.
Quite an arsenal. He felt like a one-man army, and all he
wanted to do was get out of there.

With a sense of vague surprise, it occurred to him that
instead of feeling the overpowering need to stay and fight,
to battle the forces that surrounded them as he usually did,
he wanted only to take Eden to safety. That was paramount,

a driving need that drowned out all other feelings. The familiar demon that drove him was sleeping, but instead of being comforted, his anxiety heightened. What would he do without the tiger? It had come to him so many times, taking over when his brain and muscles had ceased to function, keeping him alive. Had it deserted him now? Now when he needed it the most?

Steve's hand tightened on the rifle stock, and he realized his palms were sweaty and slippery. He shifted, wiping his hand along the material of his pants. He had to retain his composure, keep his mind focused on what needed to be done, but it was hard. His head hurt and his heart was pounding so hard in his chest that he was certain Eden could hear it.

And all he wanted was to keep her safe.

He rose abruptly, knowing if he didn't move now, he'd find himself like a greenhorn in battle—paralyzed with fright and making an excellent target.

"Come on," he said softly, and she followed with trusting obedience. He moved along the invisible trail, finding it by instinct, senses honed to screen out the slightest sign of danger. It had been difficult finding the passage from the temple mound, but his success gave them a valuable advantage. Poor Eden. The arduous climb to the top had taken almost every ounce of her strength, and the stifling heat was draining. Once they'd emerged atop the mound, she'd had to stop for a moment before going on. He didn't blame her. His own head felt as if it had been stuffed with cotton. It was difficult to think clearly, difficult to focus on what needed to be done next. If it weren't for this sense of urgency, he would have waited out the night.

But coming down this side of the towering mound put them near the lakes that fanned out beyond the ruined city. No one could follow them through water, not even the best tracker. And that was how he intended to take her, through the brackish, shallow lakes to the other side. It would cut

out the ten miles of going around them, and give them a
huge advantage over any pursuers. No one would expect
them to try it. No one in his right mind would try it. It was
generally considered to be suicide.

He had no intention of relating that information to Eden.
Best not to let her know the danger. Damn the clouds that
scudded overhead, partially obliterating the moonlight he
needed. It made for slow progress, when the need to hurry
was crucial.

"Eden," he said softly when they neared the edge of one
of the lakes, "I want you to wait here. Don't move until I
get back. If anyone else comes near you, shoot them. Trust
no one. Do you hear? *No one.* And keep your pistol primed
and ready."

"I will." She clutched at his hand blindly, and turned to
him in the smothering darkness. "Be careful."

He felt for her face and cupped it between his palms.
His mouth barely brushed her lips, then the sweet slope of
her cheek as he murmured, "I'll come for you as quickly
as possible. I just want to make certain it's safe to cross
here."

Nodding her understanding, Eden didn't protest when he
let her go. She huddled beneath the high, spreading roots
of a mangrove, half-perched atop one of the thick, twisting
stems with wide eyes faintly glistening in the murky light.

"Hurry," was all she said, and he flashed her a quick
smile as he swung his legs over a root and started down
the marshy slope. With the camp behind them and the lakes
in front of them, the need to navigate became even more
important.

The wide, flat roads the ancient Mayans had built led
from the ruined city in straight lines. Some of them led
nowhere, but others led out of the complex of jungle-hidden
structures to fairly decent roads. If he could get across the
lakes in the dark, survival would be a simple matter of
putting enough distance between them and Carter. Steve

moved from one shadowed copse of mangrove trees to another, pausing frequently to be certain no one was nearby. To his relief, there was no sign of anyone blocking off the lakes as an escape route.

The wind blew in off the lakes, carrying with it the scent of brackish water. Toucans quarreled noisily overhead, and he could hear the soft cry of an egret mingling with the plaintive call of the motmot. Then everything grew still and quiet. Only the soft murmur of water lapping at stilted tree roots and the shift of Spanish moss in a rising breeze accompanied his cautious exploration.

Uneasy, Steve made his way back to Eden. Something was wrong. He could feel it; danger vibrated in the air around him.

When he reached the mangrove tree where he'd left Eden in the shelter of its high, stilted roots, he was relieved to see that she was still there. Her pale face glowed in the ethereal light of a fitful moon.

"Come on," he said, reaching for her. "We need to hurry."

Eden didn't budge. She just stared at him with eyes looking like dark bruises in her pale face. He frowned when she didn't say anything or move. Her lower lip was quivering, and she made an aimless motion with one hand.

"Eden? Come on, sweetheart. We need to hurry . . ."

Stumbling forward a step, she lurched toward him and he grabbed for her. It was then that he saw the shadow behind her, the swift motion of an arm and the faint gleam of metal.

Instinctively, he pushed Eden to one side, bringing up his rifle.

"Ah no, señor," came the swift order, "do not be so foolish as to risk the pretty lady's life."

Startled by the youthful voice, Steve paused. Maybe it wasn't as big a shock as it should have been to see Paco step from the shadows into the moonlight. A faint smile curved the boy's mouth, mocking and derisive.

"Steve," Eden whispered, and he flicked a glance toward her. She was trembling. "I'm sorry. I didn't think . . . when he found me hiding here, I didn't imagine that Paco would betray me like this—he's only a boy. I didn't think he'd do this."

"No," Steve said shortly, "you wouldn't think so. But it seems we both misjudged him."

Paco grinned, teeth white in his swarthy face. "Sí, you were both foolish. But you are not alone." Gesturing with the rifle that was almost as long as he was tall, the boy said, "Drop your weapons, señor. I will take you back."

"I have no intention of doing anything so stupid," Steve said calmly. "Do you really think you can shoot me before I can kill you? You're not that fast. Or stupid."

Paco shrugged carelessly. "I do not have to be fast. And I am not so stupid to come here alone to search for you. It was I who thought you may try to escape by the lakes, and I brought others with me . . ."

Several shadows separated from the darkness around them, and Steve softly swore. If he had been alone, he might have tried to get away. But he couldn't now. Not with four rifles trained on them and Eden in mortal danger.

Slowly he lowered his rifle, and stood stiffly while two men approached to disarm him. There would be an opportunity to act. Once Eden was out of harm's way, he'd grab the first opening possible when they made the mistake of leaving him one.

"All right," he said softly when they'd taken away his weapons and tied his arms behind him, "you have the advantage for now."

Paco's round face wreathed in a smile. "Sí, *El Jaguar*. And we know how to keep it, I assure you."

"You seem rather young for an assassin," Steve commented, as they were prodded forward into the night. "But I suppose that works to your advantage."

"It always has. I am almost twenty, but can pass for much younger. No one suspects that a child would have his own loyalties."

"To the Cruzob, I'll bet," Steve said softly, and was rewarded with a startled glance.

Paco scowled and muttered something to one of the others, then said, "No, I work for John Carter. He will tell you so."

"I was never impressed with Carter's mental ability," Steve drawled. "Why do I get the feeling that he's in for a big surprise?"

"Silencio," one of his guards said sharply, and poked Steve painfully in the ribs with the barrel of his rifle.

Steve glanced up, and as they passed from the trees into a small clearing bright with moonlight, he could clearly see the rifle that Paco was carrying. It was a Winchester .44, with intricate scrollwork on the metal stock. It had been purchased in Abilene, Texas. And he knew exactly when—it was his rifle, the one that had been taken away from him when they'd first been captured and taken to the small village in the jungle . . .

Drawing in a deep breath, Steve knew that they were in more trouble than he'd first thought.

Twenty-four

Eden tried to stay calm. But it was difficult when she was tied to a post in the middle of the camp with Steve a few yards away and surrounded by unfriendly men. They'd seated him on a camp stool, and Sir John had planted himself in front of Steve to demand answers. Firelight gave the scene an unearthly glow.

Closing her eyes, Eden prayed silently that Steve would realize how futile it was to be so stubborn. Didn't he see their danger? Didn't he know how useless it was to refuse to answer Sir John's questions about the jaguar throne? It was sheer idiocy to remain silent when their lives hung in the balance.

Her brief attempt to convince him of that had been met with a sharp order to be quiet, and she'd subsided into silence. Mixed with her shock at discovering Paco's betrayal was the conviction that Steve knew much more than he'd been able to tell her. So she would remain quiet—at least unless it seemed like they'd kill him if he didn't tell them where to find the throne.

And then she would tell them, whether Steve liked it or not.

"So where is it?" Sir John was demanding furiously. "You might as well tell me. Unless you want to end up like Colin Miller."

Eden's head jerked up. A chill went through her, and she couldn't stop the scream when she saw where John Carter was pointing. A bonfire blazed brightly, illuminating the temple door and the stone head of the jaguar. It snarled from its place on the wall—directly over Colin's body. There, where the temple wall had been partially unearthed, fresh mortar had been poured around Colin's body. It had hardened, freezing the corpse for all eternity. She tore her gaze away, swallowing another scream.

Horror and revulsion made her weak as she heard Sir John say mockingly, "Colin wouldn't listen. Hardheaded man, and much too greedy. Paco thought he would make an excellent warning to any other man tempted to be so stubborn. Now—will you tell me where I can find the jaguar throne?"

Steve's mouth was curled in a mocking smile. "It won't matter to you before long, Carter. Believe me."

"I don't know what the hell you're talking about, you bloody sod, but it can scarcely matter to you if I find the throne sooner or later. Make it easy on yourself. Tell me how to find it, and I might be persuaded to leniency."

Shrugging, Steve looked at the men surrounding them. "Do you really think these natives will allow you to remove the throne? If you do, you're not very smart."

"What in God's name are you babbling about? This is my expedition. These men were hired by me."

"Can you buy loyalty? Sometimes it has a high price. And I have a feeling you'll discover that before another sunrise."

Sir John made a rough exclamation, then beckoned impatiently to two men to come forward. Eden cringed as one of them jerked Steve's head back while the other began to hit him with careful, calculated blows to the face that sounded bone-breaking.

"Stop it," she cried loudly, her voice faltering.

Sir John came to her and looked down. Light from the campfire gave him a demonic appearance, and she wondered why she'd never noticed it before. He smiled. "My dear, perhaps you can persuade him to cease this foolishness. We can find the throne on our own if necessary. He is only delaying the inevitable. Can't you convince him to be more cooperative?"

Eden could still hear the sounds of Steve being hit, and she shuddered. Drawing in a shaky breath, she said, "I can try."

"Very well. I'll give you one last opportunity."

Eden looked around at the leaping campfires and determined faces distorted in the reddish glow of the flames, and tried to convince herself that Sir John was more humane than this. Maybe he was right about Colin inviting disaster. Maybe he'd somehow provoked Carter into shooting him. It was possible. It had to be possible. Surely, Sir John would not cold-bloodedly command the slaying of another human being. After all, he was a civilized man. He had engineered this expedition to retrieve artifacts. Colin's face flashed uninvited before her and she shuddered. The truth was brutal, but undeniable. Even if Sir John was more intent upon personal gain than a contribution to history, maybe he could be kept from murdering them as he had Colin. If they only cooperated . . .

Steve looked up as Sir John escorted her to where he was being forcibly held. They'd hauled him up and slammed him back onto the camp stool. One man held him down with a hand on his shoulder. He had a cut over one eye and his bottom lip was split. A bruise had begun to form on his left cheek.

"No, Goldilocks," Steve said softly before she could even begin, "don't try. It's no use. Carter is too stupid to see that he's signed his own death warrant, and I'm not in the mood to accommodate him for even a moment."

"Steve, if you tell him what he wants to know, he'll let us go."

"If you believe that, you believe that Paco is Sir John's friend too," Steve said mockingly, and she frowned.

Paco. The native boy worked for Sir John. But that didn't explain why Steve seemed to think Carter was in danger from him.

Glancing at Sir John, Steve drawled, "You need to ask yourself some important questions, Carter. How is it that Paco got out of the first massacre unharmed? All the other natives who were helping were killed—or taken hostage and sacrificed later. Who recommended these men you have with you now?"

"Really. You're only stalling for time. Tell me the location of the throne, and it will go much easier for you," Carter said testily.

"Please, Steve," Eden broke in when he began to shake his head, "just tell him. It won't matter. I don't care about the throne, and neither do you. Why not just tell him and get it over with?"

"Once I tell him," Steve said, "he'll kill us. At least this way, I'm alive longer to aggravate him."

Moving swiftly, Sir John snatched Eden toward him, one arm coiling tightly around her body and the other pressing a bare knife blade to her throat.

"Very well," Sir John said softly, his breath warm against her ear as she quivered in his tight hold, "be stubborn. You can watch her die before we kill you, but it won't change anything. I will still find the throne before I leave, and you'll both be dead."

Steve had gone still and watchful. "I don't know why they're waiting," he said after a moment, "but the Cruzob will never allow you to leave the Yucatán alive. Do you think it's a coincidence that Paco survived the first attack? Stop and think—he's the one who found you more men for your expedition. He's the one who suggested that you rid yourself of unnecessary survivors by giving Richard, Colin, and Eden to the Cruzob. Only he didn't know that I'd go after them, because you didn't tell him. You thought you'd get rid of me at the same time, and knowing how superstitious some of the natives are about *El Jaguar,* you didn't tell him I was going to find them. You thought we'd all be slaughtered and that would be that. Of course, that was before you found out that I knew where the throne was, wasn't it?"

Sir John drew in a sharp breath. His hold loosened slightly on Eden, and she could feel his tension. He turned toward Paco and called him over. When the boy arrived, he stood gazing impassively at Steve and Eden. Sir John cleared his throat.

"I say, he is lying when he claims you're behind the first massacre, isn't he, Paco?"

Shrugging, the boy nodded. "Sí. He lies to save the woman. Do not believe him."

"You're going to trust him? Maybe you don't remember what happened back in '58 at Bacalar," Steve said quietly to Sir John, "but I do. Blake told me. He was there. Hundreds of men, women, and children were captured by the Cruzob and held for ransom. James Blake, a gunrunner from British Honduras, delivered the 4,000 pesos, then had to stand helplessly by while the Cruzob slaughtered every last hostage . . ."

Paco snarled something Eden couldn't understand, and one of the men stepped forward to club Steve with the butt of a rifle, knocking him from the stool to the ground. Eden stared at Paco. She had thought him a child, but she'd been wrong—he was a man possessed, a man who would stop at nothing to clear the Yucatán of white men.

Sir John's grip on her tightened, but his voice wasn't quite as certain as it had been before.

"That was then. This is now," Sir John said. "I hired some of these men in Merída. They'll do what I say."

"Will they?" Steve's laugh was mocking if a bit strained. He rolled to his back, clumsy with his hands tied behind him. "I think you're wrong, Carter. Test it—go ahead. Are there any familiar faces among these men?"

Sir John looked around him, and Eden felt his grip on her tighten convulsively. She drew in a sharp breath. Most of the faces surrounding them were native; none of them were friendly. He had to see it, had to realize that Steve was right. It dawned on her that their greatest danger was no longer John Carter, instead it was the Cruzob.

Blinding spears of pain shot through his head as Steve tried to get his bearings. That last blow had rattled his brains pretty good, he thought hazily. Maybe he should have kept his mouth shut. All hell was liable to break loose now, and he would have only himself to blame. Not that it really mattered. It would happen sooner or later anyway, and at least this way he'd be ready for it.

While Carter had been deciding upon the proper and most expedient methods of extracting information from him, Steve had been planning. It wasn't much so far as plans went, but it was all he had. And it might save Eden if nothing else. And that was, as it had been for a surpris ingly long time, all that mattered.

Now that John Carter was beginning to recognize the truth staring him in the face—the dumb bastard—the wheels of fate should begin to turn quite quickly. He'd been working on loosening the ropes around his wrists since they'd first tied him up, and he felt them give way slightly as he kept Carter distracted by talking. Almost . . . drawing his legs up under him, Steve managed to get to his knees and look up at Eden.

She was staring at him, terrified but not hysterical, and he spared an instant's gratitude for that. He tried to give her a reassuring smile, but it felt more like a snarl. He hoped she understood.

Carter still had hold of her, but his grip had slackened as he looked around him at the armed natives. "Where are the others?" he demanded of Paco, who gave an eloquent shrug in reply. Carter grew pale, and his hands shook.

Giving a laugh that sounded hollow and all wrong even

to his own ears, Steve asked, "Beginning to get the picture, Carter? I would say that the rest of your men—English or American—are all dead. Only the Cruzob are left. And I'll bet they are not at all impressed with your intention to remove the jaguar throne."

Paco didn't even glance at Steve. One of the men said something to him, and he nodded slowly. Turning to Carter, he said, "It is done. You are all here. This time there will be none left to tell the others where to search. No white man will dare come again to look for the throne."

"But I paid you well," Carter shouted. "All of you. You can't—" He drew in a sharp breath when Paco made a gesture. "Wait. If you let me go, I promise not to return. I will tell no one of this place. Or the throne. I swear it."

"We have a way of making certain of that," the Indian boy said with soft menace, and there was no hint of compassion in his eyes or his voice.

Steve was ready, and even before Paco gave the order, he'd begun to rise. Flinging his body at the slender youth, he had the satisfaction of hearing his grunt of pain as they both went down in a tangle of arms and legs. Steve flexed his muscles and jerked his hands free of the ropes around his wrists, ignoring the grating pain. Then he managed to grab Paco by one arm as he tried to roll free, and yelled for Eden to run. He hoped she was listening.

"Oh, no, you don't," he muttered in between pants for air when Paco twisted one arm free, "not quite yet . . ."

The end was inevitable, but he'd provided enough of a distraction for Carter to release Eden and make a break for it. It was up to her to seize her chance to flee, and he hoped she took it. The men around them were reaching for him, trying to free Paco from his grip. Steve fought furiously. He knew he was going to die, but he'd be damned if he'd go alone. He intended to take as many Cruzob with him as he could.

One of them kicked him in the head, barely grazing him

as he managed to twist so that Paco absorbed the worst of the blow. The natives began yelling excitedly, milling around in confusion while Steve wrestled with the wiry Paco. He was surprisingly strong for his size, but despite his loss of blood and the beating he'd suffered, Steve would have made fast work of it if not for the others. They pulled at him, none daring to shoot or strike with a machete for fear of hitting Paco. Steve smiled grimly, and heard a mutter of fear from two of the Cruzob.

But it was not enough.

Realizing that he was quickly losing ground, Steve tried one last trick. With a wrench that took the rest of his fading strength, he pulled Paco up in front of him with an arm curved around his throat to cut off his air. He intended to break his neck with a hard twist and perhaps gain Eden more time, but before he could get enough leverage, Carter responded.

Shouting furiously, the Englishman flung forward the knife he'd just been holding at Eden's throat. It caught Paco in the middle of his chest, and Steve felt the youth go stiff with impact. His body jerked in a long, convulsive spasm, then went limp. For an instant, no one moved. Pinned beneath Paco's body, Steve could see only the few faces around him, all showing shock.

The shock faded swiftly. With a concerted roar, the Cruzob rushed John Carter. Steve flung aside Paco's body and got to his feet. Not daring to pause, he raced toward Eden and grabbed her arm as he passed. Frozen with horror, she stared past him at the frenzied mob of natives surrounding Carter. They sounded more like a pack of wild dogs than men, and Steve did not need to turn around to know Carter's fate.

"Don't look," he muttered as he dragged her along. "Just run. Don't look back . . ."

Barely pausing to grab up a rifle from the ground, Steve headed for the safety of the jungle that crouched just beyond the ruined city. It would be light before long. He had to get Eden hidden. It was her only chance.

With his heart thudding, he pulled her with him. His head ached like the devil, and every step was pure torture as he fought his way through hanging vines and thick foliage. The air was thick and heavy around him, and the moonlight had disappeared. He could feel another storm approaching. It was pitch black, and he found his way by instinct before his eyes adjusted to the absence of light.

Voices sounded behind them, and Steve muttered the vilest curses he could think of as he continued. Eden didn't whimper or offer a sound, but he could hear the tortured rasp of her breath as she struggled to keep up. To stop would be certain death, and she had to know it. They fought their way through the tangle of vines and brush for what seemed like hours.

More voices sounded, closer this time. Steve set his teeth against the grinding pain in his head and moved even faster. Eden stumbled, and he stopped to lift her to her feet before pushing onward. When she fell again, a gasp of pain wrenching from her, he was barely able to help her up.

"You've got to keep going," he said between his clenched teeth, and she moaned.

"I . . . can't. Go on . . . without me."

"Like hell I will." He lifted his head as he heard the voices again, much louder this time. They would have to make a stand. There was no hope for it, and he could have wept with frustration. If he had to, he would put a bullet in her before he'd leave her for the Cruzob.

"*El Jaguar . . .*" The call echoed through the pressing heat and humidity of the jungle. Tension crackled in the hushed air. Steve pushed Eden ahead of him into a dark recess that offered the quickest hiding place.

Barely making it beneath a tangle of roots before the voices were on them, Steve took careful aim. His finger curled around the trigger as he rested the long barrel on the smooth slope of a root. Sweat beaded on his face. He could feel it wetting his shirt and trickling down his chest. Behind him, Eden was half-sobbing, and he made a mental note to leave one bullet in the chamber.

Vague shadows appeared, almost invisible among the trees and ferns. Then a loud crack of lightning split the sky, illuminating the area with a bright light. He saw the men approaching, and he paused. An insane urge to laugh welled up in him, and he tried to stifle it.

But it still crept into his voice as he half-turned to Eden. "We'll be all right, Goldilocks."

She stared at him in uncomprehending silence, and when another bolt of lightning brightened the area, he saw that she still didn't understand. "It will be all right," he repeated. "It's Yac . . ."

"El Jaguar," Yac shouted again, and Steve crawled from the tangle of roots to meet him. The Indian briefly clasped him in a greeting, then nodded in agreement when Steve negotiated with him.

"Sí, *El Jaguar.* I will do it for you. But you must go with my men back to my village while we take care of your woman. Cruzob still roam the area and it is getting light. It would be too dangerous to take both of you."

"I know." Steve put a hand on Yac's shoulder. "Keep her safe at all costs."

"Eden," Steve said softly, going back to kneel by her, "do you remember the men who brought Richard and Colin to us? This is Yac. He's not a Cruzob. He's Mayan. And friendly. He'll get us out of here. He'll get you safely to Merída."

Eden found his hand and held it tightly. When she spoke, her voice was a faint whisper. "What about you, Steve? You are coming with me, aren't you?"

His throat tightened. He put a hand on her cheek. "You know I can't. I told you—"

"But you said that's where you were taking me," she said

with a note of rising hysteria. "Just a few hours ago—you said we were going to Merída."

"Sweetheart, that was when there was no other way to keep you safe. Yac can get you there a lot quicker and safer than I can. Trust him. He can do it."

Shaking her head, Eden said stubbornly, "I won't go without you. I don't need to go back to Merída. I'll stay with you. They never bothered you before, did they? Maybe they won't any more. I don't want to leave you, Steve . . ."

Gently but firmly, he detached her hand from his arm. "You don't have a choice. Can't you see that? Yac is a godsend. He'll get you away from here. You'll be safe, and that's all that matters to me."

"Not to me," she said on a sob, and Steve swallowed hard. He couldn't stand this. It was too much.

Rising to his feet, he motioned for Yac to take her. It was the best way. If he stayed with them, they'd be too noticeable. With his injuries and exhaustion, he'd only slow them down. Yac could take care of her. He could disguise her and get her to Mexican officials who would get her home. It was the only way.

"You're a coward, Steve Ryan," Eden said furiously, tossing her hair back over her shoulder as she glared at him. "You won't go with me, and you won't let me stay. Don't do this. You know it's not what you want . . ."

"Yes, it is. Go with Yac. I told you before that I don't want you here," he snarled with painful brutality. "This isn't where you want to be, and I can't go back to civilization. I wouldn't go if I could. I belong here. You don't."

"I could," she said. "I could stay—"

"*No.* When are you going to listen to me? Get out of here. Go back to Merída or wherever you want. Go home. Just—go."

Her face paled, and he saw shock dilate her eyes. He couldn't believe he'd found the courage to say the things that would make her leave, keep her safe. It was killing him. Some part inside him that had only just begun to blossom, now shriveled and died and turned to ashes. But she wouldn't listen, wouldn't do what was needed to save herself, and he couldn't have another death on his conscience. Especially not Eden. He was saving her, even though it meant his own death. Somehow, the tiger had gone. It had abandoned him, and he wasn't sure he could keep her safe anymore. This time, he was being noble. He was thinking of her more than himself. It would kill him to lose her, kill him to watch her walk away. But he had to do it.

Still, it was not easy to move on when Eden was gone and he was left staring into the darkness. Soon it began to rain, the sky opening up like a flood of tears. For several minutes, Steve didn't move. He stood with his face tilted to the sky, drinking in the moisture. It streamed down his face in rivulets, cooling him. Rain seeped into his mouth as he stood with an upturned face, and it occurred to him that it tasted salty.

Twenty-five

Eden stared at the empty hut. One of the walls had fallen in, and the riot of flowers that had once covered it were gone. Only a few charred stones that had formed the fire pit were left. Beyond the small clearing, scraggly rows of corn had been overtaken by weeds and the jungle. Vines had even begun to encroach on the carefully cleared patch of ground in front of the hut.

Unable to resist, Eden walked into the hut. It was empty, of course, as she had known it would be. There was no sign of a hammock or mattress, or stacks of books or baskets neatly lined up around the walls. But amidst the rubble of the fallen wall, a patch of blue caught her eye.

Kneeling, she touched it lightly. It was a morning glory blossom, bravely sprouting up through the wreckage, a faint reminder of the past. She left it and went back outside.

"It is as I said," Yac murmured softly in his thickly accented English. *"El Jaguar* has gone."

"Yes." Eden did not turn around. She'd been warned. But she'd had to try. She could not leave the Yucatán without at least trying to see him once more. So much had happened since the night she'd last seen Steve. There had been an inquiry into the exploitation of Mayan artifacts, and into the deaths of Richard, Colin, and Sir John. It had been blamed upon the rioting Cruzob, and Mexican officials had been unable to catch or punish the perpetrators. That had hardly surprised Eden for she'd expected little from their investigation. What she had expected was for Steve to come after her.

She'd remained in sun-drenched Merída for five months, hoping each day to hear from Steve. But there was no word from him. The only indication that he even remembered her had come in the form of a blanket-wrapped bundle delivered to her in care of the American consulate. When she'd opened it, she'd found the gifts from the women of the Cruzob village, and recalled leaving it atop the temple of the jaguar during her last night with Steve. She'd searched the contents hopefully, but there had been no note. No message. Only the jade necklace she'd worn when she'd been pushed into the sacred cenote and the white robe of the moon goddess were there to indicate it had not all been a dream.

Despairing, she had seized her last chance to see Steve again when she'd gone to Chichén Itzá to visit the group of archaeologists living there. By chance, she had run into Yac. It had taken a great deal of pleading and persuasion, but he had finally agreed to take her to Steve's former home.

"He has gone from there," Yac had said in his halting English. "It is said that *El Jaguar* has gone to the home of the gods."

By persistence, she'd managed to learn that *El Jaguar* had been seen since the night at the temple of the jaguar, but none knew where he lived. The partial excavation of the temple had been abandoned. No white man dared go near it. Paco had at least accomplished that mission with his scheme.

Now, looking at the abandoned hut, Eden turned to Yac. "Take me to him. You know where he is."

Yac shook his head. "I cannot. It is too dangerous—"

"No, it's not. You told me that the Cruzob have left and gone back to their former lands on the Caribbean coast. Is that not true?"

Reluctantly, Yac nodded. "Sí. It is true. But there are still villages that do not want intruders in the Yucatán."

"Yes, I am certain there are. But I am with you. If you do not tell me, I'll find him myself. I think I know where he is—the home of the gods? Yes, I'm certain I can find him."

Yac smiled faintly. Eden might have worried that she'd offended him if not for the slight smile she detected as he turned away to speak to the men with him in their native Yucatec.

Now, as they started back to Chichen Itzá, Eden began to notice familiar things: the lightning-struck stump of a ceiba tree, and the way the path twisted to the left twice before turning sharply right. She looked up once to see Yac watching her—and suddenly knew.

"This is the way to the sacred cenote. He's there, isn't he." It was more a statement than a question, and Yac nodded. Eden drew in a sharp breath. The home of the gods. The gate to the Mayan underworld—the pool in the cave. So close now, so very close. Would he be angry that she'd come?

Over the past five months she'd relived her last minutes with Steve again and again, trying to find hidden meanings in all the things he'd said. Recalling everything—the guilt he felt over his father and his friend and all those he'd lost—she thought she knew what he'd been trying to do. She could only hope she was right, that he'd been trying to keep her safe and sending her on was the only way he knew how to do that.

But what if she were wrong? He'd never said he loved her, never come after her. If he couldn't come, he could at least have sent word to her, or even asked for her to come to him.

But he hadn't.

Thin streamers of sunlight pierced the sweltering shade beneath the dense canopy of trees. The heat and humidity were familiar, with no breeze stirring the leaves. Perspiration ran from her head to her heels, dampening the pink linen blouse and skirt she'd worn hoping to impress Steve. Drawing in a deep breath, Eden recognized the damp smell of decay from fallen limbs, dead trees, and rotting leaves.

Heat pressed down with familiar weight as she maneuvered the jungle trails. Eden wiped her face with a clean white linen handkerchief. Her stomach was in knots, and the closer they drew to the cenote, the more apprehensive she felt. What would he say? Would he even be there?

Lost in thought, she ducked a hanging branch just in time, narrowly avoiding the stinging ants swarming over the leaves and bark. She hardly noticed the spanish moss draped in delicate lace streamers, or the fragile orchids and other flowers clustered on some of the lower branches. The familiar clamor of birds filled the air. Their music was familiar and precious, and she realized how much she'd missed it all. Now and then she glimpsed a bright flash among the trees. Splendidly feathered scarlet macaws fluttered from branch to branch, crimson, blue, and gold feathers glittering in the sunlight as they shrilled at the interlopers below. A flock of parakeets twittered high in the treetops, looking like brilliant leaves.

Despite everything, the danger and death and fear she'd experienced, she could appreciate the tropical beauty. She'd once thought she had no pioneering spirit. Now she wondered whether that was no longer true. Maybe, after all, she could start all over.

When they paused and Yac shared his gourd of water, she drank silently. Above, a toucan gave a harsh, grating call. She looked up. Perched on a branch, the bright yellow feathers on the toucan's neck glistened in the sun as it hopped to a higher branch. The head tilted, and the huge, curved green beak opened for another raucous greeting.

"He welcomes you home, I think," Yac said solemnly.

When Eden turned to look at him, the Mayan shrugged. "The wild creatures know. It is said they have . . . souls."

Eden remembered Steve telling her that. She smiled. "I've heard that."

Maybe it was true. Maybe Steve would welcome her as well. She looked past Yac. The cenote lay just ahead. She could see the dark tumble of low rocks that hid the entrance, and the deep pit of the sacred cenote that lay in the sun. From her previous experiences, she now knew the mounds covered ancient temples, and that once this had been a thriving city. It had been reclaimed by the land, swallowed up in mystery and forgotten. Until now.

She turned to Yac. "I can go the rest of the way myself."

"Do you wish us to wait for you, señora?"

Taking a deep breath, she shook her head. "No. Now that I know where he is, I will not need your help."

It was true. She needed no help to find the cenote.

Still, Yac hesitated before asking tactfully, "And if he is not there? Do we wait for you?"

Eden paused, then nodded. "Yes. If he does not want me to stay, I will come out of the sacred cenote before the sun has set behind the trees."

"We will wait by the sacred pool, señora, though I do not think *El Jaguar* will send you away."

But Eden suddenly wasn't as certain. She approached the entrance with slow, faltering steps, aware that her entire future hung on the next hour's events. Distracted by the turmoil of her thoughts, she did not see the crouching animal half-hidden behind a rock until it was too late.

With a snarling cough, a large black shape sprang into the air and landed on Eden. It happened so suddenly she had no time to scream, no time to do more than throw up her arms to protect her face. Its weight slammed her to the soft earth of the path between the rocks, knocking the breath from her. Twisting, she fought for air and freedom.

Her flailing hand encountered soft fur, and with a shock Eden recognized Balam.

The jaguar seemed delighted to see her despite its rough greeting, and raked a raspy, smelly tongue over her face. Weak with relief, Eden managed a shaky laugh.

"You still stink, Balam," she muttered, shoving at him, and the cat batted playfully at her hair where it had come loose from her neat braid. So much for appearing her best to see Steve again. "Get off me," she said with an affectionate push, and Balam rumbled a reply as he nimbly rolled away.

For a moment, Eden ruffled the jaguar's fur, still slightly wary of his teeth and the power of his sleek muscles, but inordinately pleased too that Steve's pet had remembered her fondly. Would Steve greet her so gladly? Glancing toward the dark opening, she whispered, "Is he in there, Balam? Will he be glad to see me?"

Balam's gold eyes reminded her of Steve's as he gazed at her for a long, solemn moment. Then the cat's ears pricked forward and he grew tense, staring expectantly into the bushes beyond the rocks. Eden wasn't surprised when he exploded into action and bounded away in pursuit of a flicker of motion. Eden hoped it was not Yac and his men, or there would certainly be a protest.

Taking a deep breath, she smoothed her skirts and tried to rebraid her hair. When she finally stepped into the dim, cool cavern where water lapped softly against the rocks, she paused. Her eyes adjusted slowly from the brightness outside to the shadowed interior. Rock formations soared overhead. Light streamed down through the opening in the roof, hazy, misty, and mysterious.

There was no sign of Steve, and she drew in a deep breath as she moved forward. Her boots sounded much too loud on the rock floor. She could hear the soft rasp of her breath, and her heart pounded loudly in her ears.

When she rounded a clump of rocks on the sloping floor,

she saw him. Her heart gave a wild lurch. He was swimming. Below, in the clear waters of the pool, she saw the clean, strong lines of his body as he stroked lazily through the pool. Light from the hole above streamed over him, making his body gleam and leaving nothing to her imagination. She was glad she'd come in alone. She should have expected this, but somehow, she hadn't.

Feeling awkward and suddenly uncertain, Eden had the pressing urge to flee . . .

The light made him blink. Steve frowned slightly. He should be feeling peaceful. Serene. It hadn't been this quiet in months. So why did the damned restlessness have to return like it did? It had hit him the day before, when he'd gone hunting with Balam and found himself back at his old hut. There was a poignant sense of loss that continued to cling to him despite his best effort to shake it loose. It was a damn good thing he'd had sense enough to abandon the hut. He'd never be able to look at it without remembering Eden.

Eden. His moon goddess. Pale hair, soft blue eyes, and creamy ivory skin that embodied all the best of a female— yeah, she'd certainly known how to get to him, hadn't she? Not a day went by that he didn't think about her. And it had been five months since she'd gone from his life, disappearing into the rainy green darkness without a backward glance.

It was for the best, of course. He knew that. He'd known it even when she was with him, even when he'd held her close in the night and listened to her soft breathing while she slept. At times the memories jerked him awake, and he'd lie there in his blankets in the half-world between awareness and slumber and dream that she was still with him. He could almost feel her satiny skin, the bright silk of her hair, and her gentle curves pressed against him . . .

He should have been able to tell her how he felt. He wished he had. But there had been no time, no time for farewells, no time for weakness. Since then, he'd started for Mérida more than once. But he'd never gone. He knew better. She would be gone now, safely back in the States, living as she should live, with a roof and four walls, fine clothes and excellent food—that was how it should be for her. A woman like Eden wasn't meant for the simple life of the jungle. It had all been a mirage, a crazy dream that he had known from the beginning was foolish.

But still, when the loneliness grew unbearable and no amount of bourbon would help, he found himself wishing it had ended differently. What was it he'd said that had brought her to him the first time—?

"Oh powerful Itzamná, Lord of Life, deliver me a woman of light and beauty and independence . . ." he muttered aloud.

Yeah, that was it. The words echoed just as eerily from these rock walls as they had in the darkness that first night. He must have been insane. For a while, he'd begun to convince himself that he was actually a favorite of the ancient Mayan gods. It seemed like every time he asked something of them—

A sound caused him to jerk up his head, and he swung his legs down as he wiped water from his eyes. His throat tightened. It must be a vision. That damned Italian painter again—Botticelli.

Smiling shyly as she waded into the water with gloriously unbound golden hair streaming around her bare shoulders and down to her waist, Venus approached. Ivory skin, lush curves—a jade and gold necklace circling her throat, carved with Mayan images. It had to be another dream. He'd conjured it up too often and now it came even when he was awake . . .

"Steve?"

He closed his eyes against a painful spasm. Eden. It

couldn't be. His luck had run out long ago. Miracles happened to other men. Not to him. Never to him.

"Steve?" she said again, the whisper sounding both hopeful and tremulous.

He opened his eyes. Dear God, she was so beautiful, so absolutely damned beautiful that it made him hurt all the way to the core. From somewhere deep inside, he found the courage and the strength to move toward her.

Water streamed over his chest and stomach as he waded to where she waited for him on the shallow rocks of the pool. It clogged his lashes and his throat, and he found that he couldn't say anything. No words would come, nothing that would make any sense.

When he stopped, she looked at him, and after a long moment of silence, glanced down at her clasped hands. Her voice was shaky and soft. "Maybe I shouldn't have . . . come. I thought you might want . . . to see me."

He still couldn't force any words past the lump in his throat. He stood with his fists clenched at his sides, knowing that if he said anything or touched her, he'd make a damn fool of himself again. Hadn't he done that enough?

When the silence dragged on, Eden drew in a deep breath. "I see that I made a mistake."

No, no, no—I was the one who made the mistake. I should never have let you go. . . . Why wouldn't the words come?

With a faint, dry sob, Eden turned away, and Steve saw that he was losing his last chance. He reached for her despite the inner voice that urged caution, and his hand closed on her arm.

"Eden," he said gruffly, embarrassed at the raw emotion in his voice, "you didn't make a mistake. I just can't believe you're here, that you came all this way to me."

She halted abruptly, her back still to him. His hand tightened on her arm. He cleared his throat, words fumbling and hesitant, sounding rough even to his own ears. "These past months without you—I wanted to come to Merída."

"Then why didn't you?" she asked so softly he had to strain to hear her. "I waited for you, Steve. I hoped—" She drew in a ragged breath, and he felt that peculiar tightening in his chest again.

"Sweetheart, it wasn't because I didn't want to be with you. What could I offer you? More danger? More hiding? You deserve better."

She shook her head, pale hair shimmering in the misty light. "It doesn't have to be that way anymore and you know it."

"You're talking about the pardon." His hand dropped from her arm and he raked his fingers through his wet hair. "Are you responsible for that?"

"I do have some influence with a lawyer or two, and was fortunate that a family friend was sympathetic to your case. It isn't as if you actually stole those artifacts, and the shooting in Texas was more self-defense than murder. All it took was some time and argument to clear you."

"God. Eden." He felt helpless suddenly, helpless and uncertain and floundering for the words to say aloud what he'd thought to himself so many times. Damn. Why was he so articulate alone in the dark, and so damned clumsy when she was near him at last? He looked up and took a deep breath.

"You want to know why I never would take you to Merída? I'll tell you—it wasn't because I was worried about being seen by the authorities. It's that I didn't want to lose you. I wanted you with me."

She didn't move, and her voice was soft and husky. "You should have told me. I needed to hear that. All it would have taken was the right words, Steve. Why can't you say them?"

Taking a step forward, he put his hand on her shoulder, fingers closing on her soft skin in a caress. He closed his eyes, searching for the words that would not come. Time passed while they stood there. Water dripped in tiny water-falls down the walls into the clear pool, and the sound of silence grew heavy while he tried to summon the words that would keep her with him. He was taking such a chance, saying aloud what he hadn't even dared think, and his throat seemed to close.

Then she took a step away from him, and his hand fell free. The warmth beneath his palm was gone. Steve's eyes jerked open and he blurted, "Eden, stay with me. I—love you."

Her back was to him, and he saw the faint ripple of her muscles. After a pause that could have been only an instant but seemed more like eternity, she turned to face him. Light glittered from the jade and gold necklace. Her eyes were wide, with tear-dewed lashes blinking over them as she stared at him. Her lower lip quivered slightly. He wouldn't allow himself to look anywhere else. He kept his gaze riv-eted on her face, on the sweet oval that had haunted his dreams every night since she'd gone.

Finally, she smiled, and her voice was husky as she said, "I love you, Steve. And I never want to leave you again. Say you'll let me stay—"

Then he was pulling her to him, heedless of anything but the driving need to hold her, to keep her with him for the rest of his life. Burying his face into the sweet-smelling curls over her ear, he muttered, "I'll never let you go again. We'll go anywhere you want. I don't care. Nothing matters but being with you."

Sighing, she said, "I thought you'd never admit it."

The laughter came then, welling up inside him and dis-pelling all the darkness at last. Eden had brought the light back into his life, and no matter what happened next, they would face it together.

Still laughing, he pulled her with him into the pool, his hands stroking over her tempting curves with slow, leisurely caresses. "My goddess," he murmured against her mouth. Her arms came up to curl around his neck while she wrapped her legs around his waist. The buoyancy of the water kept her afloat as he buried his face into the damp curve of her neck and shoulder and felt her luxurious shudder. The sensuous slide of their wet bodies was arousing, and his breath came faster.

It was natural to slip inside her, the exquisite sensation taking his breath away. Eden shuddered again, and her thighs tightened around his waist as he held her intimately. "It's a good thing," he said into the space below her ear, "that I taught you to tread water. I have a feeling that it's going to be a useful talent."

"Just don't," she said with a playful nip at his shoulder, "ever sacrifice me in a well again."

"Goldilocks, I wouldn't dream of it . . ."

To My Readers

I hope you enjoyed Steve and Eden's story as much as I enjoyed researching and writing it. Those of you who have traveled to the Yucatán may have recognized the site of my fictional temple of the jaguar as Cobá. While it is true that I freely used that particular Mayan ruin as a background, to my knowledge there is no fabled jaguar throne other than the one that can be seen at Chichén Itzá. Cobá was not actually discovered until 1891 by an Austrian archaeologist, and it was thirty-five years before it was extensively explored.

While the Cruzob did, indeed, rage across portions of the Yucatán from 1858 until 1901 when they were dislodged by the Mexican Army, they were only a part of the Maya who still live in Mexico. And there were in fact instances of brutality, some of which I have recorded in the story. (For instance, imbedded in a temple wall of Tulum there are the remains of an archaeologist who did not heed the Cruzob's warnings to leave.) All in all, the Yucatán has enjoyed a colorful and varied history from the ancient Maya to the present. Thousand of unearthed temples still wait to be discovered.

Maybe there is, after all, another jaguar throne waiting for intrepid adventurers to find it . . .

Virginia Brown

Taylor-made Romance from Zebra Books

WHISPERED KISSES (0-8217-3830-5, $4.99/$5.99)
Beautiful Texas heiress Laura Leigh Webster never imagined that her biggest worry on her African safari would be the handsome Jace Elliot, her tour guide. Laura's guardian, Lord Chadwick Hamilton, warns her of Jace's dangerous past; she simply cannot resist the lure of his strong arms and the passion of his *Whispered Kisses*.

KISS OF THE NIGHT WIND (0-8217-5279-0, $5.99/$6.99)
Carrie Sue Strover thought she was leaving trouble behind her when she deserted her brother's outlaw gang to live her life as schoolmarm Carolyn Starns. On her journey, her stagecoach was attacked and she was rescued by handsome T.J. Rogue. T.J. plots to have Carrie lead him to her brother's cohorts who murdered his family. T.J., however, soon succumbs to the beautiful runaway's charms and loving caresses.

FORTUNE'S FLAMES (0-8217-3825-9, $4.99/$5.99)
Impatient to begin her journey back home to New Orleans, beautiful Maren James was furious when Captain Hawk delayed the voyage by searching for stowaways. Impatience gave way to uncontrollable desire once the handsome captain searched *her* cabin. He was looking for illegal passengers; what he found was wild passion with a woman he knew was unlike all those he had known before!

PASSIONS WILD AND FREE (0-8217-5275-8, $5.99/$6.99)
After seeing her family and home destroyed by the cruel and hateful Epson gang, Randee Hollis swore revenge. She knew she found the perfect man to help her—gunslinger Marsh Logan. Not only strong and brave, Marsh had the ebony hair and light blue eyes to make Randee forget her hate and seek the love and passion that only he could give her.

Available wherever paperbacks are sold, or order direct from the Publisher. Send cover price plus 50¢ per copy for mailing and handling to Penguin USA, P.O. Box 999, c/o Dept. 17109, Bergenfield, NJ 07621. Residents of New York and Tennessee must include sales tax. DO NOT SEND CASH.

JANE KIDDER'S EXCITING
WELLESLEY BROTHERS SERIES